VENOM'S WRATH

SPIDER-MAN®

VENOM'S WRATH

Keith R.A. DeCandido & José R. Nieto

ILLUSTRATIONS BY JOE ST. PIERRE

BYRON PREISS MULTIMEDIA COMPANY, INC.

NEW YORK

BERKLEY BOULEVARD BOOKS, NEW YORK

Special thanks to Ginjer Buchanan, Michelle LaMarca, Howard Zimmerman, Steven A. Roman, Emily Epstein, Ursula Ward, Mike Thomas, and Steve Behling.

SPIDER-MAN: VENOM'S WRATH

A Berkley Boulevard Book
A Byron Preiss Multimedia Company, Inc. Book

PRINTING HISTORY
Berkley Boulevard paperback edition / October 1998

Check out the Byron Preiss Multimedia Co., Inc. site on the World Wide Web: http://www.byronpreiss.com

The Penguin Putnam Inc. World Wide Web site address is http://www.penguinputnam.com

Check out the Ace Science Fiction/Fantasy Newsletter, and much more, at Club PPI!

ISBN: 0-425-16574-4

BERKLEY BOULEVARD
Berkley Boulevard Books are published by The Berkley Publishing Group,
a member of Penguin Putnam Inc.,
375 Hudson Street, New York, New York 10014.
BERKLEY BOULEVARD and its logo
are trademarks belonging to Berkley Publishing Corporation.

PRINTED IN THE UNITED STATES OF AMERICA

10 9 8 7 6 5 4 3 2 1

To the Children's Television Workshop
and their late, lamented kids' TV show
The Electric Company,
which introduced me to Spider-Man
all those years go.
                    —KRAD

To *Mami* and *Papi*,
who let me read under the covers.
                    —JRN

ACKNOWLEDGMENTS

Someday, a book will have an acknowledgments section that says the authors did it all themselves without any help from anyone, so there, nyah nyah. This, however, is not that book.

Keith would like to thank the Malibu Lunch crowd and the Geek Patrol for many years of fun, gossip, and really awful puns. He'd also like to thank the members of both the Cross-Genre Abuse Group and the Circles in the Hair writers group for invaluable feedback, and the Forebearance (The Mom, The Dad, John, and Helga) for all the right reasons, and probably several wrong ones as well.

José would like especially to thank friend and co-conspirator Christopher Golden; it was, after all, his evangelistic zeal for comic books that got José started in this silly business in the first place. Also: Craig Shaw Gardner, Barbara Barron, Tom Monteleone, Matt Costello, and the rest of the NECON crowd—you guys made it all seem possible.

We both would like to thank the following:

Ronald Fernandez for his book, *Los Macheteros: The Wells Fargo Robbery and the Violent Struggle for Puerto Rican Independence*, and Connie Fletcher for her book, *Pure Cop: Cop Talk from the Street to the Specialized Units*, two incredibly valuable reference tools.

In general, the creators of pretty much every comic book, novel, and short story that Spider-Man and Venom have appeared in, but in particular the writing of (in alphabetical order) Pierce Askegren, Mark Bernardo, eluki bes shahar, Kurt Busiek, Adam-Troy Castro, Gerry Conway, Peter David, Tom DeFalco, J.M. DeMatteis, Steve Ditko, Diane Duane, Craig

ACKNOWLEDGMENTS

Shaw Gardner, Paul Grist, Larry Hama, Jason Henderson, Stan Lee, David Michelinie, Dean Wesley Smith, Roger Stern, and John Vornholt.

John Gregory Betancourt, co-creator with Keith of Captain Frank Esteban, Sergeant Vance Hawkins, Sergeant Stephen Drew, and Officer Andrew Lipinski (in the story ''An Evening in the Bronx with Venom'' in *The Ultimate Spider-Man*, which you should all go out and buy right now).

Glenn Greenberg and Ralph Macchio, two of Marvel's Spider-editors, who kindly answered many a dumb question.

Steve Roman and Howard Zimmerman, without whom this book would not exist, as well as Steve Behling and Mike Thomas at Marvel Creative Services.

And our respective spouses, Marina Frants and Lisa Delissio, for putting up with us all these years.

AUTHORS' NOTE

The Cane Cutters are *very* loosely based on *Los Macheteros*, a real-life Puerto Rican nationalist group. *Venom's Wrath* is not intended to belittle either the Puerto Rican nationalist movement, or the efforts of the federal agents whose job it is to stop terrorist activities.

PROLOGUE

WEDNESDAY, 6 A.M.

The night before the kidnappings, Betty Brant dreamt of Ned Leeds, her husband, lying next to her in bed, asleep and alive. In the morning, as she struggled out from under the wool blankets to shut off her alarm clock, she could still feel the sweet weight of his hand on her back. Slowly she sat up against the mahogany headboard. She bit her thumb; the pain numbed her, cleared the touch from her mind.

It's not fair, she thought. Ned had been killed on assignment in Berlin. Back then, Betty had been J. Jonah Jameson's secretary; a pretty woman, young and naïve, living vicariously through the streetwise stringers at the *Daily Bugle*. Now she was an investigative reporter herself; she had over a dozen bylined exposés to her name. Her feature on the Latverian rebellion had made the front pages. She had grown up, moved on. Ned shouldn't be able to mess her up like this. Not anymore.

The room was dark—the sun cast but a slight glint on the window pane—and smelled of winter: old flannel sheets, dried cocoa, steam pipes. Over in the corner, next to her grandmother's dresser, the radiator belched and gurgled. Betty wiped her eyes. Turning sideways, she lazily dropped her feet onto the still-cool floor. She grabbed the robe draped over the dresser and glanced at the clock. The display read 6:05 A.M. in flickering green characters.

After a long, hot shower she dressed in a wool suit and salt-stained galoshes—her heels waited under her desk at the *Bugle*. She'd intended to hurry out of the apartment; instead she moved in a strange languor, as though wading through a deep and muddy river. Her breakfast bagel had cooled by the time she finally slipped it out of the toaster. The grapefruit juice, which she could have sworn had just been poured from the carton, felt tepid against her lips. On the radio, songs seemed to meld together, lacking endings or beginnings.

By the time Betty placed the empty dishes in the sink it was a quarter past eight; she should have left the apartment half an hour ago. Any other day it wouldn't have mattered—as a reporter she didn't need to punch a clock. Besides, she had to wait for a source in her fish market story, so chances were she would be twiddling her thumbs until lunchtime.

Today was Wednesday, though. Joe "Robbie" Robertson, editor-in-chief, held his big weekly editorial powwow first thing in the morning. Unlike the daily late-morning meetings, everyone *had* to be there Wednesday morning. Sure, veterans often brazenly wandered in fifteen minutes late, like Charley Snow waltzing in with his topped-off coffee cup and knishes from the Jewish bakery on Thirty-fourth Street. Not Betty. Just the thought of Robbie glaring at her empty chair, shaking his head as he called the gathering to order, made her mouth sour with guilt. For the same reason, she always turned her stories in early.

Compulsive punctuality—that was what Dr. Gravston, the therapist she'd seen after Ned's murder, had called it. He'd tried to convince her it was all about her mother. Hadn't she raised Betty alone, worked a very demanding job as Jonah's secretary—Betty had, in essence, inherited her mother's job—to keep a roof over their heads, food on the table, etc? How many times had Mother picked her up late from school? How many of Betty's band performances had she missed because something had come up at the *Bugle*? How often had Betty been disappointed by her mother? Betty remembered leaning back on Dr. Gravston's expensive leather couch and flashing him a patronizing smile. Soon after, she'd quit therapy altogether.

A loud noise sounded from outside, metal scraping against concrete. Betty shook her head and looked down through the kitchen window. Two sanitation workers, their red overalls bright against the dingy snow, were tossing bags into the maws of a rusted garbage truck. *Oh, great*, she thought. They never did her street before nine o'clock in the morning. Angrily she jerked into her overcoat and scooped her purse from the table. She ran down two flights of stairs and onto the sidewalk. The cold burned on her cheeks like a slap.

Almost at once she stepped onto a patch of black ice. Her boot slipped, and she fell sideways against a snowbank.

It wasn't until she hit the ground, her legs bent under her overcoat, that she heard the laughter. The garbagemen had deemed her floundering a hoot. One of them held a hand to his lips and whistled. Another clapped limply, yelling, "Bravo, bravo!"

Betty stood up, her left knee aching. Her wool overcoat, which she'd bought on sale less than a month ago, was streaked with dirty snow; she would have to get it cleaned.

She opened her mouth for a moment to respond to the garbagemen, then snapped it shut. How she would have loved to give those idiots a piece of her mind. Not today, though. It was much too cold outside to linger. Besides, she was late enough already.

She limped down a block to the entrance of the Union Square subway station. The stairs were caked with slush. She climbed down slowly, taking measured steps.

The train was delayed—the loudspeakers crackled with something about a track fire in Chinatown—and when it came it *just* happened to be the 6 train, which was a local. Betty could look forward to four jostling stops before reaching the *Bugle* instead of one. She bit her lip. Lord knew when a 4 or 5 express would be rolling by the platform. Tightening the grip on her handbag, she pushed through the impassive crowd into the car.

There was a single empty seat by the crossover door, next to an old man wearing a duster over a dingy wide-lapel suit. His face was ruddy, half-hidden by a salt-and-pepper beard. When he noticed her, the man nodded gentlemanly and shifted sideways to give her room to sit. Betty smiled. A simple act of politeness, but it brightened her mood a little. She sat down and felt a gentle tug as the train accelerated out of the station.

Soon enough, she picked up the stench. Her eyes watered. It was like vinegar, but sharper; she was reminded of the public bathrooms in the Port Authority bus terminal. Instinctively she glanced at the old man next to her. The redness on his cheeks was frostbite, she realized, and the suit wasn't just dingy, it was soiled and covered in creases like origami paper. The tie hanging from his neck was frayed into narrow ribbons. Between his legs he carried a battered briefcase spilling over with newsprint.

Good one, Betty thought, fuming. It wasn't so much the man that bothered her—only a month ago, she'd gone undercover for an exposé on a Chelsea homeless shelter—but the fact that, though she did look at him, she hadn't *seen* him. A good reporter should always be aware of her surroundings. A laser eye for the story, that was what Robbie had called it. Intuition. Instincts. Today it seemed that she had nothing of the kind.

Suddenly the man turned toward her and flashed a ragged grin. "Time?" he said. His breath smelled like roadkill.

"Excuse me?" Betty said, surprised.

"Have the time?" He pointed at his naked wrist. Betty could barely hear him over the squeal of the wheels on the tracks.

"About twenty past," she said curtly.

"Eight?"

Betty sighed. "Nine."

The man slapped his thigh and shook his head. "Stupid subway system," he grumbled. "Weren't they gonna fix the schedule, for Pete's sake? Be the death of me, I tell ya."

"Oh, sure," Betty whispered. She couldn't help be amused. *Where is this man headed? Work? The law firm of Daniels, Smirnoff, and Tanqueray, perhaps?*

"Boss's gonna fire me," he added distractedly. "Can me for good this time. Told me so, he did."

Betty swallowed and brushed the stain on her overcoat with her fingers. *Poor man*, she thought, at once embarrassed by her callousness.

Somehow she was reminded of a comment Ned had made on their first date, all those years ago, as they sipped espressos at a bistro on Fourth Street. New York's victims had a way of wearing their stories on their sleeves. Old women wrapped in kerchiefs, for instance, clutching crucifixes in their tiny fists; strung-out junkies shivering atop park benches in Tompkins

Square Park; teens cruising up and down Broadway in Lycra dresses and loose stockings; homeless, legless veterans. One glance and you knew everything there was to know about them. At first Betty had taken his words as nothing but cynical bluster, a speech meant to impress J. Jonah Jameson's oh-so-impressionable secretary. When she told him so, Betty remembered, Ned had laughed (and how she missed that laugh—the sharp little cough, the sudden flash of white teeth . . .) and said tenderly: *No, you see, it's the stories trapped inside, the ones hidden, that's what I want to write about.*

Right then, she'd fallen in love with Ned Leeds.

The train slowed down, stopped, then started again. Absently Betty reached inside the purse and toyed with her lipstick and the can of pepper spray. It could have happened to her, she now realized. Her life could have seized up after losing Ned. In fact, it almost had—she had suffered a nervous breakdown, even gone so far as to join the so-called Cult of Love. She could have become something very much like the man next to her.

Not that her friends hadn't done their best to be supportive and comforting: Peter Parker holding her as she waited at the terminal for Ned's body; Glory Grant inviting her over for dinner and gossip; Ben Urich filling her head with embarrassing stories about Ned's rookie years; Flash Thompson, who had rescued her from the Cult of Love, just being there for her. They had all done their best, but their gingerness, the zealous care with which they spoke to her, the paucity in their gestures, had made Betty feel like a cracked and useless vase. Even Jonah—thundering J. Jonah Jameson—for almost nine months after Ned's death seemed to tiptoe in her presence. Once or twice she'd even caught him saying *please*.

Joe Robertson, though, he was different. In her many years at the *Bugle* she and Robbie had never been very close, and, to his credit, he did not pretend it had been otherwise after her husband's death. His manner remained as calm and matter-of-fact as always. When Betty had recovered from her breakdown and her ordeal with the Cult, Robbie welcomed her briskly, then handed her a manila folder stuffed with photographs and legal-pad sheets. Without a hint of pity, Robbie explained that Ned had left a story unfinished upon his death. It was a small piece that he had intended to follow up on down the line—a line that never happened. Betty nodded, all the while staring at the folder, which was creased and covered in coffee stains— Ned's coffee stains. The thought stunned her for a moment. *I want to see a draft by the end of the week*, Robbie said, gesturing at the folder. And with that he returned to his office.

The article wasn't much—a Sunday Metro piece on the aftermath of a warehouse fire in the Hunt's Point section of the South Bronx. But it had been enough to give her direction. Driving through the maze of warehouses, interviewing the fire marshall, typing away on her old, cantankerous Selectric, Betty had begun to make sense of her new world.

"Seventy-seventh Street!" boomed a gritty voice over the loudspeaker. Confused, Betty lifted her gaze and watched the crowd rustle about her. The old man in the tattered suit was gone. Through the window, she saw the number 77 stenciled on a steel brace; somehow she'd managed to overshoot the *Bugle* by three stops.

Oh, please. In a single motion she scooped her bag and leapt for the exit, almost trampling a young man clasped to the handpost. The southbound train was just pulling into the station. Unfortunately, the Seventy-seventh Street stop didn't have free access between the uptown and downtown sides. She dashed upstairs (skipping over a neat pile of newspapers), crossed Lexington Avenue (nearly getting run down by a cab and a bus in the process), ran back downstairs on the other side (breaking through a teenaged couple holding hands), fumbled for her MetroCard, ran through the turnstile, and leapt down the small staircase—

—just as the doors hissed shut. Her knuckles rapped against the metal plate. "Come on!" she yelled. The conductor, a fresh-faced black man in his twenties, simply smiled and shrugged in his cabin. Helplessly Betty watched as the train pulled away from the platform and disappeared.

"That's it," she said, defeated. Her mouth tasted bitter like grass. "I'm taking a taxi." Ignoring her own watch, she glanced at the grimy clock inside the station newsstand. Twenty to ten. As much as it pained her, she would have to call in at the *Bugle*. The new City Room receptionist was sweet, but was also a terrible snoop and a gossip. Betty knew that the woman wouldn't let her go without asking her what happened. Betty hated making up excuses, but the truth—that she'd been thrown off kilter by a dream about her dead husband—was far too personal for the office. No, she would have to tell Ginny Pryce that she'd overslept. There was a first time for everything, after all.

As the crowd on the platform cleared, Betty noticed a cluster of public phones by the staircase. She rummaged through her purse—taking a moment to drop the MetroCard in—and found a single quarter hidden in the lining. Dropping it carefully in the slot, she dialed the City Room extension.

The phone rang three, four times. Betty hung up; the voicemail would click on the fifth ring, and she didn't want to lose her only quarter. She squinted. In her many years as Jonah's secretary she had never left the desk unstaffed during an editorial meeting. Things had been in kind of a mess since Kate Cushing was laid off, but still . . .

Hastily she dialed again, this time Joe Robertson's number. Just as she got an answer, a northbound train pulled into the station; the wheels screeching made it difficult to gather the voice in the receiver. What she heard sounded like, "Is that you, Robbie? Thank God!"

She waited for the noise to quell. "It's Betty Brant," she said, finally. "Listen, I'm going to be kind of late this morning and—"

"Betty!" It was Ben Urich. The cigarette-roughened snarl was unmistakable. "Are you okay? Have you heard from Robbie?"

"No I haven't. I just—I just overslept, and I was calling—"

"Never mind about that," Ben interrupted. "Listen to me. Robbie isn't here yet. Jonah called him at home, and his wife said he left Queens around eight o'clock . . ."

"Robbie's never late," Betty said. A simple statement of fact, but it resonated in her head like a curse. She wondered what Dr. Gravston would have made of *his* compulsive punctuality.

"Yeah, well, we thought maybe he'd had a flat tire or something, but Glory's been calling his car phone every five minutes, and so far nothing."

Betty felt a familiar pang in her belly. "He's in trouble," she said.

"Well," Ben said. He was quiet for a moment. "That's pretty much what I figured."

WEDNESDAY, 9 A.M.

A.J. Pierce, accountant extraordinaire, had expected a hall with vaulted ceilings, paneled in dark mahogany, filled with row after row of pews. Something churchlike, more in keeping with the significance of his information.

Instead, upon his arrival at the New York County Courthouse in downtown Manhattan, A.J. had been escorted to a deposition hall on the fifth floor, which, he quickly discovered, was nothing but a cramped, windowless meeting room. A threadbare carpet covered the floor; overhead, fluorescent lights sparked and sputtered. A conference table in the center took up most of the available space.

Disappointed, A.J. squeezed his gangly frame around the table and sat down on a chair wedged in the far corner. His escort, a balding, middle-aged court officer with hairy wrists, parked himself by the open doorway.

"Well, well," A.J. muttered, unbuttoning his double-breasted jacket. He crossed his legs and brushed the dirt off his brand new Bally loafers, a mannerism he'd picked up from a Russian gangster in Queens. "Are you supposed to keep me from escaping?"

"For your protection," said the court officer.

"My protection," A.J. laughed. "No offense, but once I'm done with the district attorney, it's going to take more than a rent-a-cop wannabe to keep me safe and sound, if you get my drift." He paused for a second, then added, "I mean, no offense."

"None taken," the court officer said, fixing his gun belt.

"Anyway, when's this Philip Castillo planning on showing up?"

The court officer gave him a nasty look. "Mr. *Carrillo* should be here soon," he said.

A.J. gritted his teeth. After four weeks of interviews, subpoenas, and negotiations, he'd grown sick of waiting around for attorneys. What was worse, today even his own lawyer, lovely Ms. Ann Weying, was running late—she should have met him on the courthouse steps at a quarter to nine.

He wasn't worried, though. Not really. He and Ms. Weying had rehearsed his deposition over a dozen times; by now he could recite every word of it like a prayer. And besides, the immunity and witness-protection package was, as Ms. Weying had assured him, a done deal. All A.J. had to do was swear over a worn Bible, name the names, and decipher the codes on Morgan Hall's computer ledger. Then his record, what little there was of it, would be wiped clean. Seemed easy enough to A.J.; just like going to confession.

All the same, he wanted to be done with it. The quicker the better.

The stenographer arrived first; he nodded toward A.J. and quickly set up his machine at the head of the table. He looked much too young for the job, with his pointy sideburns and bangs cut straight across the forehead. For some reason, A.J. had pictured a shriveled fellow who'd stop at every other page to complain about his arthritis. *Live and learn.*

After the stenographer came two men dressed in dark suits and brilliant white shirts. The second one, tall and olive-skinned, introduced himself as Mr. Carrillo. When A.J. stood up to shake the Assistant D.A.'s hand, he accidentally kicked the chair with his heel, sending it clattering against the plaster wall. Embarrassed, A.J. turned around and picked it up by the backrest. He made to sit down, but the first man—Steve Phlegas, court official—insisted on shaking his hand as well.

"Mr. Phlegas will be swearing you in," Carrillo explained, "and then we'll get started, all right?"

"But my lawyer's not here yet," A.J. said.

Carrillo grinned and carefully pulled out a seat for himself. "Oh, we'll wait a few minutes for Ms. Weying," he said. "Certainly. We're in no hurry."

For a long time nobody spoke. A.J. tried his best to stay calm; every two or three minutes, though, he would glance at the door, and at the hairy-wristed court officer standing next to it, wondering when Ms. Weying would make her appearance. Sweat beads rolled behind his ears. Once he thought he heard the chirp of the hinges, and he jerked in his seat and opened his mouth to greet his lawyer, but when he turned he found himself staring at nothing.

The court officer brushed his thick neck with his fingers. "Heating system," he said. "It's kind of noisy sometimes."

"Right," A.J. said, and settled back in the chair. He sighed. He turned his wrist and read the face of his Cartier. There was a new scratch on the sapphire glass, deep as a record groove. *Oh brother. Must have hit it against something.*

Carrillo cleared his throat, wrapping his hands around the edge of the table. "Well," he said, "how about we swear you in, if that's all right? I'm sure that Mr. Phlegas has other business to—"

"Nope," A.J. said. "I'm not doing anything without my lawyer."

"It's nine-forty already," Phlegas said. He held his tie weaved between his middle- and forefingers.

"Mr. Pierce," Carrillo started.

"Not without my lawyer," A.J. said, then turned to the stenographer as if for confirmation. The young man just shrugged.

They can't understand what I'm dealing with. Nobody understood. Nobody except for Ms. Weying.

He'd explained it all to her, and she had listened intently, so intently, and she'd nodded her beautiful head at all the right moments. He'd told her how it had started: sitting at his desk in the mutual funds company, bored and lonely, making up dummy corporations on notepad paper, then, on a whim, registering them with the state government. He'd told her how, after a few weeks, and to his surprise, he'd created a vibrant fictional economy, a system so complex and subtle that any transaction within it vanished, as it were, into thin air. He'd spent his days on client accounts, nights playing with his virtual world, opening dozens of bank accounts, writing prospectus after prospectus, drafting fanciful business plans on his PC.

It wasn't long before company security was alerted to his strange hobby—by now an obsession—and summoned him "upstairs" to be dismissed on the spot. A security guard, not unlike the court officer here in the deposition hall, stood by his desk as A.J. cleaned out the drawers and stripped his mother's picture from the cubicle wall.

Lean months followed. Often A.J wondered if things would have gone better for him had he been caught embezzling or selling inside information—something that a financial manager could understand. As it was, he received not a single response to the dozens of résumés he mailed out, and every rent check he penned brought him closer and closer to paupery. He ate canned meats and Wonder Bread. He washed his clothes in the sink.

Even as his lifestyle foundered, though, he kept working on his private world; adding subsidiaries, staging mergers, arranging stock raids and hostile takeovers. The whole thing became terribly vivid in his mind, and whenever he neglected it he felt as if he'd abandoned his subjects, as if myriad lives depended on his constant and undivided attention. He could imagine stern men like his father being laid off, drinking gin from streaked highball glasses. . . .

One day, as he walked down to a pawn shop on Fifth Street, a silver limousine pulled over next to him. Slowly the passenger window came down and a gray-haired man sporting a well-trimmed vandyke called out to him by name. Intrigued, A.J. stepped closer. There was another man in the car, he saw, leaning imperially against the opposite door, half covered in shadows, and who seemed ludicrously large. His fist, which he held clenched on the leather seat, looked the size of a cannonball. Vandyke Man introduced himself as the agent of a very important businessman who had become aware of A.J.'s "activities," and was interested in putting his talents to use.

When A.J. stared at him questioningly, the agent proceeded to explain: *We're in need*, he said, *of a good launderer.*

That was five years ago. A.J. had not heard from the big-fisted man in the last three, though his patronage—or, rather, his name—had brought him plenty of business. He would still be at it but for the racket of his money-counting machine, which for days kept his new next-door neighbors awake and bothered. Eventually the elderly couple notified the police. Two officers came to his apartment to investigate, and A.J. was caught with eight Coach suitcases full of one-hundred-dollar bills. All belonging to one Morgan Hall, on-the-rise mobster . . .

"This is ridiculous," Phlegas said, tapping the face of his digital watch.

A.J. licked his teeth and leaned back on his chair. Above him, a fluorescent bulb popped, flashed brightly, and died.

"I have to agree," Carrillo grumbled. "I've just about lost my patience. You promised to cooperate, Mr. Pierce. If Ms. Weying can't make it to the deposition—"

"She's supposed to be here, all right?" A.J. yelled. At once he regretted raising his voice. He pinched his chin and shut his eyes for a moment. Ms. Weying's delay had pushed him close to the edge. He could feel the start of a migraine, teasing at his temple, and in his stomach, acid gurgled and spit. This was trouble of the worse kind, and A.J. loathed trouble.

The Assistant D.A. grimaced. "If this is some sort of delaying tactic," he started. He didn't need to finish the sentence.

From his coat pocket A.J. fished a slim cellular phone, and with a practiced flourish he opened it and dialed Ms. Weying's number, all the while staring flatly at Carrillo. He'd learned long ago, from his underworld clients, that the best way to cover fear was to feign anger and annoyance.

There came no answer; each empty ring seemed to needle in his skull. Finally the answering machine started. Ms. Weying's voice on the tape sounded thin and weary.

A.J. tried to restrain himself once the beep came. "Hello, Ms. Weying, this is A.J. Pierce, your most important client. It's almost ten o'clock already, and I'm here at the County

Courthouse, and as you know Mr. Castillo is waiting for us for the deposition, so—''

Suddenly the machine clicked and beeped twice in quick succession. Then, a dial tone. A.J. cursed and almost threw the phone against the wall—something he'd seen Morgan Hall do countless times. Instead he simply slapped it shut.

Sitting at the head of the table, the stenographer bent forward over his machine and sighed. ''Maybe,'' he said quietly, ''maybe something happened to her. I mean, this jerk's been under police protection, right?''

At once Carrillo and Phlegas looked at each other.

''What?'' A.J. said. The question felt sharp and cold in his throat. ''What?'' he said again.

''Better get someone at NYPD,'' Carrillo said dourly. Phlegas gestured toward the court officer, who immediately rushed through the door and down the hallway.

No, A.J. thought in a panic. He needed her. Without her he wouldn't—couldn't—testify. The D.A. was just after Morgan Hall, that much had been made clear in his first interview with that awful sergeant—what was her name? Jackson? Now, A.J. didn't have any qualms about selling out his latest employer; he had never liked Hall, and he could trust the police to protect him from such a fleck of a gangster. Unfortunately, it wasn't an easy task, teasing out a single client from his money-laundering scheme—in fact, it was nearly impossible. Everything was connected. In his belabored knot there were others, much more powerful others. The man with the cannonball fist, for instance.

One word against Wilson Fisk, and A.J.'s life wouldn't be worth the jar for the ashes.

Only Ms. Weying understood. Since taking the case, she had dissected his world as if with a scalpel. She'd sifted through coded ledgers, sorted out corporate records, studied bank statements until she could list transactions off the top of her head. She'd snipped off the links and tied up the bleeders. Kept his fictional world from hemorrhaging.

Just yesterday she had promised to walk him, step by step, through the deposition. And now she was missing.

Suddenly the narrow room appeared to contract around him. The lights turned milky and diffused. A.J. felt his mouth go dry; his head pounded in earnest.

He didn't want to go to jail. He didn't want to die.

"We have to find her," he pleaded.

Squinting, Carrillo stood up and smoothed the front of his jacket. "We certainly do," he said.

"Hey, wherefore art the lieutenant?"

Somehow, Lieutenant Romeo Golden heard the uniformed officer's question amidst the cacophany of the Midtown South Precinct. "Right here."

The uniform turned to face him, revealing herself to be Officer Schwalb. "Ah, sir, Peters and Borck wanted me to let you know that they still don't have a confession out of that guy in the liquor store robbery. The captain's not in yet, so . . ."

Schwalb's voice trailed off. Golden sighed. One of the first things Golden learned in the three months since his arrival was that Captain Frank Esteban always came in fifteen minutes to an hour late. Right now, at 9 A.M., he was only forty-five minutes behind.

"Kick him," Golden said after a moment. Schwalb nodded and went toward the interrogation room.

The lieutenant continued plowing through the crowds of police officers, perps, complainants, lawyers, and other people who weaved their way through the precinct. Plowing was the only method that worked—politely waiting for a path to clear could take weeks.

Not for the first time he pined for the days when he had been in charge of a quiet squadroom in Haverhill, Massachusetts. He hadn't wanted to return to New York, but his wife Constance received a lucrative job offer here. Golden grew up in Manhattan, and had been with the NYPD for many years before finally getting fed up with trying to police a city overpopulated with super-powered types—"costumes," Golden called them.

Plus, moving again meant he had to once again break in a

new set of cops who couldn't resist jokes about his first name. True, it was actually pronounced "ruh-MAY-oh," but that would hardly cause cops to desist from lines like Schwalb's "wherefore art" crack.

Still, he could not deny Constance this job opportunity. So he put his concerns aside for the good of his marriage, returned to his hometown, and managed to get a good position at one of the busier Manhattan precincts.

"Lieutenant," bellowed Karen Jones, the desk sergeant. A good-sized African-American woman with straight black hair, she had a shout that could decalcify spinal columns when she turned it on high. This particular bellow, to Golden's relief, wasn't quite at that level, though it was enough to be heard over the din.

Golden stopped walking. Another uniform, who had been moving in the lieutenant's wake, collided with him. After the uniform extricated himself, muttered a quick apology, and moved on, Golden turned to face the approaching sergeant.

Jones held out a sheet of paper. "The captain ain't here yet, and I need you to sign off on this estimate for repairing the holding cell."

Golden took the sheet and sighed. Last week, two uniforms had brought in a DWI. It turned out that the guy had super powers of some sort. Once he sobered up, he used them to blow out the wall of the holding cell they put him in after he was booked. Incidents like that kept the turnover rate on the NYPD high—it was why Golden left the first time and why he had a relatively easy time finding a decent position when he came back.

"Yeah, it's fine," he said, handing the sheet back to Jones. The estimate was actually less than the budget allotted for such repairs, which was a welcome change.

"Thanks. You finish the paperwork on Mendoza yet?"

"I was heading to my office to work on it right now."

"Sure you were." Jones rolled her eyes.

Golden smiled. She'd heard that line before, though, in fact, Golden truly did intend to work on the Mendoza case, if he could ever actually make it to his office.

After being temporarily stymied by a logjam at the booking desk—three plainclothes cops were bringing in five querulous perps on breaking-and-entering charges and taking up all the available space in an already-too-narrow corridor—Golden did arrive at his office. Closing the door against the noise, he buried himself in the intricacies of *People* v. *Lawrence Mendoza*. Amazingly, this lasted a good twenty minutes before Sergeant Stephen Drew knocked on the door.

"What?" Golden asked.

Drew opened the door just enough to stick his pale face between the door and frame. "Sorry to bug you, Lieutenant, but you need to talk to this person on the phone."

"What person?"

"A fed. From an organization called SAFE. She says they need more copies of the paperwork on the Dr. Octopus case."

Golden frowned. "SAFE—where do I know that name from?"

"It stands for Strategic Action For Emergencies. They were involved in that mess over at the Russian embassy with the Hulk."

Golden vaguely remembered the incident. Connected with some senator or other getting blown up by a plane, but he couldn't remember the details. "And they have the Octopus case now?"

"Yeah, and they want to talk to you."

Sighing, Golden said, "Drew, this is a costume case. You know how I feel about costumes."

Drew nodded, his blond hair falling in his face. "Yeah, I do. About the same way you feel about feds."

"So why are you asking me to talk to a fed on the phone about a costume when you know full well that inside of five minutes I'll be yelling at the idiot for getting in the way of real police business, which is all feds and costumes are good for anyhow, and then we'll get the precinct in trouble and the commissioner will make me call and apologize, which I hate doing?"

"Because," Drew said patiently, "she asked to speak to the highest-ranking cop we had. The captain's not here, so, unless

Commissioner Ramos dropped in without telling me, that leaves you.''

"He *still* isn't here?" Golden's eyes widened. They had now passed Esteban's one-hour window, which worried the lieutenant.

Drew suddenly looked concerned. "Uh, no. I figured he just called in or something."

"No, he hasn't." Golden scratched his neatly trimmed beard. Esteban always let someone know when he was going to the bathroom. If he had called in, Jones would have told Golden, and if he hadn't, something was wrong. He said to Drew, "Put off that agent of Safety, or whatever it is. Tell her we're in a big meeting with the commissioner or the mayor or the Avengers or something, and someone'll call her back later today or tomorrow."

Drew nodded, and turned to leave. He almost crashed into Sergeant Jones. "Sorry, Sarge," he said with a quick smile, then continued onward to his desk. Jones opened the door the rest of the way and stood before Golden's desk.

"Karen, I'm glad you're here, I need—"

"The captain ain't here yet."

Golden blinked. *Of course she noticed too, jerk*, Golden admonished himself, *that's her job*. "I need you to call—"

"I already called his home number and his car phone, and I beeped him. Then I beeped him 911. Then I called his wife, who said he was still eating breakfast when she left."

Golden winced. "I wish you hadn't done that. Now she'll be all worried."

Jones smirked. "You ain't met Lydia, have you? Trust me, if I *didn't* call her, I'd never hear the end of it."

Shrugging, Golden moved onward. "He's up in Washington Heights, right?"

Nodding, Jones said, "That's the three-four."

"Okay, call the Thirty-fourth and have them send a car over to his place. And beep him again, but use my direct line."

"Got it."

Jones left. Golden proceeded to look at the same paragraph on one of the depositions in the Mendoza case fourteen times, pausing every seven seconds to stare at the nonringing phone. This went on for twenty-five minutes before Jones came back.

"The unit from the three-four called in," she said. "No answer at the captain's place, and his lights were off. They checked the parking lot, and his car was gone." Before Golden could ask a question, Jones typically anticipated it: "The building has assigned parking, and besides, the super saw him get in his car and drive off at a quarter to nine."

Golden cursed. "All right, put the word out—get the description of his car to every cop in the city."

"I already got Epstein handling it," Jones said.

"Good. Keep me posted."

Jones left. Golden stared at an indeterminate point on the floor between his desk and the door.

Where the hell are you, Frank?

WEDNESDAY, 9:45 A.M.

Frank Esteban awakened sprawled on a cold cement floor, shivering, his hands cuffed tightly behind his back. He'd been stripped of his jacket; the holster at his side was empty. For a minute he lay still, fighting to orient himself. His head felt distended. He smelled soot and grease. Light streamed from a crack in a boarded-up window high above. In the distance there was a sound of water dribbling, like lazy rain.

The last thing he remembered was wiping the mist off the windshield in his car and buckling his seatbelt. He'd gotten into the Plymouth in a hurry—late for work as usual—and the strap had ended up pinched under the door. When he reached down to free it, a strong arm in a down sleeve had hooked around his neck and pinned him to the backrest.

What followed was a blur; he recalled a struggle, jerking forward, shoving his elbow, and snapping his head blindly. None of it helped. There was a smell of sweat and chloroform. A burlap cloth was thrust in his face; soon the windshield began to shimmer, and he was gone.

He'd been taken to some kind of a warehouse, Frank

guessed, or maybe an abandoned loft. The ceiling was lost in shadows, and he could see several wood beams around him, spaced evenly like stakes. If there was a heating system, it barely made a difference. A frigid draft blew from the broken window and swept along the ground, right through his clothes.

More alert now, Frank rolled back and forth, curling his legs to gain momentum. Suddenly, as he settled on his left hip, his shoulder crackled. He fell back and yelped. Broken clavicle, he was certain. As a child, back in San Juan, he'd dropped from his grandmother's second-story balcony and fractured that same bone.

Maldita sea, Frank thought, wincing. The kidnappers, whomever they were, had been careless with his unconscious body. *Not a good sign.* He turned his head and with his chin tapped gently on the muscle. It felt like boiled ham.

Cuffed, injured, unarmed: the situation wasn't at all good. Any attempt at escape would have to wait. Still prone, he stared at the ceiling, heartened only by the fact that he'd been taken from the car, and not the apartment. He had to assume that Lydia wasn't hurt.

He heard a quiet moan coming from a few yards behind him. A woman's voice. *No* . . . Clenching his jaw, Frank drew sideways and clambered to his knees. The pain was excruciating, but he had to look. A slim blonde sat against one of the beams, also handcuffed, wearing a linen suit and stockings—ruffled, but still quite elegant. Not Lydia. *Thank God*, he thought. He knew that he would feel guilty later—this was another victim, after all—but right now he could not deny his relief.

The woman seemed oddly familiar to him, though. Something about the curve of her chin, the slope of her neck—he'd definitely seen her before.

''Ma'am,'' he whispered. ''Are you all right? Ma'am?''

Once again she moaned, then grimaced and licked her lower lip as if to feel a cut. She exhaled; a cloud of mist swirled around her. Frank finally recognized her, from newspaper photographs. Ann Weying, lawyer, ex-wife of Eddie Brock, aka Venom.

The sight brought a lot of sour memories: Officer Toño Esteban, broken, his body laid carelessly on a chrome slab; himself standing in full dress uniform, hot July sun bearing down on him, as they lowered Toño's casket into the ground, listening to the stiffled sobs of his young widow.

Frank knew that it wasn't Weying's fault, his cousin dying at the hands of the creature she had divorced before he even became a psychotic super-villain. It wasn't her fault at all.

What could she be doing here with him, though? Just as Frank began to consider the question, he noticed yet another figure, a man lying on his back a few feet beyond the young lawyer. Brown-skinned, middle-aged, dressed in an undershirt and black suit pants. In the dim light Frank couldn't be sure of the face, but it sure looked like Joe Robertson, editor-in-chief of the *Daily Bugle*.

What the hell . . . ? Frank swallowed and shifted toward a nearby column to steady himself. *A cop, a lawyer, and now a newspaperman?* There had to be a connection, of course, but Frank couldn't see it. Weying was all but a stranger to him, and these days Frank didn't even read the *Bugle*; the paper had misquoted his office far too many times.

"Chacho!" The name, stretched into two long syllables by the sing-song yell, echoed across the room. Painfully Frank turned on one knee and saw, by the door, twenty feet away, a skinny kid slouched in a school desk. He held an M-16 rifle at his side, pointed at the ceiling. Over his face he wore a mask made of wire mesh. There was a weird caricature painted on the front—round eyes, a grin, and a handlebar mustache.

"They're up, Chacho!" the kid cried in Spanish, knocking harshly on the door.

A faint voice answered from outside, "Should I get Sombra?"

"No, you should go and get your cousin Pino," the kid said sarcastically. He shook his head and slipped out of the desk, cradling the rifle in his arms. "Of course, Sombra."

"I was just asking. There's no need to be nasty about it, I mean—"

"Just go get him!" the kid interrupted.

Oh boy, Frank thought grimly. *Amateurs.* He took a deep

breath and sighed. In his experience, there was nothing deadlier than a novice perp. Professionals knew how far to take things, when to cut their losses and surrender. Amateurs panicked. Amateurs shot people by accident.

Maybe it *couldn't* wait, after all. The kid was alone now. Perhaps a bit of police intimidation . . .

Out of the corner of his eye, Frank noticed Weying rising. With his handcuffed hands he waved at her to stay put. His shoulder flared; Frank could feel himself slipping into a blackout. He gnawed the inside of his mouth. When his head cleared he scrambled to his feet. He took a step forward, terrified. Right away the skinny kid trained the rifle on him.

"Don't move," the kid said in English. The rifle was much too long for his arms, and the barrel dipped and wavered.

"Do you know who I am?" Frank said in his best bad-cop growl. "Do you have any idea who you're dealing with? Do you?"

"You gotta sit down!" the kid yelled.

"I'm Captain Frank Esteban from the New York Police Department!" He took another step forward. "Do you hear me? Captain Frank Esteban!"

"*Mira—*"

Frank didn't let him finish. "I'm not gonna say this twice, so you better pay attention! You've got five seconds to put your weapon down, you hear me?"

"I . . ."

Frank stepped firmly on the cement floor. "Four!"

"You have to—" the kid began.

"Three!" One more step. Frank was now only two yards away from the boy. He could see the scrawny neck flushing, the thin hands slackening around the grip. "Two," he said, quieter.

The mask remained impassive, frozen in its toothy grin. But slowly the kid let the rifle slip from his arms. *Gracias a Dios!* The barrel scraped against the concrete.

For some reason, Frank was reminded of his younger brother. He hadn't seen Carlos in years, not since he quit the army and headed back to the island.

"One," he whispered.

Suddenly he heard the sound of the door latch unlocking. "Quick, son," Frank said, glancing behind him at Weying and Robertson, both of whom were now awake and sitting tautly in the ground. "Get me out of these handcuffs, and if you cooperate—"

The kid swung the rifle over his head like an axe. Frank could only blink, and then the butt caught him square on the left shoulder. His whole body quivered, and his lungs filled with cotton.

When Frank came to, he was propped against the corrugated metal wall. Weying and Robertson huddled around him. His neck, arm, and left flank were numb.

"Captain Esteban? Captain Esteban?" Robertson said. He shook Frank gently with his hip.

"I still can't believe he did that," Weying said, her eyes widened.

"Messed up," Frank muttered and stretched his jaw. The street Spanish had fooled him—he'd expected nerve-wracked kids, way over their heads, following orders they didn't understand. None such. The perp who'd hit him had discipline, or at the very least brass *cojones*. At the moment Frank couldn't decide if that was a good thing.

"You're awake, thank goodness," Weying said, then turned round to face a man Frank hadn't noticed before. "He's going to need a doctor. That bone—"

"He'll be fine," the man said harshly. Immediately Frank recognized a Puerto Rican accent—and a thick one at that—but this character was over six feet tall, his face was pale and weathered, and his hair was a mess of bright-red curls. At either side of him stood two slight men wearing similar wire-mesh masks, holding nine-millimeter pistols in their fists. Behind them, M-16 boy was slouching against the metal door.

Frank glared at the man with the red curls. "You must be Sombra," he said in Spanish.

The man ignored him. He pulled down on his camouflage jacket, then ran a stiff finger along the collar.

"The quicker you give us the information we want," he

said in English, obviously bored, "the quicker we'll get you out of here. Then you can take him to a hospital, or whatever you want to do with him. I don't care."

He gestured toward the mask at his right. The wiry man turned around and nodded at the M-16 kid, who then, with a hurried shove, opened the door. The metal slab whined and slammed against the outside wall. Behind it was a hallway lit by bright spotlights.

"Just keep in mind," Sombra continued, "that these men are trained soldiers, and this is a war we're fighting." He smiled at Frank Esteban. "They won't hesitate. Trust me."

"Excuse me," Robertson said, "but exactly what war are you talking about?"

Sombra smiled, then glanced quickly around. "It's freezing in here," he said. He leaned toward the mask on the left and said in Spanish, "Get them some blankets, and a pillow for the pig."

Without another word, he walked out of the room.

CHAPTER 1

WEDNESDAY, 10 A.M.

Peter Parker hated winter.

As he alighted atop the Cathedral of St. John the Divine, a gust of wind sliced through his Spider-Man costume as quickly as a knife—and, he thought, as unpleasantly as one. The costume proved to be nigh-fruitless protection against the low temperatures this morning. *Maybe I should wear a leather jacket, like some of the Avengers used to do*, he thought. *Then I could be the amazing Biker-Man.*

He took a deep breath; the cold air seared his lungs. The smell of cooking pretzels wafted up from a street vendor standing in front of the church, out even in this weather, bundled up in so many pieces of clothing it obscured his face.

Spider-Man had worked his way to Manhattan's Upper West Side this cold Wednesday morning for no other reason than that the exercise kept him warm. Besides, crime happened up here, too.

Though it wasn't happening much today. The only sights he saw on Amsterdam Avenue were New Yorkers wrapping their coats tightly around themselves and hurrying to get indoors.

I should've gone back home, he thought, but knew that would have been foolish. He'd rushed to the Empire State University campus from his home in Queens for his nine o'clock lecture, arriving his usual ten minutes late, only to find that it had been cancelled. With nothing else to do for the three hours until his noon lecture, he'd decided to put in a little web-swinging.

Trying to keep his teeth from chattering under his full face mask, Spider-Man double-tapped the small stud on his palm. A line of his customized webbing shot out. Based on a chemical compound he had created in high school, the webbing had proven a valuable tool in his career as a super hero. It was incredibly strong, adhesive, and adaptable, and it dissolved into a fine powder after an hour—a feature that made it impractical for mass-market use, but kept him from littering the city with webbed detritus.

The web-line caught and held the cornice of a building across the street, then Spider-Man started his Tarzanlike swing. At the swing's midpoint, he shot another line onto another building, and so on. Initially, travelling through the air like that proved even chillier than sitting on the roof, but the constant motion required by his unique mode of travel got his circulation restarted.

After only a few moments, he found himself at the campus of Columbia University. As a bright young high school student, and part-time Spider-Man, Columbia had been one of the many places Peter Parker applied to for undergraduate study. However, he got a full scholarship from ESU—as good a college as Columbia, and more helpful to a student from a middle-to-low-income household—and so went there for financial reasons. *Financial considerations were always a factor after Uncle Ben died*, Spider-Man thought sadly.

Unbidden, his mind turned back to his four years at Midtown High School in Forest Hills, Queens. They started out normal: Peter was, as ever, the class geek, the target of bullies, and the bane of popular kids—unless they needed help with their homework. A trip to a science exhibit and the bite of an irradiated spider brought Peter down a road that kept the latter portion of that tenure—and the rest of his life—from being anything but normal.

Desiring to keep moving, and not finding anything worth Spider-Man's time in this area, he started swinging down Broadway in a zigzag pattern. Few people bothered to gawk—indeed, nobody seemed to spare him a second glance. Spider-Man was almost disappointed. *Time was they'd at least yell at me and call me a menace. I guess people have gotten used to me. Wonder if that's good or bad.*

Spider-Man had changed direction before he was consciously aware that his spider-sense had gone off. Like the agility that enabled him to swing through Manhattan's concrete canyons, the spider-bite had also given him a built-in danger sense. It alerted him now to something happening at one of Broadway's many movie theaters.

As he approached, he saw the likely source of the warning: a person wearing a suit of high-tech armor that followed the form, if not the details, of a human body. Only the helmet deviated, curving up, then down and back so it looked like someone with a pompadour haircut wearing a baseball cap backwards. No features were visible on the battleship-gray metallic surface, though the right arm had a cylinder running down the forearm and ending at the knuckles. *Probably*, Spider-Man thought, *where he keeps the ray beam. Guys in cheesy exoskeletons* always *have a ray beam.*

He landed on the theater's marquee and paused to set up his automatic camera and take stock of the situation. Years of experience had taught him never to go wading in with both barrels until you were sure that it was necessary. For all he knew, this was a publicity stunt or a show the theater was running.

A filtered voice sounded from the armored figure. "Attention, box office! You will turn over all your cash to me immediately! If you do not, you will face the terrible wrath of— *the Iron Monger*!"

Spider-Man couldn't help it. He burst out laughing.

The self-proclaimed Iron Monger swiveled its head upward toward the marquee—a lengthy process, accompanied by the *whirr* of servomotors. "Spider-Man! Long have I awaited the chance to test my mettle against you!"

Between guffaws, Spider-Man said, "Well, your metal doesn't impress the heck outta me, fella. Where'd you get that helmet, from a bike messenger with a pituitary problem?"

"No one laughs at the Iron Monger and gets away with it!" With another *whirr*, the right arm lifted. "Feel the wrath of my hydrogel blast!"

Still laughing, Spider-Man easily dodged the expected ray beam, needing neither his spider-sense nor his enhanced agility to evade so telegraphed an attack. He leapt onto a lamppost about ten feet away on the curb. The beam left a small burn mark in the marquee. *Looks like a garden-variety laser beam.*

"Stand still, wall-crawler!" the Iron Monger shouted, *whirr*ing around and firing at the lamppost.

"That wouldn't be very bright, now would it?" Spider-Man said as he leapt back to the marquee. The laser shot past the lamppost and went off harmlessly into the sky. *Better stay above him*, Spider-Man decided. *Keep the bystanders out of the line of fire*. This proved necessary, as a crowd of New Yorkers typically decided a spectacle was of more import than their personal safety and had gathered around to watch.

As his foe turned and fired at the marquee and Spider-Man leapt in response back to the lamppost, he said, "Y'know, I haven't played a good game of Monkey in the Middle since grammar school." He leapt back to the marquee, dodging another blast. "It's much more fun this way. Back then, I was always the monkey." He swung back to the lamppost. "It was usually on a day like this, some jerk would grab my wool hat and start throwing it back and forth over my head to one of his jerk friends." Back to the marquee.

"*Enough!*" the Iron Monger finally cried.

"Well, that's what *I* kept saying, but they'd keep tossing the hat."

"I shall crush you like the insect you are!"

The Iron Monger's arms lowered and the armor seemed to lean forward a bit. Then, accompanied by the roar of miniature jet engines, it lifted off the ground toward Spider-Man—

—for about three feet. The roar then turned into a sputter and the bootjets fell silent.

"Aw, geez!" Same filtered voice, but higher-pitched this time. "The stupid jets conked out again! Darn it!"

With that, the Iron Monger fell to the sidewalk on its back. *"Aw, geez"? "Darn it"? Who am I fighting here, Radar O'Reilly?* Shaking his head, Spider-Man followed him down, landing lithely on his feet. First he secured Iron Monger to the ground with a generous dosage of webbing, then found a handhold on the ludicrous helmet and yanked it off.

The face it revealed was young, male, wearing wire-rim glasses, and had short curly brown hair. *My God, it is Radar O'Reilly.*

"Don't hurt me, please!" said a whiny voice.

Tossing the helmet aside, Spider-Man leaned in close to the young man. "Let me give you a few pieces of advice, Sparky. One, an iron monger is someone who *sells* iron, not someone who *wears* it. Last guy to use the name was an industrialist, so it fit *him*. Two, hydrogel is an inert substance with no energy whatsoever, so the idea of a hydrogel blast is ridiculous. What you've got is a laser beam—just call it that."

"But laser beams are for wimps!" the young man protested.

Spider-Man resisted the obvious comment and plowed onward. "Three, spiders are arachnids, not insects. And four, if you're going to rob a movie theater, don't do it at ten in the morning. They only just opened—they haven't made any money yet."

As Spider-Man gave his speech, a police car from the Twenty-fourth Precinct double-parked next to the minivan in the space in front of the theater, right under the sign that read NO PARKING ANYTIME. Two female cops, one white, one black, came out and approached Spider-Man.

"I see you've already done the fun part," the black one, whose nameplate read DIVER, said to Spider-Man.

"Something like that," he said.

"Oh, cripes," the white one, named Greenburg, said upon seeing the Iron Monger's face. "Daniel, is that you?"

"H-hello, Officer Greenburg."

Greenburg rubbed her blue eyes. "Geez, not again."

Spider-Man asked, "You know this twerp?"

"Oh yeah," said Diver with a rueful smile. "This is the fourth time we've found Daniel wearing some kind of Iron Man knockoff and makin' a fool outta himself. He's a Columbia student—or was, anyhow. They expelled him after the first time we busted him. You'd think he'd learn."

Greenburg said, "I'm calling for a chopper. No way in hell we're gonna be able to lift him, especially with that goo all over him."

"Don't worry, Officer," Spider-Man said, leaping up to the marquee once again, "the 'goo' dissolves in an hour."

"We know," Diver called up after him. "Sure you don't

wanna stick around? Fill out some paperwork? Sign a state-ment? You know, *real* police work?"

Surreptitiously grabbing his camera, Spider-Man said, "Sorry. Places to go, appointments to keep, miles to go before I sleep, all that stuff. See ya!"

He swung off.

As he continued down Broadway, he thought, *Shouldn't have been so dismissive of the cop. After all, she's got a job to do, and that includes icky things like paperwork.*

Unlike more popular super heroes like the Avengers and the Fantastic Four, Spider-Man had not always been on the best of terms with the local law enforcement. Certain individuals treated him with a modicum of respect, such as the late Captain Jean DeWolff, but as a rule cops viewed him—and, to a de-gree, all paranormals who didn't work within the system—with disdain.

Still, he'd been the one to catch DeWolff's killer, which had improved his relationship with the cops somewhat, though not enough to make most of them happy.

Well, so be it. They do what they do 'cause it's their job. I do it because I have to.

He worked his way southeastward, eventually coming to Central Park West. *Well, heck, let's really play Tarzan for a bit.* The Park sat between him and his destination, the *Daily Bugle* offices, where he hoped to drop off the photos of his encounter with the Iron Monger. He attached a web-line to a tree, and swung past the mass of vegetation near Tavern-on-the-Green.

Working his way through assorted trees and occasional statues, he eventually came out right at the southeast corner facing the Plaza Hotel. Within minutes, he reached the *Daily Bugle* Building. Smiling, he remembered his first trip to this edifice shortly after he became Spider-Man. He'd taken a few pictures of himself fighting the Vulture in the hope of selling them to pay his and Aunt May's rising bills. He never dreamed that he'd make it into a profession, but here he was, one of the *Bugle*'s most respected crime photographers. He'd won a Newsguild Award some years back, and more recently a coffee-table book of his Spider-Man pictures called *Webs* was published.

He landed on the roof behind the access tower and put his civilian clothes on over his Spider-Man suit. *Of course, pictures of me fighting some dumb kid in an ugly gray exoskeleton won't get top dollar.* Still, every little bit helped. He and his wife Mary Jane were both students surviving on freelance work, a notoriously unreliable stream of income.

Within minutes, Peter Parker entered the cacophany of the *Bugle*'s City Room and maneuvered around screaming editors, frantic reporters, harried gofers, beleaguered assistants, and various other always-moving cogs in the newspaper's wheel. His destination was the office of the editor-in-chief, Robbie Robertson.

"How do you *do* that?" asked a voice.

Peter turned to see a petite blonde he hadn't seen in a while: Vreni Byrne. An excellent, thorough reporter, she'd come to the *Bugle* from the *Chicago Tribune*. Peter had accompanied her on an assignment to cover a space shuttle launch in Florida, which turned into an immensely complicated situation involving the Lizard, Venom, and a plot to blow up that selfsame shuttle. "Do what, Vreni?"

"Navigate like that. I can't take four steps in this room without bumping into somebody or something, but you always slide through untouched."

"Hey, I've been taking the subway since I was a kid. You get good at it," Peter said neutrally. In truth, his spider-sense allowed him to avoid even such minor collisions.

"So, did you hear?" she asked, obviously expecting a "yes."

"Uh, I don't think so. I just got here, though."

"Robbie hasn't shown up yet. Missed the editorial meeting and everything. Jonah's not very happy about it."

Peter blinked. Robbie had a well-earned reputation for timeliness. He certainly would never miss an editorial meeting without good reason.

"*Parker!*"

Few things were capable of breaking through the City

Room's perpetual wall of sound. The megaphonelike bellow of the newspaper's publisher, J. Jonah Jameson, was one of them. A lot had changed over the course of Peter's career as a *Bugle* freelancer, but one constant was regularly having his name shouted across the City Room by Jonah.

Giving Vreni a jaunty wave, he worked his way to Jameson's corner office.

Unlike most newspaper publishers—who preferred to stay in their plush offices away from the riffraff, and dealt with concerns loftier than the basics of news reporting—Jameson maintained a constant presence in the day-to-day operation of the *Bugle*. He'd started out as a reporter, and worked his way up to a top editorial position before buying the paper and becoming publisher.

Jameson had the most forceful personality of anyone Peter had ever met—and that was up against some very stiff supervillain competition. The publisher stood at just over six feet tall and was fairly thin—with his brush cut and tiny swatch of a moustache, he was instantly recognizable even if he was just a face on a television screen.

Heck, Peter thought, *if I was blind, I'd know he was in the room.* Jonah even had a distinctive smell: cheap aftershave swimming upstream against the odor of cigar smoke that hung over him even when he wasn't smoking one.

As Peter approached, Jameson leaned forward and the face with that moustache and that hair leaned close to him. "I want good news, Parker—tell me Robbie picked you up in Queens and drove you here and his car phone's on the fritz, which is why he hasn't been answering it."

Peter sighed. " 'Fraid not, Jonah. I got into the city under my own steam. Didn't even know he was missing until Vreni tol—"

"Well then, where the hell *is* he?" Jonah interrupted, straightening up.

"I don't know, I—"

"Of *course* you don't know if you haven't seen him, Parker!" Jonah said in a tone one might use on a five-year-old.

Biting back the obvious retort of, *Well, then, why did you ask?* Peter instead asked, "Has anyone called the police?"

"Not yet. We want to—" Then something caught his eye over Peter's shoulder. "*Mercado!*" he screamed.

Peter turned to see that reporter Joy Mercado had just entered the City Room. Jameson obviously hoped she might know Robbie's whereabouts.

Somehow, I don't think anyone's going to give a hoot about my pictures of a super-villain wannabe.

He wandered slowly back through the City Room, catching snatches of conversation. Most centered on Robbie, usually pertaining to where they saw him last. Apparently, no one had seen him that morning.

Well, I've still got another hour and a half before my noon lecture. Let's see what Spider-Man can find out.

Within two minutes, he had changed back into costume and leapt from the rooftop of the *Bugle* building, heading uptown toward Queens.

As he shot a web-line onto one of the many outcroppings of the Queensboro Bridge, he wondered what could have happened to Robbie. It might have been something as simple as his car breaking down or his son and daughter-in-law paying a surprise visit or a major story breaking—Robbie, too, had been a reporter once, and those instincts occasionally steered him. Still, he would've called in.

And it could be something worse. Robbie had a history with a super-villain called Tombstone, a superstrong thug who'd tried to gain a position of power in the New York mobs. The last Spider-Man knew, Tombstone was safely in prison, but his grudge against Robbie dated back to their teen years in Harlem, and it wouldn't be the first time a villain influenced events from behind prison walls.

Working his way quickly across the bridge, he then navigated the industrial complexes of Long Island City. Spider-Man spent the early years of his career living with his aunt May in Forest Hills before moving to Manhattan during his first year of college; he'd traversed the midtown-to-Forest Hills route so many times, he could do it in his sleep—*in fact, I probably* was *asleep some of those times*, he thought, remembering some particularly exhausting battles.

This time, though, he couldn't just go on years of instinct: his destination lay a trifle farther north.

The streets of the Jackson Heights neighborhood of Queens were even more sparsely populated than those of the Upper West Side had been this cold morning. No one was around to comment on the sudden appearance of a man in red-and-blue tights landing in front of the Robertson house. As Peter Parker, he had been to the modest, red-brick house several times. He also knew that Robbie kept his car in the driveway, since it didn't fit in the garage, what with everything else in it—"stuff" according to Robbie, "garbage" according to his wife Martha—and that car didn't occupy the driveway this morning.

Robbie owned a huge brown Oldsmobile that was older than Spider-Man. Though he had upgraded it with air-conditioning, a police radio, an alarm, a state-of-the-art sound system, and a car phone, many had wondered why he didn't just buy a newer, faster, more efficient car. Robbie's response was always, *Why? This one still works.*

A quick check at the windows indicated that no one was home. Spider-Man noticed two flashing lights—one was the answering machine, blinking furiously with ever-more-frantic calls from the *Bugle*, no doubt; the other the alarm system.

Spider-Man leapt up to a nearby tree and began to follow Robbie's normal route. A creature of habit, Robbie always went down to Northern Boulevard, thence to the Queensboro Bridge, and down Second Avenue to the *Bugle* building and its underground parking garage.

As he wended his way down Northern Boulevard, Queens's largest and busiest local street, he wondered what he was really accomplishing. For all he knew, Robbie's ancient car was in the shop and he had taken the subway. There could have been a breakdown on the 7 train that left him trapped between stations, and his cell phone may have run low on batteries or something. *I suppose I should've checked that out. Checked transit reports, too.* Not having done that, he had no idea if he was wasting his time or not.

But he couldn't just let it go. He owed Robbie too much, both as Peter Parker and as Spider-Man. If anything happened to Robbie, it wouldn't be because Spider-Man failed to act. He made that mistake once before.

Shortly after the spider-bite, a burglar had run past Spider-Man, but the young man—flush with his new powers—arrogantly saw no reason to stop the thief, even though he could have, easily. That burglar would go on to break into the house in Forest Hills and murder Uncle Ben. Peter Parker took a vow that day never to let something like that happen again, and he would hardly go back on that oath now.

He took it slow, leaping from lamppost to storefront rooftop to cornice to the occasional truck or van roof, all the while keeping an eye out for a big brown Olds. *Thank God Robbie didn't trade it in for a dark blue compact*, Spider-Man thought after seeing his twentieth car of that description in five minutes. *Then I'd be here all day.*

Soon enough, he found himself back at Queens Plaza and the tangle of intersecting streets leading to the Queensboro Bridge. Not a brown Olds in sight.

All right, let's check the side streets.

He intended to go in a zigzag pattern, checking one block to either side of Northern Boulevard. After that, he'd try the bridge and the Manhattan leg of the route.

That proved unnecessary. He quickly found a familiar brown Olds on Thirty-third Street, parked in front of a fire hydrant. Spider-Man did an elegant backflip and landed feet-first by the driver's side door. Inside, he saw the familiar dashboard full of high-tech items that looked as out of place in a thirty-year-old car as a VCR in a cave.

His spider-sense remained quiet, so any danger had long passed. Still, two things felt wrong. For one thing, there were dents and chips to the paint of the car's body. Despite its age, Robbie always kept the car in excellent shape. Of course, it was possible that these were the result of some other problems and Robbie just hadn't gotten around to fixing them yet. But then there was the second wrong thing: the doors were unlocked and—Spider-Man noticed after peering inside the window—the code alarm unset. Like most New Yorkers, Robbie would sooner walk down the street naked than leave his car unlocked with the alarm off.

Then he noticed something else on the passenger's seat: Robbie's briefcase and his laptop. *No way Robbie would leave his car unlocked with that stuff in it. Heck, no way Robbie would leave that stuff in the car, locked or not.* He looked around. *This can't have happened too long ago—in this neighborhood, an unlocked car with this many gadgets in it would be stripped clean inside an hour.*

A sudden *chirp* made Spider-Man tense, before he realized it was the car phone. He considered opening the door and answering it, then decided that would be unwise. It was probably Jonah. *Lord only knows what he'd make of Spider-Man answering Robbie's phone when he's gone missing.*

Spider-Man stepped back from the car and looked at it—and realized, to his great annoyance, that he had no way to figure out what had happened. All he had was an abandoned car and a great deal of supposition. This required, as Officer Diver put it so succinctly earlier, *real* police work. Forensics people, that sort of thing.

Despite his sometimes rocky relationship with the NYPD, he did know a few cops he could call on in special cases. This qualified.

Months ago, when Venom threatened a man the NYPD had in protective custody, Spider-Man had assisted the team doing the protecting, and saved the life of one Detective Sergeant Vance Hawkins, whom Venom had tossed out a window. Shortly thereafter, Hawkins's partner, Stephen Drew, assisted Spider-Man with a cellular phone fraud that was making a mess of Peter and Mary Jane's life by sending Spidey to a freelance troubleshooter named Doris Smyth. As a result, Drew and Hawkins were among the few cops whose direct phone number Spider-Man had.

He had to go back to Northern Boulevard to find a pay phone, and travel three more blocks before he found a working one. He then dialed the 800 number that applied to his calling card and dialed the complex series of digits that would charge the call to that card. When he and Mary Jane inherited the Forest Hills house from Aunt May, they also inherited the phone and its calling card, which Peter had found a great convenience. It beat having to carry change in his belt.

After two rings, a voice said, "Drew."

"Sergeant, it's Spider-Man."

"Really," was the reply, and it sounded, to say the least, dubious. Spider-Man couldn't blame him. His face mask muffled his voice, which kept people from figuring out who he was, but made recognizing his voice over the phone more or less impossible.

"Yes, really. Haven't talked to you since I kept Doc Ock from blowing up the World Trade Center."

"Uh-huh."

Drew still sounded unconvinced. Ock's bomb in the Windows on the World restaurant's wine cellar was public knowledge, so Spider-Man went for something the average person couldn't know.

"It was a good thing for me you recognized those AK-74s. That little bit of trivia was real useful." Smiling, he remembered one other detail from that case. "Oh, and Doris said to say hi to 'Stevie' for her."

Drew perked up. "It *is* you. By the way, if you ever call me 'Stevie'—"

"Understood. Listen, I'm at a pay phone on Northern Boulevard in Queens. I know that's out of your territory, but I'm not exactly on a first-name basis with the local precinct. Joe Robertson of the *Daily Bugle* has been missing since this morning, and I just found his car abandoned about three blocks from here. The car's banged up, and it was left unlocked with some valuable equipment inside, including his briefcase. I suspect he didn't exit the vehicle voluntarily," he added drily.

"Sounds pretty unlikely, yeah. Where?"

"Thirty-third Street between Northern and Thirty-eighth Avenue."

Drew paused a minute, presumably to write it down, then

said, "Got it. I'll get over there to check it out."

This surprised Spider-Man. "*You'll* go over there? Why not just call the locals in?"

"Long story." Drew's tone implied that he knew more than he was telling. "Did you touch anything?"

"Nope."

"Good. I suggest you not be around when the uniforms show up. I'm gonna send 'em over to keep an eye on things till I get out there."

"Uh, Drew, what's going on?"

"Maybe nothing. Look, thanks for the tip, okay? I'll talk to you later." Then Drew hung up.

Spider-Man stared at the receiver for a full ten seconds before hanging it up. *That was really weird. Drew doesn't usually play things that close to the vest.*

Still, there was little he could do.

As he left the pay phone, he saw two kids staring at him from the front of a candy store. They both wore thick down jackets, mittens, and wool hats—one hat, he noticed, bore the Avengers' logo. One of them asked, "Ain't you *cold?*"

Spider-Man came very close to putting on a Schwarzeneggar voice and saying, *Yes. Your clothes—give dem to me,* but decided that that would be mean. So he said, "I just think warm thoughts," and swung off.

He crouched on the roof of a nearby building, keeping an eye on the car until a blue-and-white from the One Hundred Eighth Precinct pulled up across the street. Then, after checking his watch, he headed toward the Queensboro Bridge. He had a noon lecture to get to.

CHAPTER 2

WEDNESDAY, 10:30 A.M.

"Did you check out the furniture in that lobby?" Officer Susan Doyle said as she and her partner, Lisa Hoblock, felt the tug of the upward-moving elevator.

"What about it?" Hoblock said, rolling her eyes. She knew exactly where this was going. After two years of sharing her cruiser with Doyle, Hoblock had come to recognize that shrill, indignant tone. It was inevitable: whenever she got into a fight with her husband, she would get started in one of her tedious crusades. A year ago it was tobacco companies marketing their products to teenagers; some of her BUTT OUT stickers could still be found lying around Midtown South. Just last month she'd sworn off meat altogether—her little protest against the "cattle slaughter camps," as she'd called them. That one had ended abruptly, in a flurry of curses, when she'd tried to convince Captain Esteban to give up his onion-steak lunches.

And now, furniture. If Hoblock had to guess, this time it was about—

"Mahogany," Doyle said, undoing the zipper on her overcoat. "Tropical hardwood, every piece. Do you have any idea how many acres of rainforest were knocked down to make that loveseat? Just for that tiny little loveseat, mind you."

The elevator chimed as it passed the second floor. Hoblock exhaled loudly. She tapped her muddy boot on the carpet. According to dispatch, their missing lawyer lived in one of the penthouse apartments. Twenty-three floors left.

"I don't know," she said and almost added, *And I don't care.*

"Well, let's say Belize, right? In the latest report from HCP—"

"HCP?" Hoblock asked.

"Habitat Conservation Project. They keep track of global deforestation and stuff like that. Anyway, it's something like six acres for a dinner table, so I'm guessing four for the loveseat. I mean, four acres so that some yuppster can get his butt all comfy. Unbelievable!''

Hoblock nodded in sympathy. *She's already doing research. Must have been quite a fight.*

"I mean," Doyle continued, her voice narrowing, "this may not be on top of people's mind all the time, but it seems to me that if—"

"What did Ian do this time?" Hoblock said.

"Ian?" Doyle said. She touched her lips with her fingers. "Ah, he was complaining again about my weight. But listen, this deforestation problem—"

"I know," Hoblock said, grasping her partner's shoulder. "Crucial. Very important. That's all fine and good, but why don't you tell me exactly what he did to you, huh? You know you can tell me."

Crossing her arms, Doyle just stared at her reflection on the mirrored door. For a while she didn't speak. She was a big-boned woman, five-six and a hundred and forty-eight pounds, but nobody in her right mind would call her fat. To Hoblock, who'd often describe herself as gangly, Doyle seemed imposing, powerful. She'd seen Doyle take down muscle freaks a foot taller than her—a twist of the arm, a sharp blow to the solar plexus, and the woman would have the handcuffs on the perp before he knew what hit him.

There came a chime and Hoblock glanced at the floor markers above and saw the penthouse light flicker.

"I'm so angry," Doyle muttered, just as the elevator door opened.

"We'll talk about it," Hoblock said. "Okay? We'll talk."

Doyle nodded. She checked her gunbelt and holster and stepped first into the truncated hallway—a foyer, actually, with two plain wooden doors on the opposing wall. From the ceiling hung a glass-and-chrome chandelier, and the floor was covered in crisp industrial carpeting. The air smelled faintly of lavender.

"Talk about homey," Hoblock said, slipping past her partner. As far as she was concerned, the building had all the warmth and character of a forensics lab.

"That's black maranti," Doyle said, pointing her round chin at the apartment on the left. "From Indonesia, believe it or not. Every year they clear-cut an area the size of Rhode Isla—"

"That's terrible," Hoblock interrupted quietly. "I think we want the one on the right." She reached into her shirt pocket and produced a small notepad, which she flipped open with a roll of her wrist. "Ann Weying," she read, "248 West Thirty-fourth, 25B." She put away the notepad and added, "Okay. Now, as far as we know, the lawyer just overslept and missed a deposition, all right?"

"But she didn't answer when the doorman called."

"Well," Hoblock said. Suddenly a burst of static rang from her two-way radio. She turned down the volume and walked across the foyer, her partner following closely. She knocked twice on the door to 25B. The wood made a sound deep and resonant. She waited a moment, then struck the door again.

After a minute, Doyle shuffled to Hoblock's side and, holding onto her gunbelt, leaned sideways toward the apartment.

"Ms. Weying!" she yelled. "This is Officer Doyle and Officer Hoblock, from the NYPD. Could you please open up? Ms. Weying!"

"Hold on," Hoblock said, glancing at the fancy door handle. Quickly she knelt down and examined the burnished chrome. Scratch marks spread outward from the keyhole like comet tails. Before her partner could protest, she drew a wool glove from her coat pocket and carefully, without touching the metal with her fingertips, tried the handle. The latch gave with a peculiar ratchet noise.

"Forced entry," Doyle said, stepping away.

Hoblock nodded. She felt a stream of cold air on her palms, seeping under the door. "They left through a window, though. And didn't bother to close it."

"Oh, man," Doyle whispered, "I don't know why you haven't made detective yet."

"Me neither," Hoblock said, resigned. She rose and straightened the folds in her uniform, and they both went in to check the place out.

• • •

Detective Sergeants Peter Gilman and Laura Liverakos got the call twenty minutes later. They were in the middle of investigating a convenience store holdup that, with the jerk of a finger, had suddenly turned into a homicide. Gilman hesitated at first—he'd been in the middle of interviewing the grieving Vietnamese husband—but when the name *Weying* came through the radio speaker, he and Liverakos rushed out of the store and into their banged-up Mercury Sable. They parked under a NO STANDING ANYTIME sign in front of the Thirty-fourth-Street high-rise, right behind the evidence van. Upon sighting the badges clipped to their coats, the doorman allowed them inside without hesitation.

Upstairs, next to the elevator, two uniforms, both women, talked to a nattily dressed older man whom Gilman assumed was a neighbor. As the detectives sped past them, the stocky officer tried to catch Liverakos's attention; Laura stopped her with a raised palm.

Inside the apartment they found a busy scene. Sergeant Gardner, the head evidence technician, sprinkled white dust on an upset mission chair; his assistant crawled on all fours through the open kitchen, brushing bits of porcelain into a plastic bag. A young photographer, looking trim in his leather jacket and turtleneck, wandered like a top from bedroom to living room: *snap, flash, snap, flash*. Three other uniforms—Gilman recognized one of them, David Grand, from the precinct football pool—milled around a marked ten-foot perimeter of carpet by the open east-side window.

Gilman and Liverakos said nothing; for a while they simply observed. When they passed the answering machine, which blinked insistently on a table by the bathroom, Gilman pushed the play button and listened to a shrill voice identify itself as Weying's "most important" client, A.J. Pierce. *What a whiner*, Gilman thought.

Finally, after surveying the whole apartment, he and Liverakos settled at the long stool by the northern window. They sat close together, not touching, awash in cold and harsh winter light.

"Did I ever tell you?" Liverakos said, her booted feet dangling. "My middle name is Anne." She ran a hand through her thin brown hair. "Only mine has an 'e' at the end."

"Really?" Gilman said, distracted.

"Anyway, for a lawyer, Weying certainly had taste. I could kill for these curtains."

"I don't like it," Gilman said.

Raising her eyebrows, Liverakos grabbed a fistful of fabric and brandished it at Gilman. "You think you could do better? On our salary?"

"No, no, I mean *this*," he waved his arms around as if he were swimming. "The situation here. Small space, way too many people . . ."

Liverakos looked at her partner and smiled. "Hey, you know how it is. The moment you've got possible kidnapping and Venom's ex-wife in the same sentence, the brass is gonna put the whole crew on the deal. They're not gonna take any chances."

"I still don't like it," Gilman said. "The connections, they get all muddled."

"I hear you," Liverakos said.

Gilman glanced down at the street below; a limousine weaved through a maze of double-parked vehicles—mostly police cruisers.

"So what've we got?" he asked.

"She was supposed to meet that Pierce person at the County Courthouse, right?"

"Quarter to nine, front steps. According to his message, anyway."

"Her robe was hanging from a hook in the bedroom, the dishes were piled in the sink, and there's a broken mug in the kitchen—well, there was just a dribble of coffee on the floor. The alarm clock was set for seven—set to 104.3, by the way—so I've got to put the break-in at around 7:45. She was dressed and breakfasted and ready to go when they took her."

"Agreed," Gilman said. His partner had a lousy taste in radio—104.3 was a classic rock station that Liverakos favored and Gilman couldn't stand—but her eyes were sharp as needles. *We make a nice team*, he thought. They complemented each other. She was good with details, and suspects usually underestimated her because of her height and slight build. He, on the other hand, had been known to overlook a thing or two—not often, mind you, but enough to keep Captain Esteban worried. Hence Liverakos. In fact, Gilman had long ago discovered that his real talent was finding the big picture, spotting the story hidden in the mess of facts. He was always the man with the theory. Liverakos called his method intuitive; as far as Gilman was concerned, though, what he did had nothing to do with intuition.

He'd grown up in Fairview, New Jersey, the single child of a secretary and a depressed social worker who went on a lot of vacations without their son. They came back from one such trip to Acapulco with a present: a strange parchment folded like an accordion with both words and pictures—a comic book. Gilman spent hours upon hours trying to read the stupid thing, but despite his best efforts, the colorful pages remained inscrutable. The parchment seemed to begin nowhere, and though the pictures were clear and vivid—Indians with machetes, castle walls, tied-up prisoners—the figures moved in odd, jerky progressions.

Soon after school started, he happened upon one of the plates from his comic in a world history textbook, which explained that it was actually an Aztec codex—a replica, anyway—filched by Cortez in 1519. You were supposed to read it *diagonally*, right to left, not left to right like a regular comic.

One night, after he'd gone to his room following an oppressively silent dinner, Gilman's mother called him from the kitchen. She was heating up the frozen apple pie they'd bought yesterday at the A&P. Gilman sat down, but didn't eat. Instead he pushed the crust apart with his fork. From his chair he could see his mother washing dishes in the kitchen, and his dour father in front of the TV set, smoking cigarettes and sinking into the sofa. The bitter smell of his Marlboros filled the house. Gilman thought again of the frequent trips, of the awkward silences at dinner, of the dark lines marking his parents' brows. He thought of the codex—the pictures, putting the story together.

All of a sudden the truth glowered at him, bright and painful like a flare. His parents were splitting up.

Gilman felt a strange twist in his chest. Without thinking, he cut a piece of pie with his fork and brought it to his mouth. It tasted cold and metallic.

Peter Gilman didn't know it, but he had just cracked the first case of his career. A year later he was living with his mother in Brooklyn.

"Penny for your thoughts?" Liverakos said. The glare coming from outside washed out her features, and her face looked like a pale, blank slate.

Gilman stood up and turned toward the uniforms gathered by the open window. "Well," Gilman said, "for one, this isn't Morgan Hall's work, that's for sure. His goons are not this subtle; they would have konked the doorman and brought her out through the front door. Besides, why take her in the morning? Hall must have known about the deposition for weeks."

"So you saying Venom—?"

"No, not Venom." Gilman said, squinting from the cold and sunlight. He pushed his hands deep into his coat pockets. He hated cold weather with a deep, abiding passion, and saw no reason to suffer it anymore than he had to. "Hey, David," he called out, "do me a favor, will you? Shut the window already. It's freezing in here."

The officer wouldn't budge. "Sorry, Detective," he said, quietly. He held his fat arms crossed over his belly. "Evidence hasn't checked the panes yet, and I got specific instructions from Sergeant Gardner, and you know how he gets if anyone messes with the—"

"Heard my name!" Gardner yelled. He poked his head from behind the green leather sofa. With his forearm he brushed a crisp lock of hair from his eyes, fixing a comb-over that had been a precinct joke for ages. He wore a heavy beard and mustache too, as if to distract people from his shiny pate.

"Can't put one past you, Gardner," Liverakos said with a laugh.

"Peter, Laura," Gardner said, surprised. He smiled, showing a messy row of cappuccino-colored teeth. "When did you guys get here?"

" 'Bout five minutes ago," Gilman said.

"Well, come on over here, people." Gardner stood up and rubbed the balls of his knees; after fifteen years of crouching for evidence, his legs were not what they used to be. "I have much to show you."

Liverakos slipped off the window sill and landed smoothly on the carpet. "Please tell me you've got some juicy prints for us, Gardner. Nice and clear, so we can wrap up the scene and go catch our kidnapper."

Gardner thought about it for a moment. "Yes and no," he said, finally. He nodded to himself, then looked straight at Liverakos. "Yep. Yes and no."

By now Gilman had circled the sofa and was standing a few feet away from the evidence technician. There was an ugly bloodstain running along the skirt of Gardner's coat. *Lordy, you'd think he'd get a new one after that murder scene last month.*

"What do you mean?" Liverakos said.

Vaguely, Gardner pointed at one of the down-filled cushions attached to the sofa. "My guess is that whoever took Weying must have caught her in the kitchen, right? And they kept struggling all the way to the living room, where the assailant must have knocked over that mission chair and leaned against the sofa to prop himself. Are you with me?"

"Okay so far," Gilman said.

"Now, I don't know if you know this," Gardner continued, "but leather fabrics are a favorite of the lab. I mean, you put your hand on this cushion here and it's like you dropped your wallet on the carpet with your license in it. Perfect whorls, perfect ridges—you barely have to dust for prints. They're that good."

"That's great," Liverakos said tersely. She seemed to be losing patience with the technician's caginess. Gilman couldn't blame her.

Gardner kept going, apparently unfazed by the detective's sarcasm. "So far I've gotten four fresh sets from the cushion. Four different sets. Now, fingerprints are ninety percent water, and this penthouse is dry as hell, so we *know* they're fresh."

"One is Weying's," Gilman said, "and the other three are our perps. So what's the problem?"

Without saying a word, Gardner raised his eyebrows and walked past the detectives toward the open side window. Gilman and Liverakos followed, perplexed. As the three of them approached the window, the uniformed officers stepped aside, allowing them access to the half-circle marked on the floor. For the first time Gilman noticed a pair of large footprints in the carpet, and another one on the sill. Same shoes, clearly.

"See," Gardner said, "the thing is, we've got a single point of exit. There are no footprints leading *back* to the front door. So it had to be the window. And my guess is that our kidnapper is carrying the victim by now—drugged, most likely—and handing her over to an accomplice outside."

Liverakos put her hands on her hips and exhaled. "Gardner, this is the twenty-fifth floor."

"Bear with me, all right? Maybe the guy was on a harness or something. We checked out the roof and found a cord running across the alley to the building next door. Hell, in this town, the guy could fly, like as not. Anyway, you're missing the point. There's only one pair of footprints here. One guy."

"But there are four different sets of fingerprints on the sofa?" Gilman said, holding his chin.

"Four on the cushion," Gardner said. He paused for a moment and smiled mischievously. "And six on the mission chair. And three more on the doorknob. Did I mention the eight we found in the foyer? And also seven in the elevator."

"Don't forget the eleven sets on the counter!" the assistant technician called out from the kitchen. His voice was high and reedy.

"That's—" Gilman started, then stopped himself. A chilly gust blew through the window. Shivering, he glanced at Liverakos. After a while Gilman laughed and said, "That's kind of unlikely."

"I think the word you're looking for," Liverakos muttered, "is impossible."

Gardner took a step backward and spread his coat open. "Hey, I just call them like I see them," he said.

"Boy," Gilman said. His lips ached from the cold; his eyes felt pasty and swollen. This was going to be a long day.

On a rooftop across the street, the creature crouched behind a cornice, watching. Ann hadn't shown up for her court date, so the creature went to her home to find police officers swarming the place, and no sign of Ann.

This angered the creature. Or, at least, the creature's human half.

Once there had been just Eddie Brock, and that had been enough. He came to New York's Columbia School of Journalism from his native San Francisco, hoping to become a big-time New York reporter. While there, he'd met a beautiful young pre-law student named Ann Weying. They fell in love, they graduated, they married. He got a job at the *Daily Globe*, she became a respected lawyer. And everything had been perfect.

Spider-Man changed all that. Bad enough that, for years, Brock had seen front-page stories bumped to accommodate reports on the web-slinger's gaudy exploits. But then came the Sin-Eater.

It was the story of a lifetime, an exclusive interview with the Sin-Eater, a masked man who murdered a popular police captain, a respected judge, an activist priest, and, during a fight with Spider-Man, a man who happened to be standing nearby. Brock and Brock alone got to talk to a man who had galvanized the city, the biggest murderer since Charles Manson or Cletus Kasady. It was his proudest moment as a journalist.

Or so he thought.

The very day that Brock's front-page interview hit the stands, Spider-Man revealed Stan Carter, an NYPD sergeant, to be the Sin-Eater, and the man Brock had interviewed merely a copycat. Brock was fired from the *Globe*, blacklisted from the profession he loved, and driven to an almost suicidal depression.

And it was all Spider-Man's fault.

Oh, *Globe* publisher Barney Bushkin had given all sorts of excuses—what he claimed to be a long list of unchecked facts

Brock had put into his stories and columns, that the *Globe* printed more retractions based on his stories than on those of all other reporters combined, and that to do so again on a story as big and sensitive as the Sin-Eater was the straw that broke Bushkin's back.

But Eddie Brock knew the truth. It was Spider-Man who did this to him. Spider-Man who he hated.

That hatred had drawn the alien creature to him. Now the two were one—human and alien—united by a symbiotic bond catalyzed by their hatred for the wall-crawler. They called themselves Venom.

But, as Brock observed the officers of the law prowling around his ex-wife's apartment, Spider-Man was farthest from his mind. Something had happened to Ann.

The alien twitched. A shapechanger, it primarily wore the form of an almost all-black costume that mocked Spider-Man's. But now, Brock knew, it was restless. The only love it had ever felt was for Peter Parker, with whom it had tried to bond. When Parker rejected it, it had sought out Eddie Brock instead.

But Brock was still in love with his ex-wife, and would not rest until he knew what happened to her.

"Do not worry, my other," Brock said soothingly to the symbiote. "We will find who has done this. And we will have vengeance."

The alien twitched again. It understood vengeance.

And so, the creature moved off the rooftop and into the cold winter day to learn what had happened to Ann Weying.

WEDNESDAY, 11:15 A.M.

Lieutenant Golden sat back on his chair, listened to the metal springs groaning, and stared at the clutter on his desk. *People v. Lawrence Mendoza* lay strewn across the scarred formica; with all the interruptions this morning, he'd barely put together a couple of paragraphs for the prosecution report. First Frank didn't show up, then Robertson's car, then Safety (or whatever their name was) calling *again*, then Venom's ex-wife, then some punk assistant D.A. with a jurisdiction issue that "simply can't wait." The way Golden figured it, the Mendoza report would be finished just about the time they fixed those potholes on the Brooklyn Bridge.

He sighed and flicked a finger at a sheet jutting over the edge. The thick bond paper made a dull flapping noise, which Golden found oddly amusing. He smiled, shaking his head. Frank had sure chosen the wrong day to vanish.

So far the details were scanty: a missed deposition and an abandoned Oldsmobile in Long Island City. Golden knew enough to hold off speculation till the facts were in, yet for some reason he couldn't shake the feeling that something serious was brewing. Something big. Two high-profile disappearances (three, if you counted Frank's) in a single day just couldn't be coincidence.

Well, they could be. Golden scratched the bald spot on his crown. He was still thinking like a Beantown cop—a city much less dramatic than New York. Case in point: last year, thirty-eight Manhattan cabbies had been killed in the line of duty. Boston had had a grand total of thirty-six homicides of any kind in the same time period.

Frustrated, Golden glanced at the first page of the Mendoza deposition; the words were neatly typed, the lines flushed to a sharp left margin, the paragraphs separated by precise breaks. All so crisp, so comprehensible.

Right. He picked up his pen, which had rolled off the desk and into the open drawer, and leaned uselessly over the mess of paperwork. He'd written one word—"But"—when Liverakos showed her sleek face through the doorway. Peter Gilman waited behind her, sipping from a small paper cup.

"Lieutenant?" Liverakos said. Golden smiled. He like the way she called the rank—quickly, firmly. It showed respect. So far she hadn't even cracked a Romeo joke on him.

Smoothly he dropped the pen in his pencil mug, cleared his throat, and motioned for the two detectives to come inside.

"Captain's still missing, huh?" Gilman said, then took a last swig from the paper cup.

"Good guess," Golden said, unamused.

"We've got a problem, Lieutenant." Liverakos said. She took a spot by the filing cabinet, her legs crossed, her hands squeezed into her jeans pockets. Gilman shut the door.

"Weying," Golden said, deflated.

Wrinkling his brow, Gilman nodded.

"Unless it's a troupe of acrobats," Liverakos said, "I say we've got ourselves paranormal involvement."

"Come again?"

"By the time we left," Gilman said, tossing his hand as if he were holding a cigarette, though Golden knew he'd never taken up smoking, "evidence had lifted thirty-eight different sets of fingerprints from the apartment. Every single one fresh."

"Thirty-eight?"

Liverakos grinned. "And here's the clincher: only two sets of footprints in the carpet. And one was Weying's size. Six and a half."

"Don't look at me," Gilman said suddenly, even though Golden was, in fact, looking at Liverakos. "You guys always expect me to come up with something, but this time I don't even have a clue."

"No theory, huh?" Golden said, the words tinged with irony.

Grimacing, Gilman turned sideways and tipped his head against the wall. "I hear Darwin's got a good one," he said.

"Bring him over. I'll deputize him."

Liverakos brushed back her brown hair at the part and said, "We have evidence of accomplices on the roof, but it was pretty much clean up there. No leads."

Outside, Sergeant Jones yelled Detective Peters's name loud enough to make the window blinds rattle; most probably something else with which Lieutenant Golden, in lieu of Captain Esteban, would soon have to deal.

"Well," he said, "you know how I hate this costume crap." He paused for a moment, tapping his foot under the desk. "Run the prints, I guess, and see if anything—"

Just then the phone chirped. Thinking it was Safety again,

Golden grabbed the receiver and pulled it angrily to his mouth. The base hopped a bit on the formica and made a dull ringing sound.

"What?" Golden growled.

Detective Sergeant Stephen Drew answered with a quiet, hesitant voice. "Sure hope that wasn't meant for me, Lieutenant."

For a moment Golden considered apologizing, but thought better of the idea. He exhaled and loosened his grip on the receiver. "Any news from Robertson's?"

"It's the weirdest thing," Drew said.

Golden glanced at Gilman, then at Liverakos. Both shifted expectantly from side to side.

"Don't tell me," the lieutenant said. "The car's filled with fingerprints? Different people?"

Drew went silent. His breathing sounded like static. In the background, the Queens side street blared—a kid swearing, a car with a bad piston grumbling unevenly. After about ten seconds, the sergeant smacked his lips and said, "I guess now's when I ask you how you knew about that."

"Gilman and Liverakos just dropped a similar MO on me. Ann Weying."

"Really?" Drew said, recovering a bit. "Well, anyway, Robertson's Olds must've been packed like a clown car. Forensics lifted five sets just from the dashboard."

"Same with Weying," Golden muttered. A keen thought pricked him: any time now Esteban's car would be surfacing, and Golden could safely bet his pension on what they'd be finding inside. He blinked slowly. *Oh Constance, I hope you're loving the new job.*

Before him, Gilman and Liverakos leaned forward as if attracted by the metal desk. Waiting.

"All right," Golden said. He looked at the detectives and cradled the phone on his shoulder. "Listen up," he said to them, "because this is for you, too." He picked up the mostly blank sheet he'd been using for the Mendoza case; his handwriting now appeared sloppy and childish. "Drew, you and Hawkins are now working with Gilman and Liverakos on this, okay? I'll talk to the Queens brass and get the jurisdiction settled. In the meantime, get back here and compare notes." He paused for a moment and crumpled the page in his fist. "Don't forget, though, these could still be separate incidents."

"Yeah, and I'm the Duke of Windsor," Drew said. When Golden didn't laugh, the sergeant quickly added, "But I know what you mean, sir."

"Keep me posted," Golden said plainly.

Liverakos nodded; Gilman gave him a thumbs-up. Immediately the two of them filed out of the office.

Golden hung up the phone. He burrowed his thumb into the balled sheet, teased it open, and crushed it again. Eventually he tossed the ball into a little square recycle bin by the filing cabinet.

Something serious was brewing. Paperwork would have to wait.

CHAPTER 3

WEDNESDAY, 11:25 A.M.

"I've been kidnapped before," Ann Weying said. She sat on the hard cement floor of the cold warehouse, half hidden under a thin cotton blanket, propped against a wooden column. The skin on her cheeks felt papery from the cold. Her arms were cramped and her neck throbbed painfully when she turned it. She was thirsty and exhausted. A strand of hair lay annoyingly across her right eye.

It had been over an hour, and they had yet to hear anything new from this Sombra person.

Robbie Robertson, squinting from a beam of sunlight, stirred and said, "I've been to jail myself. This is worse. At least in jail I had a bed. And a toilet."

"Hear, hear," Frank Esteban groaned. He was crouched next to the metal door, his knees spread wide apart, his healthy shoulder braced against the corrugated wall. A red blanket lay crumpled at his feet.

"What I mean," Ann said, annoyed, "is that I know how these things go. I know what you're feeling right now, but I also know that we will get out of this. That I'm sure of."

"Oh, please," Esteban muttered, glancing at the floor.

"Yes?" Ann said. "You have a problem?"

"I think this wait is—" Robbie began, but didn't get to finish.

"No offense, Ms. Weying," Esteban said, "but I've been on the force for some twenty-odd years, all right? I've handled over a dozen kidnappings, and believe me, every single one of them was different. I hear what you're saying—you've been in the same situation and so on—but I can tell you, no amount of rationalizing is gonna make this any easier. It just won't."

Ann straightened her back and tucked her legs under her skirt. "Well, perhaps the circumstances were different, but the experience of the victims . . ."

"Look, it's better not to have any expectations, Ms. Weying. Be ready for anything. I know what I'm talking about here. You could say I'm a professional at this sort of thing."

"I noticed," Ann said thinly. She gestured at Esteban's injured shoulder, which was now swollen to a round hump.

Robbie held back a laugh, snorting and shaking his head.

Grimacing, Esteban pressed himself against the corrugated wall. The metal whined and crackled. He stood up, sliding along the wall, and it seemed to Ann that the man was actually puffing himself up, spreading his feathers like a threatened peacock. She found the sight ridiculous.

"Let me make something clear, *counselor*." He almost chewed the word as he spoke it. "I don't like you. I don't like your kind. I've seen you come out of the courtroom after a trial, all smiles, shaking hands with your client. We put life and limb on the line, and for what? So people like you can put the scum back on the street?" He grimaced again, then rolled his eyes and swallowed. "People like you is why the legal system is such a joke."

"Well," Ann said, "let me tell *you* something, Captain. I don't like you, either. I don't like your methods, the way your people—and I use the term loosely—treat suspects in custody. I think it's brutal. If I had a nickel for every bruised-up client I saw ... And trust me on this, if a scumbag doesn't get convicted, it's usually because New York's Finest failed to do their job, okay? I just find the holes; you guys dig them."

"Hey, if that helps you sleep at night, counselor," Esteban said. He paused for a moment, tilting his head from side to side, then added, "Or do you take Seldane? Diazepan?"

"That's enough," Robbie Robertson said. His voice was like a slap on a blackboard. "We're handcuffed, for crying out loud. There's a bunch of wackos outside who think they're fighting a war or something. And as far as I'm concerned, this conversation is not helping."

Nobody spoke. By the door, Esteban breathed in and out, releasing a vapor cloud that hung around his face. He bent his knees and slid down to the cement floor.

"Not a war," he said quietly.

"What?" Robbie said.

"It's not a war. What they're fighting."

"That's what the man told us," Ann said.

Esteban shook his head. "A revolution."

"I'm not sure I follow," Robbie said.

"It's a bunch of *Nacionalista* wannabes," Esteban said. "You know, from the island. They think they're gonna kick the *yanquis* off of Puerto Rico."

Robbie perked up and shuffled closer to Esteban. "But here in Manhattan? Unless it's like the Young Lords in the seventies."

"No, no. The Young Lords had Geraldo freakin' Rivera for a spokesperson," Esteban said with derision. "These guys are for real. You remember in 1950, when those two Puerto Ricans tried to kill Truman? Oscar Collazo, that was the name of one of them. He was from New York. East Harlem."

"Excuse me," Ann chimed in, "I don't want to interrupt the generational bonding, but what the hell are you talking about? Young Lords? Nahtionahlistahs?"

Esteban smiled. "I guess you don't know much about Puerto Rican history, counselor."

"My name is Ann." Her stomach gurgled. Behind her back she made tight, pale fists.

"Eighteen-ninety-eight, right?" Robbie broke in. Esteban nodded, and at once the old reporter turned toward Ann and continued. "Back in 1898, we got into a fight with Spain, supposedly over a ship that blew up while docked in Havana harbor—"

"The Spanish-American War," Ann said. "Teddy Roosevelt and San Juan Hill. Come on, they did teach us *some* U.S. history in high school."

"All right. The war is over, Spain is defeated, and the U.S. is hungry for territory—manifest destiny and all. So, as part of the settlement, we get Puerto Rico. Lock, stock, and barrel. Not that anyone asked the Puerto Ricans, mind you—they thought they were getting independence out of the deal, since ours is the land of the free, right? One day they're celebrating because the Spaniards are gone, the next they've got a general from New York telling them what to do. As you can imagine, they were not happy."

"Sure," Ann said. She quickly glanced at Frank Esteban, who sat with his eyes half-closed, his left arm bound and slack against the concrete. He didn't seem to be listening.

Robbie kept going, seemingly caught in the rhythm of his own words. "Now, flash forward a hundred years. Puerto Ricans are now citizens, they have a state government, the best per-capita income in the Caribbean, etc. But they're still a colony. A third of the population has left the island and settled in the States. And it rankles. You see, for the Puerto Ricans, it's not a matter of material comforts, it's a matter of justice, of protecting their culture. Of dignity."

"Dignidad," Esteban said, smiling ruefully. He dragged the red blanket closer with his legs.

"Now, there's a pro-independence party in Puerto Rico, completely aboveboard, with candidates for governor and legislators, and all that. They get something like ten percent of the vote. But there's also a small minority who have taken up arms. In the fifties they were called *Nacionalistas*—nationalists." He glanced again at Esteban, and added, "Did I say that right, Captain?"

"Perfect," he muttered, struggling to cover his knees with the blanket. "You're pretty well informed for a *gringo*. I'm impressed."

"Actually," Robbie said, perhaps a bit abashed, "most of that was from a piece I did twenty years ago in Philadelphia. 'A Migrant Community Pictures its Roots.' It got me a Press Club award, and it was picked up by a syndicate, so it's kind of dear to my heart."

"You did that?" Esteban said, surprised. "My father was interviewed in that story. Rodrigo Esteban?"

"That's right!" Robbie said. "He was a *Nacionalista*, wasn't he?"

Esteban shut his eyes and nodded.

"I didn't know you were from Philly," Robbie said.

"I'm not. My parents broke up when I was eleven, and *papi* moved down there."

"It's amazing how well you remember that story," Ann said to Robbie. "I mean, after twenty years."

Robbie stared at her blankly for a moment. "Actually, I don't. Yesterday I got a message from one of my old sources. He said he wanted to meet with me. Since I hadn't heard from the guy in ages, I thought it'd be a good idea to refresh my memory." Slowly he breathed in and out. "Jorge," he said. "Jorge DeLaSelva."

Ann almost swallowed her tongue. "You've got to be kidding," she whispered.

"What is it?" Robbie said.

"My guy," she said, gasping. "I can't believe this." She felt a cold slick spreading through her belly.

"Spit it out," Esteban said.

"I know Jorge. I defended him a year ago on a weapons charge. A *pro bono* case."

Robbie scratched his chin with his shoulder. "So?"

"He left me a message, too," Ann said, drawing her knees together. "Four o'clock, yesterday. I was supposed to call him at a pay phone today."

A cold draft swept through the empty warehouse, stirring dust into the air, which sparkled under the narrow beam of light coming from the boarded-up window.

Robbie began, "That must be what Sombra—"

"Quiet," Esteban said harshly. "We can't talk about this anymore."

"You're right," Ann said. She wouldn't have expected to ever agree with Captain Esteban. "They're probably listening to everything we say."

"Safe to assume," Esteban said.

There was a low grating noise and suddenly the door swung open to a din of booted feet and shouts. Two masked men rushed inside; within seconds each of them stood before Esteban and Robbie, their legs spread apart, their black pistols trained on the prisoners' foreheads. The taller one, who was covering Robbie, looked jittery. He held his index finger curled tightly around the trigger of his gun.

"Don't move, *cabrón*!" he yelled, his Adam's apple jumping in his neck.

"We're not moving," Robbie said, glancing over at Frank Esteban. "Right? We're not moving."

"Wait till I get you in my interrogation room," Esteban said, his voice a low, resonant grumble. "You just wait, *so canto' eh pende*—"

"We're not moving," Robbie said, louder. Even lying on the floor his demeanor commanded authority. Esteban could only purse his lips and stare at the ground.

After a moment another masked man came in through the door. Ann squared her shoulders, and her handcuffed wrists burrowed into the small of her back. The man walked slowly toward her, strutting really, his sneakers dragging on the oil-stained cement.

No, not a man—a boy. He couldn't have been more than fourteen or fifteen. His arms were too thin, Ann saw, and he smelled like cheap aftershave.

"What do you want with us?" Ann said. She tried her best to sound frightened, even though she wasn't. She'd been through this before, after all. She knew what it was like to be kidnapped.

"You're coming with me," the boy said.

"I'm not going anywhere until you tell me—"

She was interrupted by the sound of pistol hammers cocking. Over to her left, Robbie turned his face away from the muzzle and squinted.

"You know," the boy said, "Sombra wants you breathing, but between you and me, I don't think he'd be so torn up if we capped Mr. Hero over here."

The masked man lumbering over Esteban laughed thinly and planted his gun right to the captain's temple. With the barrel he brushed the thick hairs near his ear.

"Not at all," the man said. "Not even a teeny, tiny bit."

"Okay," Ann said, defeated. "Just— Okay."

"You touch one hair on her . . ." Esteban growled.

The boy took Ann by the crook of her arm and dragged her to her feet. "Shut up, pig," he said.

Ann turned and glared at the captain. "I'll take care of myself," she said.

Once they left the large room, the boy guided Ann down a narrow hallway, past locked doors and row after row of spotlights. He squeezed her biceps, pulling her clumsily along. She wished she could see the face behind the mask, if only for a moment.

Behind her, the two armed men chattered in Spanish, their long sentences interrupted by quick fits of laughter. *They're making fun of the boy*, she thought. His neck had turned apple red and his thin fingers tightened around her arm.

They descended plywood stairs to a lower level, then walked through a beaded curtain and into another hallway, this one wide, curving, and cluttered. Exposed pipes hissed above. On the floor there were crates and piles of cardboard boxes, some with children's drawings scrawled on the lids.

Eventually they stopped before a small metal door. There was an odd symbol etched on the surface: a circle and, within it, a blade of grass and a flower. Still holding her arm, the boy rapped on the door and stepped back quickly. He straightened his legs and stared ahead—or at least he seemed to stare ahead. It was difficult to tell with the mask, which made him look somehow less than human.

"*Aguántate un minuto,*" a voice called out from inside. Ann heard a rustle of papers, a chair scraping against concrete, and then the door opened. Before her stood the man Captain Esteban had called Sombra, framed by the glare of a harsh spotlight inside the room. Ann knew little Spanish, but she assumed that the name had something to do with his red hair, or his freckles, or his fair complexion—all rare on Latinos.

"*Quítale las esposas,*" he said.

"*'Tas seguro?*" the boy said, surprised.

"*Prefiero que esté cómoda durante la interrogación.*"

"*Veo,*" the boy said. He reached into his thigh pocket and produced a small key. A turn and a click, and suddenly Ann's arms hung weakly at her side. Her wrists tingled. She brought a numbed hand to her face and scratched her nose.

"Thank you," she said automatically. It took her a second to realize how inane it was to be polite to kidnappers. By then it was too late. The boy had disappeared down the hallway, and Sombra had put a warm hand behind her neck and was guiding her to a folding chair in the middle of the windowless room. The two masked men planted themselves at either side of the doorway. Standing so still, with their faces covered and their arms crossed on their chest, they looked like wood sculptures.

Ann felt an odd tightness in her chest. She hadn't been afraid; there had been something about the boy's vulnerability that had put her at ease. Now that he was gone, she was left alone with a couple of faceless guards and another man, and her ease vanished.

"What do you want?" Ann said. "If it's money, I don't have much, really, and—"

Sombra put a craggy finger to his lips. Ann hushed.

"Yesterday afternoon," he said, struggling to speak English through a heavy accent, "you were contacted by an old client of yours named Jorge DeLaSelva. Please do not try to deny it; we know this for a fact." He stroked his jaw harshly, as if he were feeling for a crack in the bone. "Jorge DeLaSelva is a traitor. He does not deserve your loyalty."

"What was that name again?" Ann said. "Hor-hay Da Silva?"

"This man has stolen something that belongs by right to—"

"Because once I'm finished with a client all the records go down to our file room—we like to call it the morgue. Anyway, if you have a legitimate complaint against this Da Silva character—"

"—the struggle for Puerto Rican liberation. We need you to tell us where—"

"—why don't you call my receptionist tomorrow and arrange for an appointment? You realize, of course—"

"—we can find him—"

"—that everything in his file is—"

"—and collect our proper—"

"—strictly confiden—"

"Enough!" Sombra screamed, jumping to his feet and kicking the chair aside. The noise startled her, but Ann tried her best to keep still. She wasn't about to give him the satisfaction of seeing her cower.

There was something different about Sombra's face, she noticed. His nose was suddenly thinner, his eyebrows looked darker and bushier. Could it be the light? He paused for a second, then leaned over her and grabbed her cheeks in a firm grip. Ann could feel his rough fingers.

"One way or another, we'll get DeLaSelva's whereabouts from you," he said. "You can make this easy on yourself and talk now. We'll let you go. We'll let the pig and the reporter go, too. No harm done."

He flicked her face to the left and stepped back, all the while glaring down at her. His eyes, which until now Ann could have sworn were blue, had a green tinge to them. He seemed smaller also: his fatigue shirt hung loosely on his shoulders, and his pant legs were crumpled over his boots.

"I've been kidnapped before," Ann said, careful to utter every syllable. "You let me see your face. I can identify you. That means you're planning to kill me."

The masked guards burst out laughing.

"Mira, si ella es la experta," the one of the right said. Their cackle was infectious, and even though Ann couldn't understand what the man had just said, and though the circumstances made it seem completely inappropriate, she found herself smiling. Sombra grinned as well; for the first time, Ann saw that he had a tooth missing in his lower row.

"Look at me," Sombra said. His nose widened before her eyes, his forehead narrowed, and his red hair crinkled and dulled. "I am the shadow man, Ms. Weying," he said, his voice warbling. Freckles popped like buds on his skin. "My heart's *puertorriqueño*, but my shell's always changing." His jaw lengthened; his chin split into a dimple. In his eyes the irises shimmered. "Changing and changing and changing."

Ann Weying knew about shapeshifters; she'd even possessed the ability herself, after a fashion—for a short while anyway, when, to save her life, she had joined with her ex-husband's symbiote. This, though, was completely different.

With Sombra, it was as if the cells were rioting, mutating out of control.

Fixed to her chair, Ann could feel her own chest fluttering.

Captain Esteban had been absolutely right. She was scared, as scared as she had ever been.

She tried to hold it, but the pressure inside her was too much: she giggled. Air pushed violently through her nostrils. In her face the muscles twitched and jerked.

"I'm not telling you a thing," she said, cackling. Tears rolled down her neck. Leaning backward, she wrapped her thin arms around her body.

"You will," Sombra said. He laughed.

Then he broke her nose.

CHAPTER 4

WEDNESDAY, 12:30 P.M.

To Peter Parker's surprise, his noon lecture was also cancelled. A quick stop at the Biochemistry Department offices revealed why: the two professors in question, as well as four others from various scientific disciplines, had had dinner the previous night at a spiffy new Greenwich Village eatery and all came down with somewhat less spiffy cases of salmonella. He also learned, to his embarrassment, that this had been posted on the department bulletin board that morning, and he'd missed it entirely.

He considered heading over to the *Bugle* to see what they'd learned—but then, he realized, they may not know what happened. Drew might contact the *Bugle*, or he might not. And Peter didn't really feel up to pretending ignorance while asking questions, since he couldn't admit to knowing that Robbie's car had been found. Besides, with his classes cancelled, he wanted to ditch his heavy textbooks, which he'd been carrying with his civilian clothes in a backpack of webbing all day.

And, he thought, *Mary Jane should be home from her morning classes by now. She'll want to know about Robbie.* He certainly didn't object to an excuse to drop in on his wife.

For the second time that day, he wended his way Queensward from Manhattan. Starting down by ESU's Greenwich Village campus, he decided to use the more southerly Williamsburg Bridge to navigate the East River this time, and soon found himself at the Forest Hills house he grew up in.

These days, he shared the house, not just with his wife, but with her aunt, Anna Watson. They certainly had the space—Aunt May had converted the place to a senior citizens' boarding house after Peter moved out, and half a dozen people lived there comfortably then. It was certainly large enough for Anna to reside with them and still allow the married couple plenty of privacy.

That proved useful when half of that couple spent large amounts of time as a super hero. Anna didn't know about

Peter's double life. Sometimes he wondered if that was fair to her—but too many people knew whose face lay behind Spider-Man's mask as it was.

Anna wasn't home when he arrived, but MJ was. She sat listlessly on the couch in the living room, dressed in black tights and a bulky green cotton sweater that matched her eyes. She looked gorgeous, but to Peter she *always* looked gorgeous. Her red hair, presently tied back in a loose ponytail, framed a porcelain face, the green eyes of which gazed down at a massive textbook. He stared at her for a moment while hidden in one of the two trees in front of the house, waiting for his spider-sense to stop buzzing. Once it did—meaning no prying eyes would see Spider-Man entering the back of Peter Parker's house—he opened the living room window and came in.

"Hi, honey, I'm home," he said as he entered, biting back the instinct to break into a Ricky Ricardo-esque "Loooocy, I'm hooooome." The last time he did that, his wife threatened divorce.

She dropped the textbook, bounded up from the couch, and greeted him with a hug. Over the course of their relationship, Peter had come to categorize MJ's different hugs. The ones he got most often were the *you're so wonderful, I love you* hug and, sadly, the *thank God you're alive* hug. This one was the *hold me, Tiger, I'm feeling yucky* hug.

As he broke the embrace and removed his mask, he asked, "What's the matter, hon? Classes go badly?"

"No, classes are fine." MJ had decided to, like Peter, go back to school—but, where Peter was finishing his graduate work in biochemistry, MJ's discipline was psychology. "I just got a call from the studio. They *are* going to make another *Fatal Action* movie, but it might not be with me."

Peter blinked in surprise as he removed the web backpack and placed it on the floor by the end table. It would dissolve inside an hour, leaving only his textbooks and clothes.

MJ had been a top model for a few years, and recently broke into acting with a role on the TV soap opera *Secret Hospital*. After that ended, work had been more intermittent, in both modeling and acting, but she had scored the starring role in the third of the *Fatal Action* movies—a series of direct-to-video action films. It had earned her decent-if-not-great money, and the occasional residual check was always a help when the bills came in.

"Why not? I thought the movie did well."

"It did, but not as well as the first two. That's kind of inevitable, but they think it might work better with someone else. Besides, after the mess last time, they're going with a different director, and he has his own stable of actors he likes to use." The mess MJ referred to was an attack on the set by a half-dozen of Spider-Man's enemies, banded together for the umpteenth time as the Sinister Six.

Still, Peter was relieved that nothing more serious ailed his wife. "When will you know for sure?"

"Couple weeks, maybe. It's just so—so *frustrating*. I know I'm good, but—Arrrgh!" She collapsed back onto the couch. "Sometimes I just *hate* show business."

"But there's no business like it."

"Oh, hardy-har-har." Despite her sardonic tone, she grinned. "That the best the celebrated Spider-Man wit can come up with?"

"'Fraid so. It's been a lousy morning." He filled her in on the day's events, starting with Daniel-the-Dork—which brought a smile to MJ's pretty face—and then with Robbie's tardiness and Spider-Man's subsequent locating of Robbie's abandoned car—which dislodged the smile.

"Poor Robbie," MJ said.

"I know. He's already been through so much," Peter said, referring to Robbie's brief-but-unpleasant incarceration on misprision charges. He had kept silent for over twenty years about a murder committed by Tombstone. For all that time, Tombstone had kept Robbie in fear for his and his family's lives.

"So what happens now?" MJ asked.

"It kinda depends on what the cops come up with."

"And that's *it*?"

Peter shrugged. "What else can I do?"

"Well, you could start by calling Sergeant Drew and asking

him for an update. Seems to me that's the least he can do after you handed him Robbie's car on a silver platter.''

Peter scratched his chin with his still-gloved hand. "True. But he might not see it that way."

"Never know unless you try. And you owe it to Robbie to try."

"Also true," Peter said with a small smile. At the *Bugle*, Robbie had been a moderating influence, tempering Jonah's single-minded hatred of Spider-Man. Whatever positive coverage Spider-Man got in the *Bugle* was usually due to Robbie's efforts, and he was as responsible for the paper's journalistic integrity as Jonah—difficult to maintain in the age of the tabloid. Robbie was respected by both staff and freelancers, all the more because he so easily dealt with Jonah, sometimes serving as a buffer between the irascible publisher and everyone else.

He had gone out of his way to be good to Peter as well—making sure he got choice assignments, offering him the occasional lift home, even giving helpful advice one time when he and MJ had a fight. He'd elegantly walked the tightrope between good boss and good friend.

Mary Jane was right. He owed it to Robbie to do everything he could to find out what happened.

Putting his mask back on, he once again dialed Drew's number.

The voice that said, "Drew," sounded out of breath.

"Hiya, Stevie, it's Spider-Man."

"Didn't I ask you not to call me that?"

"Sorry, wanted you to know it was me without going through the *entire* rigamarole again."

"Fair enough. Good timing, I just got back from Queens. And, actually, I'm glad you called."

This was a surprise. "Really? What'd you find?"

"Oh, Robertson's car was—well, weird. We found a grand total of fifteen sets of prints on it. One is probably Robertson's—we're running them now, but—" He hesitated.

"But what?" Spider-Man prompted.

"Some of them weren't internally consistent. The same finger would alter its print about halfway down.''

Spider-Man frowned. ''That strikes me as kinda impossible.''

A chuckle wafted across the phone line. ''Yeah, our forensics guys said that, too. Besides, Robertson's a normal guy in his fifties—it doesn't take fourteen people to bring him down, y'know? Anyhow, that isn't why I'm glad you called. We got two other people missing this morning, and both of them have the same MO as Robertson's: signs of a struggle and weird prints. One of 'em is our captain—remember Frank Esteban?''

''Yeah,'' Spider-Man said. He'd met the captain during the same incident where he saved Drew's partner's life. ''Is that why you were so tight-lipped before?''

''Uh, yeah, sorry 'bout that. The lieutenant'd have a fit if he knew I was telling you this, but— Well, the problem is the third victim.''

''Why?''

''It's Ann Weying.''

Spider-Man felt as if the floor had tilted under his feet. ''Oy.''

''Oy is right. We've kept a lid on the press so far, but if word gets out to a certain guy with sharp teeth, this is gonna turn into a bloodbath.''

Drew wasn't kidding. Ann Weying may have ended her marriage to Eddie Brock, but Brock still carried a major torch for his ex, and he wouldn't take her kidnapping lying down.

Unless Venom is the one who kidnapped her. But that didn't scan. For one thing, Venom had nothing against Joe Robertson, nor did he usually go for kidnapping cops. Or, if he did, it would be a bad cop; Esteban was as good as they came. Also, Venom didn't have fingerprints, at least not while the symbiote covered Eddie Brock's entire body. It certainly wouldn't leave multiple fingerprints.

Drew continued, ''Listen, we're not gonna know a helluva lot until forensics finishes their report on the three sites. We're still not a hundred percent sure that they're connected, though—what?'' Drew's voice grew distant for a moment, then came back on full. ''Hawk just came back—one set of prints on Robertson's car was, in fact, Robertson's."

"That figures." *Of course*, Spider-Man thought, *they have his prints on file from when he was arrested and jailed.*

Drew added, "Oh, and Hawk says hi."

Spider-Man couldn't help but smile. "Well, say hi back. So what's the next step?"

"Let's see what forensics says first. Call me back in about two hours, okay?"

"Shouldn't be a problem."

"Great. Talk to you then."

Spider-Man hung up the phone, then removed his mask. "Weird."

"What's weird?" MJ asked.

"Well, even at the best of times, the cops generally treat me with barely concealed disdain. But Drew sounded like he wanted me in on this." *Then again, he has good reason, if Venom's an issue.* Indeed, the case where he met Drew and Hawkins started with Esteban inviting Spider-Man to help out, due to Venom's involvement.

He shared Drew's half of the conversation with MJ, who shuddered at the mention of Venom. "I guess it was too much to hope for that we wouldn't see him again for a while."

"No such luck," Peter said with a sigh. Every time he thought he had a respite from the psychotic ex-reporter and his pet symbiote, they'd turn up again, like a bad penny with a slavering tongue.

In many ways, Spider-Man was responsible for Venom's existence. Spider-Man first encountered the alien symbiote that made up half of Venom on an alien world where he and a dozen other heroes had been transported to engage in a staged battle with various super-villains. Over the course of his time there, his costume got shredded, and he replaced it with what he thought was a new black outfit that would obey his thoughts, change shape, provide its own webbing, and much more. Only after he'd returned to Earth and continued to wear it for some time did he learn that it was a symbiotic entity that wanted to bond permanently with him. When he rejected the symbiote, it had linked up with Eddie Brock, and they became Venom.

Since then, they'd become one of the deadliest foes Spider-Man had ever had to deal with—and that was saying something. Venom had focused more of his energies on being the so-called "lethal protector of innocents" in recent times—usually protecting them to death—but that didn't change the fact that his most fervent desire was to see Spider-Man julienned.

His second most fervent desire was to be reunited with Ann Weying, though Ann herself had made it clear that she wanted nothing to do with him even before he became a psychotic super-powered murderer. *If he finds out she's been taken, he'll tear the city apart looking for her. No wonder Drew wants me around. Regular cops don't stand a chance against him. Heck, half the time I don't stand a chance against him.*

"Drew said to call back in two hours," Peter said, "but I don't think I should wait that long."

MJ smiled. "*That's* my husband." Her brow furrowed. "I just remembered something." She went over to the pile of newspapers next to the couch, liberated Tuesday's *Bugle* from the pile, and started flipping through it. "Here it is."

She handed him the paper, and pointed to a page-five item, headlined VENOM'S EX REPRESENTS WALL STREET ACCOUNTANT. Three photos accompanied the article, a big picture of Ann Weying entering the Criminal Courts Building downtown, with two file-photo insets. One was of a bland-looking businessperson type—according to the caption, it was A.J. Pierce, the accountant of the headline. The other inset was of Venom. Peter recognized the photo as one of his own, and idly wondered how long it would take the infinitely slow *Bugle* Accounts Payable Department to process the reprint fee.

"Maybe," MJ said, reading over his shoulder, "you could talk to—oh." Her face fell into a frown. "I was gonna say you could talk to the reporter, but look at the byline."

Peter looked—the story was by Ken Ellis. One of Robbie's hires, Ellis had joined the *Bugle* shortly after Peter and MJ's wedding. A top-notch investigative reporter, he was also a thoroughly repulsive human being. While doing a story on

Spider-Man, he had decided to dig into the lives of the Watson-Parker household, to a degree not appreciated by MJ. Robbie finally got Ellis to back off. *That's another one we owe Robbie*, Peter thought.

He scanned the article, and noticed that Pierce was being held in protective custody, since he was turning state's evidence in what Ellis described as the second-biggest money laundering bust in the last year. Peter smiled, remembering his own involvement in the biggest, which was directed by Dr. Octopus.

He thought a moment. "Ellis always knows more than is strictly speaking good for him. I'm willing to bet he knows where the cops are holing up Pierce. And Pierce may know what happened to Ann. I think I'll head back to the *Bugle* and pick his brain."

"Okay, but wear rubber gloves," MJ said with a frown. "And a clothespin on your nose."

Peter chuckled and gave his wife a kiss.

After several minutes, he finally came up for air and said, "I'd better head back into the city."

MJ gave him one final, brief kiss, then said, "Keep me posted, okay? I'll be slaving over a hot textbook."

"Count on it." Peter put his mask on once again, extricated his civilian garb from the web backpack, whipped up a new backpack for them, and slung it over his back. Then he went to the window, waited for his spider-sense to sound the all-clear—*Thank God we live on a side street with minimal foot traffic*, he thought, not for the first time—and opened it.

"Move it, Tiger, you're letting in a draft," MJ said with a smile as she returned to the couch and her homework.

Spider-Man smiled under his mask, closed the window behind him, shot a web-line onto the same tree he hid in earlier, and swung out into the cold day.

WEDNESDAY, 1:25 P.M.

Utilizing the same skills remarked upon by Vreni Byrne that morning, Peter Parker navigated a straight line through the zoo of the *Bugle* City Room to Ken Ellis's desk. Peter had been worried that Ellis would be out chasing a story.

Instead, he was apparently *in* chasing one. Ellis spoke on the phone, voice dripping with his version of charm, trying, from the sound of it, to wrangle information.

"C'mon, I . . . no, I understand that you can't divulge that, but off the record . . . Of *course* I won't print it until it becomes official, what do you take me for? . . . Oh, *very* funny . . . Look, can't you— Hello? Hello?" Sighing, he hung up the phone and ran his hand through his short, curly black hair.

"No luck, huh?"

Ellis looked up suddenly, not having registered Peter's presence. "Oh, hi, Parker. No, no luck. Which means something weird's going on. Usually there's at least one cop who's willing to be 'a departmental source,' but they're all clamming up on this one."

Peter frowned. "This the Ann Weying thing?"

"Hm? No, Robertson. Some anonymous tipster called in and said he found Robertson's car out in Long Island City, abandoned. The weird thing is, I heard that a *Manhattan* cop led the investigation. That's one of the things I was trying to verify."

"Maybe the call went to the Manhattan cop," Peter said.

"It did, but that shouldn't matter, it'd still go to whatever the local precinct is."

"The One-Oh-Eighth."

Ellis blinked. "Huh?"

"Uh, that's the Long Island City precinct," Peter said quickly. "I live in Queens, remember?"

Ellis frowned, and said, "Right. Anyhow, I could *maybe* see if it was a downtown cop, but this is a local—Midtown South. Why the hell would a Midtown South cop be running the check on Robertson's car?"

"Dunno," Peter said, though he knew it probably had something to do with Midtown South's captain disappearing under much the same circumstances.

"So that's my morning in a nutshell. Now what do you want from me?"

Smiling a disingenuous smile, Peter said, "What makes you think I want anything from you, Ellis?"

"Because you don't like me very much, and you would only come over here to chat if you wanted something from me."

Peter didn't appreciate the reporter's tone—but then again, Ellis was absolutely right. "It's about Ann Weying's client—this Pierce guy."

"What about him?"

"You know where the cops are holding him, right?"

"Maybe. If I did know, it'd only be because I was told in strictest confidence, so I'd hardly tell you. Why do you wanna know, anyhow?"

"Same reason the story of a money launderer's trial is page-five news instead of page-sixty-four filler—he's being defended by Venom's ex-wife. I heard that Weying missed her court date. If she's gone missing, Venom either was involved, or is about to get involved. Where there's Venom, there'll probably be Spider-Man sooner or later, and I make my living off of being where Spider-Man is."

"And you think Venom will be able to track down an NYPD safehouse?"

Peter barely bit back the obvious retort, *Why not? You did.* Implying that Ellis wasn't any better than a disgraced, psychotic ex-reporter wouldn't exactly endear Peter to the man. Instead, he simply said, "He's done it before."

Ellis rubbed his chin thoughtfully. "Okay, fair enough," he finally said. "But there's a condition—any shots you get as a result of this information, you don't give them to editorial, you give them to *me.*"

A small flash of anger passed over Peter. "Why, so you can take credit for them?"

"No!" Ellis said, seemingly surprised at the very idea. "That would be unethical. I just want to protect my source. If the pictures come from me, then my source won't think I told anyone and I can still use that person as a source. I assume you won't mind not getting actual picture credit in the paper?"

"Not at all," Peter replied. Indeed, when he first started selling photos to the *Bugle*, it was on the condition that he *not* be credited. And he had to admit that Ellis's stipulation made sense.

Ellis rummaged through the mess of papers on his desk, finally liberating a pad of *Bugle* stationery. He took another moment to find a pen, then wrote what Peter assumed to be the proper information. He tore off the sheet, folded it in half, and handed it to Peter. "Do me a favor, don't look at that until you're out of the building."

Stuffing it in his jacket pocket, he said, "No problem. And thanks."

"Don't thank me, just get me some good pictures."

WEDNESDAY, 2:15 P.M.

A.J. Pierce was growing ever more frustrated.

Where was Ms. Weying? She hadn't shown up for the deposition, but beyond that, he didn't know anything. The court officer had escorted him out, and then the Four Horsemen had come to take him back to the suite at the Edghill Hotel that had been his home for the past several weeks. Since then, nothing.

The Edghill was a decent place of lodging in a very old building, located a bit south of the courthouse. It wasn't the Plaza or the Ritz, but his suite did have a lovely view of the Statue of Liberty, Ellis Island, and the Narrows. On any other occasion, A.J. would have sat at the window and gazed out upon the water, watching the sun reflect off Lady Liberty's torch.

But not today.

Today Ms. Weying had disappeared.

Without her, A.J. Pierce was once again alone. He didn't know if he could bear it.

The Four Horsemen, as he'd come to think of the ever-changing quartet of police officers assigned to protect him, all sat in the common room. Today, the roles of Death, War, Famine, and Pestilence were taken by four men named Heck, Honigsberg, Cleary, and Daley. At present, they were playing a game of poker that A.J. had not been invited to participate in. Not that he would have accepted such an invitation. A.J. had been a gambler all his life. Years ago, he made regular biweekly trips to Atlantic City and, unlike others who made the trip, often came home with more cash than he left with. It was how he rewarded himself on payday. It gave him something to look forward to, in the days before his phantom companies started taking up more and more of his leisure time.

He would hardly participate in a penny-ante game of "high-low," or whatever moronic middle-class variation the Horsemen insisted upon.

He had already read the day's *New York Times*, *Daily Bugle*, and *Daily Globe* cover to cover. (The Four Horsemen wouldn't let him read the *Wall Street Journal*.) He'd given up asking for a laptop. Two straight weeks of asking had gotten responses ranging from a simple no to a threat of charges. *What are they afraid of?* he wondered.

A.J. loathed television, particularly the programming options of the early afternoon, but it seemed to be his only recourse. And it might take his mind off what could have happened to dear, dear Ms. Weying.

Then he felt a draft. He turned to the window—

—to find a man in a red-and-blue leotard crouched on the windowsill of the now-open window.

After a moment, he realized that this was one of the super heroes that infested New York like cockroaches. Bug-Person, or something like that; probably one of the Fantastic Avengers, or whatever they called themselves.

A.J. Pierce loathed super heroes almost as much as he loathed television. They didn't understand subtlety or finesse or grace. They just beat on people.

"Hi there," said a slightly muffled voice. "You just have to be A.J. Pierce."

"Are you out of your mind? We're on the twenty-fifth floor."

Bug-Person leapt into the room. Actually, he did a kind of somersault, and somehow managed to close the window on the back turn, then land in a crouching position in front of A.J. "Don't worry," he said, "I'm used to heights."

Hoping like hell he sounded as confident and intimidating as he didn't feel, A.J. said, "You realize that all I have to do is raise my voice a bit, and the four police officers in the next room will come charging in here."

"Look, all I want to do is ask you a couple of questions."

A.J. smiled. "Funny, that's what the police said the day they arrested me."

"It's about Ann Weying."

"She's my lawyer, she didn't show up for court this morning, I have absolutely no idea what happened to her." He said it all in one quick, nonstop sentence, and realized that made him sound like the nervous wreck he truly was. He took a breath and forced himself to speak more slowly. Confident people spoke slowly. Morgan Hall took days to complete his sentences. "I have asked for updates, but no one tells me anything." A.J. winced. That sounded like he was whining.

Bug-Person stood up straight and came in close to A.J., putting his hand on A.J.'s shoulder. A.J. thought the gesture inappropriate, but given that the man had just wandered into a twenty-fifth-floor room from the outside under his own power, he thought it best not to complain. Instead, he affected a bored expression.

"I just want to find her. Do you have any idea who might've taken her?"

A.J. forced himself not to react to this last statement. It hadn't occurred to him that Ms. Weying was kidnapped. He assumed that she just hadn't shown up for some bizarre reason.

"None whatsoever," he said aloud. "She's just my lawyer. Two months ago, I'd never even heard of her."

"You don't know of any enemies she might have."

"She's a lawyer—she's probably got plenty of them." *Much better. That sounded tough.*

"Maybe she was kidnapped to get at you," Bug-Person said, finally removing the hand from A.J.'s shoulder.

"To do what, keep me from appearing in court?" A.J. tried a dismissive laugh, but it came out high-pitched. "All that does is put me back in this secret police safehouse. What's the point in that?"

"Yeah, well, I found out about this place. Someone else could, too."

"Look, Bug-Person, or whatever you call yourself, I would love to help you," A.J. said, "but I really don't know anything. So kindly go and fly off and beat up a super-villain or something."

The super hero looked at A.J. for a moment. At least, A.J. assumed he did. The mask he wore covered his entire head, so it was impossible to read his facial expression.

Finally, he said, "All right, fine. Sorry to have bothered you."

He opened the window and leapt onto the sill. Some kind of rope shot out from under his wrist, and he jumped out the window.

As he did so, the Four Horsemen burst into the room, guns drawn. "Freeze!" one of them—Heck—yelled.

They then realized that A.J. was now the only one in the room—a room which grew colder by the second, since Bug-Person hadn't bothered to close the window behind him. A.J. did so.

A.J. Pierce hated super heroes.

"What the hell was that?" Honigsberg asked.

"Dunno," Daley said.

"We'd better call it in," said Cleary. "Are you okay?" he asked A.J.

Keeping the tough-guy timbre that had mostly worked with Bug-Person, A.J. shrugged and said, "Perfectly fine. This is the most interesting thing that's happened in this hotel room in the last three weeks."

"Yeah, I . . . No, that's okay . . . No, really, you don't . . . Honestly, we don't need your . . . No, really . . . *Really*, it's all right."

Detective Sergeant Vance Hawkins couldn't help but smile. His partner, Stephen Drew, had been on the phone for some time, and the entire conversation had been of the same tenor. Drew sat on the rim of his desk, left foot on his chair, repeatedly running his hand through his sandy hair. Hawkins sat on the chair belonging to his desk—face-to-face with and flush against Drew's—observing the proceedings with a look of wry amusement on his dark face.

"Look, I'll check with my lieutenant, okay? Either he or I will call you back, all right? . . . Great . . . Great . . . Great . . . Thank you. 'Bye." He hung up. *"Argh!"*

"I'm almost afraid to ask who that was," Hawkins said with a small smile.

"Sergeant Steen, downtown."

"That would be Detective Sergeant Steen of Clark and Steen, heads of the Venom Task Force?"

"Yup. They're having copies made of all their files and will have them messengered up here within the hour."

"Them telling you that took *this* long?"

Drew smiled, but it was the smile of a man about to run screaming into the night. "No, that just accounted for the first ten seconds. The remaining six hours related to me convincing them that we don't need their assistance on this case."

Hawkins shuddered. The VTF hadn't exactly distinguished themselves during their brief existence, and too many of their cases wound up as bloodbaths.

"I told 'em I'd run it by Golden. Oughtta be good for a laugh, anyhow."

"What oughtta be good for a laugh?"

Hawkins turned around to see Golden approaching, Gilman and Liverakos behind him.

Drew explained, "I just got off the phone with Steen downtown. They're sending us their Venom files, and she also asked to get the VTF cut in on the case."

"Right after pigs fly out my butt."

Drew smiled. "Understood."

"Meantime, I got news. I just got off a conference call with Commissioner Ramos. The Midtown South Precinct has been given local jurisdiction for investigating the disappearances of Frank Esteban, Joseph Robertson, and Ann Weying. The other precincts have agreed, and they'll cooperate fully. Anything involving this case within the five boroughs, it's our show."

Drew, Gilman, and Liverakos's reactions ranged from

"Yeah," to "All right!" to "Excellent." Hawkins remained quiet. Something was amiss.

"Drew, Hawkins, you two are primaries; Gilman, Liverakos, you're secondaries. Whatever you need, within reason, you got. Ramos also signed off on us keeping Frank's kidnapping out of the press. Questions?"

"I've got one," Hawkins said. "Conference calls are usually with three people, and you qualified yourself way too much."

Golden snorted. "Good work, *Detective*. As it happens, you're right. The third party on that call was a lady named Buchanan, the head of the New York section of the FBI." As ever when discussing federal law enforcement, Golden practically sneered the three-letter abbreviation. "Turns out they may know who's involved in this."

"Who?" Gilman asked.

"Dunno yet—Buchanan was calling from a cell phone, so she didn't wanna go into details. They're sending two agents down to brief us at three. Anything else?"

Drew spoke up. "Uh, yeah, Lieutenant, uh—Hawk and I were talking, and, ah, we think we should bring Spider-Man in on this."

Before Golden had a chance to object, Hawkins broke in, "We know how you feel about 'costumes,' sir, but this is *already* a costume case."

"How you figure that?"

Hawkins noted that Golden's tone was not belligerent, merely questioning. Choosing to view that as a good sign, he went on: "First off, the preliminary forensics reports on all three sites indicate a high probability of paranormal involvement—specifically, that the owner of the weird fingerprints is a shapechanger. Secondly, one of our apparent victims is Venom's ex-wife. He's defended her before, up to having that alien suit of his save her from a gunshot wound. I agree totally with your assessment of the VTF, but we should get someone in here who knows Venom, and no one's dealt with him more than Spider-Man."

Golden scratched his thin beard. "Okay, say I go for it. How do we get in touch with him?"

Drew looked at his watch. "Actually, he should be calling here pretty soon." At Golden's glower, Drew quickly added, "Uh, we've kinda been in touch with him already. Or, rather, he's, ah, been in touch with us. Remember that anonymous phone tip on Robertson's car?"

Golden nodded slowly.

"It wasn't really anonymous. It was Spider-Man."

"You sure it was him?"

Drew nodded. "He knew stuff about the Octopus case that only he could know."

Golden frowned. "Like what?"

Nervously, Drew said, "I'd, ah, rather not say."

Hawkins smiled. Gilman and Liverakos both snorted.

The lieutenant scratched his beard some more, letting silence reign uncomfortably for several seconds. Hawkins smiled as Drew ran his hands through his hair again. *He always does that when he's nervous.*

Finally, Golden said, "All right, fine. If Venom is involved, we'll probably have to deal with Spider-Man in any case, so we may as well get him in on our side right off."

"That was our feeling, too, sir," Hawkins said.

"When's he supposed to call?"

"I told him to call back in two hours—" Drew checked his watch again "—about two hours ago, so any minute now."

On the word *now*, Drew's phone rang. All five looked at it. Golden said, "If that's him, I'm gonna have to kill you."

Drew picked up the phone nervously. "Drew . . . Oh, hi, Jenn . . . What? . . . Oy . . . Okay, thanks." He hung up. "That was Jenn Jackson downtown. She's in charge of the team that's keeping A.J. Pierce in protective custody."

At Golden's blank expression, Hawkins quickly added, "Pierce is the Wall Street guy that Weying's defending. We asked Sergeant Jackson to let us know if anything weird happened at the safehouse."

"I take it something weird did happen?" Golden said.

Drew nodded. "Somebody barged into Pierce's room.

Pierce insists nothing happened, but the four officers all swear they saw someone go out the window. The twenty-fifth-floor window.''

''Someone?''

Drew smiled. ''Well, that's the fun part. One said it was Spider-Man, one said it was Venom, one said it was Carnage, and one said it was the Black Widow.''

''Peachy,'' Golden said. ''Lemme know when the costume calls.''

''Got it.''

WEDNESDAY, 2:35 P.M.

Spider-Man swung over to the World Trade Center for no particular reason. He just needed somewhere to perch and think. Since the twin towers had been closed to the public for some time—ever since a rather nasty fight involving Dr. Doom, Spider-Man himself, the Fantastic Four, and the intelligence organization SAFE—it was a quiet place to woolgather.

Today it was also a cold place to woolgather, but that was true of pretty much anywhere this afternoon.

Pierce had been a washout. Spider-Man supposed he shouldn't have expected any better. Still, he had left a spider-tracer on Pierce when he put his hand on the man's shoulder, just in case. If nothing else, his prediction to Ellis might come true, and Venom might track Pierce down. Venom's symbiote didn't trigger Spider-Man's spider-sense, but the tracer did. It wasn't much, but right now, it was all he had.

I can't believe he actually called me ''Bug-Person.'' That's a new one.

He checked his watch, and discovered that it was almost 2:40. *Whoops. Shoulda called ''Stevie'' ten minutes ago.*

He went down to street level, eventually alighting atop an unoccupied pay phone. Then he performed a simple flip, landing in front of the phone, facing it. Several well-dressed New Yorkers glanced at him, but most ignored him. *Gotta love this town.*

Again, he dialed the series of numbers that would charge the call to his card. After two rings: "Drew."

"It's your friendly neighborhood Spider-Man."

"About time you called. I was startin' to think you were blowing me off."

"Oh, come now, Drew, would I do that to you?"

"You never know. Listen, can you come up here to the station?"

Spider-Man hesitated. "Excuse me?"

"Hawk and I talked to our lieutenant, and he agreed that we need to bring you in on this, what with Venom and all. And it'll be easier if you just read the reports here rather than have me read 'em to you over the phone."

Again, Spider-Man hesitated. "You sure this is such a hot idea? I mean, I haven't always been on the best of terms with the boys in blue."

" 'S'okay, the lieutenant never wears blue. Seriously, it'll be fine. Besides, with Venom being a factor, I don't think anyone's gonna complain. Besides, Esteban always said nice things about you."

"Huh," Spider-Man said, impressed with so rare a testimonial.

"We're getting briefed by some feds in twenty minutes, so move it."

Spider-Man felt like he'd missed something. "Waitasec—feds?"

"Don't look at me, I just work here. A coupla FBI agents are coming down to brief us about something. We don't know what yet, but it relates to the case." Drew sighed. "I'm kinda worried that this'll get yanked out of our hands. I hate this jurisdictional crap."

"That's the nice thing about my end of the business. I don't have those problems."

"Yeah, but you have to go out in public in a bright red bodysuit. I like my way better. Look, just get over here, okay? You know the address?"

"I think so."

"Thirty-fifth between Eighth and Ninth."

Spider-Man said, "That's what I thought. See you in a bit."

After hanging up, he leapt back up to the top of the phone booth. From below, someone muttered, " 'Bout *time* you got off. It's a *public* phone, y'know."

"Sorry," he said as he shot a web-line at a nearby building and moved to swing off. "Official government business."

As he wended his way uptown, he thought about what he was getting himself into. On occasion, he had cooperated with the NYPD, but far more often, he was on their bad side. For a long time, he had been the prime suspect in the murders of both industrialist Norman Osborn and retired police captain George Stacy. Though eventually cleared of both, the accusations hadn't exactly endeared him to the cops, especially Stacy's murder. That one hurt more, since Stacy's daughter Gwen was Peter Parker's girlfriend. Gwen was shortly thereafter killed by Osborn in his guise as the Green Goblin.

Still, relations with the cops had improved over the years, particularly when Spider-Man was instrumental in capturing the Sin-Eater, who had murdered Captain Jean DeWolff. And he had worked with the NYPD on several occasions, sometimes at DeWolff's instigation when she was alive, sometimes out of respect for finding her killer after her death. *Just never this closely*, he thought as he swung uptown through Greenwich Village. *I mean, they're letting me into the precinct house. I've been inside a precinct in costume maybe three or four times in my career.*

But recently he had worked with SAFE, and prior to that he'd worked with SAFE's de facto international counterpart S.H.I.E.L.D. *So the idea isn't patently ludicrous. Just weird. Very weird.*

Swinging past Fourteenth Street and into Chelsea—at one point swinging by the apartment he'd lived in up until marrying MJ—he decided, *It doesn't matter. Robbie's life may be at stake—not to mention Esteban's and Ann Weying's. My potential discomfort with the NYPD isn't even an issue.*

His sense of purpose reassured, if not actually renewed, he continued uptown.

CHAPTER 5

WEDNESDAY, 2:55 P.M.

"The song sucks, Laura," Peter Gilman said as he and Laura Liverakos entered Midtown South's coffee room.

"It is one of the greatest rock and roll songs ever written."

"Right, sure. That's why Robert Plant gives a different answer each time someone asks him what it's about."

"He does not," Liverakos insisted.

"Yes, he does. Besides, what kind of rock song opens with an alto recorder part? Oh, hell," he added before Liverakos could reply. He had just noticed the coffee pot.

"What?" she asked.

"Look at this." Gilman held up the pot, which held barely a quarter of a cup of coffee sloshing around the bottom amidst the dregs. "I love it. Guys leave like a micron of coffee, they figure they don't have to make more, 'cause there's still some left. Like anybody's gonna drink this." He dumped the remains into the sink and rinsed out the pot.

Liverakos folded her arms in an attempt to warm them. "Why's it so cold in here?"

"Maintenance probably thought midwinter was a great time to run the air conditioning."

"Yeah probably," she said. "So if 'Stairway to Heaven' is so awful, why does it always win those top songs of all-time polls?"

"I hate to interrupt this deep musical discourse," said a voice from behind them, completely startling Gilman, "but can one of you tell me where to find Sergeants Drew and Hawkins?"

They both whirled around. Liverakos's hand had moved to her weapon. Gilman didn't see anything.

"Up here."

Gilman followed the voice to the section of the wall over one of the windows, presently open. A grown man in red-and-blue longjohns was *walking* on the wall, crouched like a—

Like a spider, doofus, Gilman realized.

"Y-you're Spider-Man, right?" Gilman said. Instantly, he regretted saying it. *Who else could it possibly be? No two people would dress like that.*

"Hope so, I'm wearing his underwear." Spider-Man reached down to close the window with one hand. "Sorry for letting the cold in."

"Uh, that's—that's okay," Gilman stammered.

Liverakos rescued him. "They're waiting for you inside," she said. "I'm Laura Liverakos, and Mr. Eloquent here is my partner, Peter Gilman. We're secondaries on this case, working with Hawk and Drew."

Before Gilman could add anything, Spider-Man flew off the wall.

No, he didn't fly, exactly—he jumped, so fast it seemed like flying. He flipped, then landed squarely on his feet.

During the last Olympics, Liverakos had finally convinced her partner to watch the gymnastics competition—for years, Gilman insisted it wasn't a real sport. Finally, though, he gave in, and became hooked.

The best gymnast he ever saw in competition couldn't hold a candle to the compactness, elegance, litheness, and grace of the man in the gaudy red suit now standing in front of him.

"G-good move," he said.

"Thanks. I owe it all to clean living and eating my Wheaties."

"Oh," Gilman said lamely. *Oy flipping vey,* he thought. *Why not just add, "Is that so?" and complete the disaster?*

"Actually," Spider-Man continued, "I hate Wheaties. Give me Corn Pops anytime."

Liverakos grinned. "A wise and sensible man. Come on, follow me," she said, leading Spider-Man back into the squad-room.

"I'm just gonna finishing making more coffee," Gilman said to their retreating forms. "I'll let you know when the feds get here."

Liverakos made an *okay* gesture to him as they turned the corner and disappeared.

Nice work there, Gilman thought as he poured water into

the coffeemaker. *Laura goes on another classic rock dissertation, you're fine. The minute a super hero walks in the door—or window, whatever—you turn into a moron.*

Entering the squadroom, Spider-Man felt a sudden sense of déjà vu. Aurally and structurally, the place could have been the *Bugle* City Room: desks shoved together in a large space, offices on the outer edges only, people in constant motion, and continuous sound hovering over the room like a lifting fog.

Visually, of course, it was completely different. For one thing, the City Room's walls were painted a cheery off-white color, whereas Midtown South had drab walls that had started out life as an unfortunate shade of green and degenerated over time to something more like olive drab. For another, most of the City Room occupants were *Bugle* employees—middle-class professionals, primarily, resulting in a certain sameness of modes of dress. Midtown South, on the other hand, was occupied by both blue-uniformed and plainclothes officers (who sported a much wider variety of clothes than the *Bugle*'s staff), as well as perpetrators, lawyers, visitors, complainants, etc., who came in all shapes, sizes, and colors.

Few people batted an eyelash at Spider-Man walking among them. A couple of the cops gave him odd looks—whether of confusion, appreciation, or contempt, Spider-Man couldn't be entirely sure—and one little kid on a bench in what looked like a waiting area pointed at him and cried out, "Hey, look, it's Daredevil!" Spider-Man could only sigh.

Liverakos—a surprisingly short brunette, wearing a tweed jacket over a black turtleneck and jeans—tried to suppress a smile as she led him to a pair of desks, at which sat the familiar forms of Vance Hawkins and Stephen Drew. Drew, a blond-haired white man of average height and build, wore a denim shirt and red tie—thus matching Spider-Man's own colors, causing the web-slinger to smirk under his mask—while his partner, a broad-shouldered African American who had shaved his head since Spider-Man last saw him, went for the more conservative white-shirt-and-solid-colored-tie approach.

"Well, well, look who's here," Drew said.

"I'm not late, am I?"

"No, right on time—the *feds*'re late."

Liverakos shook her head. "Our tax dollars at work."

Hawkins stood up. "That's all right, it gives the lieutenant a chance to prepare the ground. He wants to see you in his office."

Spider-Man nodded. "Fine by me. Lead on, Macduff."

"That's 'Lay.' "

"I beg your pardon?" Spider-Man said, blinking.

Liverakos chuckled. "There he goes again."

"Give the guy a break, Hawk," Drew said, laughing as they started walking toward one of the offices.

Hawkins went on: "*Macbeth*, Act Five, scene eight, lines thirty-three to thirty-four. Macbeth says, 'Lay on Macduff, / And damn'd be him that first cries "Hold, enough!" ' It's right before Macduff kills him."

Spider-Man just looked at the man for a moment, then shook his head and said, "Remind me never to go up against you in Trivial Pursuit."

They arrived at Golden's office, and all four entered.

The lieutenant was a burly man with no discernable neck and a thin beard. He stood as the quartet came through the door.

"So," he said, "you're the costume."

"Not exactly. I'm the guy wearing the costume. Unless, of course, you're talking *to* the costume—which is fine, if that's what you're into, just don't hold your breath waiting for a response."

Drew, Hawkins, and Liverakos smiled. Golden didn't. "Look, costume, I don't particularly want you here. I make it a rule not to trust anybody who wears his underwear on the outside. I only okayed your being here 'cause Hawk and Drew vouched for you and 'cause Frank said nice things about you. Besides, I could use a Venom expert in case he sticks his tongue into this."

"Trust me, he will. The only thing that lights Brock's pilot light more than trying to kill me is Ann Weying."

"Be that as it may, I want you to tread real lightly here.

This is an NYPD operation, not one of your harebrained solo shots. I don't want you messin' things up like usual."

"Lieutenant—" Spider-Man started.

"Lemme tell you a story, costume," Golden interrupted, sitting down.

Out of the corner of his eye, Spider-Man saw Drew shake his head, Liverakos sigh, and Hawkins put his head in his hands. *Why do I get the feeling they've heard this all before? Oh well, might as well grin and bear it.*

"A few years back," Golden said, "some uniforms found two guys webbed to a lamppost. They had no weapons on them, no stolen merchandise, and there were no witnesses. Just two guys hanging there. To this day, we have no clue why you put them there. And *they* weren't talking. We wasted a ton of time and paperwork on those two losers because you couldn't be bothered to make a statement."

Spider-Man found himself speechless. The incident Golden described matched any one of dozens of occasions when he had stopped some kind of crime in progress. He could almost visualize it. Two guys swipe a purse or a briefcase or something, Spidey chases them, webs them to a lamppost, gives the victim his or her item back. Said victim goes on his or her merry way, Spidey goes on *his* merry way—*Probably late for a class or an appointment or a date or something, knowing me*, he thought—leaving the two guys with no actual stolen merchandise on them, and the only witness long gone by the time the cops arrive. Naturally, they'd walk.

Finally, he said, "Look, Lieutenant—"

"Hey, listen," Golden interrupted again, "it happens. Besides, you saved Hawk's life here, and you got DeWolff's killer, so I guess you ain't all bad. Just keep in mind that you doing a job halfway means more work for someone else down the line. And also keep in mind that this is our show—it's our captain who's missing. You're just helpin' out. You screw us up in any way, and I will make it my life's work to nail you to the wall, *capice*?"

Spider-Man tried to feel intimidated, and failed. He'd been hearing threats like that from people far more dangerous than any police lieutenant ever could be for years. Still, he respected where Golden was coming from, and so said, "Don't worry, Lieutenant. We're on the same side, here."

Gilman stuck his gray-haired head into the doorway. "The feds're here, Lieutenant. Jones is takin' 'em to Interrogation 3."

"What do they look like?" Liverakos asked.

Gilman shrugged. "One male, one female. The man's about six-foot-six, the woman's about a foot shorter. Both wearing suits, neither show any evidence of a personality."

Spider-Man chuckled. "Sounds like typical government issue to me."

"Yeah," Golden muttered as he got up again. "Let's see what they got to tell us."

Spider-Man felt like the proverbial fly on the wall.

Not that the feeling should have come as a surprise, of course: he was quite literally *on* the wall—the soles of his feet and back flush against the cracked plaster, crouched over the dented interrogation desk some four feet from the floor. But there was more to it than that. Golden had been right; Spider-Man didn't really belong in a team of law-enforcement officers. He wasn't a detective. Everything he knew about police procedures he'd learned from Ed McBain and Steven Bochco.

Sure, he was smart and quick-witted. He'd caught his share of crooks in the last few years. But he did it all by himself. The cops followed the chain of command. They filled out paperwork and testified at trials. They observed protocol.

Spider-Man worked alone. As far as he was concerned, protocol was the name of an outpatient procedure.

Still, Drew and Hawkins had trusted him enough to bring him into the investigation. And lives were at stake. That was all that mattered.

Spider-Man reached behind his back and shifted the seam of his costume. He was glad to be above the fray: the interrogation room had not been made to fit eight people. Somehow they'd managed, though. The woman FBI agent, looking prim in her shapeless blue suit, leaned stiffly against the far wall.

Her partner sat on a metal stool, with his much-too-long legs crossed at the knees, wagging his foot as if he were conducting an orchestra. A black briefcase stood conspicuously between them. Gilman and Liverakos had propped themselves onto the interrogation desk. Drew stood under the single barred window, while Hawkins lounged on a chair next to the door. Lieutenant Golden, muttering under his breath, joined Drew at the window.

"That's Special Agent Brandy Hauman," the tall man said, motioning toward his partner. "I'm Special Agent Glenn Phillips. That's Phillips like the screwdriver."

What a charmer, Spider Man thought.

Golden introduced himself, then quickly ran through the names of the officers in the room. Somehow he managed to skip over Spider-Man. *At least he's consistent.*

"So," Agent Hauman began, stepping forward, "I understand that you have some facts to share with us?"

Golden frowned. "Now, wait a minute. I thought it was the other way around. *You* called *us*, remember?"

"I don't know how the NYPD handles its criminal investigations," Agent Screwdriver said, "but we at the FBI are not in the habit of blathering in front of masked vigilantes."

Immediately Spider-Man started shuffling toward the door. "Just fill me in later," he said. Golden, he knew, had been looking for a good reason to get rid of him, and the federal agents had just handed it to him on a silver platter. *Might as well go play in the snow or something.*

"Hold on," Golden said, looking squarely at him. He then turned toward the agents. "The costume stays."

Surprised, Spider-Man blinked under his mask.

Agent Hauman put her hands on her hips. "This is completely unacceptable."

"We don't have a choice," Golden said. "No one in this department knows Venom better."

"Venom?" Hauman asked, glancing at her partner. "We had no idea that Eddie Brock was involved in—"

"Not yet," Spider-Man said, "but Ann Weying is. And whenever you cast Brock's ex-wife in anything, Venom is bound to make a guest appearance. They go together; you know, like horse and carriage?"

"Lame jokes aside," Golden said, "we need him."

Agent Screwdriver smacked his lips. He glared at Hauman for a moment, then said, "I trust you are aware of the Wells Fargo hijacking two months ago. The one in Hartford, I mean."

"Who isn't?" Drew said. "Eight million in untraceable, small-denomination bills. And no arrests. Your classic sweet deal."

Over on his wall, Spider-Man recalled the *Bugle*'s sparkling headline: ROBBERY OF THE CENTURY! Robbie had tried for something less sensational, but Jonah wouldn't hear of it. He'd even managed to slip a picture of the wall-crawler—from a totally unrelated story, of course—onto the front page. Only if you read the small caption could you tell that Spider-Man had been *preventing* a robbery in Manhattan.

"I always figured it was the Kingpin," Gilman said. "Two or three guys, they would had been caught already. For something that big you need an organization."

"An organization, yes," Hauman said, "but not Fisk's. We have reason to believe that the robbery was political."

"Political?" Liverakos asked. She leaned forward from the desk, resting her slight hands on her thighs.

"Look," Phillips said, "what we're about to tell you is classified government information." He glanced at Spider-Man and scowled. "It cannot, under any circumstances, leave this room. Understand?"

"Whatever," Golden said.

Spider-Man held his fists together under his chin. "Oh goody! I just looove secrets."

Hauman sighed. "For the past three years," she began, "the FBI has been investigating the activities of a violent Puerto Rican separatist group called the Cane Cutters. Now, I don't know if you know much about Puerto Rican politics—"

"Nary," Drew chimed in.

"Saw *West Side Story* once," Liverakos said.

"Zilch," said Gilman.

Hauman blinked and continued: "The Cane Cutters are a fringe within a fringe. In their manifesto they blame the United States for pretty much everything that has gone wrong on the island in the last hundred years, from government corruption to air pollution to hurricanes. And they're armed to the teeth."

"They're also completely unpredictable," Phillips added. "Last Christmas they dressed up like the three wise men and distributed gifts to the kids in the housing projects. Three days later they machine gunned a bus filled with American military personnel. You never know what to expect from them."

"These are dangerous people," Hauman said. "Fanatical. Totally ruthless."

"And you think they robbed that Wells Fargo truck," Spider-Man said.

Hauman nodded. "We can only assume that the money will be used to expand the scope of their terrorist activities. Eight million buys a lot of hardware."

"I don't get it," Golden said. "What's the connection with the kidnappings?"

"Let me show you something," Hauman said. She reached down and opened her briefcase and produced a creased manila folder. From the folder she took out a sheet of white paper, which she passed over to the lieutenant, grimacing as she stretched across the room. Golden narrowed his eyes and stroked his thin beard.

"That's just from the dashboard," Phillips said, "by the way."

Curious, Spider-Man shuffled over to Golden's wall, skipping over an empty light fixture. As soon as he noticed him, the lieutenant muttered a curse and, without looking, roughly handed Spider-Man the sheet.

Thumbprints. Dozens of them, arranged across the page in numbered boxes like comic-book panels. Each one slightly different; in fact, it was easy to discern a progression, as if the lines and whorls were describing the patterns of a shifting storm. Spider-Man's mouth went dry. Drew had mentioned shifting fingerprints before, but to actually see the transformation . . .

"Subject: Sombra," Spider-Man read aloud, the words printed along the left-hand edge in neat computer characters. Quickly he folded the sheet between his fingers and handed it to Hawkins.

"There is no birth name on record," Hauman said, sorting through the contents of the manila folder, "so that's the closest we've come to an identity."

"That's Spanish for *shadow*," Hawkins said as he skimmed over the sheet.

Hauman nodded. "It's a name the CIA culled from a Soviet communiqué they intercepted ten years ago. He's from Puerto Rico originally. Besides that, we know little about the man."

"He's a mutant," Hawkins said as he handed the sheet over to Drew. "A shapeshifter?"

"More or less," Phillips said, nodding. "According to our forensic geneticist, Sombra's DNA is highly unstable. One day he could be a stocky African-American man, the next a tall Caucasian with gray-blue eyes. You could say that he's constantly mutating. We suspect that it takes him a great deal of concentration to maintain a particular guise. He is, quite literally, the man of a thousand faces."

"I take it that this Sombra character is involved with the Cane Cutters," Golden said.

"We believe he leads them," Hauman said. "The Cane Cutters are new on the scene. Three years, tops. Started by a group of disaffected college students in Ponce, a city on the southern coast of the island. Sombra has been an operative for well over a decade at least; he even trained in Cuba during the cold war. Obviously he has the experience, but he is also supposed to be a clever ideologue and a decisive commander. People listen to him. And that makes him doubly dangerous."

Over by the window, the radiator blew a thick banner of steam. Spider-Man hadn't much enjoyed the cold outside, but in this tiny room his costume felt like cellophane. His chest was damp and his head sweltered under the mask.

"It doesn't make sense," he said. "I mean, think about it: the man's always changing. His face, his bones, his skin . . . I can see him as a serial killer, maybe some kind of loony double agent. But a revolutionary?''

From the folder Hauman slipped out a stack of sheets held together with a black clamp. ''Psych profile,'' she said. Awkwardly, balancing the rest of the file on her chest, she flipped through the report. ''It's too much to read right know, but the gist of it is that Sombra overcompensates. He has no physical identity, so he became a fanatic about Puerto Rican culture and independence.'' She glanced at Golden, then quickly at Spider-Man. ''I'll leave a copy here for you. It's pretty interesting, actually.''

''I think we've heard enough,'' Golden said. Casually he drew his pistol and checked the clip. Spider-Man hated the sound of it. ''Gilman, Liverakos, call DiFillippo, get a SWAT team ready. Drew, I want you to liaison with the feds on this.''

Hawkins jumped to his feet. ''What am I doing?'' he said.

''You stay close to the costume. I have a feeling we're gonna be running into Venom before the day is through.''

''That's a safe bet,'' Spider-Man said ruefully.

Looking over at her partner, Hauman closed the folder and jammed it under her arm. Then she turned toward the lieutenant and said, ''Where are you going?''

''Cane Cutter headquarters,'' Golden said, as if it were the most natural thing in the world. ''You're leading the way, right?''

Agent Screwdriver laughed, wagging his foot. ''We have absolutely no idea where they are.''

''That's not funny,'' Liverakos said. She jumped off the desk and stepped toward Phillips. Petite as she was, her gait showed plenty of weight and power. The federal agent clammed up at once.

''Look,'' Hauman said, holding out her hand as if to take a summons, ''don't get me wrong—the FBI is very much in favor of interdepartmental cooperation. That's why we came here. But you have to understand that this is an *ongoing* investigation.''

''We want Sombra,'' Phillips added. He smacked his lips and scratched the back of his ear. ''We have him involved in over eighteen murders over the past decade. He's our first priority."

"It's so close," Hauman said. Her voice was suddenly high and glassy. "Just last week we caught up with one of the couriers from the Wells Fargo robbery. His name is Jorge DeLaSelva, we have him under twenty-four-hour surveillance, and if we play our cards right, he's going to lead us straight to Sombra. We can't afford to have the whole situation disturbed."

"Excuse me," Spider-Man said, raising his hand like an impatient school child. He could feel blood pumping at his temples.

"Yes," Phillips growled.

"I have a little question."

"Go ahead," Hauman said, exasperated.

"What about Robertson and the others?"

"Er, well," Hauman said, leafing again through the file, "we know that Weying defended DeLaSelva last year—*pro bono* work—so there might be a connection there. Esteban and Robertson are still a puzzle, though."

"That's not what I meant," Spider-Man said. He crouched tighter against the wall, crossed his arms over his knees. "We've got three people kidnapped here. People we know. And you're telling us you've got a lead, but you're gonna sit on it? This DeLaSelva guy, if that's his real name, you've got to bring him in."

Liverakos nodded. "He probably knows where the Cane Cutters are holed up."

"No way," Agent Screwdriver said, angrily. "He's the only connection we have to Sombra. If he bolts, we're gonna be left out in the cold with our—"

"Come on!" Drew said. "It's our captain!"

"We know it's your captain," Hauman said. "Believe me, we are perfectly aware of the fact. And if it were one of ours I'd probably feel the way you do. But you have to understand that this is bigger than Captain Esteban, bigger than the editor-in-chief of the *Daily Bugle*." She glared at Spider-Man for a moment, her eyes narrowed, then added, "It's even bigger than Venom, I'm afraid. We'll keep you informed, but that's all we can do.''

Gilman snorted. ''That's the biggest crock of—''

''Shut up, Peter,'' Golden said all of a sudden. He stroked the back of his neck.

''But, Lieutenant,'' Drew protested.

Without even a glance to his underlings, Golden walked up to Phillips and Hauman and, one after the other, stiffly shook their hands.

''We appreciate the info,'' he said. ''If we figure anything out, we'll let you know.''

Agent Hauman seemed perplexed at first, but quickly recovered. ''We knew you would understand.''

''We'll get them,'' Phillips said, standing up, then pacing slowly toward the door. Hauman followed. ''Don't you worry about that. We'll get them.''

''Sure,'' Golden said.

After the agents left the interrogation room, Golden shut the door and leaned against it. His eyes were like worn marbles, dark and hazy.

''Lieutenant,'' Spider-Man said, carefully, ''I don't want to tell you how to do your job, bu—''

''Then don't,'' Golden said. He paused for a moment, scanning the room as if to offer a challenge. Everyone but Vance Hawkins stared back at him, their expressions wavering between confusion and outrage. Hawkins, who had been uncharacteristically quiet, seemed to examine his kneecaps.

''There comes a moment in a conversation,'' Golden continued, ''when you realize it's gone as far as it's gonna go.''

''The lieutenant is right,'' Hawkins said.

''What?'' Drew exploded, twisting around to face his partner.

''It's personal,'' Hawkins said in a flat voice. ''Sombra killed one of theirs.''

Gilman took a deep breath and muttered, ''What are you talking about?''

''If that's true,'' Drew said, ''why wouldn't they just come out and tell us?''

"They did. You just have to listen. Not just the words, I mean, but the pauses, the tones. Read between the lines."

Spider-Man—burdened by more than his share of the dead—understood perfectly. At first he hadn't noticed, but as soon as Hawkins suggested an FBI vendetta, the signs all but screamed at him: Hauman's moist eyes, the hateful sneer in Phillips's mouth. He recalled crouching by the old Acme warehouse where his uncle's murderer lay hidden, all those nights ago, listening to the sirens, to the tires screeching, watching as the uniformed officers milled around the structure. He remembered the hunger, the greed needling his mind, knowing that it could only be him. It *had* to be him.

"The feds are not giving up DeLaSelva," Spider-Man said. "No way."

"I agree," Golden said.

Gilman put his hands to his graying hair. "So what are we gonna do, sit around and watch it all on CNN?"

"They gave us a name," Liverakos said, settling onto the stool Phillips had just vacated.

"They gave us a name," Golden repeated. He raised his eyebrows, stepped forward, and pulled the door open. Outside the precinct was bustling, as usual: officers hunt-pecked on computer keyboards, handcuffed children spat curses, women in spandex and polyester hollered across the hall for their lawyers.

For once Spider-Man appreciated the heat of the interrogation room.

"So," he said aloud, "I take it we are not just going to sit on our duffs?"

"If the feds don't want to cooperate, that's their perogative," Golden said stiffly. "But I have been given no instruction contrary to what Commissioner Ramos told me a couple hours ago: we have full jurisdiction on this case within the five boroughs."

"Good," Liverakos said emphatically.

Golden continued, "We will therefore continue to follow any lead we have—and we just had one dropped on our laps."

Jones bellowed from across the squad room. "Lieutenant, you got a call, line two!"

"I'll take it in my office." He turned and gazed upon all five of them, even Spider-Man. "I want Jorge DeLaSelva, and I want him yesterday." And with that, he turned and plowed into the crowd in the direction of his office.

Hawkins said, "Peter, Laura, see if those Venom files have shown up from downtown yet."

They both nodded and went to their own desks.

"Isn't the Lip supposed to be checking in soon?" Hawkins then asked Drew.

Drew checked his watch. "Yeah, he's got his meet with Borck and Peters in about ten minutes."

"Sit in on it, see if he's picked up anything on DeLaSelva."

"Right." Drew then went off in another direction.

"The Lip?" Spider-Man asked.

"Andrew Lipinski. One of our undercover guys—he uses the name 'Andy the Lip.' He's got his ear to the proverbial ground."

Spider-Man blinked. "Waitasec, I know Andy the Lip. He's a *cop*?"

Hawkins nodded. "Anyway, DeLaSelva has to be holed up somewhere where the feds are keeping an eye on him. The man can't be local, and if he's a courier in that robbery, he's hot as hell, so he had to have help hiding somewhere. If we're lucky, Lipinski's heard something." Hawkins looked over at Spider-Man. "Wanna grab a cup of coffee?"

"Hm?" Spider-Man had barely registered Hawkins's words. *I got info from Andy the Lip once or twice. He's a cop?*

"Y'know, I think I finally figured it out," Hawkins said suddenly. He sat with Spider-Man in the coffee room while they waited for Drew to return. Spidey once again "sat" on the wall, the lower portion of his mask raised to just above his nose to allow him to drink the coffee Hawkins had given him.

"Figured what out?" Spidey asked. He sipped the coffee, then tried not to gag. *No wonder city cops are so cranky, if this is what they drink first thing in the morning.*

"Why nobody likes you."

Spidey had to smile. "Excuse me?"

"See, there it is—you smiled. And after you sipped the coffee, you grimaced. Two actual human gestures."

"You've lost me."

Hawkins took a sip of his own coffee—without grimacing, Spidey noticed—before answering. "Communicating with you is awkward, and almost impossible."

"Hey, c'mon, Sergeant, I talk real good just like everyone else."

"That's not the problem. Speaking is only a small part of how people communicate with each other. There's also facial expressions, gestures, body language. For instance, say you're talking to a friend. She's telling a story. She works a bad pun or a double entendre into the story, and you wince or smile. She says something that surprises you, and your eyes get wide. Or the story goes on forever and you start fidgeting or yawning. Three different responses, none of which involve any speaking on your part. People convey things by gesturing, by their posture, by moving their mouths around, by blinking, and about a hundred other ways that don't involve a single vibration of the vocal cords. And people are accustomed to that. Drew has great posture. I see him walking around with slumped shoulders, I figure an interrogation went bad or he had a fight with his girlfriend or his father's in town. The words just frame the body language.

"Now with you," Hawkins continued, "none of that applies. There's a frame, but no picture. I can't tell if you're smiling or frowning, I can't tell if you're blinking or if your eyes get wide, I can't tell if you're twitching your nose or wiggling your ears. And body language is completely out of the question, 'cause you spend most of your time crouched over like someone folded your spine in half."

Spidey blinked, then realized that that was one of those visual cues, and that Hawkins couldn't see it. He'd never thought about this before. "Would it make you feel better if I told you I can't wiggle my ears?"

"Hey, listen, it's your costume. And it makes a more effective disguise than any other hero outfit I've seen. But by covering your entire face like that, combined with the way you crouch around—well, it makes you seem almost inhuman. That's the kind of thing that puts people off.''

Spidey started to take another sip of his coffee, then decided against it. ''No, this coffee is the kind of thing that puts people off. Did, ah—did this all just occur to you?''

Hawkins nodded. ''When you lifted your mask, actually. Made me realize, among other things, that until this moment I had no idea you were a white guy. Which means I win the bet.''

Spidey frowned. *And right now, Hawkins can see that*, he thought.

This thought was proven by Hawkins answering Spidey's question before he could ask it. ''Drew was sure you were black because a black guy would have more reason to hide his whole face. I pointed out that, statistically, most non-mutant paranormals are white. Don't know why, but they are. So you probably were, too.''

Spidey shook his head and smiled, and thought that Hawkins could see that expression, too. *Great, now I'm going to be self-conscious every time my face changes. Thanks a lot, Sergeant. . . .*

Before the conversation could continue, Drew entered, grinning ear to ear. ''We got something.''

''Hey, Drew, take a look,'' Hawkins said, pointing at Spider-Man.

''Yeah, that's Spider-Man. Remember, Hawk, he was in the briefing, too,'' Drew said sarcastically.

''His face. He's white.''

''Oh, the bet, right,'' Drew said after a second, waving it off. ''Fine, whatever. Look, the Lip came through. A line on Howie the Z.''

Spider-Man put the coffee down and pulled his mask down over his lower face. *Time to be inhuman.* ''I've met this guy once or twice. He plays real estate agent for the lowlife crowd, right?''

''Exactly.''

Hawkins frowned. ''I feel like I should know this guy.''

Drew blinked. ''I don't believe it. I finally found something you don't know.''

"No, you've just found something I couldn't remember off the top of my head."

"Call it whatever you want, I'm still markin' this in my calendar. Anyhow, Howie's thing is to provide hidey-holes for people who need to lay low. We've never been able to get anything on him, though. Supposedly he provided a safehouse for Cletus Kasady the last time he was at large before he got turned into Carnage."

Spidey said, "As I recall, he was the one who kept 'Nose' Norton hidden during that whole Brand Corporation mess, too."

Hawkins nodded. "Okay, I remember this guy. He's been connected to the Kingpin, the Maggia, Montenegro, Silvermane, and any number of others. I take it he's hiding DeLaSelva?"

"Well, he didn't have him by name, but Lip heard that Howie provided a place for a Puerto Rican who did a robbery in Connecticut."

Spider-Man smiled, trying not to think about the fact that the two sergeants couldn't see the smile. "And how many of those can there be?"

"Not a lot," Hawkins said. "So where do we find Howie?"

"Lip says he spends every Wednesday afternoon at a billiards club up on Amsterdam."

Spider-Man said, "Whatever happened to the good old days when pool halls were called pool halls?"

"They died around the same time garbage collectors became sanitation engineers," Hawkins said as they moved toward the exit.

Then Liverakos came in. "Hey, guys, wait up." Spider-Man stopped and turned to see the detective walking in briskly, holding a strange-looking gun.

"What's up, Laura?" Drew asked.

"Two things. Those Venom files did finally get up here. Peter's going over them now."

Hawkins nodded. "That's good news."

"And," Liverakos went on, "they gave us a couple of presents." She held up the gun. "Sonic weapon—prototype from

Stark Enterprises. Only four in existence right now. Clark and Steen have two for obvious reasons, but they passed the other two onto us. I've got one—you two can fight over who gets this one.''

Spider-Man sighed. Once, that might have made all the difference. Venom was vulnerable to sonics. When Spider-Man first learned of the alien's symbiotic nature, it could only be removed by a sonic gun. But the symbiote had proven to be an extremely adaptable creature. He tried to keep the dubiousness out of his voice as he said, ''Uh, Venom's built up a really good resistance to sonics lately. I doubt that pop gun's gonna do a lotta good.''

''These prototypes were built precisely because he's built up that resistance,'' Liverakos replied. ''It rotates frequencies every three seconds, and goes for a higher range than the old weapons they used on him did. It probably won't stop him, but it should slow him down a bit.''

''It certainly won't hurt,'' Spider-Man admitted. Still, he had his doubts.

Hawkins took the weapon from Liverakos. ''C'mon, let's go.''

''Hey, waitasec,'' Drew said, ''who says *you* get it?''

''My higher scores on the firing range,'' Hawkins replied.

Liverakos chuckled. ''C'mon, Hawk, it's not like precision matters with this thing.''

Hawkins took a breath, then said in a very quiet voice, ''I owe him.''

Spider-Man looked at the broad-shouldered detective, remembering Venom tossing Hawkins out a second-story window. The sergeant only escaped uninjured because Spider-Man was around. The hero couldn't begrudge Hawkins's desire for a rematch.

''C'mon, let's go,'' Hawkins said. ''I'll drive. You mind sitting in the back seat?'' he asked Spider-Man.

''Uh, I think I'll pass. What's the address of this place?''

Drew was about to answer when Hawkins overlayed him. ''Wait a minute, you're going to swing around instead of riding with us?''

"Nothing personal, Sergeant, I'm just not big on cars. A little claustrophobic, y'know?"

"Our car has heat."

Memories of the cold wind slicing through Spider-Man's costume as he swung around the city came unbidden.

"No, I don't mind the back seat at all. Let's go."

WEDNESDAY, 4:30 P.M.

Jorge DeLaSelva sat on an uncomfortable bench in Washington Square Park, staring past the Arch up Fifth Avenue, his joints aching from arthritis.

Robbie was half an hour late already. Jorge hadn't seen a hair on him for years, not since the talented stringer left Philly for the big time, but if Jorge knew anything about Robbie Robertson, it was that he was punctual as a Bulova.

Something was wrong; Jorge could feel it in his swollen joints.

He spit a thick *flemón* between his legs. *No point sticking around here. If Robbie isn't here by now, he ain't gonna be here.*

Jorge got up gingerly, his hip bone cracking with the effort, and walked past a row of dead bushes, then through the Arch and up Fifth Avenue. At Eighth Street he turned right and went over to the subway station. He ambled down the stairs and slipped under the turnstile under the uninterested eye of a token clerk, no doubt enjoying the heat in her booth much more than she would filling out the paperwork on a fare jumper.

There was an acrid taste in his mouth, and his ankles ached with gout. *Give thirty years of my life to the movement, and look at me—a wreck reduced to bumming rides on the subway. ¡Ay madre!*

Across the tracks, a southbound N train slithered through the station like a bright, noisy snake. Disappointed, Jorge blew a pillow of steam, then, rocking back and forth, patted his leather jacket for warmth. When Miss Weying didn't call the pay phone on Seventy-second Street, he'd assumed that she had a good reason. Maybe she had no interest in renewing her association with a year-old *pro bono* client. Now that Robbie had stood him up as well, he couldn't deny the facts any longer: he'd been made. He already knew about the FBI tail, of course; he wasn't worried about *those* clowns. The idiots hadn't even blinked when he left his hideout in the morning through a cracked basement window.

But Sombra—now, that was something else. As a matter of fact, he hadn't expected the monster to come after him so quickly. He was Jorge DeLaSelva after all, the *abuelito* of the *Corta Caña* movement. As a kid he'd shaken the steely hand of Pedro Albizu Campos. He'd shared bitter maté with Che Guevara, as rain pelted them in a muddy ditch outside of Bogotá. Back in the seventies he'd spent five years in jail on an explosives charge. He'd given up everything for the cause: a father's love, a career, two marriages, a lovely daughter.

He'd held bleeding comrades in his arms.

Three times he'd pulled a trigger when nobody else dared.

You'd think they'd cut me a little slack, he thought.

As he considered what to do with the Wells Fargo loot— go straight to the cops, maybe drop it off at the Puerto Rican Welfare League—he suddenly felt a stabbing ache in his flank. "*¡Ay Cristo!*" he moaned. The kidneys again. Soon he would have to see a doctor about that stone. He shuffled over to a bench and sat down. His knees cracked like ice cubes. His round belly was full of acid and gas.

I'm old, he thought, not for the first time.

He needed to get out of this life, out of the cold.

After a minute a northbound R train screeched its way into the station. Painfully, Jorge stood up and, holding his flank, ambled over to the opening door. Right away he collapsed onto an empty seat.

At least it was warm and quiet inside.

WEDNESDAY, 4:40 P.M.

By the time the masked guards brought Ann Weying back to the storeroom, Robbie Robertson had recomposed the front page of the *Bugle* about thirty or forty times. There was little else to do. Esteban wasn't much company—he'd spent most of the last two hours in fitful sleep. Idleness, Robbie knew, would force him to dwell on the situation at hand, on his utter powerlessness, which would in turn choke him with worry and anger and fear. As he'd learned during his brief sojourn in prison, he had to keep himself calm and rational to survive.

Besides, Robbie enjoyed fiddling with the front page. He had a vivid memory, so he was able to picture the individual stories laid out onto proof sheets, and affix them onto an imaginary pasteboard. (Nowadays everything was done with computers, of course, but, even after years staring at cathode-ray tubes, Robbie couldn't think about laying out the *Bugle* without recalling the feel of copy paper on his fingers, the tackiness of pasteup wax.)

There was Charley's wrapup of the influence-peddling trial, and Vreni's followup on the Roxxon thing—both process stories, unfortunately, but too important to relegate to the inside pages. *Guess we could fit in a nice, juicy Parker photograph.* If Betty ever finished with that fish market piece, well, that could use a page-two leadoff. Ben had that Upper West Side double murder—ghoulish stuff, but, as Jonah would often remind Robbie, ghouls bought papers. And it occurred to him that he needed some space for Ken's A.J. Pierce story; at first Robbie had slotted it for page six, but now, with Pierce's lawyer missing, well . . .

Hell, Robbie thought, tapping his head against the wooden post that served as a backrest. There was no way to avoid it; the story snuck into the front page every time, like a mouse into a pantry. POLICE CAPTAIN, LAWYER, EDITOR-IN-CHIEF FOUND DEAD IN ABANDONED WAREHOUSE. Two columns of text, topped by a gruesome crime-scene photograph. Maybe a sidebar for the coroner's statement. (''Neat bullet holes at the base of the neck . . .'') An interview with grieving widow Martha Robertson. The inevitable jump-line to the obituary pages, where Trilby would no doubt write up something impressive for all three of them.

Might as well be planning my own funeral.

The sun had all but disappeared from the boarded-up window, and in the last twenty minutes the temperature had dropped a good ten degrees. Robbie couldn't see his watch, but clearly it was way past three o'clock. DeLaSelva must have taken off a while ago. Would it be such a terrible thing, Robbie wondered, if he told the Cane Cutters about their planned meeting? There were principles at stake, to be sure, and important ones at that: protecting sources, not giving in to terrorists. But were they worth Martha's worry, her misery? Did he have the right to risk a shared life?

He thought about Tombstone and the murder Robbie had kept quiet about for two decades. He thought about the prison term he'd served to pay for that silence.

Robbie bent over and pulled on the rough, bitter-smelling blanket with his chin. At once he felt a joint pop in his neck, and his left arm twitched, tightening the cuffs around his wrists.

He turned sideways. The blanket slipped down to his lap. Angered, cold, he cursed under his breath, then glanced over at Frank Esteban. Even in the penumbra, Robbie could see Esteban slumped against the corrugated wall, his eyes shut, his mouth half open. Every few breaths he would cough lightly and gasp for air. For the briefest moment Robbie felt a pang of jealousy. He knew it was silly, of course; both he and the police captain were in the same situation. If anything, things were going far worse for Esteban, what with his broken collarbone and crushed pride.

And yet, somehow, he'd managed to fall asleep.

Robbie wished he could sleep.

He heard footsteps out on the hallway, then a rasping sound as the metal door swung open. A short, masked guard stepped into the room. At once Robbie recognized the eager strut, the leftward swing of the hip. It was the same boy who had taken Ann away, well over two hours ago.

"Where's—?" he began. Just then, two masked men pushed past the boy. Ann staggered between them, absently clutching the taller guard's forearm. Her silk blouse was spattered with blood. Her eyes were bloated; a dark welt blossomed on her cheek. The worst part, though, was her nose, which had swollen, it seemed, to the size of a mackintosh apple.

Robbie felt his gut clench. He glared at Ann as she bent down, grasped the blanket in her fist, and slowly sank to the cement floor. The two guards stepped back and settled at either side of the door.

"I'll be fine," she said, pained, wrapping herself in the blanket. "Don't worry about me, okay?"

Robbie's heart beat wildly. He tried to speak, but his throat had constricted to a thin straw. In his mind, he heard the deep voice of his father.

He'd been nine years old at the time, he recalled. Aunt Frances had just left Baltimore to move in with Robbie's family in Harlem. One day, while Robbie's parents were away at work, Uncle James had driven his dirty Chevrolet onto the sidewalk in front of their apartment, crushing a row of new saplings, and leaned on the horn till Aunt Frances came out to the stoop. Startled by the noise, Robbie poked his head out the bedroom window. Uncle James stood alone on the sidewalk, pointing a steel-like finger at his wife. *Get in the car*, he shouted, *now!* When Aunt Frances refused, he ran to the door and grabbed her by her blue satin dress. He dragged her down the front steps and through a patch of mulberries.

Robbie held tightly to the window molding, transfixed. He watched as Aunt Frances tried to squirm free of her husband's grasp, yelling curses at him and spitting in his face. But Uncle James wouldn't let go.

Finally, in a move she could have borrowed from one of the many dance lessons she gave to the children, she kicked him in the groin. Robbie flinched. Down on the sidewalk, Uncle James bent over and groaned and stared at the cement, clutching his knees as if he were about to throw up. Strangely, Aunt Frances did not run back into the house; instead she paused, trembling like a doe, and glared at her husband. Like she had broken him, like he'd fallen from her hands and shattered.

Slowly Uncle James stood up and smoothed the front of his

shirt. With the back of his hand he wiped spittle from his lips. He stepped toward Aunt Frances, calmly, as if he were about to embrace her. She didn't move.

Before anyone could stop him, Uncle James struck her right in the jaw. It made a dull sound, like meat on a cutting board. Robbie yelped. Aunt Frances stumbled backward and fell onto the sidewalk. Dazed, she began to stand up, but Uncle James decked her again, first in the gut, then on her cheek.

That would be the last blow. When Uncle James cocked his fist again, Charlie Foster, Robbie's giant next-door neighbor, appeared, hooked his arm around Uncle James's neck, and tossed him over the Chevy.

That night, after the police handcuffed Uncle James and shoved him into their cruiser, after the city tow truck dragged his dirty Chevy from the sidewalk, after Mom took Aunt Frances to Harlem Hospital, Dad came up to Robbie's bedroom and sat next to him on the bed. He smiled as his father stroked his hair and kissed him on the crown.

Son, Dad said after a long while, *you gotta promise. Never lay a hand on a woman, you hear? Ain't no reason.*

Staring at Ann Weying, Robbie heard the voice again and again. *Ain't no reason.*

"I'll be fine," she said. Her eyes glimmered in the half-light. "Don't do anything stupid, okay? Not on my account."

"You listen to the pretty woman," the boy said mockingly, tapping a syncopated beat on the barrel of his nine-millimeter.

Over by the door, Esteban stirred and coughed into his shirt.

"Ann," Robbie whispered.

"Don't," Ann said. She paused, then lightly touched the tip of her broken nose. She muttered under her breath, "Eddie'll get them, anyway."

"What was that?" the boy asked.

"Nothing," she said. The word came out flat, rough. "Nothing."

Robbie had heard her perfectly, though. Somehow he'd completely forgotten about Ann's ex-husband, which was strange, considering that he'd assigned Ken Ellis the Pierce story precisely because of the Venom connection. Anxiously,

VENOM'S WRATH

he wondered if the creature would be able to track them down to the warehouse. Eddie Brock used to be an investigative journalist, after all. Not a very good one, granted, but still . . .

Oh, hell, Robbie thought, even as the possibility turned, almost at once, into a certainty. As if the situation weren't dreadful enough already.

"Hey *reportero!*" the boy said. "You're next, *amigo.*" Quietly he sidled up next to Robbie and tapped his combat boot on the editor's heel. "Giddyup!"

Robbie simmered. "I'm thirty-five years older than you, son," he said, without thinking, "I deserve a bit more respect than that."

Ann shut her eyes and sighed, as if to say, *Was that really necessary?*

"Sorry," the boy said. Then, in a sudden burst, kicked him hard on the foot. Robbie screamed; he felt the blow through his leg and knee, all the way to his spine.

"Giddyup, please," the boy said. "Is that better?"

The two guards at the door laughed faintly, as if despite themselves.

"Very funny," Robbie muttered. Awkwardly he climbed to his knees, pushing against the floor with his handcuffed hands. His ankle throbbed. Right away the boy grabbed him by the shirt sleeve. Robbie shook him off.

"I can do it myself," he said.

"Whatever," the boy said, giggling. He glanced over his shoulder at the masked guards.

"You hear that one?" he said. Tipping from side to side, he repeated, "Giddyup, please."

The taller guard crossed his arms. "*Chico, deja 'eh perder tiempo,*" he said.

"I'm not wasting time," the boy said, defensively. "I'm just softening him up for Sombra. You'll see; this bird right here's gonna spill his guts." He turned to Robbie; his mask rode up on his chin. "Aren't ya? Just like the lawyer."

"You wish," Ann groaned.

Robbie couldn't help but smile. He welcomed her courage,

the fact that, even after such a brutal beating, she was still defiant.

It was a good reminder. The story hadn't been written yet.

"All right," he said, bracing himself against the wooden column. "Let's go, then. I've got a few questions myself."

CHAPTER 6

WEDNESDAY, 4:45 P.M.

It took twenty minutes for Vance Hawkins to drive himself, Stephen Drew, and Spider-Man forty blocks north through early rush-hour traffic from Midtown South to the billiards club frequented by Howie the Z. Ten of those passed before the heat in the blue Ford actually kicked in, prior to which the car was colder inside than out.

Spider-Man didn't object to the concept of cars, and he knew how to drive. Indeed, for a brief time he rode around on a so-called ''Spider-Mobile''—in truth, a modified dune buggy. He abandoned that particular accoutrement in fairly short order, though. For one thing, finding a place to park the thing was murder. Besides, when one could swing across the rooftops, being streetbound proved too limiting.

This drive served to remind him of that particular limitation in spades. Plus, it was freezing in the car. *Next time*, he thought, *I ignore Hawkins and go my own way. This is just silly.*

They got out of the Ford upon arrival—not a moment too soon as far as Spider-Man was concerned—and regarded the billiards parlor, which took up the second floor of a two-story building. A health club occupied the ground floor.

''Look,'' Drew said hesitantly, ''I think we should handle this. This guy has a rep for threatening to sue and other fun stuff like that. We don't actually *have* anything on him, so I think it might be better if we try the nice-cop approach instead of the big-bad-super-hero approach, y'know?''

Spider-Man started to object, then remembered Golden's words. *This is an NYPD operation, not one of your hare-brained solo shots. I don't want you messin' things up like usual.* So he didn't actually tell the two sergeants to jump in a lake.

''If you insist,'' he said through gritted teeth.

They both nodded, and went in through the glass door that opened into a narrow stairwell.

After mulling it over for half a second, Spider-Man rejected the notion of sitting outside waiting by the car. For one thing, they'd locked the doors, so he was stuck standing in the cold waiting for them.

Unless he did something.

A woman in a leather duster exited the health club, looked at Spider-Man and said, "Aren't you *cold*?"

Doing his best Adam West impersonation, he replied, "Thoughts of justice keep me warm, citizen."

Then he leapt straight upward, landing on the roof, leaving the befuddled woman behind. *There's gotta be roof access.*

Sure enough, there was. It led to a tiny, dusty attic that smelled of dirty plastic. *You couldn't stand upright here unless you were three feet tall*, Spider-Man thought, *or can crouch like a spider.* The club obviously used this for storage, full as it was with boxes labelled CUE STICKS, POOL BALLS, etc. Crawling along the wall, Spider-Man eventually found a trapdoor toward the rear of the building. It led to a dingy room; he crawled along the ceiling of that room, closing the trapdoor behind him, to a door that led to the back of the main pool hall. Said hall took up most of the remaining space on the floor. It, too, had the dirty-plastic smell, but mixed in with cigarette smoke and beer. On the far side from Spider-Man was a bar, cash register, and a few small tables and chairs; the rest of the room was taken up with pool tables.

Remaining on the ceiling proved advantageous. This late in the afternoon in wintertime, it was almost dark outside, and the long downward-shining lamps that hung two feet over the pool tables provided the room's primary light source. That left the ceiling in almost pitch darkness. *Besides*, he thought as he crawled, *who ever looks up in a pool hall? Or billiards club, or whatever the heck they call it.*

It didn't take long to find Hawkins and Drew—they were the only people near a pool table still wearing their coats. They faced four people, the shortest of whom wore a huge leather cap. Spider-Man recognized him as the infamous Howie the Z. Howie had coffee-colored skin and a face that could belong to any of four or five ethnicities. A lit cigarette hung from the corner of his mouth.

As he got closer, he could hear the exchange between Howie and the two detectives.

"I know my rights, okay?" Howie said while setting up a shot and keeping the cigarette balanced between his lips. He emphasized the second syllable of *okay* in a manner that Spider-Man found extremely annoying. "I don't gotta talk to you if I don't wanna talk to you, okay? An' I don't wanna. So take a hike, okay?"

"Look, Howie," Drew said, "all we're tryin' to do is find someone. We heard you might know where he is."

Hawkins added, "You have the right not to answer the question, but that doesn't change the fact that we have the right to ask it."

Howie took a shot—he sank the nine ball. Then he straightened, looked at the two detectives, and took a drag on the cigarette. Shrugging, he said, "Who's the guy?" He walked around the table to take another shot.

"His name's Jorge DeLaSelva," Drew said.

Howie laughed. "Delay-what-uh? The hell kinda name is 'at?"

"Puerto Rican, as it happens," said Hawkins.

"Don't know him, okay? Now take a hike, Salt 'n' Pepa, I got a game to finish." To punctuate the point, he sank both the three and five balls with a nifty combination shot.

Drew said, "You don't know this guy?"

"I just said that, okay? Now agitate the gravel."

Spider-Man had heard enough. *The nice-cop approach is turning into a dismal failure. Let's try the big bad super hero.*

He attached one end of a web-line to the ceiling, and let the other end drop to the same level as the lamps over the pool tables. Then he slid down the line headfirst, stopping at the line's end, his knees bent, the soles of his feet flush together, making it look like he was squatting upside down. He came down right in front of Howie, who was good enough to scream, "*Gaaaahhhhh!*" The cigarette fell to the floor.

"Now, Howie, is that any way to treat the nice detectives?"

"Aw, man, not you! Since when do *you* work with the man?" One of Howie's fellow players picked the cigarette up off the floor and offered it back to him. Howie angrily slapped the butt away.

"Since a very good friend of mine went missing. My two cop chums here think that DeLaSelva knows what happened to my friend. They also think that you know where DeLaSelva is. And you know what, Howie? I think they're right. So why not just tell them?"

Howie put his cue stick down. "Yeah, okay, fine, whatever, just get outta my life, okay?"

"There are few places on this Earth that I want to be in less than your life, Howie."

Howie glared at Spider-Man for a moment, then took out another cigarette. As he lit it, he said, "Try apartment 4B at 250 West Sixty-third."

Drew looked at Hawkins. "Where's that?"

"Between West End and Amsterdam," Hawkins said without hesitation. "But that can't be right—the Amsterdam Houses block off Sixty-second and Sixty-third from going between those two blocks."

"So this little twerp is lying to us?"

"I ain't lyin', okay?" Howie said indignantly, taking a drag.

Spider-Man thought a moment, then remembered something. "No, he isn't."

"What?" Drew said.

"There's a small piece of Sixty-third that runs into a dead end, coming in from West End. Doesn't make it all the way to Amsterdam, but there is a street there, and a couple of apartment buildings."

Drew turned to Hawkins. "That true?"

Hawkins frowned. "*That's* right. I had forgotten all about it. That's where they renamed the *cul-de-sac* after Thelonious Monk."

"It's easy to forget," Spider-Man said. "Don't feel too bad. I get a bird's-eye view of the city all the time, so I remember stuff like that."

Drew chuckled. "That's twice in one day, Hawk."

"Oh, shut up," Hawkins muttered.

"Can I get back to my game now?" Howie asked.

"By all means, Howie," Hawkins said.

Drew added, "And the NYPD appreciates your assistance in this matter."

"Yeah, right," Howie said, picking up his cue stick. "*See* ya."

Spider-Man clambered back up the web-line and scampered across the ceiling toward the exit. This time, people did look up at him, but it was less of a concern now.

Hawkins and Drew started in the same direction on foot when Howie called out to them. "Yo, Salt 'n' Pepa. Somethin' you should remember, okay?" They turned around to face him, expectant looks on their faces. Howie continued, "Cops is cops, but you don't mess around with the guys in tights."

Spider-Man couldn't help but smile at that.

WEDNESDAY, 5:30 P.M.

Special Agent John J. Mack sighed as he put a replacement tape into the recorder. Since he and Paul Hattori had come on duty that morning, changing the tape was the only interesting thing that had happened.

Of course, Mack had to be the one to change the tape. Heaven *forfend* that his partner lift a finger to help him.

Hattori was great in an investigation. He was thorough, professional, and had good instincts. He did his paperwork right the first time, and followed regulations to the letter without being a hidebound twerp about it.

But having to share a stakeout with him was nightmarish.

He hummed. He bit his nails. He had a braying laugh that he used whenever he let loose with a witticism—a laugh which tended to be lonely, as Hattori was the only one who laughed at his own lame jokes. And he was the world's most boring conversationalist.

Mack had once asked his boss for a new partner, but New York Bureau Chief Buchanan always asked the same question:

Is your problem with him personal? To which Mack would reply in the affirmative, at which point she would say, *You're professionals. Work out your differences.*

All Mack could think was, *That's easy for you to say.*

"Oh, great," Mack said aloud.

"What?" Hattori asked.

Mack sighed. "The CD changed. I was hoping for a break, but no such luck. It's more salsa."

"So what's wrong with salsa? It's nice, cheery music."

"Fine, *you* listen to the tape for a while."

"You kidding, I hate that stuff."

Mack sighed. *What's the point?*

The nature of the stakeout didn't help matters. They had to keep an eye on Jorge DeLaSelva, in the hopes that some of his fellow *independistas* would contact him and lead the FBI to them. This had been going on for three days, with no bites. DeLaSelva spent his days listening to salsa music, reading, going to the bathroom, and cooking, the latter every night around seven. He'd only gone out once, on a grocery run. The only visitors he'd received were a pair of Jehovah's Witnesses, he hadn't made any phone calls, and the only calls he'd gotten were two wrong numbers and a solicitation for credit card protection.

At least we aren't likely to get made, Mack thought with grim satisfaction, regarding the various bits of high-tech equipment at their disposal. Each day, they'd come in a different type of vehicle, which also differed from the night shift's. A constant stream of exterminator vans or somesuch in the area might've been conspicuous, but the recent popularity of mini-vans—combined with holographic windows from Stark Enterprises that created the illusion of an empty van—made it a lot easier to blend. And they had mixed in the occasional moving truck or exterminator van as well, in different spots. Mack was confident they had remained inconspicuous.

As Mack heard DeLaSelva knock something over, Hattori said, "I gotta go to the can."

Mack sighed. "And you don't wanna miss nothin'?" he added in a passable imitation of Peter Falk.

Hattori squinted. "Huh?"

Why do I bother? Mack thought, as he heard yet another item being knocked over in DeLaSelva's place. The only jokes Hattori ever got were his own. "Never mind. Just go. If the Queen of England calls, I'll be sure to tell her where—"

Then Mack cut himself off. He heard something odd.

"Hold on a second, Paul," he said.

"What?"

"Something in the background. . . ." He strained to listen. "Footsteps. A lot of footsteps."

"It's probably that big family next door coming home or something."

Mack shook his head. "They haven't left their place."

Then he heard the pounding on the front door and the muffled words, "Police! Open up!"

Criminetly. "We got problems," he said, ripping off the headphones and unholstering his weapon to make sure it was loaded. "The NYPD just showed up at DeLaSelva's place."

"What the hell're they doing here?" Hattori asked, doing the same with his own gun.

Rolling his eyes, Mack put his hand to his forehead. "Hang on, let me use my incredible powers of telepathy to uncover that mystery. . . ."

"Ho ho ho. Let's move."

Mack saw no cop cars as he left the minivan, and realized that they must have parked on Amsterdam Avenue and come in through the housing project on foot. That made sense—why alert DeLaSelva with a whole bunch of cop cars in plain view when you could hide them on the other side of a set of large apartment buildings?

DeLaSelva had holed up in a comparatively small structure: six stories high, four apartments per floor. Still, Mack was winded by the time he hit the third-floor landing. *That's what I hate about this job. You sit on your butt for three days, then you suddenly have to become Jesse friggin' Owens.*

Mack took in the scene as they got to the fourth floor. Four plainclothes cops, two white males, one black male, one white female. The black male and one of the white males were just kicking the door to 4B in when Mack and his partner arrived.

Behind them were a collection of uniformed cops. Above them, crawling along the ceiling, was one person in red-and-blue tights, whom Mack recognized as Spider-Man—you didn't survive long in the New York Bureau if you didn't know everything you could about the local paranormal population. Not that anybody knew much about Spider-Man, though one thing Mack thought was gospel was that he didn't work with cops.

One of the uniforms—a woman named Schwalb—noticed Mack and Hattori just as the plainclothes cops ran in, followed by two uniforms and the super hero. "Who the hell're you?"

Mack flashed his ID. "Federal agent. You people are in serious—"

He was interrupted by one of the walls adjacent to the door splintering as a uniformed officer flew through it. The officer didn't seem impeded by the plaster and wood, continuing on an arc through the officers who hadn't yet entered, knocking them down like bowling pins. Mack, Hattori, and Schwalb managed to dodge, but still wound up on the floor.

"Uh, John, we got *major* problems," Hattori said, pointing into DeLaSelva's apartment. "Look."

Mack followed Hattori's finger to see another member of New York's paranormal population mixing it up with the plainclothes cops and Spider-Man. He wore an ever-undulating costume of all-black, save for the spider-emblem on the chest and back, the hollow white eyes, and the slobbering, drooling, sharp-tooth-filled mouth.

Venom.

"Criminetly," Mack said.

The creature snarled as the police officers broke into Jorge DeLaSelva's apartment. This had not been part of the plan.

Then Venom saw Spider-Man amongst the officers. This surprised Eddie Brock; the symbiote quivered in anticipation.

But now was not the time to indulge. Ann was more important even than killing Parker.

Still, when the uniformed officer burst into the room ahead of her comrades and pointed a gun, the creature saw no reason not to respond. Having come to this place only to find it empty, the creature was not happy.

Earlier that day at Ann's apartment, the symbiote had taken on the form of a police officer's uniform. Pretending to be "Officer Badger," an identity used to good effect once before, Venom had mixed in with the various cops patrolling the crime scene, keeping bystanders away, bagging evidence, etc.

Once everyone had left, no one had questioned an officer of the law going past the yellow crime-scene tape into Ann's penthouse apartment.

The NYPD naturally had done a thorough job of sweeping through the apartment. But sometimes cops missed things.

The creature's stock in trade was violence and intimidation, but that would not help here. Instead, Venom had called upon the journalistic instincts of Eddie Brock.

When he'd started at the *Daily Globe*, Brock had been a stringer for their Bronx Bureau. He'd helped bring down a corrupt district attorney by checking the tapes on his answering machine. Tape-based answering machines don't actually erase messages once they're listened to, but simply rewind the tape to the beginning. Subsequent messages then record over them. But sometimes messages more than two minutes in could stay on the tape for months on end. Brock had found such a message, and rather an incriminating one at that, still on the DA's home answering machine eight weeks after it was recorded. The story Brock wrote based on that item got the DA indicted and got Brock promoted to the city beat. He remembered that day well. He had even been called in to see Barney Bushkin—nobody unimportant got to see Bushkin, so Brock knew that he had it made at the *Globe* from that point forward.

And he did. Until Spider-Man ruined everything.

Fortuitously, Ann's answering machine was of a similar type to that of the former Bronx DA. The creature had been afraid that she had gotten one with a digital recording system, or had gotten the phone company to supply off-site voicemail. Venom had removed the tape and gone to her home office.

A friend of theirs from college had gotten Ann and Eddie matching handheld tape recorders as an engagement present.

Eddie had broken his six months later during a nasty temper tantrum, though he could no longer remember what the tantrum was about.

The creature had opened Ann's lovely mahogany desk (*She never had a desk this nice when we were married*, Brock had thought wistfully, then put it out of his mind) to find that same handheld recorder. Brock had realized then that it was the first item in the entire place that he'd seen that came from their time as a couple. Everything else was either something Ann had before they moved in together or something, like the desk, that she'd acquired after the divorce.

But she still had the tape recorder.

The creature had put in the tape and hit play.

"Hello, Ms. Weying, this is A.J. Pierce, your most important client. It's almost ten o'clock already, and I'm here at the County Courthouse, and as you know Mr. Castillo is waiting for us for the deposition, so—"

The message had cut off. *What a whiner.* That had to have been left that morning—probably after Ann had been taken, since Ann was never late for court dates. She was never late for anything.

Beep.

"—et to check the Sweet book, and also don't forget to bring in that novel to lend to Ariana."

That was from Ann to herself—an older message that Pierce's had recorded over the beginning of. Ann often left messages for herself as a reminder for when she got home. Not that she needed to. She always remembered to do everything she intended to do. But she insisted on leaving the message "just in case."

Beep.

"Ann, it's Ariana. Just wanted to remind you that you promised to lend me The Iron Thane. *Thanks! Seeya tomorrow afternoon. Good luck with the Pierce thing."*

Beep.

"Miss Weying, this is Jorge DeLaSelva. You defended me on gun possession charges last year. I'm afraid I need your representation again, Miss Weying. I'm in a very tight spot,

so I'm going to have to ask that you call me Wednesday afternoon at 3 P.M. to discuss the details.'' DeLaSelva gave a number with a 212 area code, meaning it was in Manhattan, then added, *''That's a pay phone. I'm afraid I can't risk giving out my own number right now. It's vital that you call me precisely at 3 P.M., Miss Weying. Thank you.''*

Two other messages had followed, both fragmentary, both personal, both from friends that Ann and Eddie had made while married, and who had stayed in touch with Ann after the divorce.

The creature had no idea who Jorge DeLaSelva was. But, given the cloak-and-dagger nature of his call, he obviously was into something important—or at least something that DeLaSelva *thought* was important.

Tracing the number DeLaSelva had left would be difficult, time consuming, and tedious—and probably pointless, if it really was a pay phone. The creature had spent the last hour masquerading as an officer of the law and the last fifteen minutes being meticulous and patient.

Both halves of the creature shared a need for action over patience.

So Venom had chosen to find Jorge DeLaSelva through more direct means.

Within an hour, four lowlifes had required emergency medical attention, and the creature had learned that DeLaSelva was involved with a group of Puerto Rican nationalists—*What did one of the lowlifes call them? ''Independistas''?*—and that he was holed up on Sixty-third Street.

Satiated by remonstrating with the erstwhile informants, the creature had used more subtle means to sneak into DeLaSelva's apartment.

That effort had turned out to be wasted. DeLaSelva's apartment was a direct contrast to Ann's. Two rooms, where Ann had five; minimal funishings, where Ann had covered every inch of wallspace with either books or wall hangings. The only signs that the place had ever been occupied were the dirty dishes in the sink, the books and magazines lying around, and the five-CD player that presently blared salsa music.

So it didn't take long to determine that Jorge DeLaSelva was not at home. Venom did find one interesting thing: a device attached to the toilet that made it flush automatically every couple of hours. Brock had seen such a device once before used by someone trying to fool surveillance into thinking he was home.

The creature was furious. The only lead to Ann was slipping through Venom's fingers.

Before Venom could consider what to do next, the police had arrived with the hated Peter Parker.

Four police in plainclothes were behind the one Venom had thrown through the wall. The creature thought two of them looked familiar, but couldn't place them.

No matter. They were impediments to finding Ann.

Venom had one way of getting rid of impediments.

The symbiote reached out a tendril and wrapped it around one of the familiar-looking cops—the black one—pinning the man's arms to his side.

The cop, oddly, said, "Not again!"

Then a red-clad foot collided with the creature's head. Brock felt it even through the protection of the alien, and the tendrils loosened their grip on the cop.

Parker.

The creature snarled. "Will we never be rid of you, arachnid?"

Spider-Man didn't answer verbally, for once, but rather responded with an impressive punch to the jaw that actually sent the creature sprawling.

Then the arachnid turned toward the cops. "Hawkins, Drew, get your people *out* of here, before he—"

Foolish, Parker, the creature thought while landing a solid punch to Spider-Man's back. *You forget once again that we do not affect your precious spider-sense.*

Venom gave Spider-Man a second kick, which sent the hated one flying across the room and into a wall, then turned to face—

PAIN!

Intense, skull-shattering, tremendous *pain* throbbing through the very core of Eddie Brock's being. Dimly, Brock registered that this was just sympathetic pain felt through the mental bond with the symbiote, and that his own pain was as nothing compared to that of his other.

Sonics. Has to be sonics. But it hasn't been this bad in ages!

He looked around the room and saw the black cop and the woman cop each holding some kind of weapon. They both seemed to be firing, but to no visible effect.

It seems the NYPD have upgraded, Brock thought angrily. Slowly, meticulously, he moved toward the cops. As he did so, he found he could not fully access his rapport with the alien. *Is my other trying to hide the worst of it from me?* he wondered. *How bad is it hurting if what I feel is only a portion?*

"Get him!" someone yelled.

Then came the sound of gunfire. Normally, the other would have protected Brock from any harm, but the symbiote now writhed in agony. It shifted and undulated across Brock's body, attempting to provide its usual protection, but unable to mount a serious defense through the horrible pain.

White-hot fire spread through Brock's leg as a bullet struck his thigh. The symbiote managed to deal with the others, and several missed as well.

Still, Brock advanced on the two cops.

Yet still more pain as another bullet hit his arm.

It can't end like this. If they take me, I'll never find Ann.

Ann.

ANN!

Memories struck with the same intensity as the bullet had: meeting Ann for the first time at Ferris Booth Hall, their first kiss, the night he proposed at that Mexican restaurant near Columbia, their wedding day.

And now she was gone and he had to find her.

Nothing would stop him from finding her.

Nothing!

Eddie Brock focused past the pain, moved beyond the agony, and commanded the being he shared his existence with to strike.

Pseudopodia flew in all directions. Some were blunt, some razor-sharp, some soft. The damage was inconsistent, but still considerable.

Then the pain stopped.

The full rapport came back—again, Eddie Brock and the symbiote were one. The creature gazed upon the room. The salsa music had stopped at some point, the victim of either a bullet or the symbiote's lashing out. Parker was struggling to rise. Several cops were down, including the woman with the sonic pistol, who clutched her stomach and was coughing.

The other cop was still standing, though. He had a nasty gash on his right hand.

The sonic pistols lay on the floor. Two tendrils reached out and snatched the weapons, crushing them.

"That takes care of your toys," the creature said to the black cop. "Now we do the same to your head."

Spider-Man struggled to get up—a difficult process, given the shooting pains in his lower back from Venom's punch. *When am I gonna learn*, he thought angrily, *that the usual tricks don't work with Venom?*

Over the years, Spider-Man had developed a particular fighting style, the uniqueness of which derived from his spider-sense. He counted on it for defense, freeing up his regular five senses for purely offensive purposes. It made him a formidable opponent—or, at worst, extremely difficult to hit—since it allowed him to take risks someone else wouldn't.

All that went out the window when he fought Venom. As a byproduct of the symbiote's tenure as Spider-Man's costume, the alien did not trigger his spider-sense. In practice, that meant that he couldn't afford to do incredibly stupid things like turn his back on Venom.

He lifted his head, and saw Venom advancing on Hawkins, the latter putting pressure on a gash on his hand and looking quite intimidated. Drew, Gilman, Liverakos, and two of the uniforms were on the floor, some struggling to rise as Spider-Man was, others down for the count.

Then shots rang out from the hallway. Spider-Man looked

over to see someone he didn't recognize shooting at Venom. *Dunno who that guy is, but he's doing more harm than good.*

Spider-Man quickly let loose with a mass of webbing at the doorway, hoping to web it up before the symbiote could absorb the bullets and ricochet them right back at the shooter. It was one of Venom's favorite tricks.

Sure enough, Venom did precisely that. Spider-Man's plan mostly worked, though: the webbing didn't have the chance to properly harden, so the bullets still went through, but their momentum—already retarded by being absorbed by the symbiote and bounced—was slowed even more. *With any luck, their force is reduced enough to keep anyone from being seriously hurt.*

At first, Spider-Man thought that blocked off the only access to the apartment, but then he remembered the hole in the wall made after Venom threw poor Officer Epstein through it.

Venom, meanwhile continued advancing on Hawkins. The sergeant was frozen to the spot, looking terrified. Tendrils started snaking toward him.

"No!" Spider-Man gathered every muscle, ignored the pain in his back, and managed a ten-foot leap to knock Hawkins out of the way. He didn't have time for anything more graceful or less painful, but his shove would hurt Hawkins a lot less than whatever Venom planned.

Then he whirled on the still-advancing tendrils, grabbed a handful of them with his left hand, and yanked downward. A surprised Venom fell forward toward Spider-Man, who then nailed Venom with a right uppercut, quickly followed by a kick to the solar plexus.

Those sonic doodads must've done some good, Spider-Man thought as Venom stumbled backwards. *Venom would never fall for that under normal circumstances.*

He then leapt forward to complete the job. *Need to keep him on the defensive. Even weakened, Venom is too tough an opponent.*

Kick to the chest. Punch to the shoulder. Punch to the head. Kick to the shoulder—

—almost. Venom's hand grabbed Spider-Man's leg by the

ankle. Then Venom extended his arm, which flipped Spider-Man head over heels. He managed to convert it into a proper backflip, but wrenched his right shoulder.

Landing on his feet, he saw several tendrils reach for Gilman, who stood with his gun ready. The sergeant fired, to no avail.

Spider-Man leapt, grabbing Gilman in his right arm (wincing as pain shot through his shoulder), while batting at the symbiote's tendrils with his left hand. He set Gilman down, then turned to face Venom again.

"Much as we would love to continue this dance, arachnid," Venom said, "we have bigger fish to fry. Since DeLaSelva is not home, and he isn't likely to return with this crowd present, we must start our search for Ann from scratch."

"You're not going anywhere, Brock." Spider-Man coiled to leap.

But as he started to spring, something grabbed his ankle and he fell forward. As his chin struck the floor of DeLaSelva's apartment, he noticed a tendril of the symbiote flowing from under him back to Venom, who said, "We warn you all—stay out of our way. The next time you interfere with us, we shall not be so merciful."

With that, the ebon figure leapt through the room's lone window, accompanied by the sound of breaking glass.

Spider-Man got up and followed, dimly registering Gilman running along behind him. He alighted on the windowsill, his spider-sense allowing him to avoid the remaining shards of broken glass.

He looked down upon Sixty-third Street and saw no sign of Venom.

Figures. The alien can change shape to look like anything. It's the perfect camouflage. He caught sight of seven people on the street, none of whose faces he could see. Any of them could be Venom. More likely, none of them were.

Two ambulances pulled up outside the building. *Looks like one of the uniforms called in the paramedics.*

"Where'd he go?" Gilman said, peering out the window behind Spider-Man.

"To look for his wife, same as we're doing."

"Yeah, well, it isn't *exactly* the same, is it?"

Spider-Man shook his head. He could try searching, but there would be little point. Unless Venom chose to make his presence known, Spider-Man would never find him. *I'm better off trying to help Hawkins and the others—and finding out who the heck those two guys were.*

As he and Gilman reentered the room, they saw various cops getting up or helping others up. One of them said to Hawkins—who had gotten up but was still putting pressure on the wound to his hand—"The ambo's here, Sergeant."

"Good." He knelt down next to Drew, who lay still on the floor.

The two strangers then entered through the hole in the wall. Spider-Man suspected they were feds, based on the fact that they were armed and because they had the same pickle-up-the-butt look that Hauman and Phillips carried. Like the other two agents, one was tall and lanky, the other shorter and stockier, though the difference was less pronounced.

The shorter of the two said, "Who's in charge, here?"

Hawkins got up from his partner's side. "That would be me. Detective Sergeant Vance Hawkins, Midtown South. Who might you be?"

"You guys are in a heap of trouble. Do you know what you've done to our surveillance?"

"You haven't answered my question, Mr.—?"

The man reached into his pocket for a wallet. The taller man behind him did the same. "Special Agent Mack. This is my partner, Special Agent Hattori."

Spider-Man sighed, his suspicion confirmed. "Is there an FBI convention in town, or something?"

"Let me guess," Hawkins said, "you two were engaged in surveillance of DeLaSelva's apartment from that minivan parked across the street."

Both feds blinked like a deer in headlights. Spider-Man couldn't help but smile, and was this time grateful that no one could see it.

"Deductive reasoning," Hawkins said in response to the

question he didn't give Mack and Hattori a chance to ask. "Well, I'm sorry, but Mr. DeLaSelva is wanted for questioning in the disappearance of three people, one of whom is our captain."

Hattori said, "You realize you've blown three days' work? You guys scared him off busting in like this."

"Try again, pal," Spider-Man said. "When we got here, Venom was all by his lonesome, and he said that DeLaSelva wasn't here."

"And you believe him?"

Spider-Man tried not to laugh; it came out as a bark. "Venom is obsessive, psychotic, single-minded, and dedicated—but he's not a liar. If he said DeLaSelva wasn't here, DeLaSelva wasn't here."

"So what the hell were we doing surveillance on?" Hattori blurted.

Mack quickly said, "Will you shut up?" to his partner.

"I don't believe this, you thought DeLaSelva was home?" Spider-Man said.

Gilman chuckled. "You guys actually fell for the music-is-playing-so-he-must-be-home trick?"

"It isn't just that," came Liverakos's voice from the bathroom. Spider-Man turned to see that she had removed her jacket and she looked several shades paler. She closed her bloodshot eyes and coughed for a minute before continuing. "I was just in the bathroom throwing up," she said matter-of-factly. "There's this attachment to the toilet that has a timer on it. Probably makes it flush every once in a while."

"Criminetly," Mack said, throwing up his hands.

The paramedics had entered. Two went to Epstein, who was still sprawled in the hallway; two more went to Drew's side.

"This guy's one step ahead of all of us," Gilman said.

"So we're back to square one," Spider-Man said.

Mack gave Spider-Man the kind of look one gives to a dead insect found in a bowl of soup. "Excuse me, but what the hell're you doing here? At least these guys are legitimate law-enforcement personnel. Far as I'm concerned, you're trespassing on a crime scene."

"Spider-Man is assisting the NYPD in this investigation due to the involvement of Venom," Hawkins said. "And the last five minutes I think amply demonstrated why his services are needed."

Hattori shook his head. "Using paranormals? S'like using a hydrogen bomb. What kinda operation you guys running, anyhow?"

Spider-Man looked at Gilman. "This from a man who spent all day doing surveillance on an empty apartment."

Moving forward threateningly, Hattori started, "Listen, you—"

Mack held his partner back. Spider-Man was slightly disappointed; he was looking forward to the opportunity to web the agent's mouth shut. He consoled himself with the thought that the opportunity may yet present itself.

"Look," Hawkins said, "obviously there've been screwups all around. We want to get our crime scene guys down here, see if we can get anything."

Spider-Man looked at Hawkins in surprise. "The way this place has been trashed—"

"No argument," Hawkins said, "but it can't hurt." The sergeant turned back to the feds. "Are you guys going to give me trouble, or—"

"This is a federal case, Sergeant," Mack said.

Hawkins went on as if Mack hadn't spoken. "—or do we call your bureau supervisor and inform her that you lost your mark?"

Mack hesitated.

Gilman picked up the ball. "We can leave the toilet doodad out of the report. Say we didn't know whether or not De-LaSelva was in the apartment, that Venom might've scared him off. Won't make you guys look quite so stupid."

In light of his earlier conversation with Hawkins about facial expressions, Spider-Man was particularly amused to watch Mack's face as it changed from angry to annoyed to thoughtful to resigned in the space of about half a second. It was a good idea on Hawkins's part: it gave the feds an opportunity to save face and freed up Hawkins's people to try to salvage something from this mess.

Hawkins's people, he thought. *Can't quite think of myself as part of the team. And maybe that's half the problem.*

"All right, fine," Mack said with a sigh.

"John—" Hattori started.

"*You* wanna explain to Buchanan that we've been watching an empty room with a self-flushing commode all day?"

Hattori didn't say anything in response to that.

"Fine," Gilman said, reaching into his trench coat pocket and pulling out a cell phone. "I'll call Gardner."

At the sight of the cell phone, an idea began to form in Spider-Man's head.

Hawkins turned to the paramedic loading Drew onto a stretcher. Drew was groaning, which Spider-Man took as a good sign; it meant he was conscious. "How's he doing?" Hawkins asked.

"Possible concussion," the medic said. "We'll know more when we get him to the ER."

" 'Ey, Hawk," Drew said groggily.

"Yeah?"

"Don' nail'a bad guy without me, 'kay?"

Hawkins smiled. "Just get better, okay, partner?"

Drew nodded as the medics took him out.

Spider-Man waited a few seconds before approaching Hawkins. "Listen, Sergeant, we need to talk."

Hawkins held up his hand. "Just a second." He walked over to Liverakos, who was picking her jacket up off the floor. She still looked horribly pale. "You okay?"

She nodded. "Puking helped. Those tentacles gut-punched me. I'll be okay in a second."

"You're lucky," Spider-Man said. "They could just as easily have disemboweled you."

Liverakos smiled wanly. "Thanks, that makes me feel *so* much better."

Hawkins also smiled, then looked at Spider-Man. "You said we need to talk."

"Uh, yeah." He hesitated, then: "This isn't working. You

guys've been together for a while, you know each other's habits, you cover for each other. I don't mix in. And, to be honest, I don't play well with others. I've never been much of a team player. Look at what just happened here—I spent more time getting you guys out of Venom's way than I did actually fighting Venom."

"The sonic guns helped," Liverakos said.

"A little, but they also got him mad enough to lash out and whup Drew upside the head, gut-punch you, cut Hawkins's hand, and knock the rest of us around. And it won't work so well next time."

"Not that there'll be a next time," Gilman pointed out, "since those pistols are toast."

"We could get the other two," Liverakos said.

Hawkins shook his head. "We were lucky to get these. There's no chance that the VTF will give the others up."

"He's right, though," Gilman said, indicating Spider-Man with his head. "I read through the VTF files. He's been hit with sonics so many times, he's building up an immunity. They did a projection, and they figured in another year or two, sonics'll be next to useless."

Spider-Man nodded; that confirmed his own suspicions on the subject. "In any case, I can't keep working like this."

Hawkins set his jaw. "Not to sound inconsiderate or anything, but it took a lot for me and Drew to convince the lieutenant to go along with this."

Holding up a hand, Spider-Man said, "Hold on, I'm not saying cut ourselves off altogether. I'm just saying that—since we're kinda stuck back with no leads again—that we should each go our own way on this, but still keep in touch. You guys do your cop thing, I do my super hero thing, and we compare notes every few hours."

"Using what," Gilman said, "the Spider-Phone?"

Spider-Man smiled. *Pity*, he thought, *that Gilman can't see it.* "Close. I, ah, have access to a cell phone. I can't give you guys the number, but I can call every three hours or so on yours and give you a status report."

"Why not just call the station?" Gilman asked.

"Caller ID," Liverakos replied before Spider-Man could say anything. "Cell phone to cell phone, neither side can find out the number of the other. At least not easily."

Hawkins chuckled. "It's funny, cell phones are supposed to be insecure, but in this case—"

"In this case," Spider-Man said, "it's the best way for me to keep in touch without compromising myself."

Nodding, Hawkins said, "All right, that's reasonable." He reached into his pocket and pulled out a card. "The 917 number is the cell, obviously." Several years earlier, the city of New York had given pagers, beepers, and cellular phones their own separate area code.

As Spider-Man took the card and tucked it into one of his belt compartments, a bearded man wearing a wool cap and topcoat entered. He carried a case that Spider-Man assumed to be some kind of kit full of crime scene investigation equipment. "Aw geez," the man said upon spying the shattered glass, "someone broke a window? It's eighty below out there."

Hawkins sighed. "It's only thirty out."

"I'm still gonna freeze my patoots off."

Gilman jerked his thumb at the new arrival. "This from the man who wouldn't let us close the window at Weying's place."

"Look at it this way, Gardner," Hawkins said, "the cold will preserve the evidence."

Gardner snorted at that.

"And on that note," Spider-Man said, moving toward the selfsame window, "I'll leave you detectives to detect while I check out some stuff on my own." *And*, he thought, *dig the cell phone out of the closet. To think I swore never to use that thing again.* During a trip to Florida, Mary Jane had gotten cellular phones for both herself and Peter. After they had returned to New York, some money launderers working for Dr. Octopus had cloned MJ's phone, sticking the Watson-Parker household with a phone bill of well over four thousand dollars. Since then, they'd tucked both phones away, deciding that they weren't worth the risk.

Now, though, things had changed. *We still don't know what*

happened to Robbie and the others, there've been no ransom demands, nothing. Working alone, he stood a better chance of finding leads, but he also knew that he and the NYPD would be more effective if they cooperated, even if at a distance, and that meant staying in touch.

As Spider-Man once again leapt onto the windowsill, Hawkins said, "We'll talk in three hours."

"It's a date, Sergeant," Spider-Man replied as he shot out a web-line to one of the project buildings. He noticed that one of the ambulances had left, and that several more police cars had arrived.

It'd be nice if DeLaSelva came home now and got nailed, he thought, but dismissed the idea. If this guy was cagey enough to dodge FBI surveillance, he wouldn't stumble into this.

Home first, he thought, wending his way through the complex to Amsterdam Avenue in the general direction of Queens. *Then check a few contacts of my own.*

Gonna be a long night . . .

WEDNESDAY, 6 P.M.

In the dream Franco Esteban, seven years old, stood on a busy sidewalk next to his long-estranged father. Nearby was a wide marble stairway, which led up to a pair of massive, bronze-trimmed doors. It was morning; the sun shone vaguely through a thick summer haze and the breeze still carried with it a remnant of the night's coolness. Franco knew he wasn't in New York City. He could see a tall, white obelisk rising in the distance behind a row of brownstones. There was a strong smell of brine in the air.

People sauntered around them, wearing wide-lapeled suits and fedoras. Frightened by the patter of feet, by the swirl of jackets and skirts, Franco squeezed his father's bony thumb. *Papi* looked young, different: he wore a trim mustache, and his brilliantined hair glistened blue in the vague morning light. In his right hand he held a straw hat. Something seemed to bother him. He stood much too still on the sidewalk (*Papi* always fidgeted; Franco's mother used to call him, lovingly, Mr. Maraca), and every few minutes he glanced up at the bronze-trimmed doors. Across the steps stood another man, slight and young, dressed in a wrinkled summer suit and panama hat. Wire-rim glasses clung uneasily to his nose. He looked familiar, but Franco was sure he'd never met him.

They waited for hours in the dream, but the sun never moved, and the midday heat never came, nor did the rain that threatened on the horizon. Through the roar of traffic, Franco heard a bell tinkling; a man in a white shirt and apron pushed an ice cream cart around the corner. At once Franco pulled on his father's thumb to get his attention. Distracted, *Papi* tousled his hair and told him to pipe down.

Just then the massive doors swung outward, whining loudly, and three uniformed policemen walked halfway down the stairway. Brusquely *Papi* yanked his thumb out of Franco's tiny fist. *Stay here*, he said, nodding at the other young man on the sidewalk. From his waistband the man pulled out a small revolver, which he promptly hid inside the panama. Franco's knees clenched.

The sun rose to the top of the sky in an instant, and the wind turned damp and warm, like a breath exhaled. Two gray-haired men, wearing beige suits and fedoras, stepped out through the doorway. The young man in the wire-rim glasses set off down the sidewalk, past the marble railing, toward Franco and his father. Again *Papi* said, *Stay here*. He headed straight for the young man, who held the panama lightly against his chest.

At the steps they pretended to collide with each other. *Papi* fell backward; the young man landed on his hip. Franco's heart stopped. Quickly his father and the young man rolled onto their bellies and clambered up the stairs. By now the policemen had gotten wind of their intent. The one furthest back gathered the gray-haired men and pushed them down to the ground. The other two crouched and drew black, gleaming pistols.

Papi fired first. An officer grasped his throat and collapsed.

Blood fanned onto the marble railing. *¡Viva Puerto Rico libre!* the young man screamed, standing up, shooting wildly at the gray-haired men crawling on the landing. The two surviving officers returned fire, even as bullets ricocheted about them.

Deafened by the many reports, Franco watched his father jerk backward and fall clumsily on his seat. Suddenly his brilliantined head burst open; a bright, red mist sprayed from his crown. Franco could only stare. A few feet away, a third shot caught the young man in the belly. Clenching, he threw his weapon at the sidewalk. The revolver clanked loudly on the cement, like an empty can.

Nobody paid heed to the shootout; men and women kept rushing up and down the sidewalk, glaring ahead, carefully sidestepping the slick pool of gore. Frank Esteban, no longer a child, pushed desperately through the huddle. His shoes splashed in blood. He knelt down next to the body, which smelled of burnt flesh and rust. *I'm sorry*, his father said. But it wasn't his father. Frank heard a high-pitched laugh. He glanced up toward Blair House and saw President Harry Truman at the landing, his bespectacled face twisted into its signature smile, brushing dirt off his beige trousers.

Then he was awake. As usual, there was no disorientation, no momentary confusion of dream and reality. One second he was in Washington, D.C.; the next he lay in the dark warehouse, handcuffed and injured, his cheek stinging from a recent blow. Next to him, the boy with the grinning mask squatted uneasily.

"What is it?" Frank muttered.

"You're up, pig," the boy said.

"Of course I'm up. You hit me."

"No, I mean you're next. Sombra's gonna talk to you."

Before Frank could reply, another masked guard came to his side and, tugging at his biceps, brought him to a standing position. By now the pain in his shoulder was a dull, constant throbbing. He couldn't move the arm and his left knee ached. There was a rattle in his chest whenever he breathed. He was exhausted. After all this was over, Frank acknowledged, he would have to take a few sick days and stay home. Lydia would want to mother him for a little while.

The light from the hallway painted a white semicircle on the cement floor, beyond which Frank could see nothing but shadows. The storeroom looked empty. For the first time he wondered how long he'd been asleep. He wondered where Robertson and Weying . . .

"Where's the young lady?" he barked, glaring at the masked kid. The other guard pulled him toward the door, but Frank wouldn't budge.

"I'm alive," Weying said, waving, and immediately Frank recognized her silhouette in the darkness.

There was something wrong with her nose.

"What did—?" he started.

"Watch out for Sombra," a low voice chimed in: Robertson. His hands were still handcuffed, but now he had them on his lap. When he gestured the links made a sharp tinkling noise.

"Don't tell them anything," Weying said urgently.

"Shut up, *putita*," the kid said, laughing.

Frank grimaced. How he wanted to break that scrawny neck . . .

"Watch out for Sombra," Robertson repeated. He groaned and tightened his forearms against his chest, as if to set a broken rib. "He's a mutant."

Just then the guard yanked Frank's arm, and his clavicle shifted, and his shoulder—the whole chest, really—blazed like a star. He almost screamed.

"He changes," Robertson said, but by then Frank had been shunted out the door and down the brightly lit hallway. The pain seemed to scramble his senses, so that afterward he couldn't tell much about the long walk through the warehouse. He remembered only details: a beaded curtain, a smell of fat and tomato sauce, loose steps on a flight of stairs.

Suddenly there was an acrid burst in his nostrils. He recoiled, then wiped a string of spittle from his lips—only then did he realize the handcuffs were off. He was in a small, bare room, curled over an old school desk, his face hovering inches above the rutted Formica. As he settled back on the seat, he noticed a broken capsule in the pencil well.

Before him there loomed a heavy-set Asian man dressed in olive fatigues. His arms were crossed over a pot belly. He held an unlit cigar between his thin lips.

"That's better," he said in Spanish. "Finally we have your attention."

Frank found the cadence of his words familiar, something about the way he pronounced his vowels.

"Where's Cheeto head?" Frank asked, the first thing that came to mind. He leaned back and settled against the backrest.

The man regarded him curiously. "Cheeto head?"

"You know, Sombra. The red-headed *cabrón* who gave us that welcome earlier."

"I don't know who you're talking about," he said, annoyed. "I'm Sombra. There's no other *cabrón* here."

Frank narrowed his eyes. He thought about arguing, but then changed his mind. Whatever games these people were playing, they did not change the circumstances one bit. He was still their prisoner. Still at their mercy.

"I see," he said. He nodded and pursed his lips. "Sombra. Right. Anyway, I caught a glimpse of your handiwork, back in the storeroom. Must have been quite a struggle, breaking that poor girl's face. I'm sure many *camaradas* gave up their lives on that mission."

"Just doing what had to be done," Sombra said without emotion. He smiled, revealing a wide gap in his lower teeth. He peered closely at the police captain and added, "I'm sure you understand."

"Oh sure," Frank laughed. With his right hand he brushed his hair to the side. The fractured bone clicked in his shoulder. Blinking from the pain, he said, "Well, better get started, then. I don't know squat, and I'd rather get the beating over and done with. I mean, if you don't mind."

Sombra grinned. "Come on, Captain Esteban," he said in a patronizing tone, "relax. Settle down." From his hip pocket he produced a shiny Zippo lighter; there was a crude map of Puerto Rico stamped on the chrome. After two tries the wick caught and, puckering dramatically, Sombra lit the cigar. Right away the room filled with a sweet, caustic smell.

"I get them from Raul Castro, Fidel's brother," he said, examining the Havana held pinched between his fingers. "He's quite a connoisseur, you know." Sombra paused for a moment, then gestured with the cigar and added, "Maybe you wanna try one?"

"Not really," Frank said.

"Suit yourself," Sombra said, clenching his jaw. A moment later Frank noticed a sharp cleft on his chin. *Could have sworn that the skin had been smooth before.*

Neither spoke for a while. Glaring at Frank, Sombra drew on the cigar, and the tip glowed orange and faded.

"My grandfather used to own a tobacco plantation," Sombra said, finally.

Frank remained silent.

"The *gringos* took it, of course. Bought the adjoining farms and cut off his water supply."

"Terrible," Frank said with deep sarcasm.

Sombra didn't seem to notice. "So, are you from the island?" he said, stepping back and gesturing self-consciously with his cigar. "You grew up in Puerto Rico, right? Was it Añasco? Nah, you look more like a *sureño* to me . . ."

"*¡Maldita sea!*" Frank exploded. "What do you want from me?"

"I want to talk," Sombra said. His eyes suddenly widened. The wispy hairs that fell on his forehead thickened to wiry curls.

Stunned, Frank shifted backward on the seat. He recalled Robertson's words as the guards dragged him out of the storeroom: *He changes.*

Could this man be the same as the one with the red hair?

"Go find yourself a friend," Frank said. "Look, why don't you just let us go, all right? It's no big deal. Just let us go. Because I'm not telling you crap. No matter what you do to me, I'm not telling you anything—all you're gonna do is bruise your knuckles."

Sombra sucked again on the cigar, then blew a faint halo into the air.

"Wait, wait," he said, "I think I've got it. Guayanilla. Am I right, or am I right?"

"Are you listening to me?" Frank said, exasperated.

"I'm listening. Hell, I even agree with you." Without warning, Sombra tore the cigar from his mouth. He rushed forward and grabbed the sides of the school desk, thrusting his face all but a few inches away from Frank's.

"That's why I was thinking," he whispered, his breath pungent and hot, "maybe I should be working on the lady lawyer instead. We both know she's holding out. Maybe I wasn't— hard enough with her the last time."

Frank shrank back and looked awry at Sombra. He could picture himself jumping from the desk and grabbing this *revolucionario de pacotilla* by his fleshy throat. Putting out that stupid Havana on his face.

Taking a deep breath, Frank said, "You're right."

"Right about what?" Sombra said. He pulled away, grinning, then reached across the room to pick up a metal folding chair. He opened it with a quick jerk of his wrist. As Sombra settled on the chair, Frank saw that his pot belly was gone. His face appeared Caucasian now, pale and angular.

"I'm from Guayanilla," Frank said. "My parents brought me to New York when I was seven."

"East Harlem?"

He nodded. "One Twenty-first and Lexington."

"You moved in with your aunt and uncle," Sombra said, deliberately wiping his lips with the palm of his hand. "They had five kids, and you had to share one room with all of them. For two years you slept on a thin mat on the floor."

Startled, Frank straightened his legs under the desk. "How do you know that?"

"And the windows were cracked, so it was always freezing in the winter. In fact, one of your cousins died of pneumonia. There were rats, too. Some nights you would lay awake and listen to them scurrying, gnawing at the doorjamb."

"How—?"

"The cops wouldn't let you walk further than Central Park North. Neither did the Italians. You took to carrying a zip-gun to protect yourself. In school the Irish kids beat you, and the black kids beat you, and when you told the principal all he did was correct your English pronunciation."

"You can't know that," Frank said, shaking his head.

Sombra paused. He glanced at the spotlight hanging from the ceiling.

"More than anything," he said, "more than anything in the world, you wanted to go back to Puerto Rico."

There was a clatter of metal outside; a woman shouted a long curse in Spanish. Rooted to the desk, Frank laughed thinly, pressing a thumb against his chin.

"You're good," he said. "You're very good."

"I'm just reminding you of the truth," Sombra said.

"Yeah, yeah," Frank said dismissively, "and now you're gonna tell me about my father, right?"

"What about your father?" Sombra asked, his eyes round in mock innocence.

"You know, how he was a hero, a *Nacionalista*. How I should help you out with whatever it is you want, because *papi* would have wanted me to."

"Believe me, Rodrigo Esteban would have despised a sniveling coward like DeLaSelva. He would have told us where that *hijo 'e puta* was hiding. Without hesitation."

"Yeah, well, *Frank* Esteban doesn't have a freaking clue who this DeLaSelva is. And even if he did, he'd rather kiss a horse's butt than tell you anything. *¿Me entiendes?*"

Sombra was losing control now: his hair straightened and darkened; his nostrils widened and his skin turned brown, then a dull copper.

"You think joining the pigs wasn't enough?" he muttered. "You need to stab your father in the back again?"

"Let me tell you something about my father," Frank said. "*Papi* was a two-timing drunk and a deadbeat. He left when my mother was eight months pregnant. Never gave us a dime."

"That's funny," Sombra answered. "Your brother, he speaks so highly of him."

Frank felt his heart clench. "Carlos?" he mumbled.

"Toro, Chacho!" Sombra yelled, ignoring the prisoner's words. Immediately the metal door swung open and two masked guards stepped inside. "Take this *pendejo* back to the holding room. He's beyond my help."

"You have Carlos here?" Frank said, bewildered, just as the guards lifted him bodily from the school desk. "Where's my brother?"

Sombra looked at him intently; blue spread through his brown irises like blotted ink.

"Don't worry," he said, "we're keeping him busy."

Dinner came by a few minutes later: mounds of rice and red beans scooped onto plastic trays, topped by thin strips of caramelized plantain. Sitting again by the metal door, Frank was reminded of public-school lunches. The food was cold and gelatinous, and the guards had not bothered to give the prisoners utensils; nevertheless, Weying and Robertson dug in at once, desperately, wincing from bruised jaws and split lips. In the pale glow of the lamp, they looked washed out and faded.

Frank nibbled on a plantain. Listlessly, he carved a trench through the beans with his thumb.

"You know," Weying said, raising her blood-stained face from her tray, "this isn't half bad."

Robertson licked the grease between his fingers and nodded. "You know what I could use right now, though?" he said. "Some good tobacco."

"Oh please. Cigarettes? Really?"

"Pipe," Robertson said, gesturing with his handcuffed hands. "My single affectation as a newspaperman."

Weying laughed; immediately she groaned and covered her mouth with her hand.

"I'm pathetic," she muttered. Tears wetted the caked blood and drew bright lines across her cheeks.

"Come on," Robertson whispered.

"It's—" she began. She held her breath for a moment, shivering. "Forget it," she said.

"Takes a few weeks," Frank said. He reached carefully behind his back and fluffed the support pillow. "I know about busted noses. In a few weeks, it'll be like nothing happened."

Weying pushed her tray aside. Angrily she picked up the blanket from the floor and covered herself.

"I bet that's what you tell suspects after you beat them up," she said.

Robertson sighed; steam rose from his mouth like a thought balloon in a comic strip. "We don't need this," he said.

"Look, I'm in no mood—" Frank said.

"Oh, I'm sorry," Weying said sarcastically. "Guess you don't like being on the receiving end, huh?"

Frank shut his eyes. He could hear a distant rumbling—probably a truck. "It's something else," he said.

"You haven't touched your dinner," Robertson noted, glancing at his messy tray.

"Don't feel like eating."

"What is it?" Weying said. All of sudden she sounded concerned.

For a few minutes Frank didn't answer. He wasn't sure how much to tell these forced companions; regardless of the circumstances, they were still little more than strangers. His was family trouble, after all.

Then again, perhaps he owed them the truth.

"Look," he said, "I think I just figured out why I'm here."

"I thought it was because of DeLaSelva," Robertson said.

"Never heard of the man."

Weying glared at him. "Why didn't you say so before, when we—"

"Didn't have a chance," Frank interrupted. "And afterward, well, I wanted to keep 'em guessing."

"If not DeLaSelva," Robertson said, "then what?"

Frank hesitated; it occurred to him that maybe Sombra had lied. The idea of Carlos . . . well, it seemed so far fetched. But, strangely, it also made sense, especially given the details Sombra knew about Frank's childhood.

"My brother," he said. "I think he's mixed up with these losers."

"Ouch," Weying said.

"I didn't know you had a brother," Robertson said.

"He's a lot younger. Ten years. And well, he hasn't quite followed the straight and narrow."

Smiling, Robertson said, "Black sheep of the family?"

"Carlos means well," Frank said, embarrassed, shaking his head, "he really does. But it's like things never work out for him."

"Sounds like half of my *pro bono* clients," Weying said wistfully.

Frank rubbed his eyes and continued: "*Mami* and I, we put him on a college track program, out in Westchester. Eight months before graduation he gets into an argument with one of his teachers, and the guy swings at him, so he swings back. Breaks his jaw. That was the end of that.

"After *Mami* died I pulled some strings and got him into the Police Academy. Now, real quick we find out that he's a deadeye dick. I mean, you've never seen anything like it—he looks at the target and *blam!* Right on. So the brass immediately tags him for SWAT training, and even before he's finished there's like eight precincts fighting over him. Well, apparently he had other plans. Two days before the final exam I get the call from the commissioner's office: Carlos's been caught with a stolen Beretta in his gym bag. Says he was getting it for a Harlem buddy of his who's in trouble with a dealer."

"Yep," Weying said, "that's the other half."

"How long ago was this?" Robertson asked.

"You never heard of it, believe me." Frank regarded him warily. "I'm talking off the record, okay?"

"Off the record," Robertson said, nodding.

"We buried that sucker," Frank said. "There was this judge who owed me a favor—don't ask—and he got him into one of those Army deals: enlistment in lieu of jail time. That's where I left him, eight years ago. Twenty-three years old and he still looked like a kid, duffel bag slung over his shoulder, stupid cowlick . . . I got a letter from him a few years ago, tells me he's quitting the Army. He wants to spend some time 'back home'—meaning Puerto Rico, of course, even though he grew up on Lexington Avenue. Go figure. Anyway, I haven't heard from him since.''

"And you're saying he's a Cane Cutter?'' Weying said.

Frank nodded. "I guess they figured I'd help them, out of family loyalty, or something.''

"Like father, like son,'' Robertson muttered.

There was another rumble, this one louder than the first, and Frank held a cupped hand to his ear. "What was that?'' he said.

"Your father, he was a revolutionary too, wasn't he? A *Nacionalista?*''

"Well,'' Frank said dismissively, "I don't know about that. Carlitos never met his father.''

Weying shifted under her blanket, as if she were trying— and failing—to find a comfortable position. "What now?'' she said. "I mean, Sombra's interrogated all of us.''

"Who knows?'' Robertson said grimly.

Frank drew his left arm, by now all but useless, close to his chest. "Sombra's running out of time,'' he said. "Whatever his deal is, he's running out of time.''

CHAPTER 7

THURSDAY, 8:15 A.M.

MISSING! blared the headline of Thursday's *Daily Bugle* in sixty-five-point type over pictures of Ann Weying and Robbie Robertson. Peter Parker knew this because a mockup of the front page had been pasted to the wall of the packed *Bugle* conference room. He certainly hadn't had the opportunity to pick up a paper for himself.

He'd spent most of the night checking his street contacts. Unfortunately, the few who knew anything had said that DeLaSelva was holed up on Sixty-third Street. The only useful thing he had done the entire night was stop an attempted break-in at a Forty-seventh Street jewelry store.

According to Hawkins, with whom he had checked in twice during the night, the apartment was no help—DeLaSelva's were the only usable prints. The only personal items were the stereo and five salsa CDs (now shot to pieces), plus copies of the newspapers *El Diario* and *Claridad*, various Spanish-language magazines with names like *Hola!* and *Vanidades*, and a complete set of Colin Maxwell's mystery novels. "So we know he was probably here alone, and he has eclectic taste in reading matter," Hawkins had said.

Eventually, Spider-Man had called it a night, heading home a bit after three in the morning. Mary Jane of course had waited up for him; he always exhorted her not to, she always promised she wouldn't, and she always did. He had filled her in while she applied a heating pad to his still-aching shoulder. He had finally gone to sleep at four. Five minutes later—though his clock insisted a full three hours had passed—the phone woke him. It was Glory Grant from the *Bugle*, telling him there was a big staff meeting at 8:15 and he'd better get down there right quick.

He got down there right quick—mainly because it was, if anything, colder this Thursday morning than it had been twenty-two hours earlier when he encountered Daniel-the-Dimwit-Super-Villain at an Upper West Side movie theater.

Lordy, that was less than a day ago, he realized. *Seems like years.* He had also checked in with Hawkins, who had reported, happily, that Drew didn't suffer a concussion, and would be checking out of the hospital and returning to work by noon, and that Gilman and Liverakos were pursuing a lead on DeLaSelva's mother.

Arriving at the *Bugle* building and changing clothes, Peter went straight to the far corner of the City Room, and found every single staffer and quite a few freelancers besides himself present and packed into a standing-room-only conference room. Many of them held mugs or paper cups of coffee, tea, or juice, and Peter regretted not grabbing something for himself. He'd gulped down a cup of hastily brewed coffee at home before departing, but with only three hours' sleep and a full day of editor/lawyer/police captain–hunting ahead of him, he needed all the help he could get.

He considered sneaking off to grab something when Jonah finally made his entrance, walking under the red NO SMOKING sign while puffing on a cigar. As soon as he arrived, everyone stopped talking.

The *Bugle* publisher spoke at a volume that made the room's quieting down irrelevant. "I take it I don't need to tell you why we're here. Our editor-in-chief, Joe Robertson, is still missing." Jonah gestured with both hands as he spoke, cigar ashes flying around him. "We know that Robbie was taken from his car in Queens, specifically in the Long Island City area. We know that there have been no public ransom demands, no one stepping forward to claim responsibility. We know that this case is being handled, not by a Queens precinct, not by the detectives at One Police Plaza, but by the Midtown South Precinct in Manhattan. We know that a lawyer named Ann Weying—who, unlike Robbie, actually lives within Midtown South's jurisdiction—has also gone missing. And we know that the cops are treating both of these incidents as a single case and that it's what is referred to in cop vernacular as a 'red ball.'

"People, this is *pathetic*!" Jonah bellowed the final word. Peter swore that the glass in the conference room door rattled.

"We're a *news-gathering* organization, and what we actually know about this case—this case which involves *one of our own*—is crap."

A young woman Peter didn't recognize started to speak. "Why don't we—"

Jonah turned and looked right at her with a gaze that was pretty much the textbook definition of *evil eye*. The woman shut up.

Continuing as if he hadn't been interrupted, Jonah said, "From this point forward, this is the only story that exists. I don't care if they declare world peace, I don't care if Skrulls invade, I don't care if Dewey defeats Truman, *this* is the only story you cover, understood?"

No one reacted verbally, but several nods went around the room.

"Understood?" Jonah repeated much louder—and this time, Peter was sure the door window rattled.

Several murmurs of assent went around the conference room.

"Good! Now, then. Urich is coordinating. Anybody has anything, bring it to him. He'll keep all the stories straight, make sure we don't repeat or contradict ourselves."

Ben Urich held up his cup of coffee in reply.

"As for the rest of you . . . Mercado, from this moment forward, you *live* at Midtown South. Set up a cot if you have to. I wanna know everything that happens there."

Joy Mercado nodded.

Ben interjected a comment. "While you're there, Joy, see if you can pry a report on Robbie's car and Weying's apartment out of them. We asked for a copy yesterday, and we still haven't gotten anything."

Joy again nodded. "I'll work the desk sergeant."

Ken Ellis said, "Uh, a word of warning, Joy. The day-shift sergeant is a major pain. Name of Karen Jones. She'll eat you alive if you're not careful."

Jonah went on: "Ellis, you've been working the Pierce story. Weying's his lawyer. Pierce was ratting on Morgan Hall. There's got to be *something* there—you find it. And see if there's any kind of connection between Hall and Robbie.''

"Okay, I'll—" Ellis started, but Jonah wasn't finished yet.

"And while you're at it, press some of those cop contacts you keep gloating about. If they can't help us here, what the hell good are they?"

Plenty when it comes to one of their own, Peter thought. Esteban's apparent involvement meant the NYPD would play this so close to the vest as to be inside their rib cage. He could also see why they hadn't released the police report. The last thing Golden would've wanted was for the funky fingerprints to get out, telling all the world that this was a "costume" case. Still, he doubted the lieutenant could keep it out of the *Bugle*'s hands for long. Such reports were supposed to be public record, and Jonah would be more than happy to talk to one of the judges he was chummy with and get a court order for them.

Jonah continued: "Snow, check out a raid that went on last night at the Amsterdam Houses near Lincoln Center. It came out of Midtown South, but there's been no statement. It might be connected. And some witnesses placed Spider-Man at the scene. Find out where in the housing project the raid was, who was being raided, and why—and what that wall-crawling weasel was doing there. If *he's* involved in this, I want details.''

Charley Snow pulled on his moustache thoughtfully and said, "You got it."

Peter sighed. *Somehow, I just knew Jonah would work an anti-Spidey angle into this.* But then, Spider-Man had indeed participated in the raid on DeLaSelva's apartment. Still, he was even more grateful now that he'd distanced himself somewhat from the NYPD. Jonah would only make hay of the connection, and that would do no good, not for Hawkins, not for Spider-Man's already-tarnished rep at the *Bugle*, and certainly not for Robbie, who didn't deserve to have his victimization degenerate into another of Jonah's endless tirades against Spider-Man.

"Byrne, you take Weying. Talk to her neighbors, see if anybody's 'remembered' anything since yesterday."

"No problem," Vreni said.

"And dig a little deeper into her background. Her immediate family checked out okay, so check extended family. Maybe she's got a crazy old uncle with a thing for breaking and entering."

Vreni jotted some notes down and nodded.

"Walters, keep on the DA's office."

Billy Walters rolled his blue eyes. "I'll do my best, but old buddy Blake's been saying, 'No comment' so much, you'd think he was running for mayor," he said, referring to District Attorney Blake Tower.

"Forget Tower," Jonah said, "work on the ADA assigned to Pierce, what's his name?"

"Carrillo," Ellis provided helpfully.

"Right, him."

Peter had to admit to being impressed. He spent so much time sparring with Jonah—as both Peter Parker and Spider-Man—that he tended to forget that beneath the old goat's gruff cheapskate exterior lay an excellent journalist.

Just then, a tall, gangly man with receding black hair spoke up. Peter thought he knew the man, but couldn't place him. "Uh, excuse me, Mr. Jameson?"

"Yes, Trilby, what is it?"

That's who that is, Peter realized, *the obituary writer. No wonder I didn't recognize him.* News photographers didn't mix much with the person who wrote the death notices.

"Um, I take it I should update the obits on Mr. Robertson and Ms. Weying?"

When Jonah had started firing off instructions, a slow murmur started to build in the room. Peter hadn't noticed it at first, but he did now, mainly because, as Trilby's words sunk in, all conversation ground to a halt.

Everyone looked at Jonah.

Peter wouldn't have believed it possible, but Jonah actually looked stricken. *No*, he thought, *"stricken" is too weak a word. More like he's been kicked in the head.* Peter felt much the same way. In all the talk about finding out what was going on, not to mention all the searching he'd been doing for the past day, the thought that Robbie might be dead had never occurred to him—nor, apparently, had it to Jonah.

After a pause that went on for an uncomfortably long time, Jonah finally said, "Do what you have to, Trilby."

"Uh, Mr. Jameson, sir?" a voice said tenatively. It was Arwen Rosenbaum, an imposingly tall blonde who had recently moved to the city news staff from the Brooklyn Metro section after the *Bugle* cut the outer borough sections as part of their recent cutbacks. "I can check the hospitals and the medical examiner's office, see if any of the John or Jane Does match either of them."

Several people shot Arwen a dubious look. She was one of the few people sitting down in the conference room, by dint of her being seven months pregnant. Ben finally put what everyone was thinking into words. "That's, uhm—that's a lotta legwork."

"I can do it from here, sir," she said to Jameson, then added with a grin: "I've got people at every Manhattan hospital *and* in the M.E.'s office who owe me a favor. This strikes me as the right time to call them in."

Jonah gave what passed for an appreciative nod—he inclined his head ever-so-slightly—and said, "Good. The rest of you, find out what you can, and coordinate with Urich." A pause. "Well, what the hell're you *standing* here for? *Get out there!*"

Peter joined the mass of humanity that moved as one toward the conference room doors. They moved so swiftly, Peter was half-tempted to just go limp and let the crowd carry him out.

Once he made it out to the City Room proper, everyone scattered to the nine winds, some moving to the elevators, pausing only to grab their coats, others going to their desks and pouncing on their phones or keyboards—or both.

A part of Peter Parker wanted to share his information—the same part that forced him to go out every day in a red-and-blue costume and do the right thing regardless of the personal consequences. Unlike the others, he knew that a third person had been taken in the same manner as Robbie and Ann, and that that third person was a cop. He also knew that the Cane Cutters were likely responsible for the kidnappings. *If*, he added to himself, *you can really call them kidnappings, considering there've been no ransom demands or anything.*

But the consequences wouldn't be personal if he did that—instead, it would hamstring an investigation that already had next to nothing going for it. The Cane Cutters were professionals. They read the papers. The more the NYPD kept out of the press, the better chance they had of tracking the kidnappers down.

Still, as he looked over at Betty Brant, staring intently at something on her computer screen, he felt a small temptation to at least tell her, to give her a scoop. Betty was Peter's first friend on the *Bugle* staff, and the first woman geeky young Peter Parker ever dated. He still remembered one particular occasion, early in his career. He and Betty were both in Jonah's office, and Jonah was ranting (about what, Peter couldn't remember—it took very little to get Jonah started on a tirade and after all these years, they started to blend). At the time, Peter only knew Betty as Jonah's secretary, and had vaguely noticed that she was pretty. Attractiveness in the opposite sex was something Peter Parker had trained himself not to bother noticing since, up to that point in his life, such attentions were consistently met with derisive laughter.

To his surprise, Betty sidled up to him. For the first time, he noticed the lilac-tinged perfume she wore. She whispered to him, *Don't feel too badly, Peter. I may only be JJ's secretary, but I think you're* wonderful.

No one had ever said anything like that to him before. He'd been called *wonderful*, by family and by teachers, but never in quite that way. Eventually, he even worked up the courage to ask her on a date.

Their relationship had been a rocky one, though. Betty had been through so much in her life—her mother's illness, which forced her to drop out of school and take her mother's job as Jonah's secretary; the deaths of her brother Bennett and later her husband Ned Leeds—but in recent times she'd bounced back wonderfully, and turned into quite a good reporter in a surprisingly short time. Peter and Betty had come through the crucible of their tumultuous relationship as good friends. *And good friends do sometimes share secrets with each other.*

But, no—tempting as it might have been, Peter couldn't compromise the investigation, not even for his first love. *Funny, how you can still be a sucker for the first person you ever kissed,* he thought with a smile. *Particularly when she's also a colleague.*

Speaking of colleagues, one such cried out, "Yo, Parker!" He turned to see Ellis walking toward him.

Peter waited for Ellis to come alongside him. "So, didja get anything?"

Oh, hell, I forgot all about my little "arrangement" with Ellis. Think fast, Parker. "Uh, no, sorry. I sat outside the Edghill for a couple of hours. Got frostbite after a while, and no one showed, so I left." Then a thought occurred, and he added, "One odd thing. When I got there, the window was open. Someone shut it after a minute, though. Thought that was kinda weird, given the weather."

"That is odd, yeah. But it jibes with what I heard. Well, it was a shot. Lemme know if anything does turn up from that, though, okay?"

"Sure thing," Peter said, wishing Ellis would share what he had heard, but not surprised that he didn't. *Probably heard of a Spider-Man sighting. At least I hope that's all it was.*

"And, uh, keep this between us, yes?" Ellis added.

"Don't worry." Peter Parker had spent most of his life since high school keeping all kinds of secrets, from the everyday white lies that were part and parcel of a dual identity to somewhat more devastating ones. This would be the least of them.

Ellis wandered off, and Peter went down to the *Bugle* morgue. As ever, Bob the computer maven stood behind the desk, his bushy silver moustache having expanded into a goatee since the last time Peter saw him. Ever since the *Bugle*'s recent downsizing—which had resulted in the departure of city editor Kathryn Cushing, along with the dress code she had imposed—Bob had taken to wearing sweatshirts with silly computer-related sayings. Today's shirt read, WE ALL LIVE IN A YELLOW SUBROUTINE.

"Geez, you too?" Bob said. "Welcome to Grand Central Morgue."

Peter frowned as he noticed that all the workstations in the large room were occupied by people with whom Peter had recently shared a conference room. "Busy day."

"Yeah, well, how often is the editor-in-chief kidnapped?"

"Good point. How long'll I need to wait?"

Bob stepped away from his counter and gestured at his own workstation. "You can use mine."

Peter was stunned. Bob never let anyone touch his keyboard. "Geez, Bob, I'm flattered, but—"

"Hey, remember when you needed that info on Osborn? You actually kept your promise and came back to tell me how the story came out, which is more than these ingrates ever do," he said, jerking his thumb back at the mass of reporters staring at the various computer screens.

Peter smiled, remembering the time of which Bob spoke. The Chameleon had gotten his hands on some of the Green Goblin's old gear and teamed up with Carnage to make Spider-Man's life miserable. Bob had proven useful on that case, and in return Peter had indeed told him how the story came out. "I even brought pizza," he said with a chuckle.

"Yup. And, despite the fact that you profaned the surface of said pizza by placing pepperoni on it, it is the thought that counts, and in gratitude I am willing to allow you to use the sacred terminal."

Peter bowed in appreciation. "You are too kind, good sir."

"Not a problem," Bob said with a grin. "One thing, though. We've still only got East Coast papers in the database, and I doubt we're gonna be able to expand beyond that anytime soon—not with all the cutbacks going on."

Peter sighed. Still, the East Coast news sources probably would suffice for what he needed. "I can live with that," he said.

"Like you have a choice," Bob said with another grin. "I'm gonna go check on these other guys. Last week, Urich almost wiped the database, so I'm a little nervous."

This time, Peter grinned. Ben Urich was a great reporter,

but he still had problems with certain technological advances. *Heck, Ben's still struggling with the voicemail system.*

As Bob wandered off, Peter went into the search program and entered in three joint searches: one for the Cane Cutters and Ann Weying, one for the Cutters and Robbie, and one for the group and Frank Esteban.

The first search gave him two hits, one from the *Bugle*, one from the *Globe*, both the same basic story. They said nothing he didn't already know, to wit, that Ann Weying defended Jorge DeLaSelva, "a known Puerto Rican nationalist with ties to several terrorist groups, including the Cane Cutters," on gun charges. The other two found no commonalities.

He then broadened the searches to include any mentions of Puerto Rico. He got the same hits on Weying, as well as three followup stories that just mentioned DeLaSelva's heritage and nationalist tendencies. For Esteban, all he got were references in several local papers to the captain winning Puerto Rican New Yorker of the Year three years previous.

For Robbie, though, he got several hits, all from Robbie's time as a reporter in Philadelphia twenty years earlier. He'd done a series on Puerto Rico called, "A Migrant Community Pictures its Roots." According to one article, he even won a Press Club Award for it. As Peter skimmed the articles, he noticed that one of the people Robbie talked to was named Jorge DeLaSelva.

Well well well, Peter thought. *The plot thickens.* He checked back to the stories on DeLaSelva's gun charge. *Maybe he was arrested at Midtown South. That would give—*

He cut off the thought when the first *Bugle* article scrolled onto the screen. DeLaSelva had been arrested in Riverside Park on the Upper West Side, "and taken to the Twenty-fourth Precinct." *So much for that idea.*

He executed several other searches, trying to find some kind of connection between Frank Esteban and the Cane Cutters— or at least with the *independista* movement, or with DeLa-Selva. But he found next to nothing. Esteban had done a fairly good job of keeping his name out of the papers, so there was little to find in the first place, and the only connection he could dig up was the award.

Unless Esteban's actually a member of the Cane Cutters and he staged his own kidnapping to throw his people off. It seemed a bit far-fetched, based on his earlier encounters with Esteban, but in Spider-Man's career he'd seen things that fetched much farther. *Or maybe they took him because he's Puerto Rican. Would they do that?*

Peter sighed and realized that—while he could quote chapter and verse on megalomaniacs like Dr. Octopus and Dr. Doom and worldwide terrorist organizations like A.I.M., Hydra, and the Ultimatum—he knew far less about terrorist organizations that set their sights a bit lower than the entire world. He decided to see what the morgue had on the *independista* movement in general and the Cane Cutters in particular.

As it happened, they had quite a lot. Realizing that to sit and read all of them would intrude on Bob's hospitality more than was politic, Peter instead chose to print out as many of them as he could. That turned out to be fewer than he'd have liked, as the printer—which had gotten a lot of use this morning—ran out of toner, and Bob insisted that he have his workstation back before the intern had had a chance to replace the cartridge.

Sighing, Peter grabbed the printouts he had been able to get and, with a good-bye wave to Bob, headed back toward the City Room.

THURSDAY, 8:20 A.M.

A long time ago, Sombra had a real name.

He could still remember it on his mother's lips as she called him in out of the rain on dreary Saturday afternoons. He remembered his sister's teasing; she would rhyme the word with some filth or other, laugh like a parrot at her own stupid cleverness. And there was his father—two hundred pounds of stink squeezed into a yellow, paper-thin *guayabera*—screaming it at the top of his lungs, grabbing him by the neck, and shoving him at a broken figurine or at a new scratch on the car.

The name had been given to him, slathered on at birth, as if with a brush. As a child he'd even convinced himself that he owned it, that it was his forever.

Fool.

Sombra sat alone in the makeshift command center, his muscular back to the wall, sipping lukewarm *café con leche* from an aluminum cup. It was his second of the morning. Already his hands were jittery, and he noticed a change in his skin—from ruddy to a deathly pallor. Sombra cursed. If there was one thing he hated about his changes, it was the way that they revealed him, put his feelings on display. *Sombra's nervous, see?*

He couldn't just blame the coffee, of course, not with the way everything was falling apart. Just thinking about it—about *him*—made Sombra tremble with rage.

The robbery had come off perfectly. He could still smell the gunpowder, feel the sweaty fear in his palms, the grime as they handled the loot. He'd picked one of his most trusted men as courier, a veteran of the movement, a man who had stood shoulder to shoulder with Che Guevara, *por Dios*! Just in case, he'd put three tails on the guy. At first they'd had no trouble keeping up with DeLaSelva as he drove from Hartford to Bridgeport, where he holed up for a week and half, as instructed, before making his way down to the New York state line. But then, with a furtiveness Sombra couldn't have expected from such a *reliquia*, DeLaSelva had vanished.

He's a quick one, Jorge, he thought. *Have to give him that much.*

Sombra cursed again. What was the metaphor in English? Defeat snatched from the jaws of victory? Something like that. In any event, revenge had been so close. He almost felt the heat irradiating from it; he pictured the smoke, the flames licking the sky. He could hear the cement splintering, cracking, and the cooling towers exploding—

—and a hesitant knock on the metal door.

"What?" Sombra said, carefully setting the *café con leche* under the chair.

"Sorry to interrupt," Carlitos Esteban said—Sombra recognized his tinny voice at once, even distorted by the hollow metal door, "but it's Paqui. He just got back from talking with Altmann."

Sombra sighed. Jens Altmann was their dealer, the one whose promised merchandise had started this whole operation. Had it been good news, Paqui would have come in person.

"Get in here," he barked.

If Sombra hadn't known the fact, he would have never guessed that Carlitos and the cop were brothers. It wasn't just age: the two men looked nothing alike. They even seemed to carry their years differently. Frank Esteban looked creased, like a leather strip that had been tied far too many times. In contrast, Carlitos could have passed for a first-year college student, even at thirty-one. He walked timidly into the command center, his narrow shoulders hunched, his cheeks covered in a faint, gleaming fuzz. There was an old office chair by the boarded-up side window, and Carlitos stood behind it and held on to the backrest. Squeezing the cushion with his fingers, he spread apart a slit on the upholstery.

"Well?" Sombra asked. He could tell that Carlitos was examining him, trying to gauge his mood.

"We have twenty-four hours," Carlitos said reluctantly. "That's it."

"Twenty-four," Sombra repeated, shaking his head.

"Apparently he's got other buyers. If we can't get him the money by nine in the morning, it's bye-bye, matter disruptor. Says he's doing us a favor, holding off *that* long."

"Yeah, right," Sombra muttered. He felt a spray of acid in his stomach, and watched his knuckles swell and shrink. "I bet you anything that the other buyer offered less money."

Carlitos stroked his beard. "Maybe," he said.

"Maybe nothing." He stared ruefully at the boarded-up window, which was covered in cracks and nail holes that shone brightly from the morning sun. The sickeningly sweet smell of rotting bananas had wafted in from somewhere.

"I take it no one has spotted DeLaSelva yet," Sombra added.

"We'll let you know," Carlitos said, embarrassed.

"How about the truth serum? Any news on that?"

"Sasa's still working on it; the thing is, sodium Pentothal isn't the kind of stuff they carry at the local pharmacy. She's got a lead, though. Soon."

"Hell," Sombra muttered. He paused for a moment, then laughed and added, "Anybody got a School of the Americas torture manual handy?"

Rooted to the spot, Carlitos didn't answer. Instead he stared at the ground and ran his fingers along the vinyl upholstery.

Sombra stood up. Slowly he walked toward Carlitos, stopping just before the office chair, mere inches away from him. "You got something on your mind, *camarada*?" he said.

"Nothing, nothing," Carlitos stuttered. His forehead glistened with sweat.

Reaching with his right hand, Sombra slapped him gently on the cheek.

"Come on," he said in English.

"It's just that—" Carlitos began. He swallowed, then glanced quickly at a shadow in the doorway. "I don't understand what we're doing. I mean, why all this trouble for a matter disruptor? The robbery, the kidnappings. Beating up prisoners."

"So, you're questioning my leadership, is that it?"

"No, no," Carlitos said, lurching away from Sombra.

"Then what?" Sombra said quietly.

"I thought we were guerrillas, you know. I thought we struck and ran away. Matter disruptors, that's a battlefield weapon. And for eight million we're getting only one of them. We can't smash the *yanquis* with just one piece of artillery."

He's a quick one, Sombra thought, smiling to himself. Most of the other *Corta Cañas* were simply excited about getting a big gun stolen from S.H.I.E.L.D. Carlitos had actually thought about it. That made him valuable. And dangerous. Sombra turned around, sauntered over to his chair, and picked up the aluminum cup off the floor. The coffee was tepid, but the bitter taste felt good in his mouth.

"Do you believe in *la independencia*?" he said.

For a second Carlitos seemed dazed by the question; he

blinked and pursed his lips. "Of course," he said, finally.

"Good. Because, you know, most *puertorriqueños* don't."

"They're cowards," Carlitos answered, this time without hesitation.

Sombra shook his head. "Our people are confused," he said. "They don't know who they are, who they owe allegiance to. They don't know what to believe. Things are too good for them, you know what I mean? With the welfare, and the food stamps, and the TV, and the shopping malls.... That's why they're so afraid of freedom. They're just standing there, dazed by all that glitter. They can't feel the chains locked on their ankles.

"But, you see, *we* know that the *gringos* are imperialist devils. *We* know that they've poisoned our land and our minds, that they shoved their leaky nuclear reactors and their English and their decadent rock music down our throats. We know that they are bleeding us dry of spirit. That's why it's our responsibility, you see, we have to make things—well, clear. That's why we need the matter disruptor."

"I don't get it," Carlitos said.

Sombra lowered his voice down to a whisper. "So far we're like gnats to them. We shoot a few soldiers, burn a radio antenna. The feds swat around, hit and miss, but nobody notices it on the island. It's not their concern. The matter disruptor, though, with that we can take out battleships. We can obliterate billion-dollar planes on the runway. You following me here?"

"So it hurts," Carlitos murmured, "like a wasp sting."

"Exactly," Sombra said, the word sharp and quick as a staple. "And with wasps the feds ain't just gonna swat around, see. They're gonna burn the nest. Arrests, reprisals, all kinds of brutality. That's when the *boricuas* hear the chains rattling. That's when they choose sides."

"Our side," Carlitos said without emotion.

Sombra smiled proudly. He could see the gleam in his comrade's eyes, the bright understanding. Right then he made a point to remember that little speech; it could very well prove useful with the others.

Now, though, there was something else he had to discuss with Carlitos Esteban.

"You should know," he said, turning to face the empty hallway, "that I'm willing to answer any questions you may have, *camarada*. There's no hangups here. You ask me and I tell you." He took a sip from the coffee mug. "As long as it's the true question, of course."

"What do you mean?" Carlitos said. He reached under his collar and scratched his neck.

"You haven't said anything about your brother. Not a word."

"*Bueno*," Carlitos began. He glanced at the ceiling, then down at the wrinkled seat of the office chair. "Well, I know why he was taken. DeLaSelva, maybe he was turning state's evidence, right? So Franco is a police captain. Maybe he knows where Jorge's holed up. Makes perfect sense."

"I talked to him yesterday," Sombra said.

"I heard. He wasn't very helpful."

"No, he wasn't." Sombra sat down and crossed his legs at the knee. "Look, I'm gonna put this as simple as possible, all right? I need to know where you stand. Because the way you talked about the pig before, you made it sound like he had one foot on our coast, and that's not what I got from him. Not at all."

Carlos held his face, squinted as if he were under a spotlight. "I thought—" he said.

"I don't care what you thought," Sombra interrupted. "What I want to know is if you're still with us. I want to know if I can trust you."

"Of course," Carlitos said, sounding almost offended. "This here's my family now. I belong here."

"Good." Sombra drained the coffee dregs, then twirled the mug once on his index finger. To his consternation, he saw that his hand had grown about an inch since Carlos had walked into the room.

"Blood ain't worth much," Sombra said, tipping his head from side to side. "Nation. *Tu cultura, ves?* Your people. That's what matters. But family?" Casually he tossed the mug over his shoulder. It rang like a cracked bell against the wall. "Frank's a dangerous one. A *Tio Tomás* like him? A *vende patria*, working for the man? That's very dangerous."

"I understand," Carlitos said.

"No matter what happens, we have to take care of him."

Carlitos took a deep breath. "I understand," he repeated.

"I haven't made up my mind about the other two. But Frank Esteban . . . Maybe he's your brother, but the man is a bad, bad seed. I'm thinking we take care of him."

For a while Carlitos stood still behind the office chair, perfectly quiet. Then, finally, he muttered, "We do what we have to." After a beat he nodded curtly and walked off through the doorway, shutting the door behind him.

Sombra tapped his fist on his brand new chin. A flurry of scenarios twirled about in his head.

After a few minutes, the door thumped again. "Who is it?" Sombra yelled.

"It's me, Sasa."

Finally, he thought, relieved. *Something goes as planned.*

CHAPTER 8

THURSDAY, 8:30 A.M.

Laura Liverakos looked at her watch for the eighth time in the last two minutes. *He's late*, she thought angrily as she stood in the freezing cold outside the Washington Heights apartment complex that—according to her partner in his phone call of an hour previous—housed Jorge DeLaSelva's mother, Esperanza. She wished Peter Gilman would get his bony butt up here already.

Liverakos lived alone in a tiny apartment in the Kingsbridge area of the Bronx, all of ten minutes north of Washington Heights via the 1 train, so she and Gilman agreed that it made the most sense for her to go straight to Mrs. DeLaSelva's place from home. Gilman, who had come in early from his Park Slope, Brooklyn apartment ("I couldn't sleep," he said, a problem with which Liverakos empathized), would come up in a precinct car.

He said he'd be here at a quarter after. Where the hell is he?

Liverakos felt more than a little exposed standing out here by herself. No woman raised in a big city would be particularly thrilled with standing alone in the midst of a housing project, even though the cold weather kept most people off the streets.

But that's only part of it, she admitted to herself. After last night, Laura Liverakos had a feeling she was extremely uncomfortable with: helplessness.

The youngest of three sisters, Laura was the only one not to take after their parents and grow up to be over six feet tall. Mother stood at just over six feet, and Father almost hit seven. He spent his life talking to the tops of people's heads. Their oldest child, Penny had become a basketball prodigy, and now served as an assistant coach in the Women's National Basketball Association. Dana, the ever-rebellious middle sister, had moved to Alaska as soon as she graduated high school, and now served as a park ranger.

At age seventeen, Laura, the youngest and by far the shortest, announced that she would become a cop, and that nothing would stop her. Father shook his head and told the top of her head, *Five-four women don't get to be cops, Laura. It just don't happen.* But then, he'd said that to the top of Penny's head, too. *Women don't play basketball. It just don't happen.* She proved him wrong. Laura would do the same.

Mother, typically, took a more passive-agressive approach. When Laura started applying for college, Mother would leave brochures in her room for places like Fordham and ESU, even though Laura would only think about the John Jay College for Criminal Justice. At the dinner table, Mother would wax eloquent about how much she loved the Art History program at Fordham when she went there. Whenever a police officer got hurt or killed, Mother always made sure to ask if Laura read the paper or watched the news that day.

Laura ignored all of it. She got into John Jay and graduated at the top of her class. By the time she hit thirty, she had worked her way up to a brown belt in *shodokan* and passed the sergeant's exam—and at that, she was disappointed. She had hoped to get a black belt before making sergeant.

However, none of that did any good against Venom. Even with the bonus of a sonic pistol, she was utterly helpless before that monster, a minor distraction at best, a punching bag at worst.

She'd spent her entire life shorter than everyone around her, but last night was the first time in her life that she *felt* small.

Cops don't get to beat Venom. It just don't happen.

At last, at 8:37, a familiar-looking Mercury Sable pulled into the project's parking lot and parked in a space labelled EMERGENCY VEHICLES ONLY.

"You're late," she said as Gilman clambered out of the car. Her partner clutched the lapels of his wool duster with his left hand in the hopes of blocking out as much cold air as possible—Peter Gilman hated winter—and carried a brown paper bag in his right.

"Sorry," he said. "There was an accident on the Henry Hudson—had to cut over to the Harlem River. Consider this a peace offering—I went to the bagel place." He dangled the bag in front of her. "Got onion and pumpernickel just for you."

A wave of remembered nausea passed over her briefly, and she waved her hand. "Please, no food. I already learned that lesson."

Gilman frowned, concern etched on his brow. "You okay?"

"I haven't been able to hold down anything solid since last night. I already experimented with an English muffin this morning, and my stomach refused delivery."

Gilman winced. "That sucks. Hope it doesn't last too long. There's too little of you as it is—you can't afford to waste away into nothing."

She smiled. "Thanks a *lot*. But hey, if it does last, think of all the money I could make marketing the Gut-Punched by an Alien Diet."

They moved toward the building. Gilman opened the glass outer door; an inner door of the same type blocked access to the main lobby. The wall to their left was occupied by a huge array of buttons with apartment numbers on them, a large board with a list of names and corresponding apartment numbers next to it. To Liverakos's great surprise, the latter had E. DELASELVA—15D listed. Rarely did one find an accurate apartment listing anywhere in New York, especially in city housing.

Gilman pushed the button for 15D. A burst of static came in reply. Unfazed—*hell*, Liverakos thought, *the fact that the speaker's working is nothing short of miraculous*—Gilman said, "NYPD, ma'am."

A second later, a buzz emitted from the inner door, unlocking it and granting the two detectives access.

The building's lobby had the same general feel as far too many such places: dank, dark, various stale odors competing for the nose's attention. The place looked like it had been cleaned with a dirty rag—the dirt and grime wiped across and streaked horizontally, but not actually removed.

Liverakos sighed when she saw that three of the four elevators were out of order.

As Gilman pushed the UP button, Liverakos asked, "So how'd we find this woman, anyhow?"

"Cooperative efforts of the Twenty-fourth and Thirty-fourth Precincts. An Officer Sherman at the two-four dug up DeLaSelva's arrest report from last year, and discovered that his bail was posted by his mother, Esperanza, who listed this as her address. Sherman first called up to the three-four to verify that she still lived here, then called down to us—I was the only one in, so I took it. The three-four's desk sergeant, whatshisname—"

"Castro," Liverakos replied. She and Castro had worked at the Twelfth Precinct together when they were both rookies.

The elevator arrived. As they stepped in, Gilman said, "Right. Castro called Mrs. DeLaSelva and told her that a couple of detectives would be stopping by this morning."

Slowly creeping upward, the elevator—danker, darker, and dirtier than the lobby—eventually came to roost on the fifteenth floor.

A constant problem with city housing was finding the apartment once you arrived on a floor, since numbers routinely fell off doors and were never replaced. The sergeants were saved this difficulty by the fact that one door stood slightly ajar, kept from opening further by the still-attached chain lock.

Liverakos had to restrain a smile when she saw who stood behind the door: a tiny elderly woman who didn't even clear five feet tall.

"Mrs. DeLaSelva?" Gilman said as they approached.

"*Si.*"

Esperanza DeLaSelva had a wrinkled face, partially hidden by thick black plastic glasses. She wore a simple house dress, and held a half-completed needlepoint in her left hand, holding the door with her right. Her white hair was tied back in a bun, and smile lines were evident in her cheeks.

She did not use those lines at the moment. Her face was set in an annoyed frown. She showed no indication that she would undo the chain lock.

Gilman indicated his badge. "I'm Detective Gilman, this is my partner, Detective Liverakos. We have a few questions about your son."

Mrs. DeLaSelva then let loose with a stream of Spanish. Laura Liverakos only understood English and Greek, which put her one up on Gilman. The only word she recognized was "Jorge." Sergeant Castro spoke Spanish fluently, so he could have spoken to her in her native tongue when he called to say two detectives were coming. This was an annoyance Liverakos didn't need.

"I'm sorry, ma'am," Gilman said, "but we don't speak Spanish. Could you—"

The next phrase even Liverakos knew: *"No hablo ingles."*

Both detectives sighed. Liverakos looked down and shook her head. The half-finished needlepoint caught her eye—Mrs. DeLaSelva wasn't quite following the pattern. Or, rather, she followed the pattern, but not the stitching method. This needlepoint called for diagonal stitching, but Mrs. DeLaSelva stitched horizontally. It resulted in a slightly distorted image, as if the needlepoint was out of focus.

Then Liverakos looked over the woman's head—*and isn't it nice to be able to do that for a change?*—and saw two more framed needlepoints hanging on the wall behind her. One said HOME SWEET HOME, the other, GOD BLESS ALL MOTHERS, both with the same horizontal stitching, but still unmistakably in the English language.

A bookcase stood next to the needlepoints. About half the books were in Spanish, the other half in English.

Of course, it's possible that she can only read English and not speak it. But that's pretty unlikely. Usually, if anything, it goes the other way around.

"Mrs. DeLaSelva," she said, "we *know* you speak English."

The woman blinked in surprise, then said, in a ridiculously thick accent, "How you know that?"

Liverakos couldn't help but smile. "We're detectives, ma'am—detecting things is our job."

"I no see Jorge for three years. He bad boy—not talk to his *mami* for three years."

Gilman bunched up his wool coat and reached into his back pocket, retrieving a card. "All right, then, Mrs. DeLaSelva, if you do hear from your son, would you please call me?"

Letting go of the door with her right hand, she took the

card. "I call if I hear, but I no hear. He bad boy."

"All right. Thank you very much, Mrs. DeLaSelva."

Before Gilman finished his sentence, she had closed the door.

"Nice lady," he muttered.

Liverakos grinned as they went back to the elevator. "Well, she was lying through her teeth."

Gilman frowned. "Yeah, but you got her in it."

"Not just that, all of it. First of all, she speaks better English than that. Speedy Gonzalez has a more convincing pidgin."

"It did sound a little fake, didn't it?"

Liverakos nodded. "*Oh* yeah. But it isn't just that. De-LaSelva was arrested a year ago. If she posted bail for him, how could she not have heard from him in three years?"

The elevator arrived and they stepped in. "I can't believe I missed that," Gilman muttered.

"That's what you keep me around for, remember?"

He chuckled. "Good point. She obviously has a problem with cops, too. Or, at least, with strangers knocking on her door. She held my card the way you hold a dead mouse."

Liverakos nodded. "I think we'd better have the Three-four put a car here, keep an eye out for DeLaSelva."

"Definitely."

As the elevator lurched to a halt in the lobby, Liverakos couldn't help but smile a giddy smile. It was a small triumph, what just happened, but sometimes that was all it took.

"Hey," she said, "you still got an onion bagel in there?"

THURSDAY, 9:30 A.M.

Upon reentering the *Bugle* City Room, Peter Parker was waved over by Ben Urich, who was in the middle of a phone call.

"Yeah, okay," Ben was saying as Peter approached the older man's desk. The phone was cradled between his cheek and shoulder, freeing up his right hand to take notes, and his left to stub out a spent cigarette into an already-overflowing ashtray. "You sure about this?" he said as he pulled another cigarette and a lighter out of a pack in his shirt pocket, stuck the cigarette in his mouth, and lit it—all with his left hand, still jotting notes with his right. "Because I don't like printing rumors. My publisher tends to get cranky when I do that—and so do his lawyers . . . You've never *met* J. Jonah Jameson, have you? . . . Yeah, *that* Jameson, the one with the moustache. He's my boss . . . All right, lemme check it out and get back to you . . . Only if the tip's *good*, Shwartz, you know the drill . . . Fine . . . Fine . . . 'Bye."

He hung up the phone, puffed on the cigarette, and dumped some ashes as he turned to Peter, who had taken a seat in Ben's guest chair. "Pete, you're the closest to a Venom expert we have around here. You got any idea why he'd be looking for a guy named Jorge DeLaSelva?"

Before Peter could figure out how to answer that, Vreni Byrne—whose desk was all of ten feet from Ben's—said, "Excuse me, Ben, what'd you say?"

"Venom was tearing the city apart yesterday looking for some guy named Jorge DeLaSelva. Why, you know him?"

"Not exactly." Vreni turned her chair so that she faced Peter and Ben. "I did a search yesterday, trying to see if I could find anything Joe and Ann Weying had in common."

"Did you find a lot?" Peter asked neutrally.

"Quite a bit, actually—for one thing, both of them have had several run-ins with Spider-Man. For obvious reasons—" she indicated Jonah's office with her head "—that's the angle I've been focusing on. But I found a couple of other, non-arachnid connections, and one of them was a guy named Jorge DeLaSelva."

"Who is he?" Ben asked.

Vreni shrugged. "A thug. He's worked for some terrorist organizations, mostly ones agitating for Puerto Rican independence. Joe interviewed him for some pieces he did on Puerto Rico twenty years ago in Philly, and Weying represented him on a gun charge last year."

"That's a pretty thin connection," Ben said.

"I know. That's why I wasn't really pursuing it. But if Venom's going after this guy, there might be more there."

"Whaddaya think, Pete?" Ben said, turning to face him. Vreni did likewise.

Peter thought quickly. On the one hand, he couldn't share information he'd gotten as Spider-Man in confidence from the NYPD. On the other hand, they'd lost DeLaSelva. *Bugle* staff finding him might not be ideal, but it beat no one finding him at all.

Still, he chose his words carefully. "Venom doesn't do anything without a reason. He isn't the type to indulge in random attacks. And he has to know that Weying's gone missing, so anything he's done in the last twenty-four hours would have to have something to do with that. He still seems to think he can effect a reconciliation with her."

That prompted a snort from Ben and a bark of laughter from Vreni.

Peter hesitated a moment. *Heck, in for a penny* . . . "And I heard that Spider-Man's looking for this guy, too. He was tearing up downtown last night looking for him."

"We'd better find this fella," Ben said.

"Don't look at me," Vreni said, holding her hands up. "I'm national. I'm only on this story 'cause Jonah didn't give me a choice. Hell, I still haven't figured the subways out yet. I wouldn't know where to start looking."

Ben sighed and took another drag on his cigarette. "Yeah, well, I'm chained to my desk." He looked around, then fixed his eyes on Betty. "Hey, Betty!" he called out. "Got somethin' for you!"

Betty Brant typed two keys on her keyboard, stared at her screen for a moment, then got up and joined the kaffeeklatsch around Ben's desk. "What's up?" she asked. Not for the first time, Peter noticed a confident timbre in her voice that had only shown up since she started reporting. He liked the sound of it.

Ben replied, "Jorge DeLaSelva. Apparently, both Venom and Spider-Man are looking for this guy *and* he's got a history with both Robbie and Ann Weying."

Vreni handed a pile of printouts to Betty. "This is what I've got on him, but it isn't much—just a couple of articles."

"Who is this guy?" Betty asked.

"A terrorist of some sort," Vreni said. "His excuse is a desire for Puerto Rican independence."

Peter frowned. "Excuse?"

"I've met a lot of terrorists in my time, Peter. Most of them are more interested in blowing things up than they actually are in getting what they say they want. I doubt this one is any different."

"That's not entirely fair," Peter said, the articles he'd just been perusing still fresh in his mind. "Puerto Ricans have a lot of legitimate complaints about still being, in essence, second-class citizens. A lot of them feel pretty strongly about it, too."

"I'm not denying that," Vreni said. "Quite the opposite, actually. Personally, I think it should've become a state decades ago. But, like any legit movement, the cause attracts nutcases who just want to practice demolition skills. DeLa-Selva's one of those types."

Ben smiled. "Since when are you an expert, Pete?"

"One of my classmates at ESU is really into this stuff," Peter lied with the ease of long practice. "He gave me an earful about the *Nacionalistas* just two days ago."

He looked over at Betty, who had a thoughtful look on her face. Then Peter realized that her gaze was fixed right on him. "Interesting," she said.

Danger, Will Robinson, Peter thought, though there was no real danger—his spider-sense remained quiet. But he didn't like the look Betty gave him, either.

"All right, I'll check into him and get back to you," Betty said. "Thanks."

Peter stood up. "Well, I'm going to head out and see what I can turn up on my own. I guess any pix I get go to you?" he said to Ben.

Ben nodded. "Thanks for the kibbitz, Pete."

Peter said, "No problem. Good luck."

"To all of us," Vreni said, and turned back to her desk.

As Peter headed toward the elevators, Betty's voice rang out: "Peter, wait up!"

He waited for her to catch up. She was carrying a wool overcoat streaked with dirt. "You need to get that thing cleaned, Betts," he said with a smile.

"Right, with all the free time at my disposal," she said, returning the smile. "I took a header into a snowbank yesterday morning."

Peter winced. "Ouch."

As she struggled into the coat, she said, "I wanted to talk to you for a minute. Why were you running a search on Frank Esteban?"

Peter sighed. That had been a risk—the *Bugle*'s mainframe allowed one workstation to see what another one was doing—but he figured everyone would be too involved in their own work to notice.

"Spying on me, Betts?" He added a smile, realizing his words may have come across as unfairly snide.

"Not exactly. I still haven't entirely figured the system out, so I wound up 'eavesdropping' on you by mistake. But I *am* curious, especially with Ben dropping this DeLaSelva guy on me." She fixed her brown eyes right on him. "You're holding onto something, aren't you, Peter?"

Peter looked right back into those eyes. Into that face. That face he fell for all those years ago.

And he knew the look on that face. It was the same one she had when she said he was wonderful.

Great. Just great. How do you say no to the first woman you ever kissed?

"Let's go across the street," Peter said, stalling.

I shouldn't tell her anything, he thought as they waited in the elevator bank. *But she already knows I was searching for Esteban. Not to mention that mini-diatribe on Puerto Rico. She knows that I know something. And one of the reasons our relationship went south in the first place was because I had to keep things from her. Because of Spider-Man. And now, again because I'm Spider-Man, I may have to lie to her once more.*

He sighed as the elevator rode down. *I can't do it.*

The pair of them went out into the cold long enough to cross the street to the Stadium Deli. Julio, the owner, said upon their entrance, "Ah, Mr. Peter, Miss Betty! Two hot chocolates, *si*?"

"*Si*," Betty said, blowing on her hands. "Cripes, just crossing the street and I feel like my entire body froze over."

There were only two seats at the counter near the constantly opening door, so Peter didn't bother taking his jacket or gloves off. Betty also kept bundled up. After Julio brought the two cups full of piping, and blessedly caffeinated, hot chocolates over, Peter said, "Look, Betts, you've got to promise to keep this to yourself. Don't tell Ben, don't tell Vreni, don't tell Jonah, nobody, okay? If you do, it could mean a lot of trouble, and could make it harder to find Robbie." Peter felt like a heel for guilting Betty this way, though what he said was entirely true.

"All right, Peter, if it's that important."

"It is." He took a breath, then sipped from his cup. Julio made it too hot, as usual—his tongue burned. Ignoring it, he said, "It isn't just Robbie and Ann who're missing. They also got Esteban."

Betty's eyes widened, and she stopped in midsip. "You're kidding."

Peter shook his head. "Nope. All three are being treated as one case."

"Wow." Betty finished her sip, then said, "I know cops like to keep a detail out of the press to weed out the copycats and crazies, but this is a little extreme."

"Not entirely. It isn't great PR to let the world know that one of your captains has been kidnapped. And—" He hesitated. *Should I tell her about the Cane Cutters?*

When his pause went on too long, Betty prompted, "And?"

"Well, let's just say that it would be a good thing if someone found this DeLaSelva guy. He's involved in this whole shebang."

"How? I mean, I see that he's got ties to Robbie and to Weying, but how's he connected to Esteban?"

Peter sighed, and once again thought, *In for a penny . . .* "I don't know about any direct ties, but the kidnappers are almost definitely a Puerto Rican nationalist terrorist group called the Cane Cutters.''

"I've heard of them. Why would they want Robbie and the others?''

"Well, among other things, they're apparently responsible for that Wells Fargo heist a couple of weeks back.''

Betty was surprised enough to again stop in midsip. "I remember that—about a dozen people claimed responsibility.'' She put the hot chocolate down. "Come to think of it, the Cane Cutters were one of those dozen.''

"Well, unlike the other eleven, they meant it.''

Betty regarded Peter with a suspicious expression. "How do you know all this?''

"Let's just say I stumbled across a reliable source,'' Peter said. *Not that far from the truth, really.* "You've got to promise, though—''

"—not to reveal this, I got it the first time, Peter. I know the drill about protecting sources and knowing when and when not to use something. I've already collected about a hundred pieces of information that will probably never leave my head. Besides, it's not like this changes anything significant. I still need to find DeLaSelva. You've just given me another reason to.'' She sipped her hot chocolate again, this time finishing it off. Then she fixed him with the *I think you're wonderful* stare again. "And Peter?''

"Yeah, Betts?''

"Thanks. You didn't have to share this at all—it means a lot that you were willing to share it with me.''

Peter looked into those brown eyes that he had spent so much time staring into when he was a teenager. He loved Mary Jane with all his heart and soul, and had no regrets about choosing to spend the rest of his life with her—but right here, right now, he understood exactly why he fell for Betty Brant back then.

"Hey,'' he said, putting his gloved hand on her unclad one, "what're friends for?''

● ● ●

Ten minutes later, they had paid Julio, and Betty went off in her search for the elusive Jorge DeLaSelva. Peter went to a side street, waited until no one was looking, then leapt over the gate to an alleyway between buildings. *I liked it better in the old days*, he thought with an internal sigh, *when people didn't feel their alleys needed better security than their front doors.* It was rare these days to find an alley in Manhattan that didn't have a padlocked gate—an attempt to keep homeless people (not to mention super heroes looking for a changing room) out.

Once he got into his Spidey suit, he clambered up the building wall to the roof, and considered his next move. This early in the morning, he wasn't likely to get much from his usual street contacts. *Besides, I ran through most of them last night and got bupkuss.*

Then he remembered his thoughts from the previous day regarding Venom: *If he finds out she's been taken, he'll tear the city apart looking for her.* And he also remembered that the NYPD wanted Spidey to cooperate with them in the first place primarily because of Venom.

Spider-Man unclipped the cell phone from his belt and switched it on in order to call Hawkins.

"Hawkins."

"It's the guy in the bright red bodysuit."

"You're early," Hawkins said, sounding vaguely hopeful. "You got something?"

"Uh, no, sorry," he said lamely, realizing that by calling the sergeant before his next every-three-hour check-in would have gotten Hawkins's hopes up. "I just wondered if that lead on DeLaSelva's mother went anywhere."

"Yes and no. Peter and Laura talked to her, and she said she didn't know anything about what her son was doing, but they're both pretty sure she was lying. There's a car from the local precinct watching the building." He chuckled. "It turns out that car was *already* there. An armed robbery suspect lives in the same building, so the two guys watching it just got a little added to their workload."

Spider-Man sighed. "Sounds like a long shot."

"Right now, everything's a long shot. Doesn't mean we don't take it. I'm trying to see if there are any local members of the Cane Cutters we can talk to." A slightly bitter tone crept into Hawkins's voice as he added, "That's a little difficult, since we already have the full lack of cooperation of the FBI, and they're the ones with the full sheets on these guys. Oh, by the way, it looks like you did some good last night."

"Whaddaya mean?"

"Well, you may not have found DeLaSelva, but your interest in him, combined with Venom's searching for him yesterday, has made him extremely hot. Lipinski reported in this morning, and said that everyone's talking about DeLaSelva with the same revulsion that people spoke of Typhoid Mary. It's probably only a matter of time before he turns up."

"Well, *that's* good news. Meantime, I'm going to keep an eye out for Venom. Check all the likely places he might go. If I can run interference on him, it'll give you guys a better shot at finding DeLaSelva."

Hawkins snorted. "You know, I was just thinking that this searching for the Cane Cutters was frustrating and annoying, but it beats the hell out of facing *him* again. I don't envy you."

"Believe me, Sergeant, it isn't on top of my list of things I want to do today—but it's gotta be done."

"Mmm. Well, good luck. We'll talk in three hours."

Spider-Man ended the conversation, then clipped the phone back to his belt after shutting it and switching it off. He then reached out his right arm and let loose a stream of webbing that stuck to an office building on the other side of Third Avenue. Firmly gripping the web-line, he leapt off the roof, swinging in an arc diagonally across the street and southward.

Okay, if I was a second-rate reporter symbiotically bonded to a lovesick psycho alien, where would I go to find my ex-wife?

He swung over the traffic coming out of the Queens Midtown Tunnel and veered southwest at Thirty-fourth Street.

As the cold air bit through his mask, Spider-Man thought about his last confrontation with Venom. *He left the fight pretty quickly. He must've been in pretty rocky shape to pass up an opportunity to chow down on my brains.*

He swung out over Park Avenue South at Twenty-eighth Street. At the top of an arc, he shot out a web-line at a nondescript white building on the eastern side of the street and swung around, letting go at the apogee and flipping to land atop a corner restaurant.

Come to think of it, he remembered, *Brock got shot twice when Hawkins and Liverakos were nailing him with the sonic guns. So he probably spent the night recuperating.*

Shooting out another web-line, he wended his way toward Madison Avenue, then attached a line to the side of the Metropolitan Life Building, swinging in a horizontal arc over Madison Square Park. He let go of the line at the southernmost part of the swing, letting his momentum carry him across Twenty-third Street to alight on the façade of a bar/restaurant.

Still, the longest he would've stayed out of it is overnight— give the symbiote a chance to recover from the sonic whammy and let it heal his gunshot wounds. Thinking of his wrenched right shoulder, which still ached a bit, that ability to heal its host was one aspect of the symbiote Peter Parker *did* miss.

He shot a line onto the north tip of the Flatiron Building and swung around and up to the roof of that famous structure, then zigzagged down Fifth Avenue.

Spider-Man thought back on what he said when Gilman asked him where Venom went last night: *"To look for his wife, same as we're doing."*

He arrived at the end of Fifth Avenue and the ESU campus, belatedly remembering that he was blowing off a lecture *and* a lab today. *Well, it can't be helped. Maybe I'll be lucky and that salmonella bug still has half the department down.*

Deciding not to examine what his definition of *lucky* was these days, he forced his thoughts back to Venom as he zipped across ESU and down into Greenwich Village.

If he is doing the same thing we're doing, he'll probably try to find some commonality between Robbie and Ann, just like we did. Crummy as he was, Brock was a good enough journalist to do that *much.*

Swinging around ESU's math building, he came to rest on the roof of a Bleecker Street jazz club, closed at this early hour. As his foot hit the roof, he recalled Gilman's reply to him the previous night: "*Yeah, well, it isn't* exactly *the same, is it?*"

"Of course!" he said aloud, startling a woman walking down the street below. She gave him a dirty look and moved on.

Venom couldn't care less about Robbie. Probably views him as part of the cabal of evil journalists that helped me conspire to blacklist him from the profession. The only thing he cares about is Ann. So what would his next step be?

He smiled under his mask as he realized what he should have thought of in the first place—A.J. Pierce, Ann's client. Spider-Man knew that to be a dead end, but Venom didn't. And, though the words had been an excuse to obtain the address of Pierce's safehouse, what Peter had said to Ken Ellis yesterday did apply: Venom would go after Ann's current client sooner or later. It behooved Spider-Man to be there as well.

Leaping off the roof of the jazz club, he shot another web-line and continued southward. *I probably figured this all out subconsciously*, he thought, realizing that the path he had taken from the *Bugle* matched the route he would have taken had he decided initially to return to the Edghill.

Less than five minutes later, he was close enough for the spider-tracer he had surreptitiously placed on Pierce to register on his spider-sense. But as he came within sight of the Edghill, his spider-sense abruptly stopped.

Uh-oh.

Then he heard gunshots. Still nothing from his spider-sense.

Obvious danger and no peep from my spider-sense can only mean one thing, he thought anxiously. *I was right, and ol' chomp'n'drool found Pierce and crushed the tracer. Gotta get in there, fast.*

He landed on the roof across from the Edghill and quickly calculated the angle he'd need in order to swing into the twenty-fifth-story window he'd used the previous day—after all these years, he made such calculations almost unconsciously and at a moment's notice. That took one second. He shot a web-line along that angle, then leapt off the roof. Two seconds.

As usual, his calculations were accurate. The swing brought him right to Pierce's window. Three seconds. Leading with his feet, he crashed through that window angling upward in an arc that brought him in with his feet at a forty-five-degree angle to his head. Four seconds. Thrusting his hands toward the floor as gravity reasserted itself and pulled him down, he pushed himself back up with his powerful arms. Five seconds. In another half-second, he landed in a crouching position and surveyed the room.

Venom stood near the center of the room, the symbiote flitting in multiple directions, tendrils undulating and whipping around like hyperactive snakes. Four such pseudopodia were wrapped around four different uniformed police officers—obviously the ones theoretically providing the *protective* aspect of the protective custody, and also obviously as out of their depth with Venom as Hawkins and the others were the previous night.

After another half-second, Spider-Man noticed the final figure in the room: A.J. Pierce, almost invisible, blocked by Venom, behind whom the pale accountant cowered abjectly, covered with cuts and contusions and muttering to himself over and over.

Venom's gaze remained fixed on Pierce as he spoke: "We had been hoping that we could avoid seeing your putrid face again when we crushed your insipid tracer, arachnid. A pity you continue to show bad judgment. You will have time to consider your folly when we dine on your spleen."

Spider-Man stayed in a defensive position—as long as Venom had the four cops in his grip, the first move belonged to Brock. "What is it with you and spleens lately? Do brains no longer carry the USDA allotment of vitamins and minerals needed to keep the symbiote's coat all nice and shiny?" *That oughtta get a rise out of him—probably a razor-sharp tentacle.*

Sure enough, such a tentacle shot out from Venom's lower back. Spider-Man leapt backward over the tendril, hoping to draw Venom away from Pierce, and also hoping that the so-called "lethal protector of innocents" wouldn't hurt the cops any more than he already had.

"Cah-*mon*, Brock, that move has whiskers on it."

"We are not Brock, we are *Venom*! And we warned you what would happen if you tried to interfere with us!"

Even under the best of circumstances, Venom always sounded two bricks shy of a wall; today it was more like twenty bricks.

Of course, the nice thing about irrational opponents is that they make stupid mistakes. Case in point, Venom did indeed move away from Pierce to fight with Spider-Man.

Venom shot out a strand of the symbiote's organic webbing, which Spider-Man ducked as easily as he had the tendril. This time he leapt forward and tried to land a punch to the jaw.

As he began the leap, another tendril came out from near Brock's thorax aimed at Spider-Man's head. With only a split second's warning, and all his momentum carrying him directly into the path of the tendril—making it impossible to even try rolling with the blow—Spider-Man could do precisely nothing to avoid the impact.

Pain shot through Spider-Man's jaw and rattled his teeth as his momentum was redirected by the blow, flipping him head over heels. More pain shot through his skull as he landed on it.

And I was expecting Venom *to make stupid mistakes?* Spider-Man thought through a haze of agony. *Where does leading with my jaw against a foe immune to my spider-sense qualify?*

Blinking to clear his swimming vision, Spider-Man saw Venom lower the four cops to the floor and wrap each one in a cocoon of webbing. Every cell in his body cried out in agony, but Spider-Man forced his arms to prop him up in preparation for rising to face Venom again.

Venom did not give him the chance. Four tendrils from the symbiote wrapped themselves around each of Spider-Man's extremities. They pulled him into the air, twirled him around, then tossed him at a far wall.

Fighting down nausea in addition to the great pain, Spider-Man twisted himself so that his side would bear the brunt of the impact, and also went limp in an attempt to lessen the damage. It may not have seemed like much, especially given the effort it took, but if he hit the wall at the wrong angle, he could wind up with a snapped neck.

He slammed into the wall and felt a familiar shooting pain in a corner of his chest. A rib had cracked. Last month, he'd chased his old enemy the Lizard to Mexico, and in the ensuing conflict had broken two ribs. They had since knit together, but the bones were still weak, and the impact had splintered one of them. The collision with the wall also undid the work MJ's heating pad had done on his shoulder.

His body refused to move. Every bone, every muscle, every joint screamed in agony. Spider-Man knew he could overcome it—he'd done it before. He'd had twelve tons of machinery dropped on his back by Dr. Octopus, he'd been buried alive by Kraven the Hunter, he'd had the stuffing kicked out of him by the Juggernaut, one of the most powerful beings on the planet. For that matter, he'd survived previous encounters with Venom. He could focus past the pain and get up.

He just needed a second or two.

Across the room, Venom made his way back to the petrified A.J. Pierce.

"Now then, where were we before we were so rudely interrupted?"

"Please, I'm begging you, I don't know anything, she's just my lawyer—"

"Where is she?" Venom demanded while backhanding Pierce across the mouth, seemingly ignoring the accountant's pleas.

Pierce continued as if he hadn't been hit. "—I just want her to come back and everything will be fine, please, don't hurt me—"

"Where *is* she?" Another backhand.

"—I don't know anything, she's just my lawyer, she disappeared, she shouldn't have disappeared—"

"*Where is she?*" Yet another backhand. This time, several

teeth and spatters of blood flew out of Pierce's mouth, but he kept talking.

"—oh God oh God oh God, she's probably dead and then they'll kill me too and I don't want to die I just want to go home, it was just a hobby don't you understand, just something to keep me occupied—"

Gotta stop this before Venom kills him, Spider-Man thought. Lifting his left arm, he shot out a web-line at Venom's fist, hoping to catch it before he could deliver another backhand punch.

The web-line made it about halfway, then fluttered to the floor. Venom's punch slammed across Pierce's jaw.

Oh, great. Left shooter's out of fluid. He'd restocked both shooters before he left for his Wednesday morning lecture, but he'd done a lot of web-swinging since then.

He struggled to lift his right hand, ignoring the pain in his shoulder, and tried again.

This time it worked. Grunting in pain, he yanked down on the web-line now attached to Venom's hand. Venom stumbled backward, then turned to face Spider-Man.

"Still with us, eh? We shall have to remedy that."

"Listen to me, Brock—he doesn't know anything. I talked to him yesterday. He's innocent."

"As if we would take *your* word for it." Venom looked over at Pierce, bleeding and cringing. "Still, we believe you are correct that he knows nothing. But innocent? Hardly. The man is filth." Three tendrils flowed out and wrapped themselves around Pierce's shuddering body. "And filth should be disposed of."

Realizing what Venom was doing, Spider-Man struggled to rise and cried, "No!"

It was too late. Venom threw Pierce at the shattered window that Spider-Man had come through. His aim was off; Pierce hit the top of the window, fell down to the sill, then tumbled out.

As soon as Venom let go of Pierce, Spider-Man forced himself to rise, ignoring the knives of pain stabbing his chest where the rib cracked, ignoring the throbbing in his shoulder, ignoring the fatigue that spread through every cell in his body. As Pierce hit the top of the window, he coiled and leapt, following Pierce out.

It was two hundred and fifty feet to the pavement. Spider-Man was one second behind Pierce in the fall to earth. All things being equal, Pierce would remain one second ahead of Spider-Man all the way down. However, Pierce was still curled in an almost fetal position, which gave him a greater surface area to provide wind resistance, particularly on this breezy winter day. Plus, the Edghill was an old building with a faceted façade, which Pierce kept skidding up against as he fell, slowing his descent even more.

Spider-Man, on the other hand, dove out the window ramrod straight, arms thrust forward, despite the howls of protest from his right shoulder at that motion, which allowed him to shoot through the air like a bullet.

After two-and-a-half seconds, he caught up to Pierce. *Luckily*, he thought as he cradled Pierce in his left arm, *it wasn't the right shooter that ran dry*. He would not have been able to hold Pierce securely with his right arm just at the moment.

Another half-second, and he lifted his right arm as high as he could and shot out a web-line—

—which went all of two feet, and then stopped and started drifting through the cold air. The right shooter had also run out of fluid.

Spider-Man wasted one second in panicking as he and Pierce—who had either fainted or fallen into a coma—continued to fall.

With the street racing up to greet him, Spider-Man then did the only thing he could: he reached out with his right hand and grabbed one of the Edghill's protruding ledges, counting on his ability to cling to any surface to counteract the momentum of their fall.

It did, but not without a price. The move almost tore Spider-Man's arm out of its socket. The pain in his shoulder prior to grabbing the ledge was as nothing compared to the white-hot agony that seared through his entire arm. He let out a scream that lasted for several seconds.

Then he started to black out. . . .

THURSDAY, 9:40 A.M.

Hell.

Sombra let the word loll in his tongue for a moment. He chewed on it till the tart morsel became unbearable, and then there was a rush of bile in his neck, and he just had to blurt it out.

"*¡Carajo!*" he screamed.

Sombra wore steel-toed boots. With a swift kick he poked a hole through the corrugated wall. He could feel his lips swelling, his chest widening against his uniform. He didn't care.

He grabbed the only piece of furniture in the room—a rickety school desk—and lifted it over his head and with a loud grunt heaved it against the floor. The lunch-box cage collapsed; the armrest popped loose and caught Chacho, who was standing five feet away, square in the temple. Yelping, Chacho slapped his hands on the wound. Blood spurted between his fingers, dark and thick.

Carlitos, Paqui, and Sasa didn't even flinch. They stood together by the easternmost wall, next to yet another boarded-up window, staring intently at their leader's rage.

Sombra struck the door with his fist so hard that the whole room rattled, and it wasn't until he paused to breathe that he felt the loose bone in his hand. The skin on his arm, he saw, was now the color of almonds. He caught a glimpse of Chacho's blood; immediately he planted his elbows on the wall and pushed against it like a runner stretching before a race.

"Could they be lying?" Sombra said, panting.

Sasa, her hair long and parted in the middle, licked her lips and opened her mouth. After a moment she said, "I don't think so, no. Not with the sodium Pentothal."

"They don't have anything, Sombra," Paqui whined. He couldn't have been more than sixteen or seventeen; his eyes were too small for his wide face, and his nose was flat and bent over a wispy mustache.

"Maybe we didn't ask the right questions," Chacho offered

hopefully. Already he'd taken off his shirt—he wore a green tank top underneath—and pressed it against his temple to stop the bleeding.

"Come on," Carlitos said, rolling his eyes.

Sombra tapped his wrist on the corrugated wall. Vividly he pictured DeLaSelva curled atop a nest of stolen bills, safe in his hiding place, laughing at him. *Come and get me! Come and get me, you freak!*

If only he'd been tougher with the woman lawyer; by then it had been early enough to have had Clarita, their mole at the phone company, run a trace on DeLaSelva's number. Then they would have nabbed him as he waited for the call. Caught him with his pants at half-mast.

He smiled grimly at the mixed metaphor. Once, long ago, his own father had said exactly the same thing to him. At the time Sombra had been a shrimpy fourteen year old, just arrested for drug possession, and his parents had come to the station to bail him out. Or at least that was what Sombra assumed at first, waiting in the juvenile holding cell, his only companion a pallid junkie frenzied from withdrawal. His mother asked, *Is he all right?* His father stroked his chin and said, *Looks fine to me.* After a moment, Sombra got up from the bench he shared with the junkie and rushed toward the tepid bars. *You'll be okay, m'hijo,* his mother said, tearfully. Then she turned on her heels and walked away from the cell. Sombra screamed, clutching the bars, *Get me out! Mami, get me out!* His father snorted into his hand and said: *Caught you with your pants at half-mast, didn't they? You think about that. Tonight. You think about that.*

"We still have twenty-four hours," Sasa said, pulling Sombra back to the present. Using both hands, she pulled back her hair and tied it into a precarious bun. "We'll scour the city. We'll search every alley and every building—"

Sombra spat at the ground between his feet. "You won't find him," he said, his voice imbued with hoarse fatalism. "If the man has any brains he's left the city already. And even if he hasn't, there just isn't enough time."

"Guess we're through here," Paqui said.

"Ding, ding, ding," Sombra said, pointing with one hand and touching his bulky nose with the other. "Get everyone ready," he added, gesturing toward Sasa. "I want everything packed up and ready to go by tomorrow at nine."

"Why wait? Maybe DeLaSelva already told the police about the hideout."

Sombra shook his head. "The cops would have us surrounded already. Besides, I want to give that *hijo 'eh puta* a chance to come clean on the situation. Who knows? He could show up before the matter disruptor deal falls through. I say guilt's biting Jorge on the butt as we speak."

"You also said he could be trusted," Sasa chimed in, smiling. Sombra grunted angrily in response.

"What about the hostages?" Carlitos asked. "I mean, now that we know they don't know anything."

"They may still be useful," Chacho said slyly. Blood, streaming in faint rivulets, painted a fancy latticework on his forearm.

"There's Pocillo Pérez," Sasa said, catching his meaning, "there's Agudo Valentín."

"A trade for prisoners? The feds would never go for that," Carlitos declared.

"They gave those weapons to the Iranians."

"That's not the same."

With the tip of his boot Sombra spread the spittle across the floor. Then he said, "I'm with Carlitos. We're gonna have to deal with the hostages."

"You mean—?" Sasa said, eyes open wide, gesturing with her thumb and forefinger.

Sombra grinned. "I don't know yet. Maybe."

"Better decide soon."

"Better get your butt in gear," Sombra said. His eyebrows flared and turned shockingly blond. "I've heard just about enough from you."

Recoiling, Sasa grabbed Paqui by his arm and hurriedly pulled the boy toward the door. Chacho tied the bloodied shirt around his forehead, then followed the other two into the hallway.

Carlitos stood still and glanced hesitantly at Sombra. Something was bothering him, Sombra could tell. He didn't like playing favorites, but ever since he found the young man, angry and lonesome, at a pro-independence rally in Arecibo, Sombra had taken a shine to him. It wasn't just his ability with the gun—there was also a level-headedness about him, a cool intelligence, which, mixed with his patriotic fervor, made him the perfect weapon in their struggle. With the others Sombra didn't feel that he had to explain himself: he gave orders, and they (eventually) obeyed. He treated Carlitos differently, though. He wanted the bright young man to understand. He wanted him to learn.

"Move it, *chico*," Sasa called out from the doorway. Carlitos took a step toward her, but Sombra blocked his path with one scrawny arm.

"I got something to discuss with him," he said to Sasa, who immediately nodded and slipped away.

"Yeah?" Carlitos said.

Sombra didn't speak. He glared at the *camarada*, feeling his skull expand, the skin tighten around his eyes.

"Something wrong?"

"I want you to put together a strike team," Sombra said, at last.

"Sure," Carlitos said. "What's the mission?"

"We need that matter disruptor. Even if we don't find the Wells Fargo money, we're getting that weapon."

Carlitos squinted. "But if we take it by force," he said fast, his tone rising, "we're gonna lose a good supplier. Altmann got us the M-16s, the antitanks we used in the Vieques hit. He even came through with the sonics. Look, if we take him down, nobody's gonna do business with us. It just ain't right."

"We're gonna have to take the risk."

"But why?"

"*Venganza*," Sombra said. He produced a cigar from his shirt pocket and offered it to Carlitos.

The young man shook his head.

Undeterred, Sombra bit off the tip and fixed the cigar, unlit, in his mouth.

"I tell you this because I've come to trust you," he said. "I am opening myself, understand? This is a pact, what I say right now: it's a contract between the two of us. Now, if that's too rich for you, then take the door and leave."

Carlitos didn't move.

Sombra nodded and continued, "For a long time, I thought it was bad luck that did it."

"Did what?"

"This!!" Sombra said, pointing at his face. At once, his lips shrank, and his earlobes bloated like seed pods. He took a deep breath. "I thought it was the bad luck, *ves*? A wrong place at the wrong time . . ."

"*Bueno,*" Carlitos said. He ran a hand through his black, tightly curled hair.

"My mother, she used to work at the nuclear reactor in Rincón," Sombra said.

"The one with the cracks?"

Sombra smacked his lips. "They built on an earthquake zone, the dogs. Only one in the island . . ."

"*Gringos* are dumb," Carlitos said, smiling.

"Not dumb," Sombra muttered. "Ruthless." He paused and breathed for a moment. "They knew it all along, see? Last time I was in Puerto Rico, I saw the documents. They knew it all along."

"Then why—?"

"*Un experimento*. They wanted to know what would happen. Patterns of radiation. Cancer rates. Mutations."

Looking down at the floor, Carlitos whispered, "*Diablos.*"

"*They* did this to me, *ves*," Sombra said, "and now I'm gonna do it to them. Are you with me?"

"I'm with you, *mano*. You know I am."

"Fine. Put together a strike team, then. Get me that matter disruptor."

Carlitos tipped his head forward, then turned to leave the room.

"Something else," Sombra said, just as Carlitos crossed the threshold.

"Yeah?" he said, turning again.

"Remember what we talked about earlier?"

"Yeah," Carlitos said. He looked at Sombra askance, as if he were standing too close to focus on him.

Sombra spoke without intonation. "I want you to take care of it. Personally."

"Okay," Carlitos said, much too quickly. He glanced at the doorway, then, trembling, and rubbed a stiff hand across his lips. Nodding, he repeated, "Okay."

"This is your next step," Sombra said, concerned, but smiling kindly. "After this, there'll be nothing but Puerto Rico. Nothing but your country."

Carlitos shut his eyes.

It was a risk—Sombra was perfectly aware of the fact. In the end, Carlitos could very well disappoint him. But if he didn't, maybe the trip to New York City would have been worth it, after all.

"*Vete, hermano,*" Sombra said, stroking the loose bone in his hand. *Go, my brother.*

CHAPTER 9

THURSDAY, 10:05 A.M.

For Spider-Man, the world consisted of the stony façade of the Edghill Hotel and pain. And the former was fading into a merciful black.

Good. Sleep. I can sleep and forget the pain. Just take a nice little nap, and then I can—

"Hey, Spider-Man, you okay?"

The voice brought him back to reality. He realized that his grip on the ledge had loosened, and he tightened it, fighting through the crippling pain in his arm.

Then he realized the voice was nearby. It wasn't Pierce; he was still cradled in Spider-Man's left arm and out like a light. *Who the heck would be yelling at me when I'm on a building dozens of feet up?*

Then he looked down, and saw a crowd of people gathered on the sidewalk about fifteen feet under him.

I don't believe it. I'm on the second floor.

He shuddered. He hadn't realized he was so close to the ground. If he'd waited even half a second longer before reaching out to grab the ledge, he and Pierce would both be very large, very disgusting puddles.

Letting go of the ledge, he let his arm fall limply to his side and fell the remaining distance to the sidewalk, landing gracefully on his feet, knees bending to absorb the impact. As he did so, two blue-and-white police cars from the First Precinct pulled up. Four cops exited the two vehicles, guns drawn. They saw Spider-Man and Pierce, and one asked, "What happened?"

Why do cops always ask that? Spider-Man wondered. "This is A.J. Pierce, the guy in protective custody upstairs," he said as he placed Pierce gently down onto the pavement. "Venom came and—"

Spider-Man cut himself off. *Venom's still up there. And my right arm doesn't work.*

He sighed. *Well, I knew the job was dangerous when I took it.*

As he leapt back up to the wall and started climbing toward the twenty-fifth floor, favoring his right arm as much as he efficiently could, he yelled down: "Call an ambulance for Pierce. Venom might still be up there." He didn't bother to look to see how the cops reacted. They wouldn't stand a chance against Venom.

Spider-Man sighed as he climbed. Venom's stunt with Pierce was a trick that practically every foe Spider-Man had faced pulled at one point or another: force him to abandon the fight by putting an innocent life in danger. It always worked, and it always would. No life would be lost because he failed to act—that's why he became Spider-Man in the first place.

When he arrived at the broken window an eternity later, he saw the four officers struggling to clamber out of Venom's webbing. Of Venom himself, he saw no sign.

One of the officers—a man with a brown goatee—saw Spider-Man at the window. "Sonova— Hey Don, you owe me twenty. Ol' Webs made it."

Another officer looked at the window. "How the hell did you survive?"

Spider-Man climbed into the room and moved to assist the officers in disentangling themselves. "You kidding? I've been falling out of windows since I was a spider-tot. What happened to Venom?"

The one with the goatee, whose nameplate read HONIGS-BERG, said, "He jumped out the window a couple seconds after you did. Except he went up instead of down."

Probably off to try another lead. Wonderful.

"What happened to the weasel?" Don asked.

"If you mean Pierce, I left him with some of your buddies downstairs. They'll probably be coming up—"

The door burst open, and three of the four uniforms Spider-Man had encountered on the sidewalk entered, ready for anything.

"—right about now."

After a second, they saw that everything was under control and holstered their weapons. "What happened?"

I guess he'll keep asking till he gets an answer, Spider-Man thought with a smile. The crisis having past, he reached into his belt and pulled out a pair of spare web-fluid cartridges.

"Webs here saved our cans is what happened, Jeff," Honigsberg said. "Venom busted in here and started beating up the weasel. We tried to stop him, but he nailed us in about half a second. Webs showed up and drove him off."

"All part of the service," Spider-Man said. Having reloaded both web shooters, he turned toward the window. "I'll leave you folks to tidy up here. I've got to get moving."

Jeff turned to Spider-Man. "Hang on a sec, what were you doing here in the first place?"

"Trying to stop Venom." *And doing a lousy job of it.* "Look, I'm on your side, Officer. Check with Lieutenant Golden or Sergeant Hawkins at Midtown South if you don't believe me."

Honigsberg moved forward. "Hey, you okay, Webs?"

"I'm fine, why?" Spider-Man lied.

"I know that tight voice. You broke a rib?"

Spider-Man sighed. He supposed that cops of all people would know the signs. "Just cracked."

" 'Just'?" Honigsberg shook his head. "I got shot once, wearing my vest, and bruised a couple. *That* hurt like hell. You oughtta go with the weasel in that ambo."

"Love to, but the local hospitals won't take my Blue Cross card." He leapt gingerly to the window. "Don't worry about me, I do this all the time."

Leaving Honigsberg and the others to mop up, Spider-Man swung out into the cold morning air. He soon realized that his right arm was now more or less useless, which meant web-swinging one-handed. And with a cracked rib.

Which meant that Honigsberg was right: he needed medical help. *Probably dislocated my right shoulder at the very least.* But, despite his facetious tone, he was quite serious about Spider-Man's inability to check into the local hospital.

So he headed back toward Queens, hoping Mary Jane was home. Resetting his shoulder and taping up his ribs by himself, one-handed, would be a real pain.

THURSDAY, 12:45 P.M.

Zachary Benjamin Silber—Z.B. to his family, "Zeeb" to his friends—struggled to keep from laughing at the little girl who left his store. It was hardly her fault, after all. The sign outside did read SILBER'S FRUIT AND VEGETABLE STAND, so coming in to ask for a head of cabbage probably seemed perfectly reasonable to her.

Zeeb owned the tiny storefront wedged in between a Mexican restaurant and a bar on Fourteenth Street between Second and Third Avenues. He'd owned it for ten years. In all that time, he had yet to actually sell a piece of fruit or a vegetable. The windowsill had a pile that included a bunch of brown bananas, two equally brown heads of lettuce, a dull batch of apples, a bunch of mushy-looking carrots, and a bag full of potatoes that had stalks growing out of them. Zeeb only rotated the produce when they started to smell.

Zeeb ran numbers, supervised an unofficial offtrack betting concern, served as a bookkeeper, provided occasional storage, and performed other small services for New York's underworld. He paid good money to keep the cops off him, and in return he'd only been busted twice in a decade—the charges dropped both times.

"Kid's gotta be new inna neighborhood," he said to his assistant, a punk named Hobson.

"Whatever," Hobson said in reply.

Zeeb sighed. *Kids. No sense a humor.*

Of course, the kid wasn't nearly as funny as the little bald yutz who came in this morning. That guy was nuts. Like Zeeb could handle *that* kind of load.

He looked at his watch. "Hey, you wanna get some lunch?"

"Whatever."

Zeeb sighed. "Go get a coupla sandwiches at the deli."

"What about Steve?"

Zeeb rolled his eyes. "Steve don't eat lunch, remember?" Last year, after an unpleasant hospital stay—the result of some customers expressing their extreme displeasure with Zeeb's handling of their contraband—Zeeb realized that he wasn't getting any younger and couldn't stand up to the punks like he used to. So he hired Steve, a burly guy who came highly recommended. He did his job, too: Zeeb had emerged from the nine months of Steve's employment completely unscathed.

But Steve never ate lunch. He had a scrambled egg sandwich for breakfast each day, and didn't eat again until dinner.

"Gemme a chicken sandwich an' a cuppa coffee," Zeeb said, reaching into the till and pulling out a twenty-dollar bill to give to Hobson.

The kid snickered.

"What's so funny?"

"That's what Captain Kirk eats." Zeeb stared blankly at the kid. "Y'know, *Star Trek*. 'The Trouble with Tribbles,' Kirk eats a chicken sandwich and coffee."

Zeeb hadn't watched television in thirty years. It just figured that the only conversation he could get out of the dumb kid was about TV. As the punk walked out the door, Zeeb called after him, "Just get it for me, plus whatever you want."

"And I'll have a pastrami on rye with just mustard on it."

Zeeb almost jumped ten feet in the air at the voice. Then he reached for the shotgun he kept at the side of the counter— only to find that it wouldn't budge. It had been secured to the ground with some kind of webbing.

Oh, hell, not him.

But it *was* him. He dropped down from the ceiling in front of Zeeb like the duck on *You Bet Your Life*, hanging upside down from another one of those webs of his. The funny thing was, he only hung onto the web with his left hand; his right arm was held by a sling.

"The hell do *you* want, bug?"

Spider-Man made a tut-tut noise. "Now, now, Zeeb, is that any way to talk to an old pal?"

"You ain't no pal a mine, bug." *Where the hell is Steve?* "An' you ain't answered my question."

"I need a little information."

Zeeb laughed. "What, from me? Get outta here!"

Spider-Man sighed. "Look, Zeeb, I'm really not in the mood for this. It's been a *really* bad couple of days. I've spent all morning trying to track some people down, and my only lead seems to have disappeared. But I *have* found out something very interesting. Word on the street is, someone wants to move a huge amount of cash—through you."

"Whaddaya talkin' about?" Zeeb said, stalling so Steve could get his butt out here. "I run a fruit an' veggie stand here. Only cash I move is from people's wallets to the register."

"Riiiiight, Zeeb, that's why you didn't have any cabbage for that little girl."

" 'Ey, cabbage's outta season. It's *winter.* Ev'ybody knows that."

Spider-Man shook his head. "Zeeb, Zeeb, Zeeb. Must we do this the hard way? I always thought our relationship was based on mutual understanding and respect. I respect the fact that you don't *really* sell fruit and vegetables here, and you understand that I might ask you for info about your clientele every once in a while, or else I knock you into next week."

Finally, Steve ran in from the back. A burly man with long black hair tied back in a ponytail and sporting a black goatee, Steve was adjusting the zipper on his pants as he entered. "Hey, Zeeb, I thought I heard somethin'. Holy—!" That last was added when he saw Spider-Man. But Steve's reaction was to just ogle the super hero.

"Don't just stand there, yutz, *get him!*"

Steve looked at Zeeb like he had two heads. " 'Get him'? Zeeb, that's *Spider-Man.* I seen him take on fifteen guys without workin' up a sweat. Only thing I'm gonna 'get' from him is punched."

Spider-Man actually laughed at that. "I never thought I'd see the day—a punk with brains. C'mon, Zeeb, I just want to know about the guy who came in this morning trying to move eight million bucks."

"Shyeah, right, like I could do *that.*" Zeeb sighed. *The hell with it.* "All right, look, someone did come in. Short, older guy with a beard. One a those losers that tries t'comb over his bald spot. What is it we're supposed to call 'em now, Hispanics? Latinos? He was one a them."

"Puerto Rican, actually."

"Whatever," Zeeb said, wincing as he realized he was using Hobson's favorite phrase. "Hey, I'm just a nickel-an'-dime guy, right? This guy wants to launder enough money to bleach Canada. I ain't set up f'that. So I told 'im t'get lost."

"Where'd you tell him to get lost to, Zeeb?"

"Nowhere! Look, I jus' take care'a my own place. If I don't handle it, I don't know from it." That was the truth. He had no idea where the little guy could go to clean his cash, just that he couldn't do it at Silber's Fruit and Vegetable Stand.

Spider-Man flipped around so that he was upright, then jumped down to the front door. "Okay, Zeeb, I believe you. Thanks for the info." He opened the door, shot out one of those webs of his, then leapt into the air and was gone.

Zeeb turned angrily on Steve. "Some freakin' bodyguard! First you don't show up f'two hours, an' then you *stand* there."

"First off, I was in the john. Second—what's my job, Zeeb?"

"T'protect me, yutz!"

Steve smiled. "That's what I was doin'. You gotta understand how these spandex types think. You give them a hard time, they give you a harder time. With the spider-geek, we're talkin' someone who eats guys like Dr. Octopus and the Hobgoblin for breakfast. Hell, he helped the FF trash Dr. freakin' Doom a while back. I mean *Doom*. I mess with him, all we're gonna get is a banged-up store and me in the hospital for three days.

"But you tell him what he wants, and that's it. These types don't brutalize unless you provoke 'em. Look around. No damage, no harm, no nothin'. He's gone. And we didn't lose anythin', and we didn't get busted." Steve smiled.

Zeeb didn't return the smile, though he had to admit that Steve was right. Giving the bug what he wanted had been the best way to go.

Still don't sit right, just tellin' *him like that.*

Hobson came in with a large bag. He took out a cellophane-wrapped sandwich and a bottle of soda and handed it to Zeeb. Inside the cellophane sat a turkey sandwich.

"I asked for a chicken sandwich an' coffee, not this crap," he said. The dumb kid couldn't even get Captain Kirk's meal right.

Hobson shrugged. "Whatever."

North of One Hundred Tenth Street, the city was deserted. Only a few senseless people, wrapped in heavy parkas and knit hats, ambled about on the sidewalks. The countless stoops were all empty. An icy breeze curled between graffitied buildings, past grime-covered cars and bare trees, through vacant lots bound by slitted chainlink fences. The sun, low and bright in the sky, cast little more than a pallid glow over the landscape. Everything in that small swatch of New York City that, earlier in the century after long waves of Puerto Rican and Cuban migration, had come to be known as Spanish Harlem looked gray and dead.

Summers here were loud, colorful affairs: front steps chockfull of young people in bright clothes, chattering and gesticulating; radios set on open window frames, blaring fast *merenges* and melancholic *boleros*; old men slouched around foldup tables, loudly snapping domino pieces on speckled Formica; children running through glittering water sprays.

Every year winter came down like a neutron bomb, obliterating the neighborhood, stripping it with such force that the coming spring rebirth, inevitable as it was, seemed but a cruel fantasy.

Back when he was a journalism student at Columbia, Eddie Brock spent many a summer evening in East Harlem. There was a great *mofongo* restaurant on the corner of One Twenty-first and Lexington, and if you loved the soft pleats of a salsa trumpet, there was Casanova's on Third Avenue, where local orchestras practiced their chops, and where Ruben Blades and Willie Colón had been known to put on surprise performances.

Once he'd even brought Ann with him. She couldn't take the greasy food; it ruined her stomach. The music, though, was something else. After a long night of dancing, Eddie had walked her back to her dorm room and, as they kissed at the doorway, he'd called her his *mambo muchacha*. She'd wet her flushed lips and laughed. Ann had been terribly clumsy on the dance floor, but Eddie didn't care. In his eyes she was always lithe and beautiful.

The human half of the creature cherished such memories, even as they made him shudder with pain. With the symbiote in the form of ordinary street clothes, Venom had been wandering the neighborhood for over an hour. So far the creature had encountered only innocents: mothers on their way back from the grocery store, a few crazed derelicts huddled around a steam grate. Ignorant, every single one of them. Somehow the creature had managed to hold back the teeth, the keen pseudopodia. Venom did not harm innocents. It wasn't their fault that they knew nothing about DeLaSelva. It wasn't their fault that Ann was still missing.

Brock took a deep breath, pausing on the sidewalk. A Chevy Impala, gleaming electric blue in the oblique sunlight, rolled slowly past him. A large Puerto Rican flag had been painted on the truck, over which a single word had been scripted: *¡Sabroso!* For a brief moment, Brock's trench coat darkened, rippling like a curtain. The toothy mask surged up his neck, crawled all the way to his jawline.

The quiet approach had seemed like a good idea at first, but the creature was getting anxious.

According to a small-time bookie in Chelsea, whose knee-caps Venom had casually pulverized, DeLaSelva owned a tiny apartment on East One Twenty-third. The creature had rushed north immediately, exhilarated by the prospect of knowledge to be gained, of vengeance to be served. Of brains to be eaten.

Instead, Venom had found the building abandoned, filled with bloated furniture and rats' nests. Distraught, raging, the creature had torn the place apart, from floorboards to plaster ceiling, then burst through a window. DeLaSelva had lived for many years in the *barrio*; there had to be someone here who knew where to find him. So the creature once again began to hunt.

Venom had started with the *mofongo* restaurant, which

Brock recalled as something of a lowlife hangout. That proved to be another dead end: the Medalla beer sign hung shattered and dark, and the windows were covered in plywood. Casanova's wasn't much help, either—even though the club seemed to be still in business, steel shutters blocked off the narrow walk-up entrance. Venom could have torn down the shutters in a second, but what would have been the use? The club was surely empty inside. The creature needed people—guilty people. Crooks. Hustlers. Murderers. Kidnappers. The symbiote's claws ached for the warmth of corrupt blood.

From Third Avenue, Venom had swung through One Eleventh to Lexington, then headed north toward the housing projects by Marcus Garvey Park. It was then that the creature hit upon a plan. Quietly dropping from a cornice and pulling into a shaded alley, the symbiote had taken on the form of a trenchcoat, button-down shirt, and jeans. As Brock made his way north, he walked with short, awkward steps, turning, meandering, trying desperately to look like a victim, another white boy lost in the wrong neighborhood. He paused every once in a while to read the myriad store signs: *Marketa Perez. Botanica Santa Barbara. Cafesito El Yunque. Comidas Criollas. Iglesia de Dios Resurrecto. Pollos Fritos y al Carbón. Londromat Quisqueya.*

Eventually, he knew, the guilty would find him.

Brock crossed back over to Third at One Twenty-third Street and glanced quickly over his shoulder. Behind him, half a block away, there was a young, intense-looking man. He wore a black parka that, with all its snaps and buckles, jiggled like a firefighter's coat. His hair was cut short, jelled, and combed forward. His sneakers looked like something out of *The Jetsons*. Right away Brock stopped and turned to face the pavement, as if fixing to bolt across the avenue.

"Hey, bro'," the man shouted.

The symbiote felt a quick jolt of anticipation.

"Yes?" Brock said meekly. The man kept strutting toward him; soon he'd come close enough to whisper.

Hidden in the pockets of his trenchcoat, Venom's claws stretched and honed.

"You lost?" the man said. "Looking for something?"

"Just hanging."

The young man rolled his eyes. "Shouldn't, bro'. Not here."

"Is that a fact?" Brock said, barely suppressing a murderous grin.

"This here's a tough neighborhood. Boy like you could get hurt."

Try it, please. I beg you. "Boy like me?" Brock said.

"Look," he said, pointing down the block at a desolate subway entrance, "if I were you I'd be rushing down those steps over there, see? Taking the 6 train. I'd be getting the hell out of Dodge, if you know what I mean."

Brock licked his lips and smiled. "What happens if I don't?"

"You do what you gotta do, bro'," the young man said, at once pulling away and raising his hands. His coat made a sharp tinkling noise.

"I'm looking for a man called Jorge DeLaSelva," the creature blurted. "You know him?"

The man wiped his nose on his sleeve. "Hey, I was just trying to help out, all right?" Shaking his head, he turned and jogged away.

As far as Venom could tell, the man was innocent. The creature had no choice but to let him go.

It was hopeless. Impossible. As a *Daily Globe* crime-beat reporter, Brock had developed not a single contact this far uptown. He had no idea where to go for information. To make matters worse, the streets around him were empty. After the young man disappeared around the corner, there was not a soul in sight, except for three young men playing stickball in a wide vacant lot a few blocks ahead. Where would the creature find guilty bones to splinter, fetid guts to wring between his black fingers?

Frustrated, Brock stood in place and watched the stickballers for some time. At first the scene struck him as quaint. He was reminded of his childhood in San Francisco, of long spring afternoons spent swinging at bottle caps with broom handles.

A warm flush of nostalgia washed over him, followed by a pang of regret. Brock imagined the son he would have had by Ann—if only Spider-Man hadn't . . .

Suddenly it hit him: nobody in their right mind played stickball in twenty-degree weather.

The game had to be a front of some kind.

A front meant criminal activity.

Criminals. The guilty.

The symbiote twitched. Black tendrils shot from Brock's collar and wrapped tightly around his shoulders, changing to a dark blue in the process. Within seconds, the white-boy victim had become once again the gruff, weathered Officer Badger.

"Badger" walked steadily toward the lot. As soon as the trio noticed him, they ran across the street and slipped into a narrow alley. They didn't even try to stay and sweet-talk the cop, they just ran at the first sight of the law.

Officer Badger exploded into a mess of tarlike tendrils. The human face vanished under a grotesque mask—white slits for eyes, jaw distended, seemingly thousands of teeth protruding like quills from carmine gums. Then there was the tongue, which rolled like a lizard's tail from the mouth, dripping a bright, green ichor onto the sidewalk.

Finally, Venom stood revealed.

With impossible strength, the creature vaulted onto a burnt four-story brownstone across the street that smelled like wet charcoal. Jumping from rooftop to rooftop, Venom ran into a wide gap between buildings, climbed over the edge, and hung upside down from a fire escape, quickly scanning the alley. The creature saw one of his three stickballers, the one wearing a Raiders parka and a clashing Mets baseball cap, dash into a doorway next to a large trash bin set on the exposed brick wall. Then a door fortified with steel plates shut behind him.

Venom laughed. From the fire escape the creature jumped gracelessly onto the bin, which made a loud, hollow thump. The metal buckled and cracked on impact.

As soon as the dust settled, Venom sent a spindly tendril to knock on the door. A small window slid open. There was a quick hubbub inside, then a single, clear voice that said: *"¡No hay nadie, chico!"*

Taking that as a cue, Venom wrapped a thick tendril around both fists and slammed the now rock-hard bundle against the bricks.

The wall collapsed. Venom leapt into the room, followed by a shower of debris.

"¡Anda pal cara—!" someone cried. Eight men—the three stickball players among them—stood facing the metal door, arms outstretched, their nine-millimeters, Uzis, and Glocks trained on Venom. Only one of them, a goateed punk barely out of his teens, had the presence of mind to turn on the creature and fire.

The symbiote absorbed the bullets. Venom smirked obscenely.

"We wonder," Venom said, "will your kidneys taste as bitter?"

Before the punk could respond, a pseudopod shot from Venom's chest and snaked into the still-hot gun barrel. The tendril wiggled through the chamber, then hooked tightly around the punk's fingers.

Venom jerked back; the hand jammed into the pistol with a sickening crunch.

The punk stared at the grotesque sculpture for a moment.

"Man," he said, staggering. Then he screamed.

At once, the other men dropped their weapons.

"We thought you were a cop." The voice came from a skinny man in a *chupacabras* T-shirt. Venom took him to be the leader.

"Oh, you shall wish we were," the creature snarled.

"Whatever you want, Mr. Venom. We'll do whatever you want." He gestured dismissively at the punk with the goatee, who was lying on the floor, writhing. "That guy's an idiot. We hate his guts. Don't we, *gente*?"

The others nodded.

Venom straightened up; the symbiote's pupil-less eyes narrowed. "Hold on a second. You know who we are?"

Chupacabras grinned. "We see you on the TV," he said proudly. "You're so dope, Mr. Venom. 'We're gonna eat your brains.' That's so freaking cool!"

The creature froze. These were drug dealers, parasites. By all rights Venom should have been feasting on their spleens. And yet, they had surrendered; they even acted with deference.

"We are looking for a man called Jorge DeLaSelva," the creature said, finally.

The men glanced at each other, shook their heads, and shrugged.

"Sorry, bro'," *chupacabras* said, "never heard of him."

Venom walked—or rather, flowed—toward the leader. With a lightning fast move, the symbiote locked a tendril around the man's scrawny neck.

"Perhaps we should explain ourselves. This DeLaSelva is involved in the disappearance of our beloved. When we think of Ann alone, in danger, we begin to lose control." The tendril tightened a bit.

"*¡Cualquier cosa!*" the man shouted suddenly, looking anxiously at his companions. "Anything you know! Come on!"

Nobody spoke.

Venom squeezed.

"Come on! *¡Por Dios!*"

After a moment, the Raiders fan stepped forward. In all the commotion, he seemed to have lost his Mets cap.

"This *chulita* of yours," he said, "is she like a lawyer?"

"She is," Venom growled.

The Raiders fan looked at his friends. "There was that *mamita*, remember? Came by in the morning looking for some of that sodium Pentothal stuff. Sasa, that was her name. *¡Estaba buenísima!*"

Another one chimed in: "Yeah, that's right. And when we asked what she wanted it for, she said something about a newspaperman and a lady lawyer."

"And a pig. She said something about a pig."

"Yeah, and she was like all James Bond and crap: 'Mission this, mission that.' Said she was *Corta Caña*. Me and Wilfredo, we are like, she ain't *Corta Caña*."

Standing by a box filled with vials, Wilfredo blanched and nodded quickly.

Venom tossed *chupacabras* aside like an empty can—he landed with a hollow thump on the ground. "Where can we find this Sasa?"

"South Bronx," Wilfredo said. "I've got a cousin with the Cane Cutters. They got this abandoned warehouse there. A safehouse."

Brock felt a brilliant spark in his chest.

"Where?" he growled.

Wilfredo recoiled. "I—I don't know. Down by the river, I think. I don't know the Bronx, man—but you could see the prison from there."

Eddie Brock did know the Bronx. He started out as a stringer for the *Globe*'s Bronx Bureau, after all. If it was near a river with a view of Ryker's Island Prison, it had to be Hunt's Point. That area consisted of mostly market warehouses, holding the produce that went to the city's fruit and vegetable stands, but there were other warehouses, too.

Obviously Ann was in one of the abandoned ones.

Without sparing the kids a second glance, the creature leapt through the pulverized wall and started to head northeast.

Soon, Ann. We'll be there soon.

THURSDAY, 2:30 P.M.

From the kitchen, Esperanza Cebollero, *viuda de* DeLaSelva, came to the living room carrying a teapot and pair of porcelain cups. Her hands trembled; a steady drip fell from the spout and marked a shiny trail on the linoleum floor.

With some difficulty, Betty Brant clambered from the loose-springed sofa. She wanted to help. Before she had taken a single step toward the spill, though, Esperanza stopped her with a shake of her jowls.

"In my home," the ancient, tiny woman said, "the guest does not lift a finger, Ms. Brant."

"Don't be silly," Betty said, smiling.

"Sit, sit," the tiny woman insisted.

"I'll get a rag from the kitchen,"

"Sit!"

Chagrined, Betty sank again into the sofa. She had never felt comfortable being served. It just didn't seem right to her. As a child she and Bennett had always taken care of themselves. Every night Mother came home from the *Bugle* after seven-thirty; she simply did not have the time to clean up after her children.

Later on, of course, when the cancer had pocked her body, she had all the time in the world. But then she could barely climb out of her bed.

Betty crossed her arms, sighed, and watched as Esperanza, with consummate care, filled her cup with hot tea. On the coffee table there were also three glass ashtrays—mismatched and meticulously clean, like everything else in the apartment— and a worn-out volume of Garcia-Lorca poetry.

"I apologize because I haven't got the coffee," Esperanza said, sitting down on a plastic-covered chair across from Betty, "but my doctor told me no, I can't have my coffee anymore. It's bad for my *arritmia*. So now is only tea."

"Tea is fine," Betty said and picked up her cup by the handle and gingerly blew on the top.

"Oh," the woman said, touching Betty's wrists with her calloused fingers, "but you should have the Puerto Rican coffee sometime. It's *divino, m'hija*! It was the only coffee they served in the Vatican, you know. *Digo*, a long time ago."

"I didn't know that."

"Oh, sure. It was the best in the world. Best, best. Maybe next time I'll buy a *librita* and hide it away from my doctor, yes? For guests, I mean. Because I can't drink it anymore." She patted her ample chest. "It's bad for my heart."

"I'm sorry," Betty said, lacking a better response.

Esperanza swatted about dismissively. "I'm an old woman, Ms. Brant. A good heart is a waste for me. Anyway, I soon be with my Rigoberto, *que en paz descanse*."

"Is that him?" Betty said, gesturing toward a sepia-toned

picture alone on the nearest wall: a stern, thick-jawed man in an Army dress uniform. He held the hat tight against his chest, as if he were listening to "The Star-Spangled Banner."

"*Mi Rigoberto*," Esperanza said, nodding. "He was a gunnery sergeant in the big war. One of the very first *estadistas*. No like Ferré and Barceló, no like those bootlickers. Back then they were all unionists, *ves*, fighting for the cause of the workers. They thought it was better in the United States. Best thing for workers was for Puerto Rico to be a state."

"Must have been hard on him, then," Betty said. "His son being a violent nationalist and all."

Esperanza laughed a bit. "Hard?" she said. Then, quietly: "It killed him, Ms. Brant. It killed him just like Jorgito put a bullet in his *corazon*."

"I'm sorry," Betty said. Again, the words felt foolish and inadequate.

To her surprise, Esperanza smiled wistfully. "But you," she said, "you were so young when you lost yours. I remember when it was in the *Bugle*, about Mr. Leeds. You look so young in the pictures. So young."

"I . . ." Betty began. She hadn't expected for Ned to come up in their conversation.

"Many months later, I read in the paper a story, about a warehouse in the South Bronx I think, and I see the name on the top—" Esperanza drew a line in the air with her hand "—*Betty Brant*, and it made so happy to see it. From then on, I read everything you write, Ms. Brant."

Betty glanced down at the faded Persian carpet. Esperanza was a fan. No wonder she had sounded so excited when Betty reached her over the phone. Betty had expected DeLaSelva's mother to be reticent, at least, if not hostile—the woman had, after all, posted DeLaSelva's bail after his last arrest. Instead, Esperanza had invited her immediately to come to her apartment in Washington Heights. At the door she had even taken Betty's hands and kissed her on the cheek. Her skin smelled like stale lavender, Betty had noticed.

"On the phone," she said, finally, "you said that you had some information for us about your son."

"*Ai, si, si,*" Esperanza said. She was quiet for a moment, then muttered, "Jorgito. He is in trouble again, isn't he?"

"I'm afraid so," Betty said. She brought the cup to her lips. She grimaced; the tea was strong and still much too hot.

At once Esperanza began to struggle out of the chair. "I forgot the sugar," she said, squinting behind her thick lenses. "You have milk, too?"

Betty reached over the coffee table and patted Esperanza's knee, surprising herself with the familiarity of the gesture.

"I'm fine," she said. "Please, do not trouble yourself."

"No trouble," Esperanza said, grunting. Then, taking short steps, she waddled away toward the kitchen.

As she waited for her host to return, Betty leaned onto her lap and looked around the apartment at the blurry needlepoints on the wall, at the Santa Barbara candles on the fake mantelpiece, at the crucifix dangling above the kitchen doorway. Esperanza kept a collection of *TV Guide*s on a bookcase by the front hallway, flanked, incongruously, by thick tomes of Cervantes and Shakespeare, both of which bore strips of tape with library call numbers. There were other books too, cheap-looking paperbacks and weathered hardcovers. Family photographs sat carefully arranged around the shelves, framed in wood and plexiglas—wizened men, young girls in party dresses, boys in bright island shirts, men in uniform, men out of uniform, and swaddled babies, held aloft by new mothers haggard and glowing. Betty felt warmed by the pictures, smothered almost. She wondered what it was like to come from such a large family. To never be alone.

After a few minutes, Esperanza set a small metal tray on the coffee table. Balanced between the sugar pot and the creamer lay a small spiral notebook.

"What is this?" Betty said.

Esperanza sat on the chair and glared at her, opening her mouth, closing it, pursing her dry lips.

Slowly, Betty picked up the notebook and leafed through the first few pages. Scribbled on every line there was a date and a phone number, followed by a few words in Spanish.

"I don't understand," Betty said.

"My son, I don't know where he is," Esperanza whispered. "He never tells me where he go, what he's doing. It's all too secret for his *mami*, understand? But he calls me. And when he calls I write down the phone number. I have the caller ID machine, so I get it right from the little thing on it, what's it called?"

"The display," Betty said.

Esperanza nodded. "I put the date and the phone number, and it's like I know what Jorgito is doing. I know when he's in *Nueva York* and sometimes—" she paused and wiped a tear from her wrinkled cheek "—sometimes I think he's gonna come visit me, but he never does."

Betty turned a few more sheets on the notebook. Every few pages she spotted a 718 number underlined. Seven-one-eight was an outer-boroughs area code. And, she quickly realized, it was always the same number.

The most recent one had come a week and a half ago.

"What about these words?" Betty said, pointing at one of the highlighted lines.

"That's what I hear over the phone. Like this, *camiones*. That means trucks. When Jorgito calls from that number, I hear trucks on the phone."

Trucks, Betty thought. *An industrial area. Maybe Long Island City? That's where Robbie was taken.*

"Can I ask you something, Mrs. Cebollero?" she said. "Why didn't you turn this over to the police?"

"The police?" Esperanza said, shaking her head. "*¡Ay no, por Dios!* I don't talk to police. You don't know what goes around here, Ms. Brant. A few months ago, Doña Ramirez upstairs call the cops because there was dealing on the next door apartment. Next day the dealers beat her up, tell her to mind her own business. Cops are no good around here."

"Well, I appreciate your trust," Betty said.

Esperanza smiled. "If you talk to my Jorgito," she said, "can you tell him his mother loves him? Please?"

"Of course, Mrs. Cebollero," Betty said, amazed. First Peter hands her a good lead, which included information that the cops had kept from the press. Now Esperanza had just handed her a *great* lead, one that she was quite certain that the cops didn't know about. She thought of her stained overcoat, hanging from a rack in the front hallway. It had been a rough couple of days, but perhaps things were turning around.

No question: she'd been very lucky. But that wasn't all of it. As Joe Robertson never tired of saying, any fool can have luck; it's what you do with the breaks that makes you a reporter.

Betty had made it happen. If Robbie were here right now, he would've been proud of her.

For the first time in the last couple of days, Betty felt a surge of confidence. She would have the number traced at the phone company. She would follow Esperanza's lead, wherever it took her.

CHAPTER 10

THURSDAY, 3:05 P.M.

Every night for the past three weeks, A.J. Pierce dreamt of the Statue of Liberty.

He could see the statue from his hotel window at the Edghill. On a clear day, he could even make out the features. Often, when the boredom set in, he'd just stare at it.

Though a native-born New Yorker, A.J. had never given the city's landmark a thought until he was placed in the Edghill by the NYPD. Now that his freedom had been taken from him, though, the symbolism of Lady Liberty had hit home. Even with his testimony, he'd be living in the Witness Protection Program for the rest of his life—it was just another type of jail.

When the monster in black had thrown him out the window, he'd thought he was going to die. His brain, unable to process that information, had chosen instead to shut down. He had expected to awaken in the burning pit of fire that Reverend Lincoln had spoken of every Sunday when A.J. was a boy. When he had awakened immobilized, he had figured that this was it. He was in hell.

His nose had told a different story—expecting brimstone, he had instead smelled antiseptic and had found himself covered in bandages and tubes.

Realization had come quickly: he was alive and in a hospital. Relieved, he had fallen back asleep and dreamt again of the statue.

But this time it was different. This time the sky behind Lady Liberty was on fire—Reverend Lincoln's fire, the fire of hell. And the monster blocked the view. He hovered menacingly in the air before A.J., that long tongue and those huge teeth and that undulating costume coming toward him, preparing to strike. . . .

Then Bug-Person showed up. And he and the monster became locked in a struggle in front of the Statue of Libery while A.J. watched.

After a moment, A.J. realized that they fought in midair. Which meant he was in midair. Which meant he should be falling.

Like a character out of a Tex Avery cartoon, the realization that one should be falling was enough for gravity to finally assert itself. A.J. plunged toward the river below.

Just before impact, he awoke with a start.

Bug-Person stood upside down before him.

"Hiya there, Piercey. Long time no see. Seems like only yesterday we were having our little chat in your hotel room."

"Am I—am I still d-dreaming?" This couldn't be real. Bug-Person was standing on the ceiling. That wasn't possible.

"Hope not," Bug-Person said, " 'cause if you are, I'll never find out what I need to know. As it is, I've been waiting here for half an hour for you to wake up."

A.J. remembered that Bug-Person came sauntering into his twenty-fifth-story hotel room the day before. Was standing on the ceiling so farfetched for someone who could do *that*? "I— I told you, I d-don't kn-know where Ms. Weying—"

Bug-Person held up a hand—or, rather, given his position, held down a hand. "I know. If you still claim not to know after Venom romped and stomped on you, I figure you're telling the truth. That's not why I'm here."

"B-but—" A.J. cut himself off. *Why am I stuttering?* he asked himself.

Because you almost died, he told himself in reply.

"Listen, I need information, and you're the only money launderer I know just at the moment."

"Huh?" A.J. was now totally confused. What did super heroes care about what he did?

"One of the people who took Ann is trying to launder eight million in stolen cash. Who would he go to?"

"E-eight m-million? I don't—I don't know. I m-mean, I'm j-just an accountant, I didn't—"

"I already talked with Sergeant Jackson," Bug-Person interrupted. "Remember her?"

A.J. remembered her quite well. A very annoying woman who persisted in talking to A.J. like he was five years old. She had been A.J.'s arresting officer, and when he didn't dream of the Statue of Liberty, he had nightmares about the interrogations Jackson put him through.

Bug-Person went on: "She said you didn't work alone. That there were others who did what you did. You handled the smaller accounts. Who handled the biggies?"

"I-it's supposed to—to be in my d-deposition. I c-can't— my lawyer isn't here, I can't—" His head swam. Why was this imbecile bothering him? Couldn't he see that A.J. was dying?

Then an image came to him. Falling out of the Edghill's window. Falling down, the hotel's faceted façade zooming past like a blur. And a red-and-blue-clad arm grabbing him just before he passed out.

"You saved my life," he whispered. "I remember now, you caught me."

Bug-Person said nothing.

"M-Michael L-Lieb," he said in a very small voice. "He works for Cox, Kindya, & McCunney. It's one of Fisk's holdings. He—"

"I know all about Fisk," Bug-Person said.

"H-he works out of his home. West Orange. D-does everything there."

The hero nodded. Only then did A.J. notice that the masked man's right arm was in a sling. "Thanks. You may've helped us find Ann."

A.J. blinked. His information would help find Ms. Weying? That was wonderful! Maybe that would help later on. That, and getting pounded by that monster. True, he was in agony, but perhaps this could all be worked to his advantage.

A nurse walked in. "I'm sorry," she said to Bug-Person calmly, as if she spoke to people standing on ceilings all the time, "but he needs his rest."

"S'okay, I got what I needed. Thanks, Pierce."

The super hero turned and walked out of the room on the ceiling. The nurse checked his IV and his chart, then also took her leave. A.J. soon fell asleep.

He did not dream of the Statue of Liberty.

• • •

When Spider-Man left A.J. Pierce's hospital room, he found the same two uniformed officers who had been on guard duty when he arrived, plus Sergeant Jenn Jackson, Pierce's arresting officer. Jackson was a tall, sturdy woman in her forties, and seemed to have a permanent don't-mess-with-me expression on her face.

Two new arrivals had shown up, as well: Hawkins and Drew.

Spider-Man took up a perch on the wall, once again adhering with the soles of his feet, knees bent, and his back up against the wall.

"Finally gave up, huh?" Jackson asked with a mild sneer. She had only cooperated with Spider-Man's request to talk to Pierce after checking with Hawkins, and even then, she barely tolerated him. Even Golden hadn't been that hostile.

"No need—he gave me a name. Guy named Michael Lieb, works for Cox, Kindya, & McCunney—one of the Kingpin's guys."

Jackson's mouth hung open. "I don't believe this. I've been trying to pry this guy open for almost a month! What did you do to him?"

Spider-Man smiled wide enough so that it would be noticeable even through his mask. "I caught him after Venom threw him out a window."

"Gratitude's a great motivator, ain't it?" Drew said with a smile.

"Yup. And you're looking a lot better than the last time I saw you."

Drew smiled a lopsided smile. "With the help of a lotta aspirin, yeah. Wish I could say the same about you. Whadja do to your arm?"

"It's how I got that gratitude you mentioned. I'll be fine," he said quickly, not wanting to get into a tangent about his health. He'd already gotten MJ's patented *be careful, Tiger* speech when she helped tape his ribs, relocate his shoulder, and put his right arm in the sling.

"I guess we tail this guy," Jackson said.

"Let me do that," Spider-Man said.

Jackson sneered again. "What the hell for?"

Hawkins said more diplomatically, "You don't exactly blend into the background."

"Tailing is something we *professionals* do," Jackson continued. "It doesn't involve slugging people, so you wouldn't know about it."

That did it. Two days' worth of frustration came boiling over. "First of all, *Sergeant*, I'm perfectly capable of tracking someone without their notice. I've done it before. In fact, I've been doing what I do for *years*, and I'd like to think I've done a decent job of it against some pretty rough competition. I just went two rounds with Venom and almost ripped my arm out saving someone in *your* protective custody. That's partly because the *professional* cops who were supposed to be protecting him spent the entire time webbed to the floor by Venom."

Spider-Man paused and took a breath. Jackson had straightened up, apparently surprised at the vehemence of his outburst. Drew tried and failed to hide a smile. Hawkins was completely poker-faced.

Much more calmly, Spider-Man added, "Secondly, Pierce said this guy mostly operates out of his home in West Orange."

Hawkins sighed. "Great. So as soon as he crosses the Hudson, we'd be obligated to call our good friends at the FBI."

"No way," Drew said. "They cut us out of their sandbox— no way in hell we let 'em in ours."

Spider-Man said, "But if the guy tailing them isn't NYPD, but some loose cannon vigilante . . ."

Hawkins smiled. "In that case, we can say it wasn't our fault. Who can control a costume, after all?"

"I dunno, Vance," Jackson said. "Can we trust this goofball? For all we know, he's lyin' about this Lieb guy."

Spider-Man resisted an urge to leap off the wall and pound Jackson into the ground. Not that it was difficult to resist, but that he even thought about it showed that he was near the end of his rope. Obviously his harangue had had no effect on the sour-faced sergeant. Just as obviously, they needed a break in this case, and soon, or he'd go crazy.

Hawkins, to his credit, fixed Jackson with an almost withering look. "Sergeant Jackson, this goofball has given me no reason not to trust him, and several reasons why I should."

Drew grinned. Jackson looked like she'd been slapped. Just then, Spider-Man could have kissed Hawkins.

Shaking her head, Jackson finally said, "Fine, do what you want, it's your case." She turned and walked away.

Watching her retreating form, Spider-Man asked, "She always like that?"

"More or less," Drew said.

Hawkins added, "She's also got one of the best arrest records in her unit. She's very good at what she does."

"As long as what she does isn't public relations, I'll buy it," Spider-Man said. "I gotta admit, though, I think this Lieb guy might be a longshot."

"Not necessarily. Between our friend in there," Drew said, indicating Pierce's room with his head, "and you bringing Doc Ock down, the number of people who can move DeLaSelva's cash is pretty limited. Most of the local financial dry cleaners are either busted or laying low. And the ones laying low aren't gonna touch something as hot as the Wells Fargo job. Fisk is about the only one who would."

"Besides," Hawkins added, "like I told you this morning, right now, everything's a longshot. Listen, you still have your cell phone?" Hawkins asked.

Spider-Man frowned. "Uh, yeah."

"Good." Hawkins reached into his pocket and fished out a card. "If you even catch a whiff of DeLaSelva, and you're in Jersey, call this number."

Spider-Man took the card. It belonged to Special Agent Screwdriver himself.

"You want me to call Phillips?"

Drew gave Hawkins much the same look Spider-Man gave him—except, of course, that Hawkins could see the look on Drew's face. "What're you, nuts, Hawk?"

"No, practical," Hawkins snapped. "Right now, the FBI

needs DeLaSelva as much as we do. If we find him, maybe they'll finally cut us in on the case, and then maybe we can get something *done*. If all of us were cooperating on this in the first place instead of playing stupid kids' games, we might've found the captain and the others by now!''

Spider-Man blinked. Hawkins generally kept his temper and spoke in an even, modulated tone. *I see I'm not the only one boiling over in frustration.*

"All right, I'm sorry," Drew said, taken aback.

Hawkins shook his head. "No, I'm sorry. I shouldn't have yelled like that. But I can't help but think that we would've put this thing down by now if the FBI hadn't copped that we'll-do-this-ourselves attitude."

"Not to mention losing their only lead," Spider-Man said. "If they'd been able to actually hang onto DeLaSelva—"

"Never mind," Hawkins said. "You'd better get to finding this guy."

"Right." He straightened and moved back to the ceiling, intending to leave. "Uh, I don't suppose you know where Cox, Kindya, & McCunney is?"

Without hesitating, Hawkins rattled off an address.

Spider-Man blinked. He had asked the question facetiously. "You're kidding."

"Nope," Hawkins said with a grin.

"You knew that off the top of your head."

"Yup. Trick memory."

Drew shook his head. "You get used to it after a while. You kinda have to, since the department frowns upon officers killing their partners."

"You're just jealous," Hawkins said with a smirk.

Chuckling, Spider-Man started crawling along the tiled ceiling toward the exit. "I'll keep you guys posted."

Vance Hawkins waited until Spider-Man was out of sight, then pulled out his cell phone and another business card.

"Who you callin'?" Drew asked.

"The feds. They're gonna need to respond quickly, and I want them in place when Spider-Man calls."

"In place where?"

Hawkins still had Hauman's card, and dialed that number. "Spider-Man said West Orange."

Drew gave his partner a dubious look. "That's a helluva risk, Hawk. What if he doesn't go there?"

"To be honest?" he said as he waited for Hauman to pick up. "I won't cry too many tears if they wind up standing around in West Orange with their thumbs in their ears."

After the fourth ring, a voice said, "Hauman."

"Agent Hauman, this is Sergeant Vance Hawkins. We met yesterday."

"Yes, Sergeant, what can I do for you?" she said in a businesslike, polite manner that Hawkins admired despite himself.

"I just thought you should know that we have a line on Jorge DeLaSelva."

"What?!" The businesslike politeness had been replaced with anxiousness.

"Jorge DeLaSelva—you know, the person you lost."

"Funny," Hauman said, "the report said that Venom scared him off." Her tone indicated that she knew full well that Mack and Hattori had lost him long before Venom showed up.

"That was a courtesy. So, for that matter, is this phone call. It is my fond hope that this courtesy might be reciprocated at some point."

"Where is he?"

"West Orange, New Jersey. At least, that's where his trail leads. Unfortunately, that's out of our jurisdiction, but we do have someone on it."

"Excuse me?" Hauman was clearly confused.

"My suggestion would be for you to hie yourself to the West Orange Police Department and wait for Spider-Man to call your partner."

"Spi—?" Hauman cut herself off and sighed. "I should've known," she said derisively. "This is a joke, right?"

Hawkins had been speaking in a jaunty tone, getting a certain amount of sadistic pleasure out of yanking the federal agent's chain. Now, however, all jocularity fled his voice when he said, "Agent Hauman, I do not joke when my captain's life is at stake. I also do not joke about red-ball cases. Spider-Man is tracking a lead on DeLaSelva. As soon as he has found DeLaSelva, which should be in West Orange, he will call your partner. Yesterday, Lieutenant Golden told you we'd let you know if we figured anything out. Well, we have, and we've let you know. What you do with that information is entirely up to you."

And with that, he hung up.

Drew regarded his partner with an amused look. "I'm impressed. From snide to self-righteous, all in one conversation."

"Let's just say I'm starting to come around to the lieutenant's attitude toward the FBI. C'mon, let's get back up to the station."

Indicating that Hawkins should go first, Drew said, "Lay on, Macduff."

Hawkins shot his partner a glance.

Drew laughed, his blond hair falling into his face like usual. "Hey, you didn't know about Sixty-third Street or Howie, so I figured the least I could do was get the quote right."

Returning the laugh, Hawkins started walking toward the elevator. "You're all heart, partner."

THURSDAY, 5:30 P.M.

In his seven years as a police captain, Frank Esteban had trained hundreds of officers in the proper ways to deal with hostage incidents. He wasn't an expert—how could anyone be an expert on something so unpredictable?—but he knew enough to keep his crew from making stupid mistakes and getting people killed. He knew how to mark a perimeter and keep the civilians safe behind barricades. He knew how to wait out a perp, how to play with his mind till he surrendered: shut off the electricity, turn up the heat (literally), ring the doorbell over and over. He knew enough not to bring the guy's estranged wife or girlfriend to the scene—he might very well be looking to shoot her. And forget the priest; that only worked in movies.

Frank knew how to be a cop in a hostage incident.

Being a victim, though, that was a new experience.

He could have expected the feeling of weakness and impotence. The humiliation. Fear was also familiar to him: it had been there whenever he'd knocked on a perp's door, whenever he'd chased an armed suspect through a crowded sidewalk. During the last seven years he'd arranged many a raid and sting operation, and he'd been afraid for every single officer involved. Scared of the worst. Talking to their families, their spouses. Breaking the news.

The one thing he hadn't expected, waiting with the reporter and the lawyer in their decrepit warehouse-cum-prison, was the boredom. They hadn't heard from the Cane Cutters since the big-mouth kid had jabbed their arms with hypodermic needles more than eight hours ago. For a while afterward Frank had been caught in a weird state—a mix of drunkenness and dreaming—that turned every question posed by his captors into a decree from the Almighty. Frank half-remembered hearing Weying talk about DeLaSelva's phone call, and Robertson blather about his aborted meeting with the man, and he recalled wondering vaguely about their candor. *Weren't they supposed to keep that a secret?*

Soon, Sombra had covered his face with his hands, even as the skin and bones changed, then quietly left the room. The masked flunkies followed, locking the door behind them.

The boredom came once the drug had worn off—blacker and more soul-draining than any Frank had ever experienced. He'd been in endless stakeouts before, sloughed through pages and pages of dull depositions. He'd even had to listen to some of Lydia's opera recordings. This was different. At least with the stakeouts you could look forward to something: a phone call, a show of evidence, a crime in progress, the end of the shift. Same with court papers. Right now there was nothing ahead of him. Nothing he cared to consider, anyway.

It was the boredom of the condemned. The kind of doldrums that made people take their own lives.

The room smelled like cold ashes.

Frank glanced quickly at his companions. From their sour countenances, it was clear that they felt no better. Neither had spoken so much as a word for hours. Somehow, Frank was relieved.

He crossed his legs and leaned sideways against the familiar ridges of the metal wall. His shoulder throbbed. Staring upward, he exhaled and watched as the steam floated up to the rafters. After a moment it dissipated in the twilight.

Over by his column, Robertson coughed and grunted.

"We're expendable now, aren't we?" Weying asked, her voice breaking. Both her eyes were ringed in yellow and black. Her once-perky nose had settled into a toadstool.

"Afraid so," Robertson said.

"If they were gonna let us go," Frank said, "they would have done it hours ago."

Nobody spoke for a long time. Then Weying straightened up and yelled, "What kind of precinct do you run, anyway? Can't find anyone—even when it's one their own—for crying out loud!"

"I'm sure my people are doing their best to find us," Frank said wearily, "but the thing is, maybe they don't even know we were kidnapped. Maybe they don't even know we're related."

"We're related?" Robertson said, snickering.

"You know what I mean."

"How could they not know we've been kidnapped?" Weying said, scrunching her face as much as she could.

"It's not like they're asking for ransom," Frank said.

Robertson raised his handcuffed hands to his chin. "Maybe they did."

"I doubt it. With ransoms they usually want proof that we're alive. Photos, recordings, something."

"But," Weying protested, "don't you think that if they were going to kill us, they would have done it already? I mean, why waste time?"

Frank smiled. If they ever got out of this jam, Weying would never believe that she'd been so sanguine.

"Maybe you're right," he said condescendingly.

"A few years back," Robertson said, his words measured and quiet, "one of our Beirut correspondents got kidnapped.

There were five or six other reporters. Some jihad faction, I forget which. Anyway, as it happened, they let him go pretty quickly, and afterward, when he came back to the states, Jonah and I had a long conversation with him—kind of an exit interview, actually. The man had had his years with the paper and decided to retire. So we talked for hours, but one thing stuck with me. He took a sip from his drink—we were at a bar on Thirty-fifth and Broadway—then he turned to look at this pretty redhead strolling across the room. After a moment he said to me, 'It was pretty simple. We were all in the same room, all of us. If they took us away one by one, we knew it was over. They were gonna kill us. We had no proof of this, you understand, but we were convinced. Now, if they got us all at the same time, then they were gonna let us go. I don't know how we came up with that rule, but in the end, that's how it happened.' ''

''So you're telling us that we should stick together,'' Frank said.

Robertson shook his head. ''I'm just saying that in the end, it doesn't matter what we believe. Things are gonna happen the way they're gonna happen.''

''God,'' Weying muttered, shutting her eyes. Then she laughed and said, ''Well, at least Captain Esteban has nothing to worry about.''

''Why is that?'' Frank said incredulously.

''You know, the family connection. Your brother?''

He lied. ''I don't know. I'm thinking Sombra made it up.''

''At least you're Puerto Rican. I mean, that's got to count for something with these people.''

''Weren't the soldiers they shot on the island Puerto Rican?'' Robertson said.

''*Boricua*,'' Frank said, ''every single one of them. Look, Ms. Weying, the moment we put on a uniform, we become traitors. That's the way these people think. You're either with them or against them.''

''Should I remind you,'' Robertson said, smiling, ''that you don't wear a uniform?''

Frank smirked. "I'm glad someone still has a sense of humor."

After a moment, Weying pursed her lips, then whispered, "I'm sorry. That wasn't fair. What I said before."

"Hey," Frank said, kindly.

"Who knows," Robertson said, with a mixture of hope and bemusement, "maybe Ann's ex-hus—"

Violently, Weying shook her head, staring at Robertson.

It was too late, though. Frank held his mouth; his eyes teetered in their sockets.

"Venom," he mumbled. He'd already lost a cousin to that monster. He'd already lost—

The door opened with a crack and a loud whine, and two masked guards marched into the room. The short one, Frank knew well—the kid. The other he hadn't seen before. He was tall, slim-shouldered, wiry; his mask fit snugly on his face.

Taking two long steps, the guard walked past Frank, then turned to face him. The kid remained by the door, his arms crossed, a nine-millimeter jammed in the crook of his elbow.

"Come on," the tall guard said, obviously disguising his voice.

Behind him, Weying and Robertson made to stand up.

The kid laughed. "Not you guys," he said, gesturing with his gun. "We're here for the pig."

"No," Weying said, firmly. Then, louder, "No."

"Mira," the kid said, *"pero si se cree jefa."*

Weying scrambled to her feet. "I'm not going to let you do this," she growled.

"Ann, please," Robertson said.

"Part of the job," Frank said, resigned. Painfully, bracing himself against the doorway, he stood up.

"Don't do this," Weying said, as quickly as she could. "We haven't seen you, we don't know where we are, it doesn't have to be this way."

"Hit the floor, lady," the tall guard said.

"No!" Weying yelled. "You're gonna have to shoot me here, because I'm not gonna let you—"

Swiftly, the guard spun around and fired. Weying screamed and fell backward against the wooden column.

Frank was deafened by the report. Then, after a moment, he heard a sharp ringing, and the kid's mulelike laugh.

Robertson stared blankly at him.

All of a sudden, Weying stirred on the floor. She touched her cheekbone, which was marked faintly with soot. There was a hole in the wall behind her, but she was untouched.

"Jeez," she muttered, glaring at her fingers, almost in shock.

"Let's go," the guard said. This time he hadn't bothered with the fake voice. *Carlos. Of course—that wasn't a bad shot, it was Carlitos and his deadeye aim, shooting to scare, not to hurt.*

Frank blanched, holding his injured shoulder. His legs trembled. His throat was dry as lint. Rooted to the spot, he watched as Robertson scurried over to Weying. Then the kid grabbed him by the pant waist and pulled him into the hallway.

They had gone a hundred yards, down a narrow corridor and through an empty doorway, before Frank could utter a word.

"I know it's you," he said.

"Shut up," Carlitos said.

"Listen to me," Frank began.

Carlitos struck him on the shoulder.

Frank grunted and swallowed the pain. "Listen to me. Whatever you do, I want you to get out of here."

He felt the barrel of a gun on his back. "You heard him," the kid said. "Shut your mouth."

Suddenly the hallway came to a set of stairs, which they proceeded to climb down to another winding passage.

"You don't know who you've taken," Frank said, unfazed.

"What, are you like RoboCop or something?" the kid said.

"The woman," Frank said. "You morons took Venom's ex-wife. He's gonna come after her."

Without breaking his stride, Carlitos turned sideways and said, "Better worry about yourself, pig. That's who I'd be worrying about right now."

The kid giggled. "Gonna be good," he whispered.

"He killed Susanita's son, for Pete's sake," Frank said, desperate. "Your cousin Toño. Broke him like an old woman's hip. I don't want to lose another Esteban to that monster. You get out of here."

They stopped at a rusted door, which opened—with a kick—to an empty loading bay. The pavement around it, four feet below, was covered in tiny, yellowed pamphlets. It smelled of vinegar; Frank felt a cold breeze on his cheek.

"End of the line," the kid said. "End. Of. The. Line."

Frank screamed, "Are you listening to me? Venom is gonna kill you! He's gonna eat your freaking brains!"

"Walk," Carlitos said, tapping Frank with the barrel of his gun, "to the end of the bay. Walk."

Frank lurched forward. "I love you," he said wearily.

He walked five steps to the ledge, then turned around to face his brother. In the past three years, the boy had become gaunt. Frank was reminded of an El Greco he'd seen at the Met. Something about his slouch, about the thinness of his wrists. He looked like an honest-to-goodness martyr.

Except for the stupid wire mask.

"Take it off," he said.

"What?" Carlitos said.

"I want to see your face. If you're gonna shoot me, I want to see your face."

"Come on," the kid whined, turning and gesticulating around the threshold. "Get over it, man."

Carlitos didn't say a word. Gingerly he fingered the trigger on his pistol. Then he reached behind his head and, with a jerk, tore off the mask.

CHAPTER 11

THURSDAY, 3:30 P.M.

Spider-Man's first step was to find out what Michael Lieb looked like. That proved a better task for Peter Parker than Spider-Man. He simply walked into the offices of the investment firm of Cox, Kindya, & McCunney (occupying the first six floors of the address Hawkins had provided) with press credentials in his pocket and a camera in his hand. The former got him into the building and sent up to the second-floor reception area.

Once there, he explained that he had been assigned to take pictures of CK&M's reception area for a piece in the *Bugle* business section. No, he didn't know what the article was about—they never tell him these things, they just tell him what pictures to take. Yes, his arm was in a sling—that's why he's taking pictures for the business section instead of his usual news-section photography. One little accident, and they give you light duty.

He took a series of pictures. Then, almost as an afterthought, he remembered that his editor wanted him to pick up a copy of their latest annual report. The receptionist smiled, said that was no problem, and handed him one.

Right there on page nine: a picture of Michael Lieb, Executive Vice President of Financial Affairs. Now he had a face.

The next step was to scope out the building. He quickly learned, to his relief, that the building had no underground parking garage, nor direct access to the subway; just two public entrances and one freight entrance, all at ground level. Anyone who wanted to leave the building had to do so through one of those three exits—unless one could fly, which was certainly a possibility in this day and age, but not terribly likely.

Conveniently, one could see all three exits from the roof of the building across the street, especially if one could use one's zoom lens as a makeshift telescope. For that matter, one could see all the windows that faced the street, so even if the guy *could* fly, he'd be seen.

And so Peter Parker changed back into Spider-Man and sat on that rooftop, waiting.

As he peered through his camera lens, he realized that he had never set up his camera to take shots at the Edghill. *Ellis is going to be disappointed*, he thought, *and so's my bank balance*. Going over the incident in his head, however, revealed that the opportunity to do so had simply never presented itself. As it was, it took five seconds to get into the hotel room. Setting up the camera would have taken another ten at least. Those ten seconds could have meant the difference between Pierce in the hospital and Pierce in the morgue.

Especially the way Venom's been acting. His two fights with Venom the last two days were as brutal as any of their encounters. *He could've finished me off either time*, Spider-Man mused, *but he must've thought finding Ann was more important. Either that, or he didn't want to risk hurting the cops anymore than he had to.* Recalling Venom's reaction to the sonic pistols, he revised the latter opinion. *Still, Ann's obviously his priority.*

Gazing down at his ribs, taped up under his costume, Spider-Man was grateful for small favors.

THURSDAY, 5:45 P.M.

Betty drove slowly past a long row of warehouses, listening to a quiet sonata on WNYC. She had been through Hunt's Point only once before—following Ned's unfinished story—and yet, for some reason, the route seemed quite familiar to her. Even in the afternoon glare she recognized the narrow lanes, the eaves covering loading platforms, the potholes that, back then, had almost ruined her suspension. She could have given a tour. *Over there I interviewed the fire marshall; in that alley, the warehouse manager flashed me a patronizing, obscene smile.* Which was strange, since, all in all, she remembered few details of the actual story.

Turning left at an unmarked intersection, Betty found herself in a private lane jammed with semi trucks and trailers. She squeezed her Volkswagen through the tiny strip of open pavement. The wheels scraped against the gutter. She winced and shook her head. Betty hated driving without directions— Frances, her contact at Bell Atlantic, had given her only a company name and a muddled address. In the maze of warehouses and driveways, she couldn't tell whether she was getting closer to DeLaSelva's pay phone.

Still, there was something about the last turn that had felt *right* to her. As if . . .

The wreck came into view, all of a sudden: sooty, half-collapsed walls, zinc panels, spattered with snow, laid out crosswise on a wide barren lot. Betty stroked her mouth and chin with her fingers. It had been quite some time since the warehouse fire; she was surprised that they had yet to clear the mess.

Once she had read about a bombed-out building in Germany or Austria, to this day kept in ruins as a memorial to World War II. Betty grinned to herself. Maybe that was why they never rebuilt the warehouse. A monument to her budding journalism career.

Hey, why not?

She eased the car onto a banked cement lot, then cut the engine and climbed out. A spotlight from a security camera glittered on the windshield. Outside, she walked a few steps toward the debris, then leaned back and crossed her arms. She heard the low rumbling of a far-away diesel truck. The wind, frigid and smelling of plastic, rushed through the artificial canyons and cut easily through her overcoat. Her ears stung from the cold; her eyes felt like rough pebbles.

"Hell," she muttered. The phone booth had to be somewhere nearby. The irony was simply too rich for it to be otherwise.

Across the lane, she saw, there was a newer building topped by a tacky, illuminated billboard. CONSOLIDATED FASTENERS. At once Betty reached into her coat pocket and produced a spiral notebook. *Not "Fasters,"* she thought, reading her own sloppy handwriting, *"Fasteners."* Somehow she had misunderstood the name Frances had grudgingly murmured.

DeLaSelva's calls to his mother had been made from somewhere within that building. Glancing at the empty streets and darkened windows around her, it suddenly struck her that this "neighborhood" would be perfect for a terrorist hideout.

Betty swallowed. Reaching into her pocket, she fingered the small can of pepper spray she always carried with her. She crouched down and, bouncing on the balls of her feet, moved toward the warehouse. At the sidewalk she circled a fire hydrant and stepped on what looked like an icy patch. Her galoshes sank ankle deep into a cold pool of sludge. Water spilled inside and dampened her wool socks. Her toes numbed at once. She cursed and shook her thin leg like a tree branch.

So much for my catlike stealthiness.

Hobbled for a moment, she walked around the structure until she spotted the lit doorway on the eastern wall. There was a tiny glass window on the door. Betty stood on tiptoes and peered inside. Sitting behind a desk, a burly, white security guard leafed through a glossy magazine.

Betty knocked on the pane. With a start, the guard reached behind the desk (for a gun?), then, apparently noticing Betty's slim face, settled down, turned sideways and pushed a button on the wall.

"Can I do something for ya, sweetheart?" he said, the voice crackling from a speaker above Betty's head.

She found the intercom after a moment; for some reason, the unit had been installed down at door-handle level. Bending over, she spoke haltingly into the mic.

"Do you happen to have a phone I could use? My cellular is on the fritz and there's no street signs, so I got lost, and—"

"You surely did," the guard laughed. When Betty, perplexed, didn't answer, he added, "I mean, you did get lost. This here's no place for a young lady."

Betty held her tongue. As an investigative reporter, she was sick of men telling her where she did or didn't belong. She would have loved to scream something foul into the intercom.

Instead, still acting the part of the helpless girl, she giggled. "Oh, I know, I know. It's just that my soon-to-be-ex-husband owns some property down here, and I wanted to take a look at it before we sorted things out with the lawyers, but then it started getting dark and I'm supposed to meet a client downtown, and the whole day's just turned into a real mess. You understand.''

"Sure," the guard said. He ran his fingers through his greasy hair, then, grinning, pressed a second button on the wall. There came a buzzing sound and the lock slid open.

Slowly Betty pushed through the door and stepped into the hallway. The security guard rose at once, brushing the wrinkles from his khaki pants. Betty started to speak, then stopped. She needed a moment to think. So far she'd been making things up as she went along, trying to bluff her way into the warehouse without arousing suspicions—after all, she couldn't quite rule out Consolidated as the Cane Cutters' hideout. The terrorists had already taken three hostages; Betty doubted that they would mind a fourth.

What next, then? Well, for whatever reason, she still wanted to see the pay phone. She wasn't sure exactly what she would get from it, but one thing she'd learned from Robbie was that, whenever a story seemed too tangled, it was best to handle one strand at a time. She'd set out to find a pay phone. Maybe after she found it, after she held the receiver in hand, something else would suggest itself.

In or around the property—that was what Frances had said. Could DeLaSelva be working for Consolidated Fasteners? His mother's "log" suggested otherwise; the calls from New York were few and far between. No, it seemed more likely that DeLaSelva was squatting an empty loft in the area. But that meant that he could be anywhere around here—too much ground to cover in a single night.

"Don't worry, lady," the guard said, misunderstanding her hesitation, "you're safe in here." Eagerly, he patted the holster at his side. "Nothing's gonna happen to ya."

Betty giggled and crossed her arms on her chest. "Thanks," she said.

"And, well, here's the phone," the guard said, clearing his throat. He pointed at a lit-up unit on the desk, partially hidden by the cover of a *Details* magazine. "Go ahead," he said.

"Are you sure?" Betty asked. "Because, I'm going to be calling long distance, and I think it's going to be a while— you can't even imagine how my clients blather. Perhaps you need to keep this line open in case of emergencies . . . I mean, I wouldn't want you to risk your job. Not on my account."

The guard paused for a moment, scratching his chin to show deep concentration. "Maybe you're right, lady," he said, clearly disappointed. Then, suddenly, he brightened. "Wait a minute. Wait a minute. There's a pay phone out back, next to the loading dock—"

Yahtzee!

"—but you really shouldn't go by yourself." The guard straightened his back and squared his shoulders, which only made his paunch more prominent. "This ain't a safe neighborhood after hours."

"Well," Betty said slyly, "would you care to be my chaperone?"

The pair of them went out to the loading dock. It was nearly six o'clock already; the sky was a dark shade of purple, and the smell of plastic in the air had been replaced by a moist, oily stench, coming straight from the East River. The guard led her to a pay phone stall that looked more or less like every other pay phone stall in the city.

Betty picked up the phone and pressed the cold receiver to her ear. She dialed her home number and listened to her own voice garbled by the cheap answering machine. She started talking a nonsense conversation that barely made sense to her, so it likely would confuse the security guard.

"All right, I'll hold," she finally said, then turned and smirked at the guard, who waited patiently by a motorized dolly.

"Writers," she said, shaking her head.

The guard smiled. He seemed to be enjoying himself tremendously, playing the resourceful hero.

Betty, on the other hand, was stuck. Her "instincts" had carried her to this point, and no further. DeLaSelva was close; that much she knew. But, as J. Jonah Jameson was fond of saying, in the newspaper business, close meant someone else brought home the Pulitzer.

"Look," she said, keeping up the charade, "I'm on a pay phone, all right? I can't hold—fine, I'll wait."

Even in the faded light, Betty could see clearly through the burnt warehouse. There was a second structure across the emptied field, boarded up, with cement walls charred and water stained. That made sense; a few of the surrounding buildings had been damaged in the blaze. She recalled a Board of Education warehouse; the fire marshall's investigation had unwittingly revealed evidence of dangerous workmanship in schoolhouse equipment. Turned into a serious scandal. By that point, Ben Urich had taken over the story, of course. A seasoned reporter.

Betty shut her eyes. Twice now, she had come to this godawful place because of Robbie. The first time it had been for her benefit—an act of charity, perhaps. An editor-in-chief feeling sorry for the wife of a dead colleague. Now, when she had her chance to return the favor, to help save the life of Joe Robertson, she'd gone ahead and blown it.

Maybe I should give Ben a call, she thought angrily. *He'd know what to do.*

"That was some fire," the guard said.

"Excuse me?" Betty said.

The guard put a hairy hand over his mouth. "Sorry, didn't mean to—"

"That's okay," she lied, "I'm still on hold."

"I just saw you lookin' at the mess," the guard explained.

"I remember reading about that."

He nodded, shoving his hands into his pant pockets. "I was here all night, helpin' the firefighters. Man, it was incredible. You could see the glow clear across the river. For a while, I thought we were goin' next."

"You were lucky," she said.

"I know, believe me."

"Still, you'd think that after all this time they'd have built something in that space."

"You'd think," the guard agreed. He scanned the field, then added, "They were doin' somethin', a while back."

"Who was?" Betty asked, her curiosity all of a sudden piqued.

"Some Puerto Ricans," he said with disdain. "Haulin' metal sheets from the wreck, draggin' 'em down to the old Board of Ed building. They'd come around once in a while, use the phone. We let 'em till a crateload of rivets went missin'."

"Is that the building?" Betty interrupted, pointing at the charred structure across the lot.

"Well, yeah," the guard said. He seemed startled by Betty's brusqueness. Even her voice had changed. "They're still workin' inside, 'cause sometimes you hear sounds. In fact, 'bout twenty minutes ago there was somethin' like a gunshot. But hey, I mind my own business, know what I mean?"

"Listen to me," Betty said, hanging up the phone, then reaching into her pocket and producing her little spiral notebook. "Listen carefully, all right? If I'm not back in ten minutes, you need to call this number for me, okay?" She scribbled Ben Urich's number on a sheet of paper, which she then tore noisily from the pad.

"Wha—?" he stammered.

Betty stepped closer to him. "I'm a reporter," she said. "Betty Brant from the *Daily Bugle*." She grabbed his cold hand and shook it. "I'm a reporter," she repeated, and stuffed the sheet into the guard's shirt pocket. She then crouched and clambered down from the loading dock and onto the short cement driveway. Her coat dipped into a small patch of oil.

Oh, well, she thought.

"Hey, lady!" the guard yelled, just as Betty started across the lot. In response, she turned around and cupped a hand behind her ear.

The guard stared at the sheet of paper.

"What you want me to say to this Urich guy?" he said, mispronouncing Ben's last name as he read it off the sheet.

Betty didn't speak for a moment. She held the can of pepper spray in her fist, played lightly with the trigger. Finally, she said, "Tell him that I think I've found Robbie."

"Just that?"

"He'll know what I mean," she said.

Frightened, exhilarated, Betty turned and advanced gingerly toward the warehouse, treading behind a pile of debris, then, once she'd made certain the area was clear, rushing at a truck parked sideways on the sidewalk. Her legs throbbed, her scalp tingled as if it were charged with static. In times like these she loved her job viscerally, with a rippling intensity that, when she thought about it after the fact, would often bother her. She had to take risks; there was no way to avoid them in this business. But she liked to think that she took them for a reason, for the story, not just because they made her heart flutter.

It wasn't only the risk, though. Secrets. Hidden in that warehouse there were likely facts that the entire *Bugle* staff—not to mention the New York Police Department—were desperate to uncover.

If her hunch was right, Betty would be the first one to know. The first one to tell. Even though she would never admit it out loud, the thought thrilled her to no end.

Shivering, she held onto the truck's oversized tire and peered down the empty lane. From twenty yards away the building seemed quiet, but she could see slivers of lights, faint and white, on several of the boarded-up windows. Were those voices she heard? She sat down on the pavement, propping herself against the wall of cold rubber. There was little to be learned from this distance. She simply had to get closer.

Funny, she thought, *that's exactly what I said to Jonah about Latveria.* On that particular assignment she had ended up a prisoner of the Dreadknight; if it hadn't been for Spider-Man and Silver Sable she would have been executed. Publicly, to boot.

Betty grimaced. She had no reason to expect anything better from the Cane Cutters.

She took a deep breath and held it till she felt her lungs jerk. All she had to do was make a run for it and find her way into the warehouse. She had to be brave. Planting her hands on the freezing pavement, she squatted and peeked again under the semi. The lane was clear.

"Here goes," she whispered. She remained still for a moment, listened to her heart pounding in her chest.

A car alarm wailed in the distance.

Then she bolted.

Suddenly he was there before her, slumped and staggering like a tired mummy. Shirt blood-stained. Left arm dangling uselessly from its socket.

Betty shrieked. At once she stopped and brandished her pepper spray.

"No," the man muttered.

Terrified, but still sharp enough to think, Betty glared at him.

"I—" he said, reaching into his front pocket and producing a small leather wallet, which came open with a hushed slap. Inside was a shiny medallion. "I'm a police officer, ma'am."

"Captain Esteban," Betty whispered, stunned. She covered her mouth with her hands. "Oh my God. I'm Betty Brant, from the *Bugle*. Oh my . . ."

Esteban faltered, reaching forward as if to catch a ledge. Instinctively, Betty grasped him by the shoulder. Esteban clenched his jaw and groaned.

"Not that one," he said, offering his right arm. "Clavicle's broken."

"I'm sorry," Betty said, suddenly fearful. "But what happened to the others? Is Robbie—?"

"Still inside," Esteban grunted, glancing back at the warehouse. "I need a phone."

"Yes, sure, I know where there's one nearby. I can help you." She took his good arm and hooked it over her shoulder. "There's bandages in my car." Pressed next to her, Esteban smelled harshly of sweat and rust.

"Please hurry," Esteban said.

Together they circled the truck and walked—or rather, waddled—across the empty lot. The cold breeze brought Betty out of her daze, and once they'd reached Consolidated Fastener's driveway, she halted and signaled at the security guard on the loading dock. Seemingly thrilled by the turn of events, the guard nodded and tapped the phone with his palm.

Betty looked again at the injured police captain, hesitating, wondering if she really had the guts to be a reporter.

"Listen," she said, finally, "I'm helping you right now, but I'm expecting to get an exclusive on this. I want the whole story. You hear me?"

"The phone," Esteban muttered.

"I need to know," Betty said. "On the whole kidnapping. I want the exclusive."

Esteban leaned sideways and stared at her, eyes half closed, mouth curled into a puzzling smile. Then he shook his head and laughed.

"God, you sure are a tough one," he said.

"Well," Betty began, "it's my jo—"

"Jeez!" the security guard yelped. He teetered backward and crashed against the motorized dolly.

"What is it?" Betty asked.

The guard pointed over their heads. "Check . . . it . . . out!" he said.

Betty spun around. At first she didn't see anything out of the ordinary. Just as she was about to complain, though, she caught sight of a figure, about a quarter of a mile away, hurtling from one rooftop to another. Even from such a distance, and in the fading twilight no less, Betty recognized the monster immediately. Fangs glistened. Black tendrils danced about him. She watched in rapt fascination as Venom tore into the plaster at his feet—woodchips and dust rising above the roofline like a small mushroom cloud—and plunged into the structure. He surfaced but a moment later, crashing through a mess of insulation and electrical wiring, only to leap fearlessly over the lane and land on another warehouse.

"Who'd have thought it?" Betty said, trying to hide her fear. "Eddie Brock being systematic."

"Th-that's that Venom guy," the guard said, stammering.

"In the flesh—or whatever."

"Let me tell ya somethin'," the guard laughed, "whatever he's lookin' for, I'm sure glad I ain't it."

Just then Esteban pulled away from Betty and rushed toward the loading dock. At the foot of the stairs he paused and caught his breath, then, dragging himself up by the handrail, careened past the security guard and nearly collapsed at the pay phone.

Concerned, Betty followed him to the platform.

"Not this time," he muttered, clutching the receiver. "*No, señor*. Claimed the last Esteban, you bastard."

As night fell, Spider-Man began to worry that Lieb would be putting in a late night. The temperature had dropped significantly since the sun went down and Spider-Man found that his teeth were chattering under his mask.

Just as he started to debate with himself as to whether it was worth leaving his perch to get some hot chocolate, a person with a face matching the one on page nine of CK&M's annual report stepped out of the side entrance. Michael Lieb wrapped a scarf tightly around his neck as he made a beeline for the limousine that had been sitting under the NO STANDING ANYTIME sign for the past ten minutes. Spider-Man smiled. *It's good to be the executive vice president.*

Putting down his camera, Spider-Man stretched out his left arm and aimed the spider-tracer shooter on top of his wrist. With a blast of compressed air, the tracer went flying, adhering to the bumper of the limousine.

He packed up his camera, which gave the limo a decent head start, but Spider-Man could pick it up with no trouble. He had no other outstanding tracers since Venom crushed the one on Pierce's shoulder. Besides, it was better if he kept his distance.

Before long, Lieb's limo joined the veritable army of cars queuing up for the Holland Tunnel. This left Spider-Man with a decision to make. Unless he went into the tunnel itself—which would result in the very problem of conspicuousness that Hawkins had raised—he had no way of crossing the Hudson River to New Jersey this far south. The Holland Tunnel was located at the southwest part of the island of Manhattan. The only above-water crossing to New Jersey was the George Washington Bridge, some eight miles north. The Lincoln Tunnel was much closer, but he still had the problem of being conspicuous.

The other problem was his right arm. The traffic on Canal

Street leading to the tunnel was sufficiently dense that Spider-Man figured it to be at least twenty minutes before the limo came through to the other side. Under normal circumstances, he could make it up to Thirty-eighth Street and the Lincoln Tunnel, go through the tunnel, then head down the Jersey coast to the Holland Tunnel's exit in twenty minutes. With only one working arm, it would take much longer, and he might lose Lieb.

He had perched on the roof of a very tall building on the corner of Canal and Varick Streets, and was about to convince himself to try the Lincoln Tunnel and hope for the best, when something caught his eye on the river about three-quarters of a mile south. The lights from the city were mostly absorbed by the dark water once night fell, but he did catch a reflection off a small white ferry chugging out from Manhattan, heading toward Jersey.

''Of course!'' he said aloud, mentally kicking himself. A couple of years back, the Port Authority instituted a ferry to go between the World Financial Center and Exchange Place in Jersey City. Conveniently, one was just heading over now. *First thing that's gone right in two days*, he thought ruefully.

He swung down West Broadway toward the World Trade Center's twin towers as fast as he could. Then, when his distance to the towers was roughly equivalent to what he figured the ferry's distance from them to be, he shot out a web-line at the tower's upper wall and leapt westward as hard as he could. With the tower as the fulcrum, he swung around in an arc that would take him directly over the ferry. He let go of the web-line about thirty feet before he came over the ferry, letting his momentum carry him the rest of the distance horizontally and allowing gravity to bring him down to the ferry's upper deck.

Said upper deck was almost deserted, most passengers preferring the warmer confines of the enclosed lower deck. The exceptions were a couple with their arms around each other staring southward, and an official-looking woman making a beeline for Spider-Man, who remembered that the ferry had a toll.

"Spider-Man!" the woman said. "What're you doin' here?"

"Uh, hitching a ride?" he said tentatively. "I, ah, need to get to Jersey. What's the fare?"

She waved him off. "Don't worry 'bout it. With all you done for the city, least we can do is give you a free ride."

Spider-Man blinked in surprise—and gratitude, especially after Sergeant Jackson's attitude. "From your mouth to J. Jonah Jameson's ears, ma'am."

"Please, I ain't no 'ma'am.' It's Michelle. What happened to your arm?"

"Old tennis injury. Always acts up when the weather gets cold."

Michelle rolled her eyes. "Fine, don't tell me. Look, I gotta check on the folks downstairs. Do me a favor, stay up here, okay?"

"No problem," he said. The last thing he needed right now were either a pack of adulating fans or of people out for his blood. He'd probably get both if he went to the lower level.

Instead he took a moment to enjoy the view of the brightly lit Manhattan skyline to the east. At one point, one member of the couple walked over and asked, "Uh, excuse me, but— aren't you *cold*? I can lend you my scarf if you want."

Spider-Man chuckled. He'd kept moving enough since Lieb got into his limo—and would be doing so again shortly—to keep toasty. "I'm fine, really. But thanks."

After a few more minutes, the ferry was close enough to Exchange Place for Spider-Man to disembark on his own. With a jaunty wave to Michelle, he swung off of the boat, over the plaza next to the Exchange Place PATH train station, and out into Jersey City, heading north toward the New Jersey mouth of the Holland Tunnel.

His spider-sense buzzed just as he approached the entrance to both the New Jersey Turnpike and Routes 1 and 9. He then sighted the limo, which still sat in traffic approaching the stoplight at that entrance.

Perched on the roof of an apartment building, Spider-Man dialed Hawkins's cell phone number.

"Hawkins."

"It's your friendly neighborhood Spider-Man. Our boy just crossed into Jersey. He's pulling out of the Holland Tunnel now."

"All right, the *minute* you see DeLaSelva, call the feds. But, uh, keep me posted, too, okay?"

"No problem."

He closed the phone, switched it off, and put it back on his belt just as Lieb's limo headed onto the entrance ramp for Routes 1 and 9.

From here on, the challenge was to find the right vehicle to adhere to without letting Lieb or his driver know that the limo was being tailed. Unlike his usual city swinging, he had a very low concentration of buildings to work with. So instead he relied on the backs of trucks, minivans, and buses, all the while making sure he stayed behind the limo.

Lieb travelled onto a local route, then onto Interstate 280. Spider-Man leapt off the back of the minivan that went off in a different direction and found a Jumbo's Jelly truck that was also pulling onto 280. *If I remember my Jersey geography, this'll take us to West Orange.*

The limo got off at Pleasant Valley Way. The Jumbo's truck continued down 280, so Spider-Man leapt off it and over the huge stone wall that ran alongside the highway—*probably to block the highway noise from the residences,* he assumed—and once again got to play Tarzan. Suburban New Jersey was low on buildings, but high on foliage, so he was able to follow Lieb by swinging and leaping through the trees. *Pity it's winter, otherwise I could get closer to him and count on the leaves for cover.* Instead, the bare trees forced Spider-Man to continue keeping his distance, lest Lieb notice his red-and-blue costume in the glare of the streetlights. He'd need to be discreet even more now—this was hardly Spider-Man's usual territory, after all.

That fact hammered home when he alighted on one tree and took a deep breath of cold air that seared his lungs. What he noticed as he shot out a web-line to another tree was the comparative absence of smells. In Manhattan, dozens of odors competed for the nose's attention, from the exhaust fumes of too many vehicles plodding down Fifth Avenue to the stink of wet garbage in an alley after a rainy day to the cornucopia of different foods emanating from half a dozen kitchens in the same apartment building in Chelsea. Over the years, Spider-Man had learned to tune out the smells, distracting as they were; out here in the suburbs, though, he didn't need to. The only smell was that of grass and evergreen trees.

The limo came to a stop on Pleasant Valley Way alongside a park, and then Lieb got out and went into the park, headed toward a large lake. Spider-Man situated himself in a concentration of trees a good distance from Lieb, hoping the branches and the darkness would be enough to hide him. *That, and how often do people look in the trees twenty feet behind them and ten feet up?*

Spider-Man unpacked his camera and peered through its lens. Lieb looked at his watch several times and started pacing back and forth at the lake's perimeter. On the other side, Spider-Man saw a boathouse, now closed for the winter, but still lit up, and thus providing the only illumination aside from the distant streetlights on Pleasant Valley Way. He made a mental note to take MJ here when the weather got warmer. *A boat ride here would probably be romantic as all get-out.*

Finally, a car approached. Through the lens, Spider-Man could see Lieb mouthing the words, *What the hell is he doing?* This park was not set up for cars the way, say, Central Park was.

Then Lieb shouted, "Watch out for that tree!" loud enough for Spider-Man to hear.

The car—a dark blue compact—came within a few inches of hitting one of the trees, but it skidded to a stop in time.

And, to Spider-Man's great satisfaction, a man stepped out from the driver's side. A short, Latino man with salt-and-pepper hair—several strands combed over the round bald spot on top of his head—and a matching beard. A man who perfectly fit both Zeeb Silber's descriptions and the photo in the file Special Agents Hauman and Phillips had left behind at Midtown South.

Jorge DeLaSelva.

It's about time.

He hesitated before leaping into action. Hawkins *did* ask him to call the feds. Besides, he intended to get the location of the Cane Cutters's HQ out of DeLaSelva, and the instant he did, he was going there. Which meant he needed to leave DeLaSelva and Lieb with someone.

So he called the number on the card Hawkins had given him, then cradled the phone between his ear and right shoulder while he set up his camera to take pictures of whatever might happen next.

"Phillips," came a familiar voice before the first ring could end.

"It's the masked vigilante you blathered in front of."

"Well, it's about time, where are you?"

Spider-Man blinked. "Uh, the park that runs along Pleasant Valley Way in West Orange."

"Hang on." A pause. "That's Verona Park. We'll be there in two." And then he hung up.

Spider-Man looked at the phone for several seconds, wondering what was going on.

Then he put it together. *Hawkins must've called the feds right after I left the hospital. That a helluva chance you took there, Sergeant.*

After checking to make sure his camera was secure and starting the timer, Spider-Man leapt down at Lieb and De-LaSelva.

He landed two feet away from the pair of them. When he did, Lieb jumped like someone had attached electrodes to his feet. DeLaSelva, though, just rolled his eyes and put his hands up.

"I give. I'm too old for this crap."

Spider-Man blinked in surprise. *That's twice today that someone just gave up without trying to mix it up with me. Maybe thugs* are *getting smarter.* He thought about it a moment, then: *Naaaaah.*

Lieb found his voice: "Y-y-y-you're Spider-Man, aren't you?"

"Give the man a cigar."

"I—I just want you to know that I've never seen this man before in my life."

DeLaSelva shook his head. *"Ay madre,"* he muttered.

"It's the truth!" Lieb said indignantly. "I was just standing here—"

"By a lake in midwinter in a near-abandoned park at night," Spider-Man said, smiling.

"—minding my own business," Lieb continued, overlaying Spider-Man's comment, "when this lunatic came out of nowhere and tried to run me down! I swear to you, I just was standing here, and he came barrelling down—"

Spider-Man had heard enough. He raised his left arm to eye-level and shot out a glob of webbing at Lieb's face. "Ah, shaddap," he said in a passable imitation of Sylvester the Cat as he webbed the executive's mouth shut.

Then he turned to DeLaSelva, who still had his hands raised. "You can keep the hands down, Jorge," he said.

DeLaSelva shrugged. "Force of habit. Actually, in a sense, I'm kind of glad this is over. At least it was you who found me and not that *tosta'o* Sombra. At least you'll leave me alive."

Spider-Man shook his head in confusion. "Waitasec, you *work* for Sombra. You were gonna launder his loot through bozo, here."

"Mmmmm! Mmmmm!" Lieb cried, shaking his head anxiously.

DeLaSelva laughed. "Why do you think Sombra took Robbie and Miss Weying? I took the money and ran."

"I'm still missing something, here."

"You know what Sombra was gonna do with the money? Buy some kinda ray-gun somebody stole from S.H.I.E.L.D. Gonna blow up the Pentagon, or something. I been with the movement all my life, but this—this was too much. Used to be it felt like what I did meant something, that we might be doing some good. Now—now, it's just kids who can't count higher than ten if they got shoes on, and old *reliquia* like me."

"So you kept the money for yourself?"

DeLaSelva shook his head. "No, *estupido*, I was gonna turn it in. But Sombra screwed that one up. See, I didn't want to just give the money over to the feds, and let them pull their brush-under-the-rug *mierda*. I wanted protection, and I wanted everyone to know that it was Jorge DeLaSelva who turned it in, and I wanted them to know why."

Spider-Man finally put it together. "So you called the lawyer who got you off those gun charges and an old acquaintance who happens to be the editor-in-chief of an influential newspaper and could plaster your story all over the front page."

"Exactly. But they didn't show up for their meets. Then *someone* found my hideout," he added with a glare at Spider-Man, who ignored it. DeLaSelva went on: "I tried to get Howie to set me up with a new place, but he wouldn't even talk to me. Then I find out that you and Venom *and* the cops are all after me. Not the best day of my life, you know?"

"So you decided the hell with it, you'd keep the money."

"I see in the *Bugle* that Miss Weying and Robbie are both missing. I'm down to *nada*—so yeah, I decided the hell with it, I'd keep the money."

Spider-Man sighed. Now it all made sense: why Robbie and Ann were taken, and why no one had taken credit nor made any demands. The Cane Cutters needed information out of them, not a ransom. *Doesn't explain Esteban, though.* Aloud, he said, "So you tried to launder the cash through Zeeb Silber, who laughed in your face, then you went to Chuckles over here."

"You're not as dumb as you look."

Spider-Man shrugged. "Well, I couldn't be, really. One question: what's your connection to Captain Esteban?"

"Who?"

"Frank Esteban, NYPD—Midtown South Precinct? This rings no bells?"

DeLaSelva frowned, then a look of realization spread over his face. *"Ay Cristo,"* he muttered, *"es más estupido que lo que creía."* Louder, he said, "Esteban's *hermano*, Carlos, is part of the movement. So was his father. I guess Sombra figured he'd help the cause.''

Sirens could now be heard in the background, getting closer. *Probably Agent Screwdriver, et al*, Spider-Man thought. *Time for the $64,000 Question.*

''Where are the Cane Cutters holed up, Jorge?''

DeLaSelva seemed to be ignoring him. ''I can't believe that *morón* kidnapped a pig. Why not just a paint a freakin' target on his face?''

The sirens grew closer. ''Jorge? Where are they?''

Then four police cars labelled WOPD pulled into the park, surrounding the trio. Lieb started gesticulating and crying, ''Mmmmm!'' some more.

Eight members of West Orange's Finest, plus Hauman and Phillips, came out of the cars, some with guns drawn. However, they soon realized that the situation was under control, especially since DeLaSelva had put his hands back up.

Hauman made a beeline for DeLaSelva. ''Long time, no see, Jorge.''

''Not long enough, *chula*.''

''You, my friend, are under arrest.''

''I'm not your friend, Agent Hauman.''

''You have the right to remain silent,'' Hauman continued, undaunted.

As she went on with the Miranda litany, Phillips walked up to Spider-Man. ''What happened to your arm?''

''Nothing. Us masked vigilantes sometimes handicap ourselves so lesser mortals like yourself feel better.''

Phillips just fixed Spider-Man with a look, then asked, ''Who's the stiff?''

Spider-Man resisted the urge to burst out laughing. *Stiff* suited Special Agent Screwdriver far better as an adjective. ''This is Michael Lieb—Executive Vice President of Financial Affairs for the investment firm of Cox, Kindya, & McCunney by day, the Kingpin's pet money launderer by night.''

''I don't suppose you caught him in the act of doing anything.''

'' 'Fraid not. Not that it matters—he could've been paying

off the mayor in the middle of Yankee Stadium, and Fisk's lawyers would still have the charges dropped and him back on the street in a day.''

Phillips actually chuckled at that, an expression Spider-Man would not have credited the agent capable of based on the previous day's experience. "We'll haul him in, anyhow. Consorting with a fugitive or something." He indicated Lieb with his head while looking at one of the officers, who proceeded to cuff Lieb and read him his rights, Lieb crying "Mmmmmmm!" the whole time.

Hauman came over with a now-cuffed DeLaSelva.

Spider-Man said, "Two things you guys should know. Jorge here isn't running with the Cane Cutters anymore—he bolted with the Wells Fargo money. Plan A was to turn the money in, after he got in touch with his lawyer and the *Daily Bugle*. Unfortunately, the Cane Cutters got in touch with them first. So he went to Plan B.''

Nodding, Hauman said, "Dry clean the money through laughing boy?''

"Yup. Now then, Jorge," Spider-Man said, looking down at the diminutive terrorist, "we have one little bit of unfinished business. Where are the Cane Cutters hiding out?''

DeLaSelva smiled. "Agent Hauman here just told me I have the right to remain silent. I'm exercising my right.''

"What, *now* you're gonna clam up?''

"That's right.''

"Oh, c'mon, we've been having such a pleasant little chat.''

"Yeah, we *were*. And you wanna talk some more, be my guest. Just lose the *federales*.''

Hauman shook her head. "We're not going anywhere, Jorge.''

"Then I'm saying *nada*," he snapped, turning his head as far around as he could while cuffed in an attempt to look at Hauman. "Sombra may be *tosta'o*, but the Cane Cutters are still my *camaradas*, and I'll die before I turn them in to *you*.''

Spider-Man was briefly taken aback by his vehemence. Before the feds showed up, DeLaSelva was fairly quiet and even tempered—and, in an odd sense, *tired*. Now, though, it seemed to be all he could do to keep from spitting at Hauman and Phillips. *Should've asked him about the hideout first thing*, he admonished himself.

Aloud, he said, "Frank Esteban's one of your *camaradas*, too."

"Don't worry," Phillips said. "We'll get it out of him."

"In your dreams," DeLaSelva said, and this time he did spit.

Hauman's cell phone rang. Handing DeLaSelva over to her partner, she answered it, "Hauman."

Her eyes widened, then she said, "Got it." She hung up and turned to one of the local cops. "Officer, I'm afraid you're going to have to hold these two until we can come back for them. Glenn, we're gonna need a chopper to take us to the Bronx right away."

"We got 'em?" An almost desperate tone had creeped into Phillips's voice, like someone being told they're getting the Christmas present they always wanted, but not quite willing to believe it.

Hauman actually smiled. "We got 'em."

"Consider the chopper here," Phillips said, pulling out his cell phone.

"Uh, excuse me?" Spider-Man said.

"That was your friend, Sergeant Drew," Hauman said, pocketing her cell phone. "They just got a call from Captain Esteban."

Spider-Man felt the ground tilt under him. *"What?"*

"He escaped from the Cane Cutters and called the cavalry in. They're in a warehouse in the South Bronx."

DeLaSelva let loose with a string of rapid-fire Spanish, which Spider-Man assumed to be invective of the nastiest kind. Ignoring it, he asked anxiously, "Where?"

"Hunt's Point."

Spider-Man shot a web-line to the tree that had his camera. "I'm there."

As he leapt up to the tree and retrieved the camera. Hauman called after him, "Venom's been sighted in the area, too. We'll meet you there!"

Spider-Man barely heard her. He headed northeast as far as he could go, then pushed himself to go faster. He used anything he could—trees, buildings, trucks, billboards, trains, buses, aerial towers—mostly using his powerful legs to leap from place to place, ignoring the cold wind that sliced through his costume, disregarding the throbbing in his right shoulder, setting aside the fatigue that had set in after two days of fruit-less searching mixed in with brutal fights against one of his deadliest foes.

He had no idea how long it took him to reach Fort Lee, New Jersey and its buildings, but once he did, he fell into his more usual web-swinging pattern toward the George Washington Bridge, and thence to the South Bronx.

Been going around in circles for thirty-two hours, but now it's finally all coming together, he thought grimly.

One way or another, it ends at that warehouse.

CHAPTER 12

THURSDAY, 6:15 P.M.

By the time Spider-Man arrived at Hunt's Point, there were already four cruisers parked in front of the Cane Cutters' hideout. There would be more, soon—he'd seen at least six other cruisers on the way, sirens blaring, speeding south on the wide center lane. From the rooftop of a nearby warehouse he watched as two SWAT vans skidded on the icy pavement. Rear doors flew open, releasing small gaggles of helmeted, flack-jacketed, well-armed officers spreading a line around the perimeter, ducking behind Dumpsters and police cars, and training their long-range weapons on the boarded-up windows. Blue lights brightened the officer's faces and fell upon the warehouse walls like splashes on a blank canvas.

An impressive production, Spider-Man thought. *Hold Venom for a few seconds, at least.*

Leaning over the edge of a warehouse, he shot a line of webbing at a lamppost and swung down and landed quietly behind the nearest SWAT van. He crouched, scraping his right arm on the pavement, and peered between the tires. There were four uniforms—three men and an unusually tall woman—and a plainclothes detective on the other side, all staring intently at the warehouse. First thing, Spider-Man decided, was to get their attention; it wasn't wise to startle a police detail in the middle of a hostage situation. Unless, of course, you enjoyed dodging bullets.

With a single, startling leap he climbed onto the SWAT van. He webbed his camera on the rack of emergency lights—hoping that they would stay off for the duration. Then he knocked loudly on the metal roof and cleared his throat.

"Excuse me," Spider-Man said, "is this the Esteban residence? I have a package here for Captain Frank Esteban?"

The four officers spun around and thrust their pistols at the van.

Immediately his spider-sense screeched like a dentist's drill. His leg muscles coiled.

"Hold it, hold it," the detective growled, waving wildly with his open hand. He had a round, wrinkled face, and his eyes were spaced wide apart. At his command, the uniformed officers stepped back, bent their elbows, and breathed. The tall woman rubbed the base of her neck.

"You should know," Spider-Man said, his mask suddenly cool and damp, "I'm all paid up on my good-guy dues."

For what seemed like a long while, the officers glared at each other, not saying a word. Finally the detective said, "Are you insane? Come down from there!"

"Nice to meet you too," Spider-Man muttered. Then, with a quick flourish, he rolled off the van and landed heels first on the sidewalk—smoothly, as if he'd just taken a single step down a flight of stairs.

The detective snorted and shook his head. "Cute trick." He stepped forward and offered a hand. "Lieutenant Flaherty from the Forty-first Precinct. Hostage negotiator. My daughter's a big fan of yours, actually."

"Thank you," Spider-Man said, grateful for the quick acceptance.

Before Flaherty could say anything else, a young, freckle-faced officer stepped through the small crowd and said, "Mr. Spider-Man?"

"Present." Again he raised his hand like a school child.

"Oh, okay," the young officer said, sounding perplexed. "I'm Officer Braswell, from Midtown South? I'm supposed to take you to the captain. Gotta hurry, 'cause I need to report to perimeter security."

Spider-Man glanced at Flaherty and smiled, even though the gesture was wasted under his mask.

He then turned to Braswell and said, "Take me to your leader, Earthman."

Captain Esteban sat in the doorway of one of two Midtown South police cruisers, his shirt torn, his arm cradled in a bloodied, makeshift sling. Next to him, crouched on the pavement, Betty Brant scribbled hurriedly in her notebook—seemed she was getting a hell of an exclusive. If Esteban minded the intrusion, he didn't show it. Spider-Man hadn't seen him since that Venom incident in the Bronx a little while ago; back then he'd been the perfect image of the composed, take-charge policeman, so it was a bit of a shock to see him in such disarray. Still, considering what the man had been through . . .

"Excuse me," Esteban said, turning to Betty and patting her gently on the shoulder. "I need to talk to our super hero friend over here. I'll be just a moment."

"Sure," Betty said. Quickly she glanced up at Spider-Man, gave him a quick nod, and shut her notebook. She stood up and sauntered away toward a clump of SWAT officers.

Spider-Man squatted close to Esteban. "Good to see you again, Captain. Wish it were under better circumstances."

"Same here," Esteban said wearily. "What happened to your arm?"

"Fell from a building," Spider-Man said, giving a straight answer for once. "How 'bout you?"

Esteban pointed at his own shoulder. "Kidnapped," he said.

"So," Spider-Man said, quickly scanning the perimeter. "Where'd you put the rest of the crew?"

"They're out with Golden; got 'em working the SWAT team and the South Bronx detail. I want everyone informed as to the nature of the situation." Esteban paused for a moment and scratched the thick stubble on his cheek. "But also, I wanted to have a chance to talk to you. Alone, I mean."

"Shoot," Spider-Man said.

Esteban smiled. "You shouldn't say that to a cop, friend."

"A sense of humor," Spider-Man said, nodding. "I'm stunned."

"The thing is," Esteban said, suddenly earnest, "I've got a brother inside."

"I know," Spider-Man said. "DeLaSelva told me when I nailed him." For some reason the thought made him feel guilty, as if he'd just peeked through a neighbor's window.

"*Ay Dios,*" Esteban muttered. "Who else knows?"

"The feds might," Spider-Man said. "DeLaSelva told me just before they showed up to take him into custody." When Esteban cursed under his breath, Spidey added, "Look, it's none of my business, but people were gonna find out anyway. Once this thing is over—''

"You have to save him," Esteban interrupted.

"I—" Spider-Man began, stammering. Absently he rubbed his injured arm. "There's—if he's with the terrorists, I mean, there's nothing—"

"That's not what I'm talking about. He's gonna get arrested, believe me. He'll get put away. What I'm worried about is Venom."

"When was the last time you saw him?" Spider-Man asked.

"Not since the Bronx detail showed up, 'bout twenty minutes ago. He was two blocks away. My guess is that he sneaked inside already. And you know what that means."

"The Cane Cutters don't stand a chance."

"Not without your help," Esteban said.

"My first responsibility," Spider-Man said, inching away from the captain, "is to the hostages."

Esteban grimaced. "I know that. So is mine. But I already lost a cousin to that monster."

"I'll do my best," Spider-Man said, standing up.

"Wait a sec," Esteban said. "There's about twenty perps inside. The guys we saw had M-16s and nine-millimeters, but I wouldn't be surprised if they've got heavier stuff. All right?"

"Got it," Spider-Man said.

"One more thing. Are you sure you can sneak inside without anyone spotting you? I don't want a bigger mess that what we've got already."

"I once broke into the Pentagon, Captain." Spider-Man said, then turned to leave. Before he'd taken his second step, though, he glanced over his shoulder and said, "Carlos, right?"

"That's it. Thanks."

Spider-Man smiled under his mask. Spider-sense silent, he started running toward the warehouse, then vaulted off the hood of a patrol car and, flipping twice in the air, shot a web-line and snapped himself over the SWAT line. He landed gracefully on the warehouse roof, crouched, surrounded by an expanse of blue-black tar. The cold wind whistled through him, slipped between his aching ribs.

Suddenly, from street level, there came a loud popping noise, followed by a growl and an annoyingly long crackle. Spider-Man glanced over the edge and saw Lieutenant Flaherty strutting towards the SWAT line, bullhorn planted on his lips.

Now, this *should be interesting.*

"Hello?" Flaherty yelled into the bullhorn. "This is Lieutenant Guy Flaherty from the New York Police Department! You've gotta free the hostages, you hear! Throw down your weapons and come out with your hands over your heads, and I can guarantee that you will not be injured!"

A lonely voice screamed from inside: *"¡Los Corta Cañas no se rinden!"*

Then came a barrage of machine-gun fire. Spider-Man jerked backward, startled. Downstairs, Flaherty slapped himself on the ground and covered his head with the bullhorn. The SWAT team scattered about like pigeons. Bullets skittered loudly on the pavement, burst tires, perforated one of the vans.

Taking advantage of the distraction, Spider-Man crawled onto the side of the structure. He found a dark boarded-up window and smacked it with his fist. At once the plywood splintered, the boards clattering into an empty hallway. He grabbed onto the rotting molding and disappeared inside.

When the gunfire stopped, Frank crawled from under the cruiser and called out to Betty Brant, who lay hidden behind a brightly painted Dumpster.

"I'm okay," Brant said, her voice high as a whistle.

Frank climbed to his feet, wiping the wet dirt off the makeshift sling. Before him, the SWAT line was reforming itself officers staked out positions, knelt down again on the sidewalk checked their weapons. Two uniforms shuddered on the pavement, a third sat perfectly still, arms slack at either side, head bloody and slit.

Within seconds, five South Bronx officers ran into the inner perimeter and dragged the wounded out of the line of fire.

Hell, Esteban thought. His ears throbbed from the noise. Grimly, he wondered how long he'd be able to restrain the SWAT team, now that there had been casualties. While the hostages remained inside, attacking the warehouse was simply out of the question. They had to wait. Unfortunately, revenge-minded cops were not commonly known for their patience.

He just hoped that Spider-Man had enough time to do his job.

"I don't get it," Betty said from her Dumpster. "They have to know they're surrounded, right? So, if they can't escape, why don't they just give themselves up?"

"Don't hold your breath," Frank said.

"I'm just trying to figure it out," she said, annoyed.

Out of the corner of his eye, Frank spotted Gilman and Liverakos advancing toward the cruiser carefully, skipping from cover to cover.

"These aren't criminals, Ms. Brant," he said. "They don't weigh their options and decide on the best course of action. These are revolutionaries. And Puerto Rican revolutionaries have this nasty habit of martyrdom."

"I see," Betty said. "Something you've seen before."

"Too often," he muttered. He paused and wiped his nose with the back of his hand. "Betances, Albizu Campos, Braseti, Collaso, Terrasola, Soto-Arriví. On and on. We have a deckful of martyrs, Ms. Brant."

We. Frank shook his head; perhaps he was being too comfortable with the word. He recalled that stupid Lone Ranger joke: *What do you mean* we, *kimosabe?*

Pistol in hand, Gilman leaned sideways against the cruiser, which rocked back and forth with the weight. Liverakos creeped around him and crouched on the pavement.

"Are you guys okay?" she said.

Frank nodded distractedly. He thought of the station, the huddle at the booking desk, the crisp uniforms and haggard faces. Then there was Lydia, of course. *Mi bella Lydia.*

"Here," Gilman said, reaching behind his back. From his belt he produced a small walkie-talkie.

I've got my own "we," Frank thought.

"You need a gun," Gilman said.

Frank nodded and gestured with his hand. "Who's commanding the stormtroopers?" he asked.

"DiFillippo," Liverakos replied, pressing a Beretta on her superior's hand.

Frank sighed. Eddie DiFillippo had an unfortunate tendency to get impatient. But there was nothing to be done. Then he straightened his back and said, "Listen, from now on everything comes through me. I don't care what the Bronx guys say, I'm in charge here. And I want everything smooth and clear; no surprises, *me entiendes*?"

"Sorry?" Gilman said.

Frank felt uneasy all of sudden. "Understand. No surprises, understand?"

"Yeah," Liverakos chimed in.

They heard a loud *flop, flop, flop*, blades cutting the air above them. There was blustering cold breeze, and Frank put his arm up to shield his eyes. Through his bloodied sleeve he saw the helicopter swoop down and hover over the open, burnt field.

"Who asked for the air support?" Frank screamed. He could barely hear himself over the racket.

"Oh great," Liverakos said, pointing at the two figures that emerged from the aircraft. "Scully and Mulder are here."

"Feds?" Frank said. He felt his throat souring at the thought.

Gilman smiled sheepishly. "We had to call them. Long story, but it was the only way to reach Spider-Man."

"*Carajo,*" Frank murmured, tapping his fist against his cracked lips.

Venom barely noticed the intrusion: as soon as the masked terrorist stepped into the hallway, a heavy tendril flew outward and clamped about the young man's head. With a twist, the neck bone snapped; the Cane Cutter fell to the floor in a clump. Venom stepped over him and quietly advanced further into the warehouse.

Should have asked him about Ann, the creature realized, much too late. Third time already. Venom glanced backward and cursed. *Have to be smart.*

Not that it mattered. The building was a circumscribed structure. Eventually, Eddie Brock would find his beloved.

The creature had torn through the previous warehouses like a wrecking ball, demolishing floorboards and tearing down walls. Not this one. The tight cordon of police outside had reminded Venom of the need for caution. Ann was at the mercy of these scumbuckets; they could kill her at the slightest provocation.

Venom moved carefully through a plywood door and down another long passageway. There were sliding panels at either side, made of corrugated metal sheets held together with copper knots. The creature could hear shouting, a loud rustle of belongings.

With a solid kick, the creature knocked down the panel on the right. Inside, a slight man and a young woman packed pamphlets into a carton. The pair froze for a moment. Then the man screamed, and the woman reached for a pistol lying on the unmade bed. The action brought the sheets with it, like tissue from a box.

Venom pounced and bit the gun from her hand.

"*¡Hijo eh' puta!*" she yelled, clasping her fingerless stump against her chest. Blood drenched her pale green T-shirt.

The man, covering his head with his arms, shrank into the farthest corner of the room. Useless.

Venom smiled, displaying a bramble of blood-stained teeth. "You have taken our Ann, our beloved, and you will tell us where she is. Now."

The man, curled against a stack of papers on the floor, stammered hysterically, "Down the hallway! Sombra has them down the hallway! Don't hurt us, please!"

"*Cobarde,*" the woman sneered, glancing at her partner. The man flushed brightly and looked away.

Satisfied, Venom turned to leave. Just as the creature was about to step through the door, though, there came a pathetic shout, and the symbiote felt the weight of the puny man as he pounced on the creature's back. Venom swatted him with an elbow, perfunctorily; his ribcage collapsed like an empty box.

"No!" the woman yelped. As Venom walked out into the hallway, her cries mingled with the broken wails of the injured man.

Ann, the creature thought, dismissing the wounded pair. *We will find you.*

Venom rushed down the long, makeshift hallway, crawling along the walls and the ceiling. Five or six times, the creature encountered masked terrorists carrying weapons, lugging equipment, shouting orders into darkened rooms. The few who put up a fight were dealt with swiftly; their blood slicked the rough floorboards behind. Venom moved on, sparing them for now—there would be time for punishment later, once Ann had been rescued.

After taking a set of stairs to a lower level, Venom came immediately upon a plywood door, which opened—or rather, splintered—to a wide room filled with tables and chairs. A mess hall. It looked as if it had been abandoned in a hurry. Emptied trays were spread across the Formica tops, shiny with grease; plastic cups rolled around on the floor. Beyond it, Venom could see yet another passageway.

The creature growled, smashed the nearest table into a messy pile. By now Venom felt like a rat in a gigantic maze. Whomever had put the Cane Cutter complex together had done it in the most haphazard, disorienting way possible. To what purpose, the creature could not guess. One thing was certain, though: Venom would have enjoyed feasting on the builder's addled brains.

Shooting a line of organic webbing at the ceiling, the creature swung across the mess hall, then rolled through the narrow doorway into the hall, which was lit by a long row of spotlights. The passage ran straight for about fifty or sixty yards, then turned abruptly to the left. Halfway along the right-hand wall there was a single door—a metal one, reinforced with plates and rusted bolts. From behind it, Venom heard a low, strangled sigh.

Ann.

Angrily the creature pushed razor-sharp claws into the metal sheet, then, with a forceful heave, tore the door apart like a curtain.

Ann sat in a cavernous storeroom, half-slumped against a tall wooden column. For a moment all the creature could see was her face: swollen, bloodied, bruised to a pale ocher.

She'd been hurt.

No. Venom stood motionless, stilled by rage, glaring. Didn't notice Joe Robertson, editor-in-chief of the *Daily Bugle*, crouched beside her. Didn't notice the tall, blond man in the shadows, slowly training an odd-looking weapon—casing lit with green diodes, parabolic plate spreading out from the barrel—at the symbiote's chest.

"*¡Aquí está tu antídoto,*" the man yelled triumphaly, "*so canto 'eh imperialista!*"

At that, Venom paid attention. But it was too late.

A blast of sound, so loud it was inaudible.

And pain.

In his career, Spider-Man had been to some fairly revolting places, from the humid swamps of the Florida Everglades to the fetid darkness of the New York City sewer system. He'd pulled himself up from being buried alive and he'd survived more than one trip to the prehistoric jungle aptly known as the Savage Land.

Despite all that, the type of place he hated going to most was a warehouse at night.

It had been a warehouse much like this one where he cornered the burglar who murdered his uncle—the man he could've stopped. With all the deaths he'd seen in his young life, the one that still hit him the hardest, still haunted his dreams the most, was Uncle Ben's. And every time he went into a warehouse, it reminded him of that awful night.

After a few minutes of crawling along the ceiling, he caught sight of a man and a woman kneeling by a window. They wore bulky jackets and gas masks, and held shotguns, with what appeared to be nine-millimeters in holsters, just like Esteban promised. *Dollars to donuts, they're wearing kevlar un-*

der the jackets, too. They probably think they're ready for anything. Spider-Man smiled grimly. *Time to disabuse them of that notion.*

He positioned himself on the ceiling so that his immobilized right arm was pointed at the face of one of the Cane Cutters. He aimed his left arm at the other one, then shot a glob of webbing from each shooter, aimed at the bottom of their gas masks. The webbing hardened, securing the masks to their faces.

They both whirled around in surprise at this action, raising their shotguns. Fast as they were, Spider-Man was faster, leaping at them from the ceiling, kicking their shotguns out of their hands. He rebounded off the wall and flipped. In midflip, he shot out more webbing at the pair.

By the time he landed back on his feet, the two Cane Cutters were webbed neck to toe. That, combined with the fact that their gas masks were now attached to their faces, left them immobile and silent—without Spider-Man having to throw a punch. When dealing with nonpowered folk, he preferred to avoid physical confrontations if possible.

He gazed down upon the pair, struggling futilely against the webbed cocoon they found themselves in, making quiet "mmmph" noises—probably not loud enough to alert any of their *camaradas.* Spider-Man put his left index finger to his lips and whispered, "Shhhh! Be vewy vewy quiet—I'm hunting tewowists."

The Cane Cutters looked less than amused.

"Tough room," he muttered as he leapt back up to the ceiling and continued around the warehouse, performing the same stunt on several more, all of whom wore the same type of clothing and carried the same brands of weapons. One of them stood guard at a door, behind which Spider-Man hoped to find the hostages. Instead, he found a room full of sealed boxes labelled TEXTBOOKS and open boxes containing a rather impressive collection of weaponry—rifles, shotguns, hand-guns, Uzis, and something that looked like a rocket launcher.

He webbed the room's one window shut, then closed the

door and did likewise with it, sealing the room off. *No sense letting them get at their backup ammo.*

As he leapt back up to the ceiling, he heard an odd noise. After a moment, he placed it as belonging to a very high-powered sonic weapon. Whatever it was, it was several orders of magnitude more powerful than the pop guns Hawkins and Liverakos had used the previous night.

It wasn't coming from outside, but further into the warehouse—from below.

He scampered across the ceiling in the direction of the noise. *It's gotta be Venom. But if the Cane Cutters have sonics, it means they were ready for him—which makes sense, really. The fact that Ann is Venom's ex isn't exactly a secret.*

He just hoped that Venom's presence didn't bode too ill for Robbie and Ann. . . .

The creature writhed under Sombra's sonic beam—pseudopodia uselessly flailing, obscene tongue flicking about like windswept flame.''You thought you gonna get yourself some Rican brains, huh?'' Sombra laughed, his bones stretching under caramel-colored skin. ''Here you go, *cabrón*! You like? Tasty, huh? Better than all that white bread you've been eating.''

The reporter stood up and, holding his ribs, paced slowly toward Sombra. ''Stop it!'' he yelled over the loud hum of the sonic accelerator. ''There's a man under that thing! Please!''

Still firing the weapon in his right hand, the *Corta Caña* commander glanced at Robertson.

''Don't worry, Mr. Reporter,'' he said. ''You're gonna get the story of a lifetime. 'Imperialist beast killed by Puerto Rican revolutionaries.' Can't you just picture—''

At once Sombra reached into his waistband with his left hand, pulled out a pistol, and whirled around. He caught Weying, as *papi* would say, with her pants at half-mast. She'd tried to sneak up on him; her delicate fingers were twined into a double fist, her arms coiled over her head.

Sombra grinned. He tapped the gun barrel against her swollen nose. Slowly Weying retreated, brought down her fists.

With the pistol Sombra gestured at her to come around and join the reporter. In better circumstances he would have had a second guard with him, keeping an eye on the prisoners, but with the cops salivating outside, Sombra wanted every hand busy with the evacuation.

"How you doing, friend?" he said, turning to Venom, who could only respond with a series of sickening spasms. Then its knees buckled, and its arms slapped against the cement floor. "*¡Ay bendito!* You see, once we had to take your *jevita* here, we knew you'd be sticking your ugly mug into our business. So we got ourselves a little prevention. Supposed to be a guidance system jammer, but guess it works on *monstruos imperialistas* too."

"Please," Ann said, steadying herself against Robertson.

Sombra ignored her. "But the thing is, I've been looking forward to this little meeting. Believe it or not, *chico*. 'Cause you're like the United States in one disgusting little package."

He paused, as if he were waiting for the villain's reply. Venom reached forward with a single tendril, which wavered for a moment, then snapped back into the creature.

"No, no I'm serious," Sombra continued. "See, you're like this *asquerosa* thing that says it's gotta 'defend the innocent.' But we all know you're just a killer, and we can't stop you, so we just smile and bear it. *Gringos* are the same. Say they're gonna help you, but they just wanna eat your brains."

From somewhere in the weapon there came an insistent beeping sound. Batteries running low. Much too quickly, it seemed. Sombra glanced at his watch and realized that the second hand had stopped—Altmann had warned him about the possibility of electronic disruption. No matter; he would soon get the signal to retreat. If everything went according to plan, a Mustang parked six blocks away would burst into flames, drawing the attention of the NYPD. Then, once the bulk of the Cane Cutters had left through the secret tunnel, a special code would come by two-way radio, and Sombra would know that it was safe to join his *camaradas* outside.

The *Corta Cañas* would survive today's debacle.

On the ground, Venom rocked with convulsions. The symbiote mask shrunk back—teeth melting, blank eyes tearing away like threadbare fabric—revealing a face underneath, a human face, stuck in such a rictus of pain that for the briefest instant Sombra felt pity for Eddie Brock.

For the briefest instant, anyhow. The man inside Venom, Sombra quickly realized, was reddish blond-haired and blue-eyed.

Pure, unadulterated *yanqui*.

Sombra wasn't surprised; pleased, rather. Tempted, too. The creature was obviously incapacitated, which meant that his mission had already been accomplished. And yet . . . such a propaganda victory . . . better than the robbery itself . . .

The beeping grew faster, louder. Disgusted, Sombra released the trigger and let the weapon, which hung on a vinyl strap from his shoulder, drop under his arm.

Brock lay motionless on the ground, face down, the symbiote draped like a blanket over his body.

"Please," Ann Weying whispered, "don't kill him. I beg you."

"The cops'll be here any—" the reporter began.

"You know," Sombra broke in, waving the nine-millimeter in his left hand, "I'm getting really sick of you two."

Glaring at Sombra, Robertson put a long, bruised arm around Weying's slim shoulders.

Pathetic. The oppressed protecting the privileged.

"Get out of here," he said. When the pair didn't move, Sombra took a step towards them and yelled, "*Qué?* You thought I was gonna kill you? What you think I am? A murderer?" Then, softer: "Get out."

Robertson nodded at Weying, then, gently, pulled her by the arm toward the door. When they reached Brock's body, though, Ann knelt down to stroke her ex-husband's hair.

"I'm not moving," she said flatly.

"There's nothing we can do," Robertson muttered, leaning close to her.

"He's right about that," Sombra said. His neck stretched and his chin flattened and his forehead grew suddenly wider. He reached for the second weapon strapped on his back. At this stage of the game it seemed that he could have simply put a bullet in Brock's head, but Sombra wasn't taking any chances. *Corta Caña* intelligence had identified two methods of defeating Ann Weying's ex-husband. One was ultrahigh-decibel sound.

The other was fire.

He unhooked the gun from the fuel tank and lifted it over his shoulder. Gripping the handle, finger curled around the trigger, he pointed the barrel down at the still figure

In Sombra's hands, the flamethrower smelled caustically of gasoline.

He thought of pictures he'd seen of the Vietnam War, Asian comrades burning like candle wicks.

Weying looked up and smirked defiantly at Sombra. "I'm not moving."

"What about you?" Sombra asked Robertson.

The reporter shook his head. "Well, I can't carry her—my ribs hurt too much—so I guess I'm staying, too."

"Suit yourselves," he said without emotion. Maybe it was better this way. Cleaner.

The prisoners squinted and looked away.

Sombra squeezed the trigger.

Suddenly, just as the barrel sparked, igniting the first spittle of napalm, the whole weapon jerked out of his hands and flew backward. Flames spread wildly inside the storeroom, drawing a crooked circle on the cement floor.

A voice echoed from the ceiling. "I'm sorry, is this a private event? Or was anyone with a spider on his skivvies invited?"

Sombra looked up, just in time to see the red-booted foot about to crash on his forehead. He shuffled sideways, but not quickly enough—the kick caught him glancingly above the ear. His brain seemed to jostle in the skull, and the warehouse wavered and popped around him. He raised the nine-millimeter in his left hand. Another, ludicrously swift kick knocked it into the flames. His trigger finger snapped like chalk. Sombra had never seen anything like it. In the sudden heat from the fire, his nose narrowed and lenghtened, and his arms grew stockier. He heard a sigh of relief from the reporter, and a distinct *whoosh* as a fist landed on his temple. It was then that the pain—in his hand, in his neck—finally hit him, like a train long delayed.

"I guess you're the one they call Sombra," the red-blue whirlwind said. "What're you doing, though? You're beautiful just the way you are. Don't go and change for me."

"*Cabrón!*" Sombra muttered. The word sounded strange to him, as if he'd spoken it through a funnel. He swung blindly; his fist bounced against rock-hard biceps. The sonic accelerator twirled under his arm. Spinning around, he struck the air with his elbow. At once an open hand smacked him on the back of the head, and Sombra stumbled forward and crashed facefirst against a wooden pillar.

His legs trembled. In his mouth, he tasted the salt-rust of his own blood. A tooth lolled about on his tongue; he spat it at the cold cement. He remembered a row with his father, long ago, losing another tooth to a sharp blow. Grasping the pillar, he peered under his arm and for the first time caught a real glimpse of his opponent.

El Hombre-Araña.

Sombra cursed. He couldn't believe it was going to end like this—by the freaking bug.

"*Las Corta Cañas,*" he said, watching the flames gasp on the floor. The heat washed upon him like Caribbean waves. "The Cane Cutters will fight again."

"Not for a while, they won't," Spider-Man laughed, "unless, of course, you mean fighting for the good seats in the prison cafeteria. I hear it's murder getting a table by the window in Ryker's."

"This ain't over," Sombra said and, with much difficulty, straightened himself against the column.

"Yes it is," Spider-Man said, without intonation.

The lawyer stepped a few feet in front of Venom, breathing loudly. "Hit him again," she said.

"Ann," Robertson pleaded.

"I left the other ones for the cops," Spider-Man said, "but you, you I'm taking in myself." He stopped for a moment, then added darkly, "I can't believe you were gonna roast them. I had a tiny bit of sympathy, you know. A tiny bit.''

All of a sudden, a familiar high-pitched voice came from the darkened hallway.

"Let him go!" the young man screamed, then, running past the torn-up doorway, opened fire into the storeroom. Five quick reports, bright like soldering sparks, rang deafeningly against the ceiling. Sombra ducked and turned around and watched as Robbie and Ann sought cover behind a nearby column. Spider-Man leapt onto the corrugated wall above the doorway.

Sombra heartened for a moment. Carlitos had finally made it. The human bug had lied; the *Corta Cañas* were safe.

"*¡Déjenme!*" Sombra yelled. He was moved by the young man's loyalty, but right now the *camarada* would do better by leading the rest of the team to shelter. To be honest, he was the only one of the bunch Sombra really trusted.

"You gotta be careful," Spider-Man admonished, "you don't want to shoot your leader by accident."

"Don't you worry about that," Carlitos cried from the hallway.

Crouched on the floor, Robbie pressed a hand to his ribs and whispered, "That's him. That's the one who killed Esteban."

"Killed Esteban?" Spider-Man said jauntily. "Oh no! You wouldn't do something like that, Carlos? Would you? Kill your own brother?"

Carlitos didn't answer for a moment; in the meantime, Spider-Man crawled silently along the wall, pressing his ear against the metal panel.

With a start, Sombra gathered the arachnid's strategy: *He's strong enough to grab him through the wall.*

"Keep quiet!" Sombra shouted, to no avail.

"You bet I did," Carlitos said, hesitantly. "Shot him in the head three times. Made him like a bowling ball. And I'm gonna do the same if you don't let the *comandante* go."

"Get out of here!" Sombra yelled. "That's an order!"

"Stop pretending, Carlos," Spider-Man said, raising his fist. "Your brother's alive and kicking outside. I just talked to him.

And I'm guessing that it was you who helped him escape.''

No, Sombra thought, tapping his forehead against the wooden column. He'd expected Carlitos to hesitate, maybe even refuse. But, a betrayal? No. Never.

"That's not true! I killed him! I put a hole in his head!''

"How do you think the cops found out about this place, huh?'' Spider-Man asked, shifting a bit on the wall. "How do you think I knew that Captain Esteban's your brother?''

"Shut up,'' the young man said. But his heart wasn't in it.

Sombra spat blood on the floor. *"Traidor,"* he murmured under his breath.

"It's all over, buddy.'' Spider-Man said. "Why don't you just go ahead and put down your weapon? Your brother, he's worried about you.''

"I—'' Carlitos began. Suddenly he gasped as if he were about to dive underwater. Then he screamed. The wall thumped and rattled. Steel bolts popped from the corrugated sheets and sprinkled on the ground.

Spider-Man shot a web-line and sprang toward the ceiling.

Venom no longer lay unconscious at the doorway. Both Sombra and Spider-Man noticed at the same time, and for a second they glared at each other, as if to confirm a mutual understanding.

Enraged, disappointed, Sombra knelt on the floor and shouldered the sonic accelerator.

The wall collapsed. Carlitos flew into the storeroom, a flapping mess of gangly limbs. Spider-Man reacted instantly; the traitor landed on the web cushion with a loud *paff*.

The room was quiet for a moment. Then, roaring, Venom clambered through the ragged gateway, hunched but still imposing, dagger-teeth gleaming, tongue flicking about like a leech.

"We will juggle your kidneys,'' it hissed, immediately finding Sombra in the shadows. "We will pop your eyeballs in our maw like so many grapes.''

"You wish,'' Sombra said.

He fired the weapon, pushing the activator button with his thumb. Venom staggered backward. Tendrils sprouted from its chest, squiggled halfway toward Sombra and dropped flaccidly on the ground.

Within seconds the beeping started again; soon it turned into a long, annoying tone. Sombra smacked his elbow against the accelerator. No use. The battery was finished.

Venom recovered, rolled its neck from left to right, pretended to crack its knuckles.

"Ouch," it said sardonically.

Sombra started shaking—whether from anger or fear, he himself could not tell. As if in reply, his body shrank; first the backbone, painfully, then his shoulders, which tapered to a spadelike slope. His legs shortened, and suddenly his feet seemed to float inside his combat boots.

Sombra flung the useless accelerator at the creature. Like a lizard's tongue, a tendril shot from Venom's armpit, tagged the weapon in in midair, and broke it in half. It tossed the pieces over its shoulder at the corrugated wall. Sombra felt the loud, hollow clang in his stomach.

"Any other toys?" Venom asked. The tongue slavered with each word.

Sombra didn't answer. Police lights flickered outside, blue and red, and search beams streamed through the cracked windows. The effect was eerie, maybe even sublime. He smiled resignedly.

It was fear all right. In the distance he heard Spider-Man's harried voice—first something about the way being clear and running away, then a line about "proper authorities." When Sombra opened his eyes (he did not recall closing them) he saw the bug wrapped like a backpack around Venom's shoulders, hitting the creature's head with astounding force; every blow brought the creature closer to the ground.

The reporter and the lawyer had left.

"You have interfered for the last time, arachnid!" Venom screamed, then rolled forward and sluggishly threw Spider-Man against a wooden column. But the bug-man would not dismount so easily; he hooked his arm around the beam and swung around it and kicked the creature right on the solar-plexus.

"Lay on, MacVenom," Spider-Man said, "and damn'd be him that first cries 'Hold, enough!' "

The bug knocked Venom aside—and cleared an escape route for Sombra.

Clipped to Frank's belt, the walkie-talkie hissed and sputtered.

"Gilman to Captain Esteban," the tiny speaker called.

What now? Frank thought. So far the news had not been good. The Cane Cutters had refused to negotiate. Earlier Frank had arranged for the power lines leading to the warehouse to be disconnected, only to discover that the terrorists ran their own generator. What was worse, with all the recent noise inside the warehouse—torn metal, the weird piercing shrill—he'd had a rough time keeping the joint detail in check. The SWAT team was itching for a fight. Every few minutes DiFilippo would scurry over to the Midtown cruisers and try to convince him to order an assault; he'd even threatened to go over his head and call up the commissioner.

Let him try, Frank thought. He and Ramos went back a long way, back to Frank's rookie years. No way he'd take a SWAT cowboy's judgment over a captain's.

"Captain? Are you there?"

Frank yanked the walkie-talkie from his belt and brought it close to his mouth.

"I'm here," he said, "Now, tell me something: what part of the term *radio silence* don't you understand?"

"Sorry, Captain, but we're coming by with the feds. Thought I'd warn you."

"Thanks," Frank said grimly. He lifted his gaze and looked at the warehouse. It was difficult for him to believe that just half an hour ago he'd been a hostage inside. Obviously he preferred to be out here, running the show; still, there were a few things about being a captive of the Cane Cutters he'd appreciated. For one, not having to deal with the feds. It was funny: before Golden joined the precinct Frank had had no opinion about the FBI. The lieutenant's distaste was apparently catching.

More important, though, had Frank remained inside he

would have been able to keep tabs on Weying and Robertson
The lack of information unnerved him. Clearly Frank had had
no choice about leaving the two of them behind. He'd probably
even saved their lives by calling in the cavalry. Didn't matter
as he leaned against the still-warm cruiser, waiting for news
his belly rumbled with guilt. He should have been there to
protect them. He should be sharing their fate.

Dressed in kevlar vests, with loose gas masks hanging from
their necks, the federal agents looked like low-rent astronauts—
the kind you'd see in bad fifties science fiction films. Frank
watched them as they stiffly skipped from cover to cover
flanked by Gilman, Liverakos, and Golden. The get-up was
new, and Frank didn't like it. He'd already had a long talk
with Phillips about jurisdiction; the grim-faced agent had
seemed to take it to heart. Now, for whatever reason, the two
agents had readied themselves for an incursion.

Well, not if Frank Esteban has anything to say about it.

As soon as the group scampered around the cruiser, Hauman
put her hands on her hips and declared, "We've waited long
enough, Captain."

"Hostage situations are about waiting," Frank replied, an
noyed. "We wait, and they surrender. You're just gonna have
to be patient."

"We're going in," Phillips said, nodding.

"I don't think so."

"With all due respect, Captain," Hauman said, "we're no
here to ask for your blessing."

Golden and Liverakos rolled their eyes. Gilman mouthed
curse.

"We have just received authorization from headquarters,"
Phillips said, reaching behind his back to fix the buckle on hi
vest. "Sombra cannot be allowed to escape."

"Why are you talking to me, then?"

"The FBI believes in cooperating with local law enforce
ment," Hauman said, as if she were reading from an instruc
tion manual. "We're keeping you abreast of the situation."

Frank felt a vein pop at his temple. "If you think that I'n

going to allow you to put this whole operation at risk because—"

"How can we make this any clearer, Captain?" Phillips said, disdainfully. "You simply do not have a say in the matter."

"The hell I don't," Frank muttered. He signaled to Golden; at once the lieutenant and the two detectives surrounded the FBI agents. Their hands rested easily on their holsters.

The feds gave the detectives a quick once over, then looked at each other. After a moment, Hauman stepped closer to Frank and said, "Can't you see the conflict of interest here?"

"What?" Frank laughed, "because I'm Puerto Rican?"

"Because of your brother," she said.

Frank licked his teeth. He started to respond, but found that he was too angry to utter the words.

Golden came to his rescue. "We can't allow you to endanger the hostages. That's clearly out of the question."

But Hauman and Phillips seemed suddenly distracted, as if they were watching a television set perched on Gilman's shoulder.

"Hostages?" Phillips said, pointing in the direction of the warehouse. "You mean like those over there?"

Instinctively Frank turned and saw, in the distance, two figures staggering, shivering in the floodlight. They moved slowly toward the SWAT line, a black man holding his ribs, and a young woman with her face battered.

"Get them out of the line of fire!" Frank shouted as soon as he recognized Robertson and Weying.

To their credit, the SWAT team reacted instantly: the officers drew a cordon around the two victims, then all but carried the pair over to the nearest paramedic unit.

Two down, Spider-Man, Frank thought. *Please, make it three.*

"All right," he said, exhaling loudly. He watched his steam curl and pucker about him. "We go all out. Tear gas, the works. Gilman, Liverakos, you guys go with the feds. Take a couple of uniforms with you. Golden, get Flaherty and put together a sweep-up crew with the folks from the Bronx. Make

sure the perimeter is covered. And for Pete's sake, be careful
We don't want a bloodbath in there.''

Hauman grinned, then drew a pistol from her side holster
''Follow our lead,'' she said. Then, almost as an afterthought
she added, ''Time you guys learned how it's really done.''

''Right,'' Golden said sarcastically.

Sombra ran through the broken door, slicing his arm on a tab
of metal, and followed the hallway to a staircase that took him
down to the first floor. He scampered past a loud beaded cur
tain that he shoved aside disdainfully; he'd always been dead
set against such sentimental flourishes. He pressed his hand
against the cut and sidestepped into a narrow passage tha
smelled of leaking batteries. It looked like it hadn't been used
in ages: strewn along the path were empty cardboard boxes
which, when Sombra squashed them with his boots, burst into
sparkling clouds of dust. Sombra couldn't understand it. Mos
of the *Corta Cañas* should have gone through here already
Spider-Man had lied.

He found the hatch covered by an old, burnt PET computer
Angrily he tossed the unit aside—the screen cracked agains
the plaster wall—then yanked open the metal lid and squeezed
his suddenly thick legs into the access tunnel. He made it only
to his buttocks; in his flight from the storeroom his body had
grown much too wide at the hips.

Hell, Sombra thought. He smacked the floor with an open
hand. It wouldn't help him to calm down—what he needed
was a surge of emotion, something that would kick-start an
other change in his system. He tried to remember past mis
sions: failed ambushes, narrow escapes from the authorities
The Wells Fargo robbery. It didn't help. He felt too detached
from them—past victories, failures, nothing more.

He needed to concentrate. In his mind he pictured his cel
at juvenile prison. The bars were rusted from the salted ai
but still solid. His bunk was short and at night his feet dangled
like fishing rods from the mattress. He remembered his firs
beating: two brothers from Arecibo had pounded him wit
broom handles because he'd neglected to nod as he passed

them in the yard. He could still feel the bruises on his back, the crick on his neck where Gonorra had kicked him.

His pelvis shrank. Soon Sombra slipped down the tunnel into a maze of refuse ducts and insulation equipment. It had been months since Sombra had been down in the depths, as the Cane Cutters called their escape route, and he wasn't quite sure how to get to the emergency meeting spot. In fact, he'd expected to see some kind of marked trail.

Within minutes Sombra had lost all sense of direction. He was exhausted and cold. His jaw had almost swollen shut. His whole hand crackled with pain. Before he'd been raging, but now his anger had been replaced by a dull melancholia that seemed to drain him of energy. It was clear to him now that the other *Corta Cañas* were still in the warehouse—captured by Spider-Man or dead at Venom's hand. He was alone.

Groping about in the near darkness, he ran into a cool metal rung attached to the wall. Sombra started climbing, then suddenly cracked his head against a metal lid. After rubbing his crown, he pushed upward with his hand and shoulder and scanned the area around him. He was out on the street, behind the warehouse, but he could still see several uniformed pigs in the vicinity—he hadn't made it past NYPD's siege. Luckily, it didn't appear that anyone had noticed him. The pigs milled back and forth, flapping their arms from the cold, comparing weapons, exchanging racial epithets for laughs, or so Sombra imagined.

He could still make it. All he needed now was the opportunity, which was handed to him when all but one of the cops—a young white officer with a shiny, freckled face and an awkward demeanor—abandoned their posts and slowly, looking around as if to spot a superior, rounded the warehouse. Sombra almost laughed at the lack of discipline. Most likely they were curious; the clatter of Spider-Man's and Venom's fight could be heard in the distance. Or maybe they got tired of waiting in the cold. Whatever the reason, Sombra silently thanked them on behalf of the Puerto Rican revolution.

Clambering into the frigid night, Sombra skulked toward the ripe-looking officer. Quickly, undetected, he crossed the empty lane. The pig glanced in his direction. Sombra flattened himself against the curb, counted to five, then rolled onto the sidewalk. He peered at the cop, who examined his watch and fiddled absently with his two-way radio.

Good.

Sombra jerked to his feet and ran. The officer noticed him and, startled, reached for his gun. Sombra tackled him before he could unholster it. Once on the ground, the *comandante* acted on instinct—or rather, training. He hooked his arm around the thin neck and twisted it around.

A loud crack and a quiver.

Sombra dragged the body behind a nearby Dumpster, just as the other officers began to amble back to their position. He held his breath, so as to hide the telltale cloud of steam. At this point Sombra's plan had smacked against the proverbial brick wall. His mutant ability made it easy for him to disappear in crowds. He was the shadow man, after all, everyone and no one at the same time. But here, in this desolate place, just being around made him automatically a suspect.

He could hear sirens only a few blocks away. To his right, the East River lapped and gurgled against the canal wall. He glanced at the broken boy on the ground, and suddenly felt the jolt of an idea. He'd never tried this before and wasn't completely sure he could do it. In desperation he focused on the cop's features: on the slope of his nose and the folds of baby-fat under his chin and the sharp cut of his hairline and on his eyes, blue-green under the harsh lamppost glare. Sombra felt his own body reforming, coalescing, like wax settling at the base of a candle.

For some reason he remembered his last day in juvenile prison. Standing with a guard at the covered gate. He was thirteen at the time. His parents came an hour and a half late. *Papi* looked aggravated, like always; *Mami*, though, she seemed at once sad and embarrassed. She hid her face behind an embroidered handkerchief, which she held in place until she, alone, had walked up the driveway and joined her son under the wide cement awning. Sombra had wanted nothing from his father, but from *Mami* he'd expected a kiss, an embrace. A reunion. Instead, she looked curiously at him, then, confused, glanced up at the prison guard.

This is not my son, she said. The guard grabbed Sombra by his shirt collar and yanked him closer. *You sure?* he said. *This is not my son,* mother repeated. She seemed certain now. Sombra started to protest, but the guard rapped him in the crown and yelled: ¡Cabroncito! *Trying to sneak out, huh? Who are you? What's your name*? Flabbergasted, Sombra couldn't reply. Immediately the guard dragged him to the main office and pushed his hand into an ink pad. A burly secretary found his file in a rusted cabinet and compared the two sets of fingerprints. Even from a few feet away Sombra could tell that they didn't match. *What you trying to pull?* the guard screamed, slapping his face with the folder. *Who are you*?

Sombra thought he knew.

The Dumpster smelled like rotting wood. Sombra looked at his pale hands: the fingers, the nails, they matched exactly those of his victim. Hurriedly he stripped the young man's uniform. He read the nameplate pinned to the chest pocket.

Braswell. He tried pronouncing the name.

He liked the sound of it.

For a moment, Spider-Man actually thought he was getting the upper hand.

Then the tendril grabbed him around the neck and threw him at a window.

He went through the large single pane with a crash and landed outside on the cold pavement amidst a sea of broken glass. Thanks to the space heaters the Cane Cutters had placed around the warehouse—not to mention the use of a flame-thrower—it was rather warm inside, so being thrown into the well-below-freezing air was like getting a bucket of icewater in the face.

He clambered to his feet, ignoring the pain from the various lacerations the broken glass made on his back and legs. The fight had, at this point, shredded the sling, leaving his right arm more vulnerable.

However, there wasn't time to web up a new one, as Venom came charging out of the warehouse.

"It is long past time we killed you, arachnid!"

Spider-Man leapt over the attack easily. *He's sluggish, moving way too slowly*, he thought as he got in a kick to Venom's head on the downward arc of the leap. *Sombra took a lot out of him. Pity I'm not exactly firing on all thrusters myself—otherwise I might actually be able to bring him down.*

Out of the corner of his eye, he noticed a phalanx of cops, keeping their distance. *Hope Esteban has the brains to keep them back. Even at less than a hundred percent, Venom'll eat these guys alive.*

Then Venom leapt straight at him, pseudopodia flailing wildly around like snakes. Spider-Man managed to deflect the direct attack with a good old-fashioned punch to the jaw, but the tendrils proceeded to wrap all around him and start to pull. *Oh great, he's trying to draw and quarter me.*

Having recovered from the punch, Venom leaned into Spider-Man's face. The hollow white eyes seemed to glow, and the slavering tongue that protruded between the sharp teeth flicked at his face.

Though his legs and right arm were secured, Spider-Man managed to break his left arm out of the symbiote's grip. Before Venom could recover, he grabbed the tongue and pulled downward as hard as he could given his poor leverage.

The move surprised Venom, and the tendrils loosened. Spider-Man flexed his muscles and broke the symbiote's grip, let go of the tongue, kneed Venom in the jaw, then punched him as hard as he could with his left fist. Venom went flying toward another warehouse.

Gotta admit, he thought with a small smile as he pursued Venom, *I always wanted to do that.*

Venom got to his feet and let out a scream. "Always you interfere! First you ruin our lives! You reject us and ruin us! And now *this*! If you had left well enough alone, we would have freed Ann! We would have found her before those vermin tortured her! *We would have been together if not for you!*"

Oh, great, now his divorce is my fault, too? Spider-Man

thought as he attacked. The two of them became a tangle of limbs and tendrils. After a few seconds, Spider-Man couldn't even see his surroundings—the world consisted only of an undulating black target and his own red-and-blue fists trying to hit that target.

"Give 'em room!" Frank shouted over the din of the battle. But he needn't have worried: the SWAT team had already made a wide semicircle around Venom and Spider-Man. Flaherty, more cautious than curious, kept the bulk of his Bronx detail at a reasonable distance, while the Midtown contingent—Hawkins, Drew, plus three other uniformed officers—clustered around Captain Esteban and awaited instructions.

Frank combed his hair to the side and brooded. He didn't know what to do. All along he had expected something like this. Now that the two super-beings were at it in earnest, though, he felt weirdly powerless, as if he were watching not a fight but a storm brewing in the horizon. He could seal up the windows, make sandbag barriers, prepare for the worst. But the storm itself, there was nothing to be done about that.

Suddenly he understood why Golden hated costumes.

The rest of the Midtown team was still inside the warehouse. The assault had come off quietly—not a peep from the Cane Cutters, even after DiFillipo had flooded the building with tear gas. Wearing breathing masks, the FBI-led squad had advanced to the loading dock, scrambled onto the platform, and slipped into the structure through a makeshift metal door. Frank could do little but wait. He checked his watch. He turned up the volume on his walkie-talkie—hell of a time for Gilman and Liverakos to comply with the rule about radio silence.

"Captain Esteban?" the walkie-talkie finally cried. "Anyone?"

Frank recognized Liverakos's voice immediately. "This is Esteban," he replied, squeezing the radio so hard that the casing split.

"What's all the noise outside?"

"Spider-Man and Venom. Are you guys okay in there?"

"Everything wrapped up," Liverakos said. "I repeat, wrapped up and ready to go."

"Good job," Frank said, unable to contain his surprise and relief.

Liverakos was quiet for a moment. Then she said, "Fact is, Mutt and Jeff did most of the work for us. Though I'd be hard pressed to call what Venom did work—more like fun with gore."

Hell, Frank thought. "How about Sombra?"

"The feds are still looking for him. But, Captain?"

"Yeah?" Frank said.

"I think we've found your brother."

Frank blanched. "Is he . . . ?"

"Alive," Liverakos said, "but he looks pretty bad. Apparently had a run in with Venom."

"*¡Ay Dios!*" Frank cried. Then, calmer, he added, "Keep me posted. Over and out."

Spotting Drew and Hawkins in the small crowd of uniformed officers, Frank cleared his throat and said, "We're going over to the SWAT line; Venom's not getting away this time. Drew, Hawkins, you stick close to me, understood? I may need your help moving around."

"You should be seeing an EMT," Hawkins said quietly, sounding as if he knew it was pointless but trying anyhow. "That's what you *should* be doing."

"Not with Golden still inside the warehouse," Frank said. "I don't wanna leave DiFillippo in command."

"Wise choice," Drew said, nodding.

"Now," Frank continued, "I think we're missing someone. Has anyone seen Braswell?"

"He was with the Bronx crew," Epstein, one of the uniformed officers, said, "securing the rear. Last I saw him, anyway."

"There he is," Hawkins said. He glanced past Epstein's shoulder at a young officer hanging back with the Bronx detail, trying to catch a glimpse of the fight.

"Get him up here with us," Frank said. "I want as many

of my own people around me as possible. I'm gonna talk to DiFillippo.''

Vance Hawkins watched the fight with something like fascination. He and Drew now stood behind the line of SWAT guys who held the line fifty feet from the melée. To his right, Schwalb, Epstein, and Braswell stood ready, Braswell looking like he wanted to be somewhere else. To his left, Esteban conversed with DiFillippo.

In his previous two encounters with Venom, months ago at an NYPD safehouse and again last night at DeLaSelva's apartment, Hawkins saw him up close. This time the detective had some distance, and could truly observe without the distraction of fearing for his life. Despite himself, he had to admire the way Venom moved. The actions of Brock's human body dovetailed with those of the alien creature—not quite moving in tandem, but not completely separate, either. They complemented each other with an elegance Hawkins would not have expected from a psychotic.

Right now, he and Spider-Man seemed evenly matched. The wall-crawler's superior speed and agility were made up for by Venom's greater dexterity—thanks to the alien—and his sheer ferocity.

Sheer ferocity? he thought. *Hell, the man's nuts. What Aunt Cornelia used to call "binky bonkers."*

The fight carried them further away, toward the river. DiFillippo noticed this, and ordered his people to move the perimeter up accordingly.

As they moved forward behind the SWAT team, Drew asked, "Hey, Hawk, you ever watch tennis?"

Despite everything, Hawkins laughed. "You ask me that every August when the U.S. Open comes to town and you want to go out to Flushing Meadows to catch some games, and I *always* tell you that I hate tennis."

"All right, all right, but—" He hesitated, then ran his hands through his hair. "Couple years back, Steffi Graf and Monica Seles faced off against each other in the finals. It was either Wimbledon or the U.S. Open, I forget which. Anyhow, Graf had, like, half a dozen bone fragments in her feet. Seles had shin splints, and it was her first tournament back after getting stabbed.''

''I just know there's a point to this,'' Hawkins said impatiently, not looking at Drew in order to keep an eye on the fight.

''Those two could barely walk. And despite that, they played some great tennis—they beat everyone else, and fought down to the wire in the finals. Even at half-mast, they were quantum leaps ahead of everyone else. I didn't think I'd ever see anything like that again.''

Hawkins saw where his partner was going. ''Until today.''

Nodding, Drew said, ''Yeah, until today.'' He pointed at Spider-Man and Venom, who were a blur of red, blue, and black. The punches, swipes, kicks, and flailing pseudopodia all started to overlap. ''I mean, look at that. We know that the web-head is running on fumes, and Venom's moving like a forty-five record at thirty-three—and still, we gotta stay fifty feet back or we'll get frapped.''

At the sound of footfalls, Hawkins turned around to see Gilman jogging up to join them. He hefted what looked like an giant economy-sized flamethrower.

He pulled up between Hawkins and the captain and held the flamethrower up for Esteban to look at. ''Laura found this inside,'' Gilman said, out of breath. ''The Cutters were probably usin' it in case Venom showed up. There was a sonic weapon, too, but the battery was shot.''

''Figures,'' Esteban said. ''Sombra's nuts, but he's no fool.''

''Great,'' DiFillippo said. ''We can use 'at on Smiley over there an' get this crap overwith.''

Esteban rolled his eyes. ''Good idea, Eddie. After all Spider-Man's done for us, the least we can do is crispy-fry him.''

DiFillippo gave the captain a withering look. ''Yeah, I know that, Frank, but they'll prob'ly separate sooner'r later.'' He turned to his people. ''Anyone certified on one'a these?''

One member of the team, whose nametag read ST. JOHN, stood up. ''I am, sir.''

"Good," DiFillippo said. "You get a clear shot at Smiley, you nail 'im with this, got it?"

St. John nodded and took the flamethrower from Gilman, who seemed relieved to be rid of it.

Hawkins turned to look back at the fight, just as Spider-Man kicked Venom in the jaw, which sent the creature sprawling. Spider-Man then leapt forward and pounded Venom with a series of punches. Venom managed to yank Spider-Man off him with a pair of tendrils, but Spider-Man got in another punch.

Then, as Venom staggered backward, Spider-Man charged ahead to bodyslam Venom with his left shoulder. The two of them were now only a couple of feet away from the wooden waist-high fence that kept people walking amongst the warehouses from falling into the East River.

As Spider-Man charged, Hawkins noticed that Venom had relaxed himself. "Oh no," he muttered.

"What?" Drew asked.

Spider-Man collided with Venom. Venom fell more than stumbled backward—but Spider-Man also seemed to stumble, as if moving forward farther and faster than anticipated.

"I was right," Hawkins muttered. "Venom went limp so Spidey's bump—"

The pair of them went over the fence and into the river.

"—knocked them into the river," Hawkins finished.

Esteban's eyes went wide. "*Ay, Cristo*—move in!"

Hawkins, Drew, Gilman, Esteban, and the uniforms followed DiFillippo and his people as they ran to the fence and took up position.

To St. John, DiFillippo said, "Have that thing ready t'go." Then he turned to another person and said, "Jourdan, get back over t'the truck and get one a the floodlights."

Nodding, Jourdan got up and ran back toward the Cane Cutter warehouse.

Peering over the fence between the heads of two SWAT members, Hawkins saw the water sloshing around a bit, but no sign of life otherwise. He knew Spider-Man couldn't breathe underwater. *Can Venom? Who knows what that alien thing can do for him?*

Raising his voice, Esteban said, "Make sure you look before you shoot. If you see black, shoot—if you see red, *don't shoot.*"

An interminable time passed. Hawkins figured it was probably only about ten seconds, but it seemed like days. The murky water, lit by the odd glow of the sodium lights that dotted the Hunt's Point Market area, grew ever more calm.

I don't like this, Hawkins thought. *I don't like this a lot.*

"He should've come up by now," Gilman said. "Shouldn't he?"

Nobody replied to that.

After several more seconds, Braswell spoke up. "This is stupid. They're probably both dead."

Esteban turned sharply on Braswell and said, "We wait."

Braswell just shook his head and muttered, *"Estupido."*

Hawkins blinked. Luckily, Esteban didn't hear him, but muttering *stupid* in Spanish regarding the captain was an invitation for trouble. Braswell had never struck Hawkins as the insubordinate type in the past.

Jourdan returned with one of the portable floodlights that they had been using to supplement the sodium lights' illumination during the siege of the warehouse. Epstein and Schwalb helped Jourdan set the thing up and shone it on the water in the area where the two combatants had fallen in.

Hawkins frowned. "You know, Captain," he said to Esteban, "the way they were going at it, they could come up anywhere."

Esteban sighed. "Yeah. Shine the light around, Eddie, see if they come up anywhere else. Peter, get on the horn to the divers, we may need 'em."

"Right," Gilman said, pulling his cell phone out of his coat pocket.

Then the water started to churn. Hawkins pulled out his nine-millimeter; next to him, Drew did likewise. The SWAT guys all tensed and peered into their 'scopes. *If it is Venom, he's gonna get one helluva reception*, Hawkins thought grimly. *But then, it's no less than he deserves.*

A red-clad head broke through the water. Hawkins could hear a sharp intake of breath.

"Hold your fire!" Esteban said.

"Careful," DiFillippo added, "it could still be Smiley."

A left arm also broke through the water and reached for one of the wooden posts of the fence. "Nice reception," came what sounded like Spider-Man's voice from behind the mask.

It could still be Venom, Hawkins thought. *That mask muffles his voice too much.*

Then the figure started to climb the post. The costume was soaking wet and covered with the various bits of gunk one finds in the East River.

"Hold it there, pal," DiFillippo said. "Don't move till we know it's you."

"Venom's gone, Lieutenant," he said, sounding exhausted. "I searched for as long as I could hold my breath, but he's gone."

Hawkins made a connection in his head, then lowered his weapon. "It's him. Let him up."

Esteban didn't take his eye off Spider-Man as he said, "You sure, Vance?"

"Venom's symbiote can change shape, but it can't make Brock smaller. This guy's too lithe—Venom's a lot bulkier than that."

Nodding, Esteban lowered his Beretta and said, "Let him up."

Spider-Man climbed up the post, clambered over the fence, and half-landed, half-collapsed next to Hawkins. He and Drew knelt down beside him. "You okay?" Drew asked.

"Not especially, no." His voice sounded a bit scratchy, and his impromptu swim left him smelling awful. Hawkins considered trying to ascertain what the odors were, then decided he didn't want to know.

"You sure he's gone?" Esteban, standing behind Drew, asked.

"I think so, yeah. He wouldn't have deliberately let me

dunk him like that if he didn't want to get away. He's single-minded, but he's not stupid. He knew I had a chance to take him down in the shape he was in.''

''Well, I can't take that chance.'' Esteban turned to Gilman. ''Peter, how soon'll the divers be here?''

''Ten-fifteen minutes.''

''Eddie, keep your guys on the water, just in case.''

Spider-Man shook his head. ''Waste of time.''

Hawkins smiled. ''Hey, it's procedure. Gotta do a sweep, just in case.''

''If he didn't want to leave, he would've kept the fight going. But he did what he came here for. Single-minded, remember? Ann's safe.'' He looked up. ''She is safe, right?''

''Mhm,'' Hawkins said, ''paramedics are taking care of her and Robertson.''

''Good.'' He shivered. ''Venom came here to rescue Ann. She's rescued, so he's gone.''

Drew turned around and called out to one of the uniforms. ''Hey, Schwalb, can you rustle up a blanket?''

Schwalb nodded, and started to move off, but Braswell grabbed her by the arm. ''I'll get it.''

''Whatever,'' Schwalb said with a shrug.

Next to Hawkins, Spider-Man looked straight at Braswell and tensed. No, it was more than that—his entire body seemed to come to attention and point at Braswell.

Then he leapt at the officer.

Hawkins couldn't believe it. Spider-Man had been half-sitting, half-kneeling on the pavement. If Hawkins were in that position, it would take him two seconds just to rearrange his legs so he could get up. In less time than that, Spider-Man jumped ten feet and pounced on Braswell.

Confusion ensued. Esteban yelled something. DiFillippo shouted that it was Venom. Braswell started saying something in Spanish. Epstein and Schwalb grabbed at Spider-Man. Drew cried out, ''What the hell?''

Spider-Man brushed the other officers aside and said, ''This isn't who it looks like.''

Then it hit Hawkins: *Braswell didn't speak Spanish.*

The freckle-faced officer cried out, "My name is Braswell! I'm a cop, you jackass!"

Then the freckles disappeared off his face and his nose got bigger. Images of the file provided by the feds the previous day mixed in Hawkins's head with the forensics reports on multiple fingerprints at three crime scenes.

"*¡No me tocques, cerdo!*"

Esteban's eyes grew wide, and he cried out, his words mirroring Hawkins's thoughts: "It's Sombra!"

Hawkins whipped out his weapon and aimed it at "Braswell."

Drew grabbed his partner's arm. "Hawk, what're you, nuts, that's—"

Then the face under the blue police officer's hat changed completely to that of a pale, drawn Asian man. "I'm a cop! I'm Braswell, *I'm a cop!*"

Spider-Man webbed him up as he yelled.

"What the hell's that?" DiFillippo asked as Sombra's face changed to that of a chubby African-American man.

Shaking his head, Esteban said, "That's the *commandante* of this little band of *Nacionalistas*."

"I'm not a *Nacionalista*, I'm a cop! A cop!"

Spider-Man shook his head. "I'd say he's lost it. Assuming he ever had it in the first place."

Esteban looked on the raving face that changed again, this time to a pudgy white man with a moustache. Hawkins wasn't sure if the captain's face was full of pity or disgust. "When we were inside, his face kept changing—like it is now. It looked like it was random, that he couldn't control it."

"In that case," Spider-Man said, "having to hold a specific form might've driven him over the edge."

"It was a short drive," Esteban said, and Hawkins decided that it was definitely disgust.

Hauman and Golden approached just then.

"We can't locate Sombra," Hauman said.

Golden added, "And we found a body, with the uniform taken. It was—"

"Braswell?" Spider-Man interrupted, pointing at the webbed-up figure of Sombra.

The eyes of both the lieutenant and the federal agent followed Spider-Man's finger to see the ever-changing face of Sombra, who now muttered the same phrase over and over again in Spanish.

Hauman's jaw set as she approached the leader of the Cane Cutters. "Well, well, well. Sombra. I've waited a *long* time for this."

The face of an elderly Latino man cried, "I'm not Sombra, I'm *Braswell*! Why won't you believe me?" By the time he finished asking the question, he was a baby-faced Native American.

The agent grabbed him by the shoulders—which had been left uncovered by the webbing—and maneuvered him back toward the command center.

Golden, meanwhile, looked at Spider-Man and wrinkled his nose. "What the hell happened to you?"

"Such a nice night, I decided to go for a swim. Hey, have they taken Ann and Robbie away yet?"

Golden shook his head.

Hawkins stepped forward. "C'mon, I'll walk you over."

The two of them walked back about ten paces behind Hauman and her new detainee. "Thanks," Spider-Man muttered. "I'm about ready to collapse as it is."

"I could tell."

Hawkins heard a chuckle before Spider-Man replied, "I thought you couldn't read my body language, Sergeant."

Grinning, Hawkins said, "Hey, the fact that I can read it is a pretty good indicator of how far gone you are."

"Yeah." Suddenly, the wall-crawler's voice had a faraway sound to it.

When they arrived back at the command center, the place was crawling with uniforms, most from the four-one, as well as a pair of ambulances. Joe Robertson and Ann Weying had both been placed onto gurneys. Hawkins also saw the *Bugle* reporter who had found Esteban, who now had an Asian woman next to her, taking pictures. She was talking to Wey-ing.

Spider-Man approached Robertson, though not too close, as his costume still dripped.

Robertson looked up at him and said, "You look like hell, son."

Spider-Man laughed. "You've looked better yourself, Rob-bie. Still, I'm glad you're okay."

"Me, too. Thanks for coming to get me."

"Hey, just looking out for number one—after all, if you're not around, there'll be *no* stopping Jonah from running me out of town on a rail."

Robertson chuckled. "Good point."

"Feel better, okay?"

Hawkins regarded Spider-Man with surprise. He had as-sumed that the hero's concern in this case related to Venom. He had no idea that there was any kind of personal relationship with Robertson—but it was patently obvious that there was, at the very least, some serious mutual respect between these two.

Then Spider-Man went over to Weying just as the *Bugle* reporter finished with her. The young lawyer had a pressure bandage on her nose that covered most of her face, and she was hooked up to an IV.

"Eddie?" she said in a hazy voice—obviously, the para-medics had painkillers in the IV.

"He's gone. Went into the river and disappeared. I'm sorry."

She shook her head slowly. "S'okay. Did—best—I know." Then she fell asleep.

Hawkins frowned. "Did she think that was good news or bad news that he got away?"

Spider-Man shrugged. "Hanged if I know, Sergeant. Listen, it's going to be a zoo here in a minute, and I'd just as soon not be one of the caged animals. I'm gonna head out."

"Okay. But do me a favor—meet up with me and Drew tomorrow morning, okay? Final debrief, or something." He was about to suggest they meet at Midtown South, then thought better of it. "Say eight-thirty, quarter to nine at the Seventy-ninth Street Boat Basin?"

"It's a date, Sergeant," Spider-Man said, raising his left hand, presumably to shoot out a web-line.

"Hey, my friends call me 'Hawk.'"

Spider-Man shot out the web-line and leapt into the air. "Fair enough, Hawk—just don't start calling me 'Spensaaah.'"

Within seconds, he had swung off into the night.

EPILOGUE

DAILY BUGLE

NEW YORK'S FINEST DAILY NEWSPAPER

Partly cloudy, chance of snow. High 25-30. Details p.2

50¢

...mber 1998

...AREHOUSE SHOWDOWN!

...TERS
...DOWN

...rant
...e Staff Writer

...ters, the Puerto
...ation that is al-
...r dozens of terror-
...the kidnapping of
...hief Joseph Robert-
...es over a dozen
...were taken

A. YIN—DAILY BUGLE

...lawyer Ann Weying, and
...t. Esteban were all
...ehouse. ...whose

Also on th...
super-villa...
Weying's...
rescue o...
several...
injurie...

FRIDAY, 8:45 A.M.

Spider-Man sat at the Seventy-ninth Street Boat Basin, reading over the day's copy of the *Daily Bugle*, complete with a front-page photo of Spider-Man fighting Venom, as well as a photo of Sombra being taken into custody, both credited to Angela Yin. The byline for the lead story belonged to Betty Brant. The first five pages were taken up entirely by articles on the bust and related stories, from the page-two story by Vreni Byrne and Ben Urich on the arrest of Jorge DeLaSelva and Michael Lieb, which had two pictures credited to P. PAR-KER—*DAILY BUGLE*, to the special editorial on page five by publisher J. Jonah Jameson on the evils of terrorists, which inevitably managed to turn into an anti-Spider-Man diatribe by the second paragraph.

He sighed wistfully at the lost income by not getting the higher-paying front-page shots. He of course had pictures from Hunt's Point, but he could sell either those or the Verona Park ones, since he'd have had a hard time explaining how Peter Parker got from West Orange to the South Bronx in fifteen minutes. And the Verona Park shots had the advantage of being exclusives.

Besides, he liked Angela and didn't really begrudge her the front page.

His right arm felt a lot better—he kept it out of the sling, though he still favored it as much as he could. The weather had taken a turn for the warmer, getting up into the forties this Friday morning, for which Spider-Man was immensely grateful.

He looked up when a sedan approached from the Henry Hudson Parkway entrance ramp and pulled up alongside the wall-crawler's perch. Hawkins and Drew exited the car and approached.

"Geez," Drew said, looking around, "I haven't been down here since that crazy arms bust with the Silver Surfer. Remember that, Hawk?"

Hawkins nodded. "Very well."

Spider-Man folded up his copy of the *Bugle*. "The Surfer?"

"*Long* story," Hawkins said, cutting Drew off.

"It was a coupla years ago. You really hadda be there," Drew said, smiling. "Catching up on your press notices?" he added, indicating the newspaper.

"Something like that. Wanted to make sure they got my good side in the photo."

"Hey, you did good," Drew said. "Even took Jameson two whole paragraphs before he got around to bashing you."

"Well, Jonah's always been pro-cop, even if he is anti-vigilante, and he could hardly go against all the nice things you said about me."

"I haven't seen the paper yet," Hawkins said. "How much did they quote?"

Spider-Man turned to page sixteen, where Betty's article jumped to from the front page. "One thing in particular that I think kept the leash on ol' JJJ." He found the paragraph he wanted and read aloud, " 'Detective Sergeant Vance Hawkins, who, along with Detective Sergeant Stephen Drew, was the primary investigator into the kidnappings of Robertson and Weying, said that Spider-Man's involvement was "invaluable." If not for his assistance, Hawkins added, that final confrontation would've turned into a bloodbath.' "

Hawkins's eyes widened. "My God."

"What?" Spider-Man asked.

"That's what I said."

"Of course it is, it's a quote from—"

Hawkins waved his hand. "No, you don't understand, in twelve years on the force, I've *never* been accurately quoted in a newspaper before. That's amazing."

Spider-Man smiled. "Well, that Brant lady's a good reporter," he said with a certain amount of pride. "In any case, I want to thank you for saying that—really, it meant a lot."

"No problem," Hawkins said. "You did the work, you get the credit."

"I'm really sorry about Officer Braswell."

Drew waved him off. "Not your fault."

"Still, I should've been able to prevent it. If Venom—"

"Hey, c'mon," Hawkins interrupted. "If you hadn't been there, it would've come down to a shooting match. I've done enough hostage negotiations in my time to know when there's no chance of negotiating, and this was it. I don't know if you noticed what kind of hardware they were carrying, but they had teflon-coated bullets—'cop-killers.' I wasn't exaggerating to that reporter—it would've been a massacre."

"I suppose." Still, the death rankled on him, as all deaths did, whether it was Uncle Ben or some cop he never met. "In any case, I really do mean those thanks. After all the times people have called out for my head on a platter, it's nice to get some support from the NYPD."

"Listen, we gotta get back," Drew said. "You sure you don't wanna come to the station with us?"

Spider-Man smiled under the mask. "Nah, I better not. Even if we did work okay together, I think keeping my distance was the right idea. I'm just not comfortable in the precinct house, y'know? Besides, the coffee's *terrible*."

Both detectives smiled at that. Drew added, "We didn't just work okay, we worked great. Gives you some hope for the future, anyhow."

"Maybe."

As Hawkins moved back to the driver's side door of his car, he said, "Oh, you'll be happy to know that the lieutenant has promised to try and stop calling you guys 'costumes.'"

Spider-Man laughed at that. "Thank him for me."

After the two sergeants drove off, Spider-Man shot out a web-line and headed southward. He had a nine o'clock lecture to get to.

In his long career at the New York Police Department, Frank Esteban had spent many a morning at the hospital. Rarely as a patient; he'd been lucky enough for that. But subordinates, colleagues, perps—he'd seen dozens wheeled down pale corridors.

It seemed strange, then, that the caustic smell of the waiting room reminded him of nothing but his mother. Maybe it was the fact that she'd spent so much time in the oncological unit. For almost a year Frank had come to visit her every other afternoon; sometimes twice a day, whenever he managed to drag his younger brother to the hospital. She always welcomed him with a tired smile. When she finally returned home to die, she carried with her the smell of disinfectants—sometimes, as she lay on the heirloom mahogany bed, shriveling under piles of quilted blankets, she would joke that she could clean a room by her mere presence. Frank would laugh, but only for her.

The nurse before him was dressed in scrubs and head cap, and for a second Frank confused her with a doctor. But then she knelt down to speak to him at his level. Only nurses did that. Doctors couldn't help but talk down to cops.

"He's awake," she said, quietly, as if to keep his privacy in the crowded room. "You can go in a see him now if you want."

"Thanks," Frank said. With his one good arm he grabbed his coat, then stood up and followed the nurse into the elevator.

They got off at the fifth floor; only a few doors down the hallway there was a U.S. Marshall sitting on a spidery chrome chair, leaning backward—so far that the metal legs creaked under his weight. Officer Friesner—that was the name pinned to his jacket—nodded at the nurse, then glared suspiciously at Frank's badge, which hung from the pocket of his rumpled suit.

"He's from the NYPD," the nurse explained. "That's his brother inside."

"I'm gonna take your sidearm," Officer Friesner said. His voice was gruff, weathered. Once Frank handed the marshall his Beretta—his own, which they'd actually recovered from the warehouse—the man hurriedly stepped forward and opened the door.

"If you need me," the nurse said, walking away, "just ask them to page Nurse Garcia, okay?"

Frank nodded.

Inside, Carlos lay uneasily on the orthopedic bed, pained, his left leg raised and scaffolded. The worst damage was internal, though: a broken rib had pierced through his spleen, which quickly swelled him with blood and fluid. It'd taken eighteen transfusions to stabilize him—several of which had been donated by Frank himself. Even then, the surgeons had patched him up with only seconds to spare.

Carlitos regarded him with something like wistfulness. Frank started to speak, but then heard the sound of a gurney behind him, and realized that the door was still open.

"Could we have a moment?" he said to the marshall without turning.

"I'm not supposed to—" Officer Friesner began.

"Please," Frank said, exasperated.

The door snapped shut. Frank sat down on a chair by the bed and crossed his legs.

"How are you doing, *m'hijo*?" he said.

"Don't call me that," Carlos grunted in Spanish. "You're not my father. You think you are, but you are not. You never were."

Looking down at the worn sole of his shoe, Frank waited to reply. Eventually, Carlos wetted his lips and tapped his fingers on the mattress.

"I'm hurting," he said, "but the doctors said I'll be making a full recovery. So that's okay."

"I'm glad," Frank said, switching to Spanish as well. The words felt hard in his mouth, like gristle.

"Well," Carlos said, shifting sideways on the bed. "Go ahead. That's why you're here."

"Go ahead what?" Frank said. Having dealt with so many criminals in his job, he'd gotten very good at pretending innocence.

"Ask me," Carlitos said. He lost his breath for a moment; regained it with a quick gasp.

"Ask you what?" Frank said.

"Come on! You wanna know why I did it! You wanna know why I'm a *Corta Caña*."

"Well, I know it wasn't upbringing," Frank said, barely controlling his anger, "*Mami* did an excellent job raising your sorry ass."

Carlos smiled a bit. "That's appreciation for you. After I save your life and everything."

"Yeah, and shoot your *camarada* in the process. Do you know what kind of position that puts me into? If there's an inquiry about that murder, I don't know what I'm gonna do. I really don't."

"*Ay Dios,*" Carlos whispered. He wiped the moistness from his eyes and spoke with a hesitant, awkward voice. "It wasn't my fault about Paqui. Sombra made me take him, and the idiot wouldn't listen to me when I said he should take a hike, said he wouldn't miss a cop execution for the world. What else could I do?"

"That's a real good question," Frank said grimly. "A real good question."

Carlos didn't speak for a long while. Then he ran a hand through his thick hair and said, "What's gonna happen to me?"

"I don't know," Frank said in earnest. "If you cooperate with the feds, maybe they'll cut you a deal. You gonna have to talk, though. Give them something they want."

"I'm not doing that," Carlos declared, shaking his head.

"Look, *mano,*" Frank said. He uncrossed his legs and leaned closer to his brother. "You made some mistakes, bad mistakes, but right now maybe you can do something about 'em. You can rectify, know what I mean? Put things right. You're still a young man; there still a life ahead of you. Do yourself—hell, do *me* a favor, all right?"

"You'd never understand," Carlos said, smiling.

"Well, then explain to me!" Frank shouted.

Carlos smiled.

"What?" Frank said.

"Did I tell you I met *Papi* in Puerto Rico? He's living in a little farm in Comerio. Raising chickens. He's got a few acres of *plátanos*, too."

"Good for him," Frank muttered. Just thinking about him made his guts clench.

"See," Carlos said, "you and *Mami* wanted to make a life for me, putting me in school and in the police academy, but you never told me about my past. You never told me about where I came from. Who I was, *ves*? You kept it from me. My father could have been a plantain tree, as far as you were concerned.''

Frank took a deep breath. ''At first, *Mami* and I didn't think *papi* had left,'' he began. ''Not for good, anyway, The feds were putting heat on the local *Nacionalista* cell, that's what he told us, so he had to go underground for a little while. A political thing, *me entiendes?*''

''Look, you don't—'' Carlos began, but Frank hushed him with a wave of his hand.

''All I knew was that it was Philadelphia,'' he continued. ''I heard him mention the city to a friend of his over the phone. So I took out a few books from the library and read all about the Liberty Hall and Benjamin Franklin and the Declaration of Independence and all that. Soon afterward I started having these nightmares. *Mami* was on her eighth month with you, and every night I would dream about *Papi* making a revolution. I'd see him get shot, blood spewing everywhere. And it got into my mind that I was the only one who could save him. I mean, I was ten years old at the time. I didn't know any better.

''So I ran away. I took some money I'd saved from shoe shining and bought myself a one-way ticket to Philly. I was gonna save my father, see. I thought it was possible I could make the ultimate sacrifice; better not waste the money from the return ticket, right?

''I left in the morning, but it was pretty dark by the time the bus pulled in to the station. Of course, I didn't know where I was going, so I just wandered around the ticket counter, clutching my school bag—*Mami* thought I was headed for school—and, I don't know, hoping I would spot him in the crowd. What can I say. I wasn't all that bright, even for a ten year old.

''Eventually, the woman at the ticket counter came over and asked if I was lost. I said no. She asked if I was looking for someone, and I just blurted out my father's name. And that was when the whole strangeness began, because the woman just pulled out the white pages from under her desk, flipped through it quickly, and dialed a number on the courtesy phone. Next thing I know, I'm talking to my father on the line. He tells me to wait with the lady by the counter. He's going to pick me up.

"Don't get me wrong—I was happy to hear from him after two months. But I'd thought he was hiding. I thought I would have to search for him. The fact that his number was listed in the phone book just sent my head spinning. It was simply unbelievable.

"He came by about a half an hour later. As usual I could smell the *ron* in his breath. He was very happy to see me. What a surprise! *Mami* had said nothing about it. I kept my mouth shut about the mission, guessing that he was only pretending—I'd seen a couple of police officers in the area, and you just couldn't be too careful.

"The drive was quiet. Once we got to his place, *papi* ran around the car and opened the door for me, then took my hand and led me up the stoop. We climbed a staircase that I thought would never end. Then down a hallway, third door, if I remember right. We walked into the apartment, and there in the kitchen there was a woman. She looked a bit younger than *Mami*, a bit thinner too, but her hands were rough like *Mami's*, and when she held my face and bent down to kiss me, it was—for a moment at least—just like I'd never left home.

"But then, of course, I understood."

Sensing a pause, Carlos finally spoke. "Margarita. They're still together, you know."

"He lied to me," Frank said, "he lied to *Mami*. All this talk about loyalty to the *patria*, and he was running around with that *putita*."

"Well," Carlos said dismissively. "Look, you've got your own demons. I can accept that. Being *Corta Caña*, that's how I made peace with mine."

Frank was stunned. He'd expected the story to have some effect on his brother. He thought he could still save him.

Defeated, Frank stood up and straightened the skirt of his jacket.

"Please consider it," he said. "Think about talking to the feds. Don't throw away your life."

"Don't worry," Carlos muttered in English, "I won't."

Somehow the words did not prove reassuring.

Just as he was about to leave, Carlos called out to him.

"Is it true what I hear about Sombra?" he asked. "Went crazy and turned himself into a cop?"

Frank nodded yes.

Carlos smiled. "Makes you think, doesn't it?"

FRIDAY, 9 A.M.

Vreni Byrne was the first person to sight Robbie as he entered the *Bugle* City Room, and she was therefore the first to cheer and applaud.

The whoops and clapping spread quickly throughout the entire office, building to a standing ovation—even Arwen Rosenbaum hauled her pregnant self up from the ergonomic chair Robbie had gotten her.

Robbie felt his face go flush. He had expected a warm reception, of course, but nothing like this. He flashed back to his first day back after his abortive prison stay. Everyone seemed to be dancing on eggshells, not sure what to say to him. For the entire day, people would tentatively walk up to him, mumble a quick, "Welcome back," then ask him about work in that flinching manner people usually reserved for Jonah. It had taken him weeks to get people comfortable around him then.

Now, that didn't look like it would be much of a problem.

A sharp voice cut through the ovation like a buzzsaw. "All right, all right, that's enough," said J. Jonah Jameson, and Robbie couldn't help but smile. "This is a newspaper, not Shea Stadium."

Of course, when he came back from jail, the one person who hadn't treated him at all different was Jonah.

"About time you got here, Robertson. The place is going to hell in a handbasket without an editor-in-chief."

"I know," Robbie said. "I saw the way the comp was mangled on the opening news story. Obviously, whoever put the spreads together didn't know that we'd agreed that your 'publishorials' would only go on a left page."

"Er, uh, yes, well, I'm sure that was an accidental oversight," Jonah thumped, thus confirming Robbie's belief that the publisher himself had put the editorial on a right-hand-side page, where the more prominent stories usually appeared. "When you get settled, we need to talk about next week's Sunday Supplement."

"Of course," Robbie said with a nod.

"See you in my office in five," Jonah said. He then turned on his heel and walked back to his office, pausing to upbraid the occasional staffer who appeared to be slacking off—in other words, anyone who had paused to take a breath. Robbie made his way to his own office, amidst various congratulations and welcomes that were more sedate, if no less enthusiastic, than the applause upon his arrival.

By the time he reached Betty Brant's desk, the City Room had once again settled into its usual chaos. *Hmm*, he thought, *settled chaos. Have to remember that one.*

Betty looked up from her monitor and gave Robbie a smile. "It's good to see you up and around again."

"Good to be up and around."

"I figured you'd be taking the weekend off."

Robbie shrugged. Martha had already made that suggestion—rather more forcefully and loudly than Betty had—but he wanted to get back into his routine. Joe Robertson had always gotten through life, from growing up in Harlem to being a reporter in Philadelphia to being an editor in New York, by sticking to certain routines. Prison life was actually relatively easy for him to grow accustomed to because it, too, had a set routine, albeit an unpleasant one.

To Betty, he said, "I thought about it, but sitting around at home for three days after sitting around in that warehouse for two . . ." He trailed off and shivered, feeling a phantom chill from the memory of that cold room where he lost two days of his life to the ravings of a shape-changing lunatic.

"I see your point," Betty said softly.

Composing himself after only a second, Robbie continued: "In any case, I wanted to congratulate you on getting the story. That was really good work." He hesitated—the words, *Ned would've been proud of you* were on the tip of his tongue, but he bit them back. That wasn't what Betty needed to hear.

He put his left hand on her right shoulder and said, "You should be proud."

She blinked her brown eyes for a moment, then smiled. "Thanks."

"You're welcome. Now get back to work," he said in a mock stern voice. "For one thing, I'm still waiting for that fish market story."

"You'll have a draft by lunch."

"Good."

Several other people called out to him as he went to his office—some offering yet more welcomes, others with work-related information, such as Vreni telling him that the followup to the Roxxon/Acme merger was ready for him to look at—and his assistant Glory Grant informed him that he had several dozen messages. "Later," he said as he went into his office and closed the door.

He looked around. Everything was more or less as he left it, except for the much bigger pile in his in-box.

After turning on the computer, he sat at his oak desk. A couple of years back, new fire codes had required that all wooden desks be removed from the building. Jonah, however, refused to do so for the editor-in-chief's oak desk, nor the beautiful mahogany one in the publisher's office. Those two desks had been with the *Bugle* since Jonah started there as a cub reporter, and he steadfastly refused to get rid of them as long as he owned the paper.

Robbie stared out the window. It faced south, so he couldn't see the Bronx, getting instead a view of the Williamsburg, Manhattan, and Brooklyn Bridges and the southeastern tip of Manhattan beyond it. *Maybe that's for the best. Last thing I want is to be reminded any more than I have to.*

He called up Vreni's article on his screen and started to read.

This is the right way to go, he thought with a satisfied smile, *get right to work. There's just something missing.* He frowned.

Then it hit him.

He opened the desk's second drawer, where he kept his office supply of pipe tobacco. Pushing past the various blends from Dunhill, he reached into the very back for the Latakia. A fancier brand of tobacco, he rarely indulged in it, partly because he preferred to save it for special occasions, mainly because Glory constantly complained about the smell. She once said that the Latakia was the one thing in the world that smelled worse than Jonah's cigars. But today certainly qualified as a special occasion, and he kept the door closed for Glory's benefit.

Very meticulously, not wanting to be sloppy about it, he filled the pipe that always lived in his shirt pocket when he wasn't actually smoking it. Then he lit it.

After three or four puffs, he sat back in his chair and continued reading Vreni's piece. He smiled. *Smoking my pipe, reading an article—finally, everything's back to where it should be. Back to the routine.*

FRIDAY, 9:35 A.M.

It really is like coming home, was Frank Esteban's first thought upon re-entering the Midtown South Precinct. The chaos, the noise, the constant movement—he didn't realize how much he missed it until he came back.

He could have gone back home after his visit with Carlos, but that would only mean going through the press gauntlet; about a dozen reporters had taken up residence in his apartment building's parking lot, and he didn't have the stamina to deal with them at the moment. At least at the precinct, he could get in through one of the side entrances and avoid the lights, microphones, tape recorders, and endless stupid questions.

As soon as he entered, people greeted him—uniforms, detectives, all saying how good it was to have him back.

"Hey hey, his royal highness returns," said Detective Peters, shaking Frank's hand gingerly.

"Kneel when you say that, Helga," he said with a smile.

Her partner, Detective Borck, said, "I though you weren't coming back till Monday, skipper."

Before Frank could respond, a familiar booming voice came from behind him. "He wasn't *supposed* to." Grinning, Frank turned to see Sergeant Jones and her patented don't-*make*-me-whup-you-upside-the-head look. "Mind telling me why you ain't home resting like a sensible person—sir?" The last word was tacked on as an afterthought.

"I missed the sound of your voice, Karen."

"Yeah, right. Well, since you *are* here, you should get over to Interrogation 3. The commish is in there with the lieutenant, Hawk, Drew, Gilman, and Liverakos."

Frank blinked. *Wilson Ramos himself. He hasn't come by here since Golden's first day.* Given the personnel involved, the meeting probably had to do with Frank's kidnapping, so he went over to the room in question.

Everyone was just settling in when Frank entered.

"Frank!" Golden said with a rare smile. "What're you doing here?"

"Slumming." He returned the smile and went on, "I couldn't just stay home, so—" he hesitated; he didn't really want to get into his family problems with his people, so he skipped over his visit to his brother "—I decided to start getting back into the swing of things here."

The others all expressed their greetings and salutations, until Wilson Ramos's voice cut through the chatter, quieting the others down.

"I'm glad you're here, Frank," Ramos said. New York's "top cop" was a stocky man, about ten years older than Frank and with a cut-through-the-crap attitude that Frank had always found refreshing. "This relates to you after all."

Ramos stood at the head of the table; Frank took a seat at the other end. Gilman stood leaning against the window, and Golden went over to join him. Hawkins, Drew, and Liverakos took the three remaining seats.

The commissioner held up a piece of paper. "I have here a fax from FBI New York Bureau Chief Buchanan. It says, and

I quote, 'The FBI would like to thank Lieutenant Romeo Golden, Sergeant Vance Hawkins, Sergeant Stephen Drew, the officers of the Midtown South Precinct, and the New York Police Department for their invaluable assistance in apprehending the Cane Cutters.' "

Liverakos turned to Gilman, standing behind her. "How come *they* get named?" she asked, jerking her thumb to the two detectives sitting across the table. "What're we, chopped liver?"

"Apparently," Gilman said, shaking his head.

Drew smiled. "Hey, it's that whole black-guy-white-guy motif. Y'know, Riggs and Murtaugh, Bayliss and Pembleton, Hill and Renko, Hawkins and Drew. It's a pop culture thing."

"Oh, *very* funny," Liverakos said.

Once again, Ramos's voice cut through the side conversation. "The fax goes on to say," he said, as if the three sergeants hadn't spoken, "that they promise to keep us apprised of all developments regarding the Cane Cutters. Now, I don't often agree with the FBI, but in this, at least, I can safely say, what they said. In spades. You all did excellent work."

A murmur of thank-yous went around the room.

Ramos's face then darkened. "The fax then commends you for involving Spider-Man in the case, as his assistance proved most useful." He set the fax down and picked up a copy of today's *Daily Bugle*. As he did so, Hawkins started to shrink in his chair. Frank suspected that the sergeant had been caught in an impolitic quote, which surprised him—Vance usually had more sense than that. "And then," Ramos continued, "there's today's *Bugle*, with this lovely quote from Detective Sergeant Hawkins."

Ramos read the quote. Frank frowned. He didn't see Ramos's problem, but based on the commissioner's tone, he most definitely had one.

"Should I assume that the paperwork to deputize Spider-Man just hasn't made it to my desk yet?" Ramos asked sardonically with a withering gaze at Golden as he tossed the paper unceremoniously back onto the table.

Golden asked tightly, "Do I take it that the commissioner

is not satisfied with the way my people handled the investigation of this kidnapping?''

"Like I said, I don't always agree with the FBI, and I certainly don't agree with what I read in the *Bugle*. I'd expect that kind of boneheaded stunt from Frank, but I thought you knew better, Lieutenant."

Frank stood up faster than he should have, given his injuries, but ignored the pain when he said, "Now wait a minute—"

Ramos's face softened slightly. "Settle down, Frank. Nobody's criticizing you, it's just—"

"Like hell you aren't!" Frank snapped, then reined in his temper. *I guess Carlitos got me more worked up than I thought.* In a softer tone, he continued, "I'm responsible for the actions of this precinct, so if you have a problem with how they handled it, then you have a problem with me. And I'm still trying to figure out what the problem *is*."

"The problem is that this is the New York Police Department, not the Avengers. We don't work with costumed weirdos."

"Yeah, well, we don't do so well against them, either. Have you read the file yet, Wilson? I did, last night. Venom showed up on three separate occasions. Each time, Spider-Man was the only one who could deal with him, and each time, officers' lives would have been lost if it wasn't for Spider-Man's assistance."

"Officer Braswell would disagree on that," Ramos said with maddening calm.

"Spider-Man didn't kill Braswell, Sombra did!" Frank realized that he was shouting again, and took a breath to calm down. "Sergeant Hawkins's statement was right on the money. At DeLaSelva's, at the Edghill, and at Hunt's Point, Spider-Man's actions saved the lives of members of this department. That's the bottom line. And I might remind the commissioner that he gave Lieutenant Golden full jurisdiction over this case within the five boroughs. You gave him the authority to do what he did. Furthermore, *Spider-Man didn't do anything wrong*. Quite the opposite, actually. So again, Commissioner,

I ask you, what, exactly, is your problem with how my people handled the case?"

"Spider-Man is a loose cannon. He has no ID, no social security number that we're aware of, no fingerprints on file. Nothing. We don't even know if it's the same guy who helped nab DeWolff's killer—as it is, he's changed costumes at least twice."

"C'mon," Gilman said, shaking his head, "how many people can do what he does?"

"I can think of two off the top of my head," Ramos said with a glower at the sergeant. "We don't even know if he's white, black, Latino, or what."

"Actually, he's white," Drew said. Realizing he spoke out of turn, he finished lamely, "I mean, he, uh, he had some coffee and had to, y'know, raise his mask slightly. So we saw part of his, uh, his face."

Ramos's glower only intensified. Frank knew that this would get out of hand in a minute. He could sense the severe discomfort and anger on the part of his people, who felt like they'd been slapped in the face for doing a good job. The commissioner obviously had a bug up his butt about Spider-Man, and he had let it screw up his perceptions.

"I'm not saying we should deputize Spider-Man," Frank said. "I am saying that this was a special case, and that he was needed here. If the confrontation at Hunt's Point had gone down without Spider-Man, we'd have a lot more dead cops than Braswell."

"You don't know that."

Hawkins said, "Sir, they had cop-killer bullets, and these people have already killed a federal agent. I don't think they'd have had any compunctions about shooting us down."

"Commissioner," Frank said, laying his cards on the table, "are you reprimanding this precinct for bringing Spider-Man into this case? Because if you are, you should know that I intend to make that reprimand public. Be real interesting to see how the press reacts to that—especially after all the positive coverage we've gotten for how we handled it, not to mention the kudos from the FBI."

Ramos didn't answer at first. He stared angrily at Frank for almost ten seconds before finally saying in a very tight voice, "No, no reprimand, Captain. But in future, *any* use of paranormals by this department *must* be cleared through my office first. Is that understood?"

"Perfectly."

"Good. Do yourself a favor, Captain Esteban," Ramos added as he gathered his belongings to depart, "go home and get some rest. You look like hell."

Ramos left. As soon as the door closed behind him, the tension broke. Drew threw a pen at the closed door, and everyone started muttering angrily.

"I do *not* believe this," Gilman said. "What the hell was that?"

"He's never been big on paranormals," Hawkins said.

Drew said, "So what? We needed help here—even you thought so, Lieutenant."

Golden didn't reply to that directly, but instead turned to Frank. "Thanks for the support, Frank. It meant a lot."

"No problem. I wasn't about to let him hang you out to dry because he didn't like the way you saved my life."

"Probably killed your shot at a promotion," Golden added with a rueful smile.

Liverakos said, "Hell, I think we all killed our shots at it. And I really wanted to make lieutenant, too."

"Is that why you kept your mouth shut?" Drew asked with a grin.

"Well, you were doing such a good job of shooting your mouth off, Drew, what could I possibly have added?" Liverakos said with a sweet smile.

Good, Frank thought, *they're already joking with each other.* "Forget about Ramos," he said. "He's not gonna do anything to make the department look bad, and ripping into you guys would do that, and he knows it."

"I don't think he liked being reminded of it, though," Gilman said.

"Maybe not," Frank said with a mild shrug, "but that don't

matter. What does matter is that the case was put down. You all did good. Even the costume.''

"Hey," Golden said, gravely serious, "you shouldn't call them 'costumes.' It's offensive. Call them super heroes or paranormals, if you call them anything."

Frank did a double take.

Then Golden's face split into a grin.

Cathartic laughter spread throughout the room. "Very cute, Golden," Frank said, patting his lieutenant on the back. "C'mon, let's get back to work."

FRIDAY, 5 P.M.

The creature relaxed in the armchair that had been discarded by some West Eighty-eighth Street apartment dweller despite being in excellent shape, and switched on the television found in a garbage can on Ninety-seventh Street and Columbus Avenue. The reception was lousy, but it was as good as could be expected given that the signal had to penetrate underground.

Venom had set up several makeshift homes below the city streets. This particular one was in the abandoned Ninety-first Street station on the Broadway line. Every once in a while a train would go by and fuzz out the TV's reception—more often now, during afternoon rush hour—but the creature had rigged up an antenna that provided a mostly solid black-and-white image and good sound.

Of course, getting cable was out of the question, so Venom settled for the local news. Unsurprisingly, the top story was the capture of the Cane Cutters and the rescue of Captain Frank Esteban, Joe Robertson, and Ann Weying. Venom had already read the newspaper accounts in the *New York Times* and *Daily Bugle*—Eddie Brock refused to even look at the *Daily Globe*—during the day while recovering from the fight with Sombra and the subsequent scuffle with Parker. The creature had not wanted to run, but Parker had actually started to get the upper hand. Whatever else one could say about the arachnid, he never gave up in a fight, and Venom knew that victory would only be attained at full strength. After Sombra's vicious assault, the creature wouldn't be at full strength for some time.

Venom shifted uncomfortably in the chair until the news showed the impromptu press conference that Ann held on the steps of the hospital where they had taken A.J. Pierce. Ann had, according to the anchor, just overseen the taking of Pierce's deposition in the latter's hospital room.

Eddie Brock's heart sank when he saw Ann on camera. She looked awful. A bandage covered her nose, and the skin around it appeared discolored. *Perhaps that's just the reception*, he thought, not entirely convinced. Once again, Venom cursed Parker for interfering with the creature's application of justice—Sombra didn't even begin to pay for the crimes he perpetrated on Ann.

"*Ms. Weying,*" said one of the reporters at the hospital, "*how do you feel about the fact that your ex-husband Venom, a known super-villain, participated in your rescue?*"

Ann blinked once, then spoke slowly, her voice taking on a nasal tenor because of the broken nose: "*I was rescued by the New York Police Department and Spider-Man, and I am grateful to them for their efforts. I owe my safety to them, and to no one else.*"

"*Ms. Weying, do—*"

The reporter's question was cut off by a black tentacle that smashed the television screen.

"Betrayed! Again!" the creature cried out, voice echoing off the graffiti-covered tiles of the dark station. "Everywhere we turn, we are betrayed!"

It's all Parker's fault, the creature thought, getting up from the chair and pacing about the filth-strewn floor. *If he had not interfered, Ann would have seen the truth—that we found her, that we rescued her from that madman. And Parker gets to go home to his wife, while we continue to lurk in the shadows, cut off from the love of our lives.*

As a train roared by, rattling the shattered television on its stand, the creature bellowed, "We shall have our revenge, arachnid! Someday soon, you shall die at our hands!"

* * *

When Ann Weying's press conference ended, Peter Parker hit the MUTE button on the remote control and leaned back on the couch. Next to him, Mary Jane leaned over and rested her head on his left shoulder.

He had had a long day of classes, which included a grueling lab session, on top of the previous two days' craziness. All he wanted to do tonight was be a couch potato at home with his wife.

Still, he had wanted to see the television coverage of the whole Cane Cutters incident. There were so many aspects to the case—the Wells Fargo robbery; the ongoing *independista* movement in Puerto Rico; the kidnapping of a police captain, a prominent lawyer, and a prominent journalist; the death of a police officer; the endless rigamarole surrounding the King-pin related to the arrest of Michael Lieb; the involvement of both Spider-Man and Venom—that this story would stay in the forefront of the news for days.

But, of course, the TV news focused most of their energy on Venom, Spider-Man, and Ann Weying.

"That was mighty harsh," Peter said after Ann's answer to the first question.

MJ sat up again and looked at her husband with a look of surprise. "Harsh? We're talking about *Venom* here. If anything, she was being too kind."

"The thing is—she stayed behind. Robbie, too. After Sombra let them go, they refused to leave because they wouldn't let Sombra kill Venom. *She* saved *his* life. Besides, I always thought she was Brock's best shot at redemption. That if they—"

"Oh, puh-*leeeze*," MJ said, throwing up her hands and looking to the ceiling in supplication. Then she fixed Peter with her jewel-green eyes. "Listen, Tiger, men are only redeemed by the love of a good woman in trashy novels and Hollywood movies. Eddie Brock chose his way of life. He chose to run the Sin-Eater story, he chose to blame you for it. It's not Ann's function in life to save him from that—redemption only comes from inside. Keeping that guy from shooting him is one thing—that's basic compassion—but to let him dominate her is a whole other thing.''

Peter regarded his wife, and noted the expression on her face. It was the same one most of his lecturers wore when they were in full didactic mode. ''Those psych classes are really paying off, huh?'' he said with a smirk.

MJ smiled, showing her perfect teeth. ''Better believe it, Tiger. But seriously, I think Ann's just trying to get on with her life. I mean, she doesn't really have an identity of her own—she isn't Ann Weying, she's Venom's ex-wife. She gets headlines for her latest case because she's Venom's ex-wife, she gets arrested by those lunatics in the Venom Task Force because she's Venom's ex-wife, the press calls her 'She-Venom' when Brock sics the symbiote on her because she's Venom's ex-wife. What was the first thing you thought of when Sergeant Drew told you she was kidnapped?''

Peter frowned. ''I'm not sure, I—'' He hesitated.

''I bet it was that Venom would be on the rampage—not that she might be hurt, but what Venom would do.''

Peter sighed, embarrassed at the fact that she was absolutely right.

''It's okay,'' MJ said before he could say anything, ''it's natural. I think she knows it, too. That's why she said what she said to the reporters—she's trying to move on as best she can without that drooling, slavering lunatic hanging over her every move.''

On *drooling, slavering lunatic*, the lecturer face fell, to be replaced by a look of pure disgust. Venom first introduced himself to Spider-Man by terrorizing Mary Jane—not one of MJ's fondest memories.

''I suppose you're right,'' Peter said, turning away from his wife to stare out the living room window at the trees in front of the house. ''And I hope she manages it. We should all be so lucky.''

Thinking of Ann trying to carve out an identity led Peter's thoughts to Sombra. His powers stripped him of identity, and he used the cause of Puerto Rican independence to provide a new one.

Then he thought about his featureless, faceless mask that kept his own identity a secret from the world. *Is that a danger for me?* he wondered. *Does this mask make me as identity-less as Sombra? Hawkins said the mask made me inhuman— one step removed. Sombra's powers did the same thing. Could I wind up like him?*

He looked back at his beautiful wife, who had stuck with him through traumas a fraction of which might destroy another marriage. *No, it won't happen. Not as long as I have MJ to remind me of what I have.*

"Have I mentioned lately that I love you?" he asked his wife.

"Oh, it's been several minutes at least," she replied with a smile. "Howzabout a reminder?"

He took her in his arms, still favoring the right shoulder. "Your wish is my command, memsahib."

KEITH R.A. DeCANDIDO left home at the age of sixteen to pursue a career in fisheries, but came home an hour later when he realized he forgot to pack a lunch. He left home again at the age of twenty-one to pursue a career in publishing, at which he's had a bit more success. His most recent short fiction appeared in *The Ultimate Hulk* and *Did You Say Chicks?!* and he's also contributed to *The Ultimate Spider-Man*, *The Ultimate Silver Surfer*, the *Magic: The Gathering* anthology *Distant Planes*, the *Doctor Who* anthology *Decalog 3: Consequences*, and *Untold Tales of Spider-Man*. His editorial résumé includes co-editing the anthologies *Urban Nightmares*, *OtherWere: Stories of Transformation*, *The Ultimate Alien*, and *The Ultimate Dragon*; editing original science fiction and fantasy, as well as books based on comic books and role-playing games; and helping bring Alfred Bester back into print. With Christopher Golden and Nancy Holder, he co-wrote *Buffy the Vampire Slayer: The Watcher's Guide*, and he is working on a Buffy novel. He is also the percussionist for the Don't Quit Your Day Job Players, a rock/blues/folk/country band whose first CD, *TKB*, was released in 1996. He lives on the Upper West Side of Manhattan with his lovely and much more talented wife, Marina Frants, where he is currently plotting either his next Spider-Man novel with José R. Nieto or how to make the perfect tomato sauce, depending on his mood.

Born in Puerto Rico, **JOSÉ R. NIETO** is a graduate of the NYU creative writing program (though he may have to return his diploma once it gets out that he has written a super hero novel). His work has appeared in a number of magazines and anthologies, including David G. Hartwell's *Christmas Magic*, *Washington Square*, *The Ultimate Super-Villains*, *The Ultimate Silver Surfer*, and *Untold Tales of Spider-Man*. He is currently at work on a weird literary novel as well as a sequel to *Venom's Wrath* (again with Keith R.A. DeCandido). Though you could probably find him in Boston if you really tried, José can be much more easily reached at jnieto1@ix.netcom.com.

New York–based cartoonist **JOE ST. PIERRE** is the co-creator and artist of the Image comic book series *MegaHurtz*. His other comics work includes a whole bunch of Spider-related material for Marvel: *Spider-Man 2099*, *Venom: Along Came a Spider*, and *Venom: Tooth and Claw* (where he got to draw Wolverine slicing Venom's tongue off, a lifelong dream). His other work in book illustration includes *The Ultimate X-Men* and *Untold Tales of Spider-Man*.

CHRONOLOGY TO THE MARVEL NOVELS AND ANTHOLOGIES

What follows is a guide to the order in which the Marvel novels and short stories published by Byron Preiss Multimedia Company and Berkley Boulevard Books take place in relation to each other. Please note that this is not a hard and fast chronology, but a guideline that is subject to change at authorial or editorial whim. This list covers all the novels and anthologies published from October 1994–December 1998.

The short stories are each given an abbreviation to indicate which anthology the story appeared in. USM=*The Ultimate Spider-Man*, USS=*The Ultimate Silver Surfer*, USV=*The Ultimate Super-Villains*, UXM=*The Ultimate X-Men*, UTS=*Untold Tales of Spider-Man*, and UH=*The Ultimate Hulk*.

If you have any questions or comments regarding this chronology, please write us.

Snail mail: Keith R.A. DeCandido
Marvel Novels Editor
Byron Preiss Multimedia Company, Inc.
24 West 25th Street
New York, NY 10010-2710
E-mail: KRAD@IX.NETCOM.COM.
—Keith R.A. DeCandido, Editor

X-Men & Spider-Man: Time's Arrow Book 1: **The Past [portions]**
by Tom DeFalco & Jason Henderson

Parts of this novel take place in prehistoric times, the sixth century, 1867, and 1944.

"The Silver Surfer" [flashback]
by Tom DeFalco & Stan Lee [USS]
The Silver Surfer's origin. The early parts of this flashback start several decades, possibly several centuries, ago, and continue to a point just prior to "To See Heaven in a Wild Flower."

"In the Line of Banner"
by Danny Fingeroth [UH]
This takes place nine months before the birth of Robert Bruce Banner.

X-Men: Codename Wolverine ["then" portions]
by Christopher Golden
The "then" portions of this novel take place while Team X was still in operation, while the Black Widow was still a Soviet spy, and while Banshee was still with Interpol.

"Spider-Man"
by Stan Lee & Peter David [USM]
A retelling of Spider-Man's origin.

"Transformations"
by Will Murray [UH]
"Side by Side with the Astonishing Ant-Man!"
by Will Murray [UTS]
"Assault on Avengers Mansion"
by Richard C. White & Steven A. Roman [UH]
"Suits"
by Tom De Haven & Dean Wesley Smith [USM]
"After the First Death . . ."
by Tom DeFalco [UTS]
"Celebrity"
by Christopher Golden & José R. Nieto [UTS]
"Pitfall"
by Pierce Askegren [UH]

CHRONOLOGY

"Better Looting Through Modern Chemistry"
by John Garcia & Pierce Askegren [UTS]
  These stories take place very early in the careers of Spider-Man and the Hulk.

"To the Victor"
by Richard Lee Byers [USV]
  Most of this story takes place in an alternate timeline, but the jumping-off point is here.

"To See Heaven in a Wild Flower"
by Ann Tonsor Zeddies [USS]
"Point of View"
by Len Wein [USS]
  These stories take place shortly after the end of the flashback portion of "The Silver Surfer."

"Identity Crisis"
by Michael Jan Friedman [UTS]
"The Liar"
by Ann Nocenti [UTS]
"The Doctor's Dilemma"
by Danny Fingeroth [UTS]
"Moving Day"
by John S. Drew [UTS]
"Out of the Darkness"
by Glenn Greenberg [UH]
"Deadly Force"
by Richard Lee Byers [UTS]
"Truck Stop"
by Jo Duffy [UH]
"Hiding"
by Christopher Golden & Nancy Holder [UH]
"Improper Procedure"
by Keith R.A. DeCandido [USS]
"Poison in the Soul"
by Glenn Greenberg [UTS]
"Here There Be Dragons"
by Sholly Fisch [UH]

CHRONOLOGY

"The Ballad of Fancy Dan"
by Ken Grobe & Steven A. Roman [UTS]
"Do You Dream in Silver?"
by James Dawson [USS]
"A Quiet, Normal Life"
by Thomas Deja [UH]
"Livewires"
by Steve Lyons [UTS]
"Arms and the Man"
by Keith R.A. DeCandido [UTS]
"Incident on a Skyscraper"
by Dave Smeds [USS]
"A Green Snake in Paradise"
by Steve Lyons [UH]
   These all take place at various and sundry points in the careers of Spider-Man, the Silver Surfer, and the Hulk: after their origins, but before Spider-Man got married, the Silver Surfer ended his exile on Earth, and the reemergence of the gray Hulk.

"Cool"
by Lawrence Watt-Evans [USM]
"Blindspot"
by Ann Nocenti [USM]
"Tinker, Tailor, Soldier, Courier"
by Robert L. Washington III [USM]
"Thunder on the Mountain"
by Richard Lee Byers [USM]
"The Stalking of John Doe"
by Adam-Troy Castro [UTS]
"On the Beach"
by John J. Ordover [USS]
   These all take place just prior to Peter Parker's marriage to Mary Jane Watson and the Silver Surfer's release from imprisonment on Earth.

Daredevil: Predator's Smile
by Christopher Golden

CHRONOLOGY

"Disturb Not Her Dream"
by Steve Rasnic Tem [USS]
"My Enemy, My Savior"
by Eric Fein [UTS]
"Kraven the Hunter Is Dead, Alas"
by Craig Shaw Gardner [USM]
"The Broken Land"
by Pierce Askegren [USS]
"Radically Both"
by Christopher Golden [USM]
"Godhood's End"
by Sharman DiVono [USS]
"Scoop!"
by David Michelinie [USM]
"The Beast with Nine Bands"
by James A. Wolf [UH]
"Sambatyon"
by David M. Honigsberg [USS]
"Cold Blood"
by Greg Cox [USM]
"The Tarnished Soul"
by Katherine Lawrence [USS]
"Leveling Las Vegas"
by Stan Timmons [UH]
"If Wishes Were Horses"
by Tony Isabella & Bob Ingersoll [USV]
"The Silver Surfer" [framing sequence]
by Tom DeFalco & Stan Lee [USS]
"The Samson Journals"
by Ken Grobe [UH]
   These all take place after Peter Parker's marriage to Mary Jane Watson, after the Silver Surfer attained freedom from imprisonment on Earth, and before the Hulk's personalities were merged.

"The Deviant Ones"
by Glenn Greenberg [USV]

CHRONOLOGY

"An Evening in the Bronx with Venom"
by John Gregory Betancourt & Keith R.A. DeCandido [USM]
   These two stories take place one after the other, and a few months prior to The Venom Factor.

The Incredible Hulk: What Savage Beast
by Peter David
   This novel takes place over a one-year period, starting here and ending just prior to Rampage.

"On the Air"
by Glenn Hauman [UXM]
"Connect the Dots"
by Adam-Troy Castro [USV]
"Summer Breeze"
by Jenn Saint-John & Tammy Lynne Dunn [UXM]
"Out of Place"
by Dave Smeds [UXM]
   These stories all take place prior to the Mutant Empire *trilogy.*

X-Men: Mutant Empire Book 1: **Siege**
by Christopher Golden
X-Men: Mutant Empire Book 2: **Sanctuary**
by Christopher Golden
X-Men: Mutant Empire Book 3: **Salvation**
by Christopher Golden
   These three novels take place within a three-day period.

Fantastic Four: To Free Atlantis
by Nancy A. Collins
"The Love of Death or the Death of Love"
by Craig Shaw Gardner [USS]
"Firetrap"
by Michael Jan Friedman [USV]
"What's Yer Poison?"
by Christopher Golden & José R. Nieto [USS]
"Sins of the Flesh"
by Steve Lyons [USV]

CHRONOLOGY

"Doom²"
by Joey Cavalieri [USV]
"Child's Play"
by Robert L. Washington III [USV]
"A Game of the Apocalypse"
by Dan Persons [USS]
"All Creatures Great and Skrull"
by Greg Cox [USV]
"Ripples"
by José R. Nieto [USV]
"Who Do You Want Me to Be?"
by Ann Nocenti [USV]
"One for the Road"
by James Dawson [USV]

These are more or less simultaneous, with "Doom²" taking place after To Free Atlantis, *"Child's Play" taking place shortly after "What's Yer Poison?" and "A Game of the Apocalypse" taking place shortly after "The Love of Death or the Death of Love."*

"Five Minutes"
by Peter David [USM]

This takes place on Peter Parker and Mary Jane Watson-Parker's first anniversary.

Spider-Man: The Venom Factor
by Diane Duane
Spider-Man: The Lizard Sanction
by Diane Duane
Spider-Man: The Octopus Agenda
by Diane Duane

These three novels take place within a six-week period.

"The Night I Almost Saved Silver Sable"
by Tom DeFalco [USV]
"Traps"
by Ken Grobe [USV]

These stories take place one right after the other.

CHRONOLOGY

Iron Man: The Armor Trap
by Greg Cox
Iron Man: Operation A.I.M.
by Greg Cox
"Private Exhibition"
by Pierce Askegren [USV]
Fantastic Four: Redemption of the Silver Surfer
by Michael Jan Friedman
Spider-Man & The Incredible Hulk: Rampage (Doom's Day Book 1)
by Danny Fingeroth & Eric Fein
Spider-Man & Iron Man: Sabotage (Doom's Day Book 2)
by Pierce Askegren & Danny Fingeroth
Spider-Man & Fantastic Four: Wreckage (Doom's Day Book 3)
by Eric Fein & Pierce Askegren

Operation A.I.M. *takes place about two weeks after* The Armor Trap. *The "Doom's Day" trilogy takes place within a three-month period. The events of* Operation A.I.M., *"Private Exhibition,"* Redemption of the Silver Surfer, *and* Rampage *happen more or less simultaneously.* Wreckage *is only a few months after* The Octopus Agenda.

"It's a Wonderful Life"
by eluki bes shahar [UXM]
"Gift of the Silver Fox"
by Ashley McConnell [UXM]
"Stillborn in the Mist"
by Dean Wesley Smith [UXM]
"Order from Chaos"
by Evan Skolnick [UXM]
These stories take place simultaneously.

"X-Presso"
by Ken Grobe [UXM]
"Life is But a Dream"
by Stan Timmons [UXM]

CHRONOLOGY

"Four Angry Mutants"
by Andy Lane & Rebecca Levene [UXM]
"Hostages"
by J. Steven York [UXM]
These stories take place one right after the other.

Spider-Man: Carnage in New York
by David Michelinie & Dean Wesley Smith
Spider-Man: Goblin's Revenge
by Dean Wesley Smith
These novels take place one right after the other.

X-Men: Smoke and Mirrors
by eluki bes shahar
This novel takes place three-and-a-half months after "It's a Wonderful Life."

Generation X
by Scott Lobdell & Elliot S! Maggin
X-Men: The Jewels of Cyttorak
by Dean Wesley Smith
X-Men: Empire's End
by Diane Duane
X-Men: Law of the Jungle
by Dave Smeds
X-Men: Prisoner X
by Ann Nocenti
These novels take place one right after the other.

The Incredible Hulk: Abominations
by Jason Henderson
Fantastic Four: Countdown to Chaos
by Pierce Askegren
"Playing It SAFE"
by Keith R.A. DeCandido [UH]
These take place one right after the other, with Abominations *taking place a couple of weeks after* Wreckage.

CHRONOLOGY

"Mayhem Party"
by Robert Sheckley [USV]
This story takes place after Goblin's Revenge.

X-Men & Spider-Man: Time's Arrow Book 1: **The Past**
by Tom DeFalco & Jason Henderson
X-Men & Spider-Man: Time's Arrow Book 2: **The Present**
by Tom DeFalco & Adam-Troy Castro
X-Men & Spider-Man: Time's Arrow Book 3: **The Future**
by Tom DeFalco & eluki bes shahar
These novels take place within a twenty-four-hour period in the present, though it also involves travelling to various points in the past, to an alternate present, and to five different alternate futures.

Spider-Man: Valley of the Lizard
by John Vornholt
Spider-Man: Venom's Wrath
by Keith R.A. DeCandido & José R. Nieto
Spider-Man: Wanted Dead or Alive
by Craig Shaw Gardner
"Sidekick"
by Dennis Brabham [UH]
Captain America: Liberty's Torch
by Tony Isabella & Bob Ingersoll
These take place one right after the other, with Venom's Wrath *taking place a month after* Valley of the Lizard, *and* Wanted Dead or Alive *several months after* Venom's Wrath.

Generation X: Crossroads
by J. Steven York
X-Men: Codename Wolverine
by Christopher Golden
These novels take place one right after the other, with Codename Wolverine *taking place less than a week after* Crossroads.

CHRONOLOGY

X-Men & Spider-Man: Time's Arrow Book 3: **The Future** [portions]
by Tom DeFalco & eluki bes shahar
   Parts of this novel take place in five different alternate futures in 2020, 2035, 2099, 3000, and the fortieth century.

"The Last Titan"
by Peter David [UH]
   This takes place in a possible future.

SPIDER-MAN®